THE BOX OF DEATH

TALES OF CASTLE RORY
BOOK 1

R. MARSDEN

Hurogol
press

Copyright © 2024 by R. Marsden

All rights reserved.

No part of this book may be reproduced in any form or by any electronic or mechanical means, including information storage and retrieval systems, without written permission from the author, except for the use of brief quotations in a book review.

Published by Hurogol Press 2024.

ISBN: 978-1-917063-00-5 (Paperback Edition)

ISBN: 978-1-917063-01-2 (Ebook Edition)

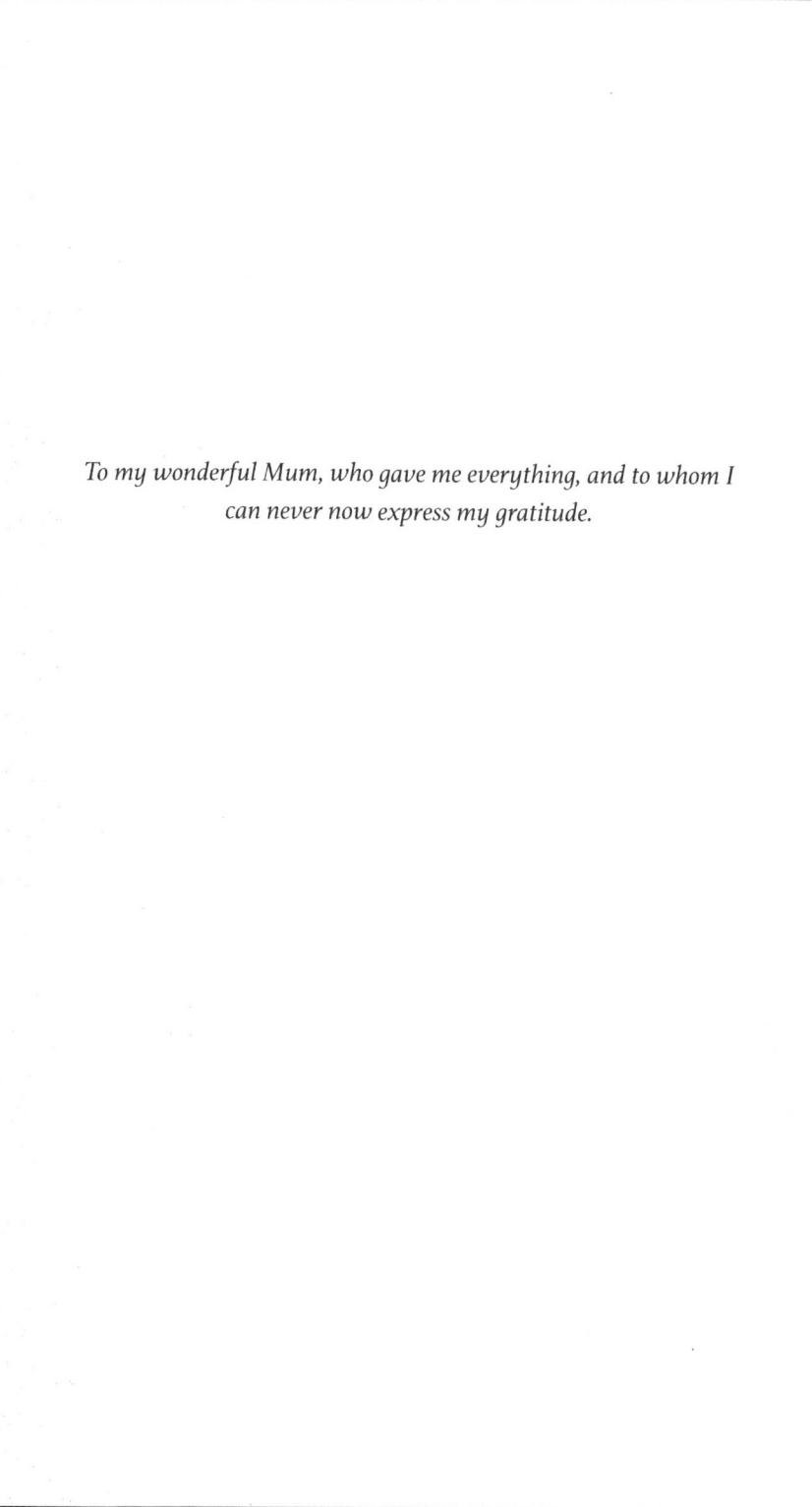

To my wonderful Mum, who gave me everything, and to whom I can never now express my gratitude.

CONTENTS

Join The Household! vii
Also by R. Marsden ix

Prologue 1
1. Some questions will always remain unanswered 5
2. Damage had already been done 11
3. Let's get on with it 20
4. No sort of an answer 28
5. Do as I tell you 37
6. Joan and Anthony 43
7. I would have loved him 51
8. Take me to him 57
9. Pies or no pies 66
10. We called it the Box of Death 74
11. Three days 86
12. His pretty boats 95
13. I just needed to sleep 106
14. My poet and my page 117
15. Shame for the rest of his life 125
16. His name is Quinn 133
17. How could you ever know the man? 146
18. They wanted their revenge 158
19. And then supper was served 167
20. We command the hill for now 175
21. And now he's dead 187
22. After the battle 195
23. Safe for the night 202
24. I whispered my own goodbyes 213
25. My draughty great hall 227
26. It doesn't make any sense 239
27. Chalk lines on a deerskin 251
28. Who dug it up? 260

29. I'll hang the bastard myself	276
30. An evil thing	284
31. No resignations	293
32. This new Kyown-Kinnie	304
33. Diplomacy	313
34. I know where it's buried	321
35. I intend to find treasure	332
36. Could anyone be so scrupulously honest?	341
37. The punishment seems entirely fitting	350
38. I wish he'd said so in the first place	358
39. We are going to York, you and I	369
40. It was no longer there	379
41. It was ready	391
42. This is what he meant	400
43. Crowbars and hammers	410
44. The only thing to do	422
Epilogue	433
Acknowledgments	445
Author's Note	447

JOIN THE HOUSEHOLD!

Join **The Castle Rory Household — an exclusive and free club for my newsletter subscribers!**

Members of **The Household** will receive *Mansurah: Jonny's Tale*, an ebook *only* available to **The Household**.

You'll also get my newsletters, full of exciting medieval facts, quizzes, stories and background information.

All you need to do is click here to subscribe to my newsletter and that's it, you're in!

If you would like to know more about Lord Rory's adventures, please go to: www.talesofcastlerory.co.uk

Join The Household!

ALSO BY R. MARSDEN

Tales of Castle Rory Series

Book 1: The Box of Death
Book 2: The Soldier of Fortune
Book 3: The Man in the Moon
Book 4: The King's Ransom
Book 5: The Paradise Garden
Book 6: The Foucois Legacy
Book 7: The End of Time

———◆———

Exclusively available to members of
The Household:
Mansurah: Jonny's Tale
(your free e-book when you join **The Household**!)

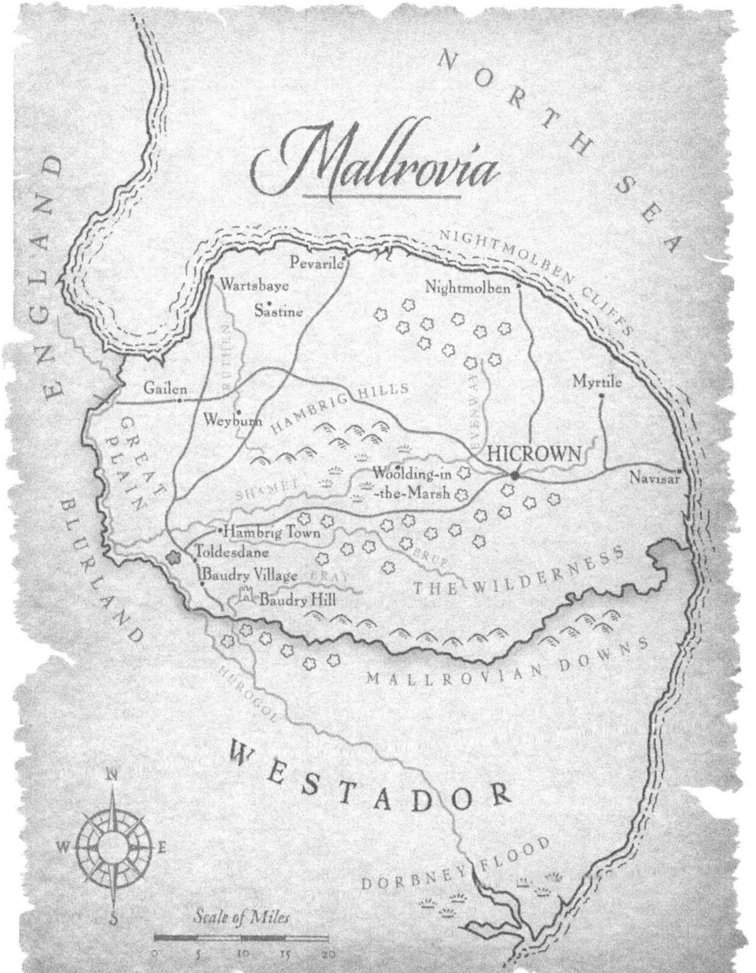
Mallrovia
NORTH SEA
ENGLAND
NIGHTMOLBEN CLIFFS
Pevarile
Wartsbaye
Sastine
Nightmolben
RUTHEN
Gailen
Weyburn
HAMBRIG HILLS
EVENWAY
Myrtile
GREAT PLAIN
HICROWN
Woolding-in
-the-Marsh
Navisar
SHAMET
BLURLAND
Hambrig Town
Toldesdane
BRUE
Baudry Village
ERAY
THE WILDERNESS
Baudry Hill
MALLROVIAN DOWNS
HUROGOL
WESTADOR
N
W
E
S
DORBNEY FLOOD
Scale of Miles
0
5
10
15
20

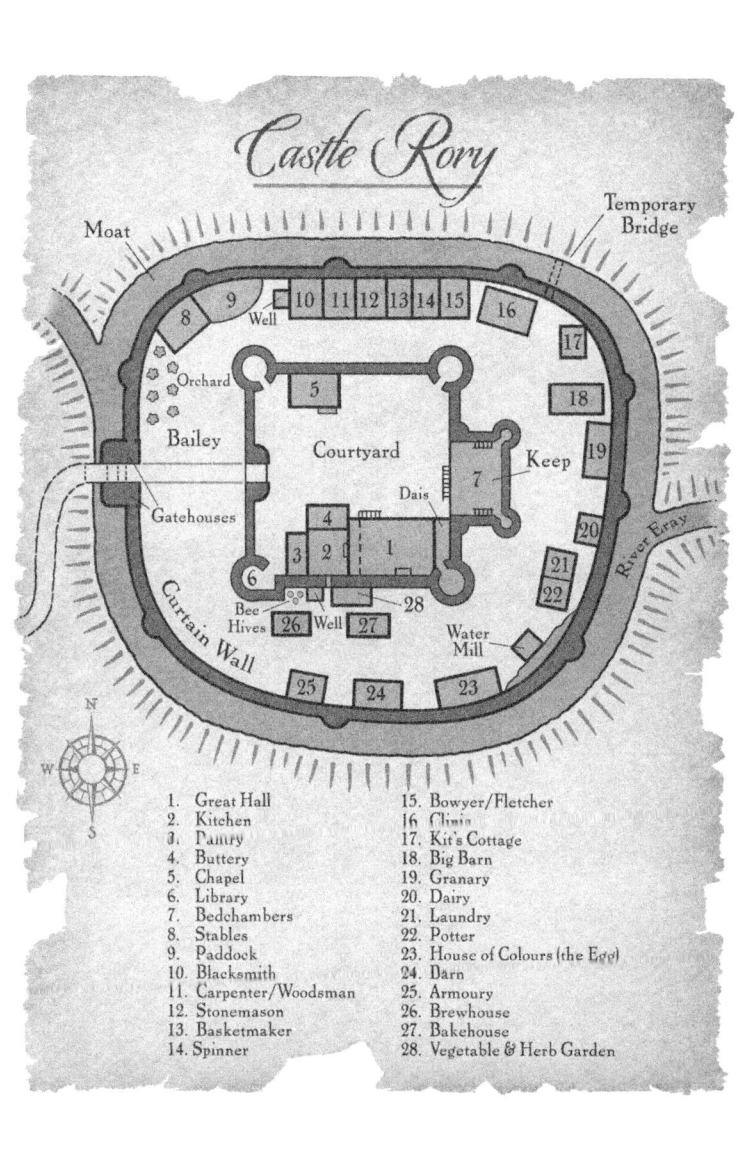

Castle Rory

1. Great Hall
2. Kitchen
3. Pantry
4. Buttery
5. Chapel
6. Library
7. Bedchambers
8. Stables
9. Paddock
10. Blacksmith
11. Carpenter/Woodsman
12. Stonemason
13. Basketmaker
14. Spinner
15. Bowyer/Fletcher
16. Clinic
17. Kit's Cottage
18. Big Barn
19. Granary
20. Dairy
21. Laundry
22. Potter
23. House of Colours (the Egg)
24. Barn
25. Armoury
26. Brewhouse
27. Bakehouse
28. Vegetable & Herb Garden

PROLOGUE

October, AD 1248

On a rare night of calm waters and soft moonlight, a coracle glides across the River Hurogol.

Three trainee warriors have broken out of their garrison in the castle on the hill. Full of mischief, and desperate for a change from the boredom of drills, parades and endlessly watching sheep from the wall-walk, tonight they are off to find the enemy.

On the other side of the river, having left their small boat on a mud weight, they wade through the reed-beds into the swamplands, deep into enemy territory. Their mission: to raid the enemy unseen, steal something of value and be home by daybreak. A joke, nothing more. So long as their commanding officer never finds out.

And now the enemy dwellings are in sight, a collection of wattle and daub huts, grouped around a central square of flat, well-trodden mud, where the enormous firepit still pulses with faintly glowing embers. There's a lookout, of course, but Alex fells him expertly to the ground.

The largest hut, over there on the right, must belong to the chief of the tribe. Kerry, Bess and Alex look at each other. With silent gestures, they decide they will steal from the chief himself.

The door to the hut is guarded only by a heavy rush curtain, a servant woman asleep outside. Bess gags the woman, ties her hands and pulls her out of the way.

The chieftain and his wife are asleep on a large wooden platform. Bess points to the woman, and Alex's eyes widen in astonishment. Seriously? They will kidnap the chieftain's wife? That was never the plan, but Bess is still pointing, so Alex gathers up the sleeping woman in one swift movement. She can't fight, or even scream – Alex has his arm pressed tightly over her mouth. The chieftain is dead to the world, his breath smelling of liquor. Kerry stuffs a rag into his open, snoring mouth, while Bess binds another cloth over his eyes. They spreadeagle him, roping him helplessly to the four corners of his bed.

The young warriors sweep their eyes around the hut, noting the evidence of chieftainship – the carved chair in the corner; woven rugs on the floor; fleeces hanging on the walls and covering the bed. Though primitive, this is a high-ranking dwelling. The audaciousness of their actions almost overwhelms them.

They hurry back to the swamp, carrying their prize. Bess has decided to leave the woman, unharmed, at the edge of the reeds where she will be easily found. Into the reed-bed and the swamp they all tumble, out of sight and earshot of the enemy village, and here Bess, Kerry and Alex explode into laughter and exaggerated back-slapping. Their prank has been a huge success. They have outdone themselves!

Prologue

On the boggy ground, the woman opens her eyes. She looks round in terror. Her breathing is ragged and harsh. To their dismay, the recruits see that the young woman is ill. They frown, disconcerted. Should they take her back to her husband? They cannot, after all, leave her in the swamp. But they don't have time. They are concerned for their coracle, the need to get home.

In the just-dawn light they notice another boat nearby, almost hidden in the reeds. It's a flat-bottomed fishing punt, not in good condition, but the inside is dry. They will place the woman in the punt, and surely the enemy tribesmen will find her soon. The sky is growing lighter now. They must get back before they are missed.

Paddling furiously home, they just about make it, falling in with the rest of Training Company on parade after breakfast. They never think about the kidnapped woman again.

1

SOME QUESTIONS WILL ALWAYS REMAIN UNANSWERED

May, AD 1263

The Sacred Gecko of the Nahvitch.

They say it can talk.

They say the Swamp-People tamed it, made it learn their language.

They say its gaze will kill you stone dead – unless you are of the Nahvitch tribe.

The Nahvitch, who are the Swamp-People, have given their deadly lizard a name: *Fiorello*

And now this creature is here, within my walls. Inside my home.

An hour ago, King Philip, newly arrived from the palace, was seated in my great hall, and he was furious.

'Is it true, then?' I asked him. 'What they're saying about Prince Barney?'

THE BOX OF DEATH

'It's true he's been a little fool,' Philip growled. 'He's been told enough times, but he just doesn't listen. Doesn't *want* to listen. It's a miracle he's still alive.'

Well, he was definitely that – I'd seen him with my own eyes, riding his proud Arab stallion into my courtyard, his cloak swept back off his shoulder, revealing its lining of ermine.

'As you can guess, my son went "adventuring". He took your servant lad, Sammy, did you know that?'

I didn't know it, and I didn't see how he could have done so.

'They met at the landing stage. Sammy was the bribe to get a boatman to sail Barney to the other side of the River Hurogol and guide him through Blurland into the heart of Nahvitch country.'

The swamp-dwelling tribe of Celts over the river. A persistent thorn in our side. The Nahvitch are our enemy; they always have been. Blurland is the name of the swamps where they live.

'How was Sammy a bribe?' I asked, but then suddenly understood. We'd all but forgotten Sammy is the son of a Nahvitch woman. Many years ago, one of our fishermen had ventured into the enemy swamplands on the hunt for pike. He found a small abandoned punt floating in the channel, and on it, half dead, lay a tribeswoman. The fisherman pulled the woman into his boat and brought her back to our side of the river. The woman recovered and married her rescuer, but later she died giving birth to a baby boy. The baby survived.

When Sammy was seven the Nahvitch came to our shores. They didn't find Sammy, but they knifed his father, leaving a message pinned to his body. The message was a promise that the Swamp-People would come back for their

Some questions will always remain unanswered

boy. Frightened out of his wits, Sammy ran up the hill to the castle and sought sanctuary and protection. In her workshop down by the curtain wall, the Lady Joan took him in.

'The Nahvitch want Sammy back,' I said.

'It was like this.' Philip's voice was harsh. 'Your squire arranged with Sammy that he would visit the Nahvitch with Prince Barney. Davy and Sammy rode to the boatmen's landing, where they met up with Barney. Davy and Barney had communicated in secret about everything.'

Philip stopped to take a deep breath. 'The boatman had been briefed. *Bribed* by your wretched squire, Rory! How much freedom does that boy have, for God's sake?'

'Philip, Davy has no more or less freedom than he should have. And if he has abused the little he had, he will be punished. But what of your son? What happened?'

'Barney and Sammy embarked on the Spiderboat. The boatman, who's disappeared by the way, took them across the River Hurogol, then nosed his boat through the swamp, along numerous dykes and ditches. Barney says he *must* have done it before, for he was unerring in his direction. This whole business has made me question the allegiance of the Spiderboatmen. They've always been a special group, and perhaps I have been too trusting. That, among other things, will be changing.'

I could hear the pain in the King's voice. His trusted Spiderboatmen. His network of couriers and spies, his eyes and ears throughout the kingdom, travelling swiftly along the Rivers Hurogol and Shamet, and all the many waterways that criss-cross the land, bringing news, bringing supplies, bringing us all together. *Could* they be working for the enemy? At the very least it was suspicious.

'Anyway,' Philip continued heavily, 'the boatman finally

arrived at a small jetty, and Barney and Sammy scrambled ashore. It's right over on the other side of the swamp, of course, and what's beyond *that* I guess only the Romans knew. They managed to get everywhere, didn't they. We, cooped up here in tiny Mallrovia, what do we know?'

He was bitter. Philip, like his father before him, and no doubt generations stretching back to the very Romans of whom he spoke, regretted and resented our apparent backsliding from the civilisation represented by the greatest empire that ever was. I do not believe in any such backsliding. Did the Romans ever build castles like ours? Did they have our system of fiefdoms and vassalage, a system that works in perfect harmony? No, they did not. We have moved on from them, or so I believe. But it's not my place to contradict a king.

'Well,' Philip went on, 'who do you think was standing on the jetty? Who was the welcome party?'

I shook my head.

'It was the Kyown-Kinnie himself!' Philip smacked his fist into his other palm in disbelief at what he was saying. 'The Kyown-Kinnie! Prince Barney and young Sammy were received by the High Chieftain of the Swamp-People! Now, why would that be? Why do *you* think that would be, Rory?'

'They were expected,' I said at once, for surely it must be so. 'Barney and Sammy were expected. And the Kyown-Kinnie was doing you honour. He knew he was meeting a king's son.'

'Pah!' snorted Philip. 'He wouldn't give a fig for that. The Kyown-Kinnie wouldn't care if it had been I, the King of Mallrovia, landing on his foul jetty. It wasn't *Barney's* status that drew him there, it was Sammy's.'

'*Sammy's*? What, just because his mother was a disgraced Nahvitch woman? Surely not!' For we had all long

Some questions will always remain unanswered

since deduced that Sammy's mother had been a Nahvitch whore, probably poxed, and that was why she had been left for dead in a drifting, rotten swamp punt.

'Ah well, that's not how Barney tells it,' Philip sneered. 'According to Barney, Sammy was given a hero's welcome, and was hurried away into the bosom of his family.'

'How did your son return? Did the boatman bring him back?'

The King rose and began to pace up and down. He seemed agitated.

'Barney was highly praised for escorting Sammy to his people. Barney was told he was welcome among the Nahvitch any time. And then he was given a large wooden box. The Kyown-Kinnie gave it personally to Barney, and told him not to open it until he was back in the palace. He said it was a great and precious gift, a thank-you from the tribe. It should be opened in front of the King and the entire royal family, so that all could marvel at it.'

'Where is this box? *Did* Barney open it in front of you?'

'The box is unopened, Rory. We have brought it with us in one of our wagons.'

'Unopened, sire? Why still unopened?'

Philip gave a strange high-pitched laugh. 'Before Barney returned with the boatman, Sammy ran out to say goodbye to him. And whispered secretly to him that he must never, ever open the box. Do you want to know what's in it? *Fiorello!*'

The lizard. The Sacred Gecko of the Nahvitch.

I was angry. 'Sire, why have you brought the box with you? Why not just destroy it?'

Castle Rory is my stronghold. The drawbridge was lowered for the royal family to visit us in peace and friendship, not to bring danger and death inside the curtain wall.

'I will tell you exactly why we have brought the lizard with us,' the King began, but at that moment a strident horn blared in the courtyard, drowning all other sounds and summoning my household to dinner in the great hall.

So far, I've had no answer to my question.

It's 8th May, Anno Domini 1263, and in my private journal I am writing an account of all that has taken place. I am the Lord of Hambrig, a frontline shire in the tiny kingdom of Mallrovia. England, a much bigger nation, lies to the west, and to the north and the east we are bounded by the sea. South of us lies little Westador, an unfriendly principality.

This is not the official record of Castle Rory, my home. It's personal to me, and private, for I have shown it to no one, nor will I. It is my dream that one day, maybe a long time from now, someone will read my *Tales of Castle Rory* and understand how and why we did what we did. As for *this* Tale, hopefully by the end of it we will know why King Philip thought fit to visit my home, bringing with him the deadly lizard. But then again, maybe not. It's my belief that some questions will always remain unanswered.

2

DAMAGE HAD ALREADY BEEN DONE

Once the roast meats, the rich gravy and the baked pies had all been consumed, we could sit back and relax. The candles and torches had been lit, and the huge fireplace seemed alive as the logs crackled and sparked, the flames throwing their light on the whitewashed stone walls. It was time for some entertainment. My bard emerged from the shadows, carrying her harp.

Accompanied by chords of great beauty, Amie's high, clear voice rang out, but it was not so much a song as a strange, rhythmic chant, and after I'd heard the first few lines, I found myself sitting up and looking around in alarm to gauge everyone's reaction – not least the King's.

'Twas in the night the Nahvitch came,
With spears and torches all a-flame.
They put our women to the sword,
And slew our good and noble lord.

Our skilful soldiers, tightly knit,

THE BOX OF DEATH

Defending Hambrig, made them quit.
Our warriors were a fearsome sight,
The Nahvitch pissed themselves with fright!

But later on the Nahvitch sent,
To say they'd get new armament;
Their brand-new weapon did arrive,
And, so they boasted, 'It's alive!'

We sent our spies to flnd out more,
They died upon the swampy shore.
We found out they'd been ripped and scissored
And cut to death by some great lizard!

How could a lizard murder men?
Our warriors approached again.
The Sacred Gecko turned and said,
'All those on whom I gaze are dead!'

Some soldiers fled and scattered wide
(Though many stayed and many died.)
The Gecko hissed its wicked spell,
And watched, unblinking, as they fell.

We know it's crossed the Hurogol,
Thus bringing peril to us all!
To take such risks would make us wince,
Had we not trusted in our prince!

Its eyes, its teeth, its open jaws,
Its sticky feet and grippy claws,
With skin of iridescent yellow,
Beware the Gecko - Fiorello!

Damage had already been done

As Amie screamed out the last word of her song, there came a thunder of applause, amplified a hundredfold by pewter goblets banging on tables, booted feet stamping, everyone shouting, yelling, fists in the air. I held my breath. The noise went on and on, as Amie stood triumphant on the hearth and took a mocking bow.

A mighty roar came from my left. Everyone turned to the high table, and an angry, edgy silence fell. The King was on his feet. With terrible strength, he lifted and overturned the mighty table itself, hurling dishes, leftover food and flagons of wine onto the floor. King Philip stood before us, our greatest warlord, his arms raised, his palms flat towards the people, while the firelight threw a huge shadow of his form onto the wall behind, making him look ten feet tall. Prince Barney had also risen, a stunned look on his handsome face. He ran furiously from the hall.

I hadn't realised the presence of the gecko in the castle was common knowledge. I should have remembered nothing is secret in such a close-knit circle of people. The distinction between rumour and fact is never a high priority among the gossips and the tongue-waggers.

Amie had told them the Sacred Gecko was here among us, and she had mocked Prince Barney, also here among us. I was suddenly alert to the very real possibility of a riot, right here in my home.

Instinctively I looked round for my steward and found him right beside me. Sir Patrick of Myrtle. Tall, spare, old enough to have served my father before me, a wise advisor and a man of few words, all of them to the point.

'At least nobody's armed,' he murmured. Which was indeed a blessing, but of course no one is allowed to bring weapons into the great hall.

'Patrick, close the castle. Lock everything and raise the drawbridge.'

'Already done.'

'Where's the Lady Joan?'

'Gone. But she knows something she's not telling us – something about Sammy, I believe.'

The huge iron-studded door at the other end was slowly closing. If the company noticed, if there were a stampede to get out, we would not be able to contain them. I looked over at Amie and found her eyes locked with mine. I beckoned to her.

'What the *hell* was that all about?'

Most lords would have bundled her straight into the dungeon, her harp snapped into pieces before her eyes. The King had already accused me of being too lenient. If Amie had taken advantage of me, she would pay for it.

Amie dropped a respectful curtsy. 'Lord, this gecko has been brought to your castle. It is here, in our midst, and it is a killer. Would you allow a murderer within these walls? We who live here have always felt safe under your protection. So why has the Nahvitch animal been allowed in? They say it only has to look at you, and you fall down dead! They say Prince Barney brought it here.'

'They say a lot of things. Do you have to believe everything you hear?'

'No, lord. But I do believe this because Prince Barney has spoken with your squire, who told your page, who told the kitchen, and then—'

'And then it was all round the castle,' I finished for her. 'Look what you've done, girl!'

'I'm not sorry, lord. They have a right to know!'

I thrust Amie into Patrick's arms. 'Take her somewhere safe. Make sure she's alone and contained.'

Damage had already been done

King Philip had dropped his arms to his sides and was talking to Queen Julia, who had remained remarkably calm throughout everything. I leant over and asked the two of them to sit down. Servants were righting the table, picking up the debris.

I called on my household to listen to me.

'We need some restraint! Rioting and panicking will not help. I am going to find out what the situation is, and I will tell you myself later.'

'Where's the gecko, lord?' someone shouted.

'As I've just said, I need to investigate. You may all go from the hall, but no one leaves the castle. I will summon you back here when there is news.'

And now the great hall was empty of all but the royal family and me.

I bowed to the Queen. 'Your Majesty, we need to talk to the prince.'

'Indeed we do. I will send one of his sisters to fetch him.'

'No, ma'am, that will not do. For one thing, none of us knows where the prince has gone, and for another, it would not be safe. We had best wait for Patrick. He will find a way to bring Prince Barney to us.'

And Patrick, as on so many other occasions, anticipated my needs, and entered the hall with Barney firmly clasped at the elbow. The young prince sat down opposite me.

I addressed him sternly. 'Prince Barney, where is Fiorello, the Sacred Gecko of the Nahvitch?'

'He is in a box in our wagon in the courtyard.' Barney's voice was low but clear, his gaze direct. 'I haven't done anything wrong, Lord Rory. I went adventuring, that's all. I did meet the Kyown-Kinnie, and he was very nice to me. That's all that happened.'

'What of Sammy?'

'Sammy stayed with the Swamp-People. They said he was one of them. He wanted to stay, he's not their prisoner. He wanted to go back to his own people.'

'And the gecko? Why have you brought it here?'

'Lord, the gecko isn't even dangerous! Everyone thinks it can kill you just by looking at you, but it can't, it's just a lizard. The Kyown-Kinnie gave it to me in friendship. It's a gift.'

The King interrupted. 'Why would the Nahvitch chief give anything to you?'

The boy shrugged. 'They were just being friendly. And also I'd brought Sammy back to them, so they gave me a pet lizard in gratitude. What's wrong with that?'

I wondered if Barney really believed it. The gecko was harmless? Well, there was only one way to find out.

'Have you opened the box?'

'Not yet.'

'But why not? If the gecko's harmless, why not have a good look at it? Let it out, watch it walk around. What have you done about feeding it?' I watched his Adam's apple bobbing nervously in his throat.

'Oh, I'm going to do all that.' It didn't sound convincing.

'Perhaps you could go and get it now,' I suggested.

'No!' gasped his older sister. 'He can't! Don't make him do that, Lord Rory. What if he's wrong? Fiorello will kill him!'

The King and Queen looked at each other in consternation. The youngest child looked bored. Barney didn't seem particularly eager to fetch his gift.

I stood up. 'Sir Patrick will look after you. I am going to find the Lady Joan.'

The King and Queen turned to Patrick, and he smiled reassuringly at them as I strode from the hall and walked

Damage had already been done

quickly down to the bottom of the bailey where Joan's textiles workshop stands.

On the lintel of the door is a wooden sign with painted wobbly letters declaring *Got Egg Need Teacher*. It was Sammy's attempt at writing, after his teacher, the Lady Joan, had sent him to fetch eggs from the hen house. She was so proud of his achievement, she mounted the sign over her door, and her workshop has been known as the *Egg* ever since. Inside, the Lady Joan was busy preparing some sort of mash for her chickens. She had her back to me, but she knew I was standing in the doorway.

'Where's Sammy?' I asked. 'What do you know?'

Joan turned. 'I expect you know exactly where Sammy is. He's with the Nahvitch.'

'Why?'

'They're his people.'

'No more than we are. He has a Nahvitch mother and a Mallrovian father.'

'But he has never seen his mother's folk! He must have been desperate to make contact, and after all he's fourteen now. I'm sorry he didn't let us know, but it may be a good thing he's gone to see his family.'

All these statements made sense, but the Lady Joan had taken Sammy in when he had no one. She'd mothered him, cared for him, taught him everything he knew. I didn't believe either of them would want to part from the other so easily.

'What was your part in Barney's adventuring?' I asked her. 'Did you set it up?'

'I didn't need to set anything up, lord. Your squire did it all.'

I frowned at the formal address she was adopting.

I moved inside and shut the door behind me. 'You and I

are old friends, Joan. Let's have no more "lord" when we speak.' I'd known this woman since I became Lord of Hambrig, and she'd been a friend of my father's before that. 'Now tell me. What really happened?'

Joan sat down at her table and gestured to the stool opposite. I noticed the table was covered in a new cloth. It was a beautiful colour, something between blue and green. I'd never seen anything like it. When I looked up, I saw she was amused. 'It's called pavonalilis,' she said. 'Well, that's what we call it, anyway. Lapis lazuli, together with some herbs and grasses, ground into a paste in water, then boiled in a copper urn.'

'It's beautiful,' I murmured, fingering the fabric. 'The colour – so bright and vivid. Is it just for the table? Do you have a gown in this shade?'

Joan laughed. 'No gown, Rory, no. It was just an experiment, something for Sammy to try once.'

'*Sammy* did this?' I was incredulous. 'Well, that brings us full circle, doesn't it. You were about to tell me what happened to him.'

'Sammy went without my permission. I've long wanted him to see his people, his mother's people I should say, but I was going to ask you for an escort for him. I didn't know anything about Barney's "adventure". As I understand it, it was Davy's idea anyway.'

'Joan, I know you know more than you're saying. What is it?'

She was silent for a few moments, almost as if she were wondering how much to tell me. I cursed under my breath.

'I really don't know much more.' Joan put both hands flat on the table. 'Sammy turned fourteen last month, and he knows our custom here. A fourteen-year-old boy, especially if he's the son of a noble family, is sent away to learn to be a knight. Sammy wanted something similar for himself. He had itchy feet. He needed to explore the wider world, to expand his horizons.'

'Then why didn't the silly child talk to me?' I cried. 'I'd have arranged something for him here in Mallrovia. He didn't need to put us all in danger with a trip to the swamps!'

'I'm sure he didn't think he was doing that, Rory. And *of course* he should have spoken with you first. If you talk to Davy, you'll probably find the three boys put their heads together and decided Barney's "adventure" and Sammy's itch to travel could usefully be combined. Davy was the link between the palace and here. He has more brains than Barney and more experience than Sammy. He cooked the whole thing up.'

'And what about the gecko?' I growled, furious with the lot of them.

'The gecko, yes. You know, I never really believed in that legend. A gecko that talks? That kills just by looking at you? It's not likely, is it?'

'Yet apparently it was given to Prince Barney. The Kyown-Kinnie gave it to him in a box, telling him the lizard isn't dangerous at all.'

'Well there you are then!' Joan said triumphantly. 'I said it couldn't happen. The lizard's just an ordinary reptile, it can't kill you and it can't talk. The Kyown-Kinnie says so!'

'And of course we believe everything the enemy tells us,' I said sarcastically, rising from the table with its colourful covering. 'Joan, it's getting late. I'm going back to see that everything is all right and that no one's burnt the place down in their excitement at Amie's song this afternoon.'

My last remark was meant to be flippant, but as I walked out of the *Egg*, I thought that between Barney, Davy, Sammy and Amie considerable damage had already been done.

3

LET'S GET ON WITH IT

I knew Patrick would have made sure the Watch was set and the fires doused. My household would be preparing for bed. Except, perhaps, for Amie, who would be fretting about her fate. The royals, too, had much to think about.

In the great hall, Patrick was waiting for me with his report.

'All is well,' he said in his measured voice, and together we began to walk across to our bedchambers in the keep. 'Your poet is secured for the night. The King and Queen are in the solar. It is unfortunate, but Prince Barney found your squire before I could get to either of them and they have been talking. Naturally, they would not repeat their conversation to me. I have now ensured that Davy and the prince are separated, but who knows what devilry passed between them before that?'

He left, his own chamber being next to mine. I quickly stripped off my clothes and fell, exhausted, into bed.

Let's get on with it

In the morning we were all in chapel, and Laurence, our elderly chaplain, read to us from the Bible. The Latin words rolled around the building, carried by the weight of centuries which even Laurence's reedy voice could not lighten. Afterwards, Laurence would paraphrase the text, adding his own homilies and tedious chastisements. I remember Laurence in this very chapel from my boyhood, and he seemed ancient to me even then. But chapel is a good place to be every morning; it gives me a daily opportunity to observe my household in an attitude of prayer. So, while they all had their eyes closed, or penitently on the ground, I had mine on them. Laurence shuffled distractedly in front of his lectern, his crabby fingers picking at the parchments that lay there. He didn't need them; he knew all his scriptures by heart. I decided the old man was probably desperate for a piss.

I looked over at the bard, Amie. She was more penitent than anyone, prostrate on the floor, her head turned to the left, eyes tight shut, arms flung wide. The shape of Christ's cross. Patrick stood next to her, and, briefly, his eyes met mine, before he looked dutifully down, contemplating his sins. As we were all supposed to be doing. I examined my conscience, but found nothing there that would not wait.

After Mass I sought out Prince Barney. He had been crying. Perhaps his sinful behaviour had overwhelmed him, but more likely it was because he'd been given a thorough bollocking by his parents.

Out in the sunny courtyard, I asked him if the gecko were still alive.

'I don't know, lord,' he answered miserably, scrubbing his arm across his face. 'It can breathe, I think. I'm sure there are tiny holes in the lid of its box.'

'Has it water to drink?'

'I – I was told it doesn't need water.'

'And we still don't know if it will kill us,' I reminded him.

'It won't, lord,' Barney said earnestly. 'It's harmless. I told you.'

'And yet you couldn't listen to Amie's song. If that was all nonsense, why did it upset you so?'

'I was upset *because* it was nonsense. Amie was making everyone believe that poor Fiorello is a monster. I know he isn't.'

'Barney, you are lying. What really happened in Blurland?'

'It was very confused on the Nahvitch jetty,' Barney said desperately. 'The Kyown-Kinnie gave me the box. He said there was a precious gift inside it. Then Sammy ran over and whispered that I shouldn't open the box until I had returned home.'

'Until you'd returned home? I thought he told you not to open it at all.'

Barney said with sudden passion, 'I don't believe the Kyown-Kinnie would trick me like that. He embraced us! He had his servants bow to us! I liked him.'

'Go and fetch the box,' I commanded, and watched panic spread over his face.

'I – it's in the chapel. We put it there. My sisters helped me. We put it in the chapel so that God would protect us all.'

Clearly Barney wasn't convinced by his own argument that the gecko was harmless.

'Then let us go and see it there,' I said, and we retraced our steps to the chapel. I was wondering where they'd put it,

Let's get on with it

as I certainly hadn't noticed a large wooden box around during Mass. No wonder. They had placed the box behind the very altar, and I was appalled. I stared at Barney, for some moments quite unable to speak.

'This is a desecration,' I said at last. 'You have placed this evil animal at the spot where the Host is consecrated.' I took a step back from him.

'Lord,' Barney began, on the verge of tears again, but I interrupted.

'Get it *out* from here.'

Between us, we carried the heavy box outside. I heard the animal scrabbling about inside it, and we could feel its weight shifting from side to side as we manoeuvred the thing through the chapel and out into the sunlight. We set it down on the stump where logs are split for the various fireplaces in the castle. We could hear the animal's claws on the wood, and we could hear it breathing and snuffling.

'Send for Laurence,' I said to Barney. 'We need a priest here. And get Master Peter and Doctor Bethan as well.'

Peter of Redmire has been practising alchemy and other mysterious skills for years. I didn't know how well informed he was on the habits of geckos, but I decided he should be here, just in case. And our physician knows much about medicines, herbs, potions and liniments. If anyone was going to get hurt – or worse – it would be Bethan who either patched them up or declared them unpatchable.

We waited, and eventually we had our little gathering. Around the stump and its teetering wooden box stood Laurence, wringing his hands in distress (fat lot of good he's going to be, I thought); Peter, who looked both curious and excited; Bethan, with her bag of gruesome tools and a box of herbal remedies; Barney, who was extremely anxious; Sir Jonny, general in command of the garrison, though I hadn't sent for him and don't know why he turned up; and myself. We were a silent and nervy group.

Suddenly a messenger arrived: my page, younger brother of my squire, both sons of Baron Giles of Wartsbaye.

'Lord, I have a message from his Majesty the King,' squeaked the child. He could not take his eyes off the box on the stump, and his mouth gaped wide in horror as he heard the lizard shifting inside.

'The message, Gael?' I asked.

'Oh! You are to send Prince Barney to his Majesty forthwith.'

This was not unexpected. The King was absent because of the great risk to him when we opened Fiorello's box. And Barney is his heir. I jerked my head at Barney to tell him to leave.

'I think I should stay,' the young prince said, his voice quavering but his gaze steady, holding my own. 'I brought the gecko here. I should be here when we open the box.'

And suddenly I found some respect for him. Barney is a good-looking young man, with thick brown hair and well-proportioned features. He always looks fearlessly at you, his back straight, his head held high. Throughout his childhood he was mischievous and unpredictable, and over the years this mischief has developed into the so-called 'adventuring', but at sixteen he should be turning his attention to learning the art of kingship. Wayward behaviour is not what we want from our ruler.

'It is your decision,' I said. It wasn't of course, but I decided to make it so. When the prince did not move from his place, I turned back to my page. 'Tell his Majesty that Prince Barney is too much of a man to leave his post. Make sure you use those exact words, Gael.'

The small boy nodded, but couldn't seem to tear himself

Let's get on with it

away from the box on the stump. Exasperated, I shooed him off.

We all turned our attention once again to the box. 'We should wear masks!' Laurence said unexpectedly. 'For protection, lord. We should all wear masks!'

Sir Jonny gazed at him pityingly. 'Laurence, you addled old fool, if the gecko can kill us with his gaze 'twill make no difference that *we* cannot see *him!*'

There was a chuckle from the assembled company, and poor Laurence flushed red. Jonny was right, of course – firstly that the priest was indeed an addled old fool, and secondly that the gecko would kill us all stone dead if the rumours were true. And that would be the end of Castle Rory, the end of Hambrig, and the end, most probably, of the kingdom itself. *The end of time*, said a voice in my head, though I had no idea why.

'Then – what if we open the box in the dark? So that the creature cannot see us?' This was our physician, Doctor Bethan. There was a murmur of support for this suggestion. I considered it.

'We don't know if the gecko can see in the dark,' I said finally. 'In addition, we would be at a disadvantage, not being able to see it ourselves, not knowing where it was and what it was doing. And aside from all of that, we still wouldn't know its powers. At some point we would *have* to let it see us.'

'No!' cried Laurence, clutching at his robes in agitation. 'No, we cannot take the risk, we must not. Let us throw the gecko, box and all, into the river. Quickly now! We must kill it before it kills us!'

And this from a man of God!

I seized him by the cowl of his robe, almost pulling him off his feet. 'I brought you here to say prayers for us,' I snarled, 'not to spread alarm and panic. You have not understood what we are doing here.'

I released the miserable priest, who whimpered and massaged his neck.

'But perhaps t' holy man is right,' spoke up Peter the alchemist. 'It'd solve our problem. No more Fiorello, no more danger.'

'Or *burn* it,' screamed Laurence suddenly, hopping up and down. 'Set fire to it! Get rid of the evil thing now!'

'He is right,' stated a new voice, and we all turned. The Queen was among us.

Instinctively, I bowed. 'Ma'am!'

'Lord Rory, it is your duty to protect this stronghold and your people. This creature, this evil lizard, must be destroyed. I do not want my son's foolish behaviour to be the death of him or anyone else.'

Laurence's head was bobbing in agreement. Peter nodded earnestly too. Sir Jonny was looking directly at me, his soldier's face inscrutable. Bethan, the observant physician, missed nothing, her eyes darting from each of us to the other. Prince Barney, humiliated, looked at his mother and shook his head, but she was taking no notice of him. Her eyes were on me.

'Lord Rory,' she said again, 'his Majesty and I received the message from your page. We understand that Prince Barney has shown great courage and we commend him. We do not believe he now needs to give his life to prove himself. We are convinced of his bravery and his honour, and we command you, as lord of this castle, this estate and all Hambrig, to destroy the gecko. We cannot, *we must not*, take the risk of opening the box. Your bard, for all her disrespectful and seditious chanting, at least made the position very clear to us all last night. The gecko is death.

Let's get on with it

Both I and his Majesty your King order you to destroy it. Go now to the river. Throw the box and its evil contents into the water.'

So. It was an order. I bowed to her again. 'As your Majesties wish.'

I picked up the box. The lizard moved weightily inside and everyone gasped as the thing rocked in my arms. 'Prince Barney and I will see to this,' I informed them. 'We shall need neither blessings nor medicines, as it turns out. Laurence, Peter and Bethan, you will return to your normal duties.' And, with Barney hovering anxiously at my side, I turned to leave.

But Sir Jonny stood before me. 'I will come with you. As commander of your household troops, I have a duty of protection second only to your own. I shall be a part of this, to make sure we are all safe.'

I nodded. 'Come on then. Let's get on with it.'

4

NO SORT OF AN ANSWER

My marshal brought us our horses saddled and ready. The three of us mounted and rode off in silence. Sir Jonny had already assured me that the guard had been turned out, and his best officers, Captain Kerry and Sergeants Bess and Alex, were on duty in the gatehouse. He takes no chances, and I knew what he was thinking. Jonny and I go back a long way – to Louis IX's Crusade fifteen years ago, in fact.

As we rode along, I examined the box perched precariously in front of me. Barney was wrong, there were no holes in the lid. I wondered what else the young idiot had been lying about. Instead of holes, the lid was decorated with strange marks, lines carved into the wood in a pattern, much repeated. I traced the carved lines with my forefinger. They had been deliberately made, there was no doubt about that. And then I realised. The marks made a rather strange letter F, though with only one horizontal line. But maybe the Swamp-People write their letter F like that. F for *Fiorello,* of course. The box itself was very well made, using oak planking with neatly butted joins, and the lid had a deep

No sort of an answer

overhang, making sure the contents were safe. There were no rough edges, and no splintering. It may have been varnished at one time, but the resin remained only in patches. A pity – a beautifully crafted box like that deserved to be cared for. Well, it would hardly matter now, if we were just going to throw the whole thing into the river.

I chose a place where the river shoals and there's a shallow slope down to the stony shore. We dismounted at the top of the slope, and I handed the box down to Jonny, who placed it carefully on a large, flat stone. Even though the sun still shone and the day was bright and warm, the Hurogol looked grey and cold. It almost always does. I shaded my eyes to see the shoreline on the other side, but the Hurogol is swift-flowing and wide, and the land is flat. It's hard to make out the division between land and water. No wonder the swamps have always been known as 'Blurland'.

Barney stood behind me. I could sense his nervy fidgeting. 'I – I need to tell you something, lord.' There was an ominous wobble in his voice.

I'd been expecting this, and indicated that the three of us should sit. We each found some sort of stony surface and made ourselves reasonably comfortable, the gecko's box in the middle. It felt as if we were about to make some sort of religious sacrifice, and perhaps we were. The sun was high overhead now, and I thought it a shame we couldn't let the lizard out to enjoy the sunshine one last time. I know geckos come from hot climates and enjoy warm weather. Fiorello would have liked to bask in the sun – after killing us stone dead, no doubt.

'Lord Rory,' Barney began, 'we can't just drop the box in the water. There's a reason. But I'm not supposed to tell you about it.'

'Yet you must, mustn't you?' I answered, and he nodded glumly and frowned at the racing tide.

Then he looked up. 'Sammy spoke to me, as I told you. But he didn't say I should never open the box. I made that up because I didn't want anyone to open it. I never imagined your chaplain would say we should burn it or drown it. I just thought we'd leave it alone. Then I had to say the gecko's harmless. I was trying to stop the panic, but that didn't work either.' He stopped, and poked around in the pebbles with his shoe.

'Go on, Barney,' said Jonny, encouragingly. 'What did Sammy actually say?'

'He gave me a note, and he told me to read it in private. He said I mustn't show it to anyone, nor reveal its contents, until I had proved myself. That's what he said when the Kyown-Kinnie gave me the box.'

I held out my hand, and Barney reached into his tunic and pulled out a small, folded piece of scraped parchment. With a hiccup, he handed it to me.

I unfolded it carefully and read it aloud.

Fiorello is death to those he looks upon. Only a person of great courage and determination will open this box, but if such a one can be found, a great reward will be his. This message comes from Hope, Endurance and a New Beginning.

I looked up in consternation. Jonny was gazing at Barney, who looked like death.

'It means I am to open it,' Barney said wretchedly. 'That's what Sammy meant when he said I have to prove myself. I am to be the brave person who lets the gecko look at him. And it will kill me.'

'But who or what are Hope, Endurance and a New

No sort of an answer

Beginning?' I asked, bewildered. 'And if the gecko kills you, then what's your great reward? It doesn't make any sense.'

'It's probably not meant to,' said Jonny at once. 'It's a nonsense. And we all know what Sammy's like. He likes to pretend he's more important than he really is. This will be some rubbish he's invented, for sure.'

'Well,' I said robustly, standing up, 'I'm not so sure it's rubbish. And if you think Sammy is capable of writing a message like this, you don't know him very well. It's not Sammy's work, so we don't know what it is or who it's from. Personally, I'm for finding out what the great reward is!'

They scrambled to their feet and stared at me in disbelief.

'The message says a person of great courage and determination will open the box,' I explained. 'I daresay that between the three of us, we've determination and courage enough. Let us hold hands, linking our courage and our lives, and see what the gecko does.'

'We will all die,' whispered Barney.

I don't know why, but I didn't believe we would. For where would be the reward in that?

Jonny moved forward, his eyes alight, and suddenly we were reckless young men and it was the Holy War all over again. 'Let's do it!' He grasped my left hand in his right, and Barney's hand on his other side. I reached out for Barney, and we linked up around Fiorello. But with our hands in each other's, we couldn't open the box. Again, it was Jonny who moved, letting go of Barney and me, then bending down to examine the fastenings.

'See? There are four bolts, one on each side. I am going to release each bolt carefully. Then it should be possible to prise off the lid, perhaps with a foot.'

And he slowly and carefully wriggled each bolt

downwards through its shaft and into its bed. When all four had been drawn, he stood up, and again we all clasped hands. I hitched the toe of my boot under the lip of the box's lid and lifted it slightly. The lid moved. I knew then that if I jerked my foot, the lid would fly off. I reported my findings to the other two. We were ready.

'I'll count to three,' I told them, and hoped Barney's nerve would hold. 'One. Two. Three!' I jerked the toe of my boot hard, and the wooden lid tipped backwards and clattered onto the stones. The box was open.

An extremely angry rabbit leapt out, bounded up the grassy slope and was gone before any of us could blink. I almost laughed. Jonny's mouth had fallen open, his clammy hand still in mine. He seemingly couldn't move. Barney fell suddenly to the ground and lay curled up in a tight little ball. And we were all, quite definitely and quite wonderfully, still alive.

Some time afterwards we were back on our stones in our little group, gathered around the wooden box as if nothing had happened. There was a flagon of wine in one of my saddle bags. My thoughtful marshal, Branca, must have put it there, and we took turns to drink from it. It revived us.

'But what actually happened?' Barney asked. It had taken time for him to be able to speak at all. Jonny and I had tried to uncurl him, but he was convinced the deadly gecko was nearby. He had become hysterical, and in the end Jonny had cupped his hands in the river and had thrown cold water on the lad. Yet he'd shown courage when it mattered. Gripping my hand like a vice and gabbling the Lord's Prayer, he had stood totally still while I levered the lid off the box. I think it was the sight of the rabbit, and the suddenness of its jumping out that did for Barney. But he came round eventually, and now sat between us with a

No sort of an answer

woollen blanket around his shoulders, shivering but cheerful.

'What happened?' I repeated. 'What happened is that, being fools, we were fooled.' Barney gazed blankly at me. I looked over at Jonny and saw that he, too, was in the dark. I sighed. 'You see, the message never said that Fiorello was in the box. You were never told that, were you, Barney? The Kyown-Kinnie didn't say it. You assumed it when you read the note, which said that Fiorello will kill you if he looks at you. But it didn't say he was inside the box! The writer of the message knew we'd assume the two things were connected; we would assume a deadly creature was in here. And so only a person of great courage would dare to open the box.'

For a few moments I watched the two of them digest the idea that Fiorello had not somehow turned into a rabbit. That he had never been in the box at all.

'And the "great reward"?' breathed Jonny.

'Ah yes. The reward.'

I inched forward to the box. Not one of us had touched it or its lid since the rabbit's escape. I peered into it, then lifted it, shook it, and finally turned it upside down. A few rabbit droppings fell out, and then it was, quite simply, an empty box. Disappointed and puzzled, I put it back on the shingle.

'Looks like there's no reward for us after all,' I said lightly. The other part of the puzzle also remained unsolved. What had the writer meant by 'Hope, Endurance and a New Beginning?' And who had written the message?

I turned again to Barney. 'It was Sammy who gave you the parchment?'

He nodded.

'Did he say how he came by it, who gave it to him?'

Barney shook his head.

'Well,' I mused, 'it didn't come from Sammy, that's for

sure. I know he's been working hard for Joan, but she hasn't managed to get him to write like that yet. He's still at the "cat sat on the mat" stage. So he must have got the message from someone else. But who?' I paused for a moment. 'Here's the thing. You are both to be silent about this afternoon's events. No one is to know Fiorello was not in the box. No one is to know we did not just throw the box into the river, as instructed by the Queen. You are both sworn to absolute secrecy until I have had a chance to speak to their Majesties.'

They bowed their heads and placed their hands within mine, as when swearing allegiance. The wine being finished, we climbed into our saddles and headed slowly home in the afternoon sunshine. I barely noticed the ride back, and my mare, Guinevere, needed no cues from me to find her way home.

I knew I would have to account for disobeying my King and Queen. Then there was Davy, my squire. I compressed my lips. Davy has a lot of explaining to do. And what of Sammy? The Lady Joan seemed remarkably calm about his disappearance, his apparent defection to the enemy. As for Fiorello – does he even exist?

It took Jonny's hailing me twice before I heard and saw the party of troubadours tramping along the road towards us, a group of three, carrying their instruments and chattering as they walked. They seemed cheerful, and I thought it would be good to book them for the evening. Amie would not perform again for some time, if ever, and we needed a diversion, something to bring us all together in merriment,

No sort of an answer

song and dance. I reined Guinevere to a halt and slid to the ground. The troubadours doffed their hats.

'Noble lord,' said one, bowing extravagantly low. 'We are travelling musicians, and need only our food and a bed for the night in return for as much music and song as you wish!'

I introduced myself: 'I am Lord Rory of Hambrig.' But I saw at once that they already knew me. 'You've been to the castle?'

'We have indeed,' said their spokesman, 'and were told you were away. And so we were sent away too, in short order, by your guard!'

'Then retrace your steps, musicians. We'll have your best work in our great hall tonight!'

I walked with them, leading Guinevere, letting Jonny and Barney ride ahead, and I learnt their names – Master Kit, Master Christopher and Mistress Annis. I was intrigued at their instruments. Master Kit plays tambour and gittern, while Mistress Annis sings the songs. She told me the words of each song could be changed to fit the occasion and the company. How bawdy would we like them?

I smiled at her. 'Not too bawdy, mistress. We have the King and Queen of Mallrovia with us!'

At that, their faces were a picture, and I laughed aloud.

'You are joking, lord?' asked Master Christopher anxiously.

'Indeed I'm not,' I assured him. 'The royal family are visiting Hambrig for a short while. And one of the riders up yonder is Prince Barney, the heir to the throne.'

'We are not from these parts,' Master Kit said hastily. 'We have come from the south.' He was a young man with an exuberant expression, curly black hair and dark, deep-set eyes.

'How far south?' I asked, curiously. 'And how did you get here?'

At that, Master Kit did an extraordinary thing. He turned around and began to skip backwards, twirling a wooden stick in the way wizards and conjurors do. And as he skipped, he sang a very strange song.

Over the mountains and onto the Downs,
Crossing the plains and then passing the towns,
Looking at treetops and under the ground,
Pretty things hide, but they want to be found!
On through the water, but not through the sea,
Splishing and splashing, the travelling's free!
Only a minstrel! I'm not some great lord,
Tiptoeing through, that's all I can afford!
Dirty and murky and chiefly I go,
Hither and thither, but you'll never know.
Places and faces and spaces I've seen,
Prancing along like a merry machine.
What a good boy, taking Mother's advice.
You gave me everything, wasn't that nice!
These are my friends who've been waiting for me,
Having a grand time with posh royalty.
So I've returned and I want you to know,
'Mission Accomplished' is still 'way to go'.
Dancing or singing or boxing in fun,
Now I've arrived and my journey is done!

Master Christopher and Mistress Annis laughed uproariously, and I joined in so as not to appear churlish, but I didn't understand the song, and as for my question – well, it was no sort of an answer.

5

DO AS I TELL YOU

We'd arrived at the foot of Baudry Hill and needed all our breath to climb up the stony path that leads to the gates of Castle Rory, so nothing more was said.

I lifted my hand to Jonny in the gatehouse, and to Captain Kerry and her two sergeants. Gael appeared, and was sent to find the cook so she could decide which barn the minstrels should use for the night. Marshal Branca hurried out to take Guinevere from me, for she would allow no one but herself to have the care of the castle's bloodstock, and I remembered then that I'd picked up the oak box and its lid and brought them back with me. Barney had wanted to hurl them as far into the murky Hurogol as he could, and Jonny had agreed, not seeing the point of bringing the empty box back to the castle. I didn't see any real reason to bring it either, but there was also no reason not to. And now I lifted it down from Guinevere's saddle. Branca glanced at it, but said not a word.

Annis, Christopher and Kit went off to wash their dusty feet and faces, while Branca took Guinevere away for a well-deserved grooming. Unobserved, I stowed the box in a shadowy corner of the gatehouse. I would retrieve it later, and perhaps take it up to my library. I had an idea I should inspect it a bit more closely, and in private. I'd only just emerged from the gatehouse when Master Kit approached me.

'You will want to read my song,' he declared, proffering a rolled parchment. 'If not now, then later...'

I took the parchment, somewhat mystified. 'Your song? The one that didn't answer my questions about how and why you came to Mallrovia?'

'The one that answered those very questions,' he said with a skip, a wink and a laugh.

I smiled politely, but he was talking rubbish, so I ran up to my library and threw the rolled parchment into the desk drawer. The thing had made no sense to me when I heard it sung, and reading it wouldn't make any difference. In any case I had other things to think about. I hailed Alex on the ramparts and asked for Master Davy to be sent to me. Before supper, I wanted another word with the Lady Joan, so I hurried down to the *Egg* by the little River Eray. Davy would find me there.

The Lady Joan was creating more colours for her fabrics and she held out her hands to me, hands stained purple and pink. Indeed, she was purple to the elbows!

'Woad and madder,' she said succinctly, waving to indicate I should come in.

I sat at the table with its flaring pavonalilis cover and fingered the material again. My eye was caught by the squirls and spirals of lighter and darker shades of the shimmering blue-green. The coloured patterns draw your eye, and it's hard to look away from them. I was intrigued as to how this was achieved, but I had not come here to talk about design, and I knew Davy would soon catch up with me.

'Joan, you must tell me what Sammy is up to.'

But at that moment, Davy burst into the *Egg*, his face red with exertion. He must have run all the way from the keep. No doubt he'd been told I was not in the mood to be kept waiting.

I swung round to face him. 'Why did you take Sammy to the Nahvitch?'

'I didn't, lord. I took him to the boatmen's landing and handed him over to Prince Barney.'

'But you knew Barney was planning on crossing to Blurland? You knew they were going to the enemy?'

'Yes, lord. I knew that was the plan. But I *trusted* Prince Barney. It was in Amie's song! *We trusted in our prince.*'

'So you're going to hide behind Amie? What exactly was the plan, Davy? What did Barney hope to do, and why did he need to take Sammy with him?'

Just as I had done earlier, Davy fiddled with the tablecloth. Joan sat in the far corner and wound yarn on a spindle. Round and round went her arm, and the bobbin of bright red wool grew fatter and fatter. I looked over at her, but she was watching the fleece twist in her hand. Joan was behaving as if neither Davy nor I were there. I waited for Davy to answer my question.

'Lord, Barney didn't tell me much. I'm not hiding behind Amie, because it was I who gave her that line. I *did* trust him. He wouldn't say what he was going to do, he just asked me to bring Sammy to him at the river. When I asked why, he just said *trust me.*'

'So you wrote Amie's poem?'

'We wrote it together, lord.'

I hadn't realised that. It would make a difference to how Amie was treated. To her punishment.

'Lord,' Davy continued earnestly, 'what Amie said – it was how I felt too. I didn't know Barney was going to bring the deadly lizard to the castle. It was treachery! He made me help him do something bad, and I didn't know it was bad when I did it because I trusted him. Please, please believe me, lord. I would never, ever have helped Prince Barney if I had known Sammy wasn't going to come back to us, and that Barney was going to bring the Box of Death here.'

The Box of Death! I'd not heard it called that before, but it doesn't take long for epithets like that to be bandied about.

'Is there anything else I should know about this?' I looked coldly at my squire. I did not want him to think his plea of ignorance and trust would make me lenient with him.

'Well, there was something Sammy said when we rode to meet the Spiderboat. He said, "You will have a surprise when you see me next. You will all have a great surprise."'

'Anything else?'

'He said one other thing, but I didn't understand it at all. It wasn't in English. It sounded like *Keeshiv.*'

'*Keeshiv?* Are you sure?'

'That's what it sounded like. I couldn't ask him about it, because we'd arrived at the river by then and Prince Barney was already there, and so was the Spiderboatman. The Spiderboatman was in a terrible hurry and he kept swearing at us. Sammy and Prince Barney jumped on board the Spiderboat, and before I knew it Lillian and I were just left on the riverbank. She went back to the palace, leading Barney's horse, and I brought Sammy's pony back to the castle.'

So the elder princess had been involved in the scheme

Do as I tell you

as well. Of course, someone would have been needed to deal with Barney's beautiful Arab. I rubbed my forehead. I didn't seem to be getting very far with this investigation. Davy, sitting opposite me, was still twisting the edge of Joan's tablecloth. I guessed he was wondering how far he would be held responsible for bringing the so-called Box of Death to the castle. As yet, he didn't know it had contained only a harmless rabbit. For all his shifting of responsibility to Barney, he must have realised that his part in the matter would be held against him. Another thought struck me.

'Davy, were you *just* there to bring Sammy's pony home? Was that your only part in the matter? Come on, lad. You know you must tell me the absolute truth.'

Davy has been a difficult and rebellious child, and he is a free spirit still, but he has never been dishonest with me.

'I was asked to bring Sammy to the river, and then take the pony back,' he replied at last. 'I was also asked to say nothing about any of it. Barney told me he was going adventuring, and I didn't think it was serious, 'cos usually it isn't. Sammy had to go too because the Nahvitch would only pay the boatman if Sammy went over the water, at any rate that's what Sammy said. He said he was valuable to the Nahvitch, and they'd pay good money to see him. That was how we got the boatman to take them there. And then the Kyown-Kinnie gave Barney the Box of Death, but that would've been because the Nahvitch have always been our enemies, and they would've wanted to use their Sacred Gecko to kill us!' Davy's voice suddenly rose hysterically. 'Barney should *never* have gone into Blurland, lord, and he should *never* have brought the Box of Death back with him. And the King and Queen should *never*—'

'Stop there!' I commanded him, before he could talk treason. 'Have a care, Davy.'

It was then I noticed that the rhythmic winding of red yarn had stopped. How long had it been stopped? I looked across the room, but the spindle had been laid on the stool and Joan was no longer there. I cursed. Where was she? What was she up to? But when I asked Davy if he'd noticed the Lady Joan's departure, he just shook his head.

Someone was blowing a horn in the bailey. I signalled to Davy that we would return to the courtyard. Supper would shortly be served in the great hall. 'And,' I told the boy, my hand on his shoulder, 'there is a troupe of minstrels waiting for us! They are visiting Mallrovia. It will be good to have some fresh music and song and perhaps dancing too.'

I steered my squire up the hill towards the hall. Although I spoke of minstrels and dancing, and although my hand was but lightly upon his shoulder, my message was clear: *Stay with me and do as I tell you.*

6

JOAN AND ANTHONY

First thing this morning, Amie was brought to my library for interrogation. She was tearful, fearful, and utterly repentant. I sat in my carved chair. They say that seated is the position of power, and my father confirmed this to me on the many occasions I stood before him in the great hall and nervously awaited his judgement.

Amie's eyes were cast down, as I was sure Patrick would have reminded her they should be.

'Tell me about your relationship with my squire.'

It was unexpected. 'My – my relationship?'

'Don't lie to me, Amie, and don't pretend you don't know what I'm talking about.'

'But lord, I don't know him! He is your squire – he is far beyond me to know.'

And that was true, or should have been. Davy is destined for great things. Within two or three years he will be dubbed knight. One day he will inherit Wartsbaye Castle, and all its household, lands and tenants. Amie is just a stray orphan, taken in by a kindly lord, although it is possible she no longer thinks of me as 'kindly'. At any rate, there can be no liaison between Davy and Amie.

'Davy is telling me a different story,' I said sternly.

'We have talked, but only once or twice. That's all, lord, I swear.'

'I don't believe you. Did Davy write your seditious song?'

'He – he helped me.' The girl sounded as though she could hardly breathe. 'He suggested some of the words.'

'Some? Or all?'

'No, lord, not all of them! I wrote it, I swear I did. Davy only made a few suggestions!' She prostrated herself on the floor.

'Get up, girl,' I said roughly. 'There is no need for prostration. And you are, I know, trying to protect my squire, but you cannot. He has told me the truth, as he always does. If your story doesn't match with his, then it's you who are lying, and for that you will be doubly punished. Get up now.'

Amie rose slowly to her feet.

'Let's start again. What is your relationship with my squire?'

Amie bit her lip, and I watched as she tried to muster the courage to admit serious fault.

'We see each other,' she faltered eventually. 'We like each other, lord.'

'How much do you like each other?'

'A lot, lord, but not in the way you think. Davy's good at making up words, and he did help me write the song. He told me to put in the bit about trusting our prince. He told me Prince Barney shouldn't have brought the gecko here, and we should have been able to trust him to keep us safe, and now we're not safe, because he brought the Box of Death right into the castle.'

I sat back in my chair. Amie had gabbled her way through her speech, as if she knew she could only say it at top speed. She snuffled and sobbed quietly while she waited for me to speak.

'The Box of Death. Why do you call it that?'

'I don't know, lord. I think Davy called it that. Or perhaps it was Gael.'

'Well, no matter. You will not see or speak with my squire again. You will not perform music in the hall. From now on, your duties will be in the kitchen and the dairy. You will help Rachel and Eliza with preparation of food and drink, but you will not serve in the hall. You will keep the company only of women.'

I dismissed her.

She has been foolish, there's no doubt of that, but the greater responsibility lies with Davy. He must have encouraged her to feel fond of him, and he must have sought her out. The greatest sin, of course, is being found out. An illicit liaison does no great harm to anyone, provided nobody knows about it and no babies result from it. Davy didn't bother to ensure the first condition was met, and I can only hope he's taken more care with the second one.

My next job today was to talk to their Majesties, the King and Queen of Mallrovia. I found them sitting in the great hall, conferring quietly with each other. I asked first if they had spoken with Prince Barney, but they hadn't even seen him. I guessed he was avoiding them. They asked what was happening to my bard. I described her punishment and they seemed satisfied. Finally, the question I'd been waiting for, and it was Queen Julia who asked it.

'And so, Lord Rory, you have disposed of the box with

the gecko in it? You have thrown it into the river and the animal is dead?'

'Your Majesty,' I answered, 'I did not need to throw the box in the river, for there was no gecko inside.' The King opened his mouth in astonishment. The Queen merely stared at me. 'Your Majesties,' I continued calmly, 'inside the box, there was a rabbit.' It sounded so comical as I said it, that I had to turn a sudden laugh into a coughing fit.

'A rabbit?' The Queen frowned. 'And how do you know that? You must have had to open the box to find out, and why would you do that, believing it to be instant death?'

I had my answer ready. 'I could tell it wasn't the gecko, ma'am. The movements were wrong, and so I investigated. I spread my thick woollen cloak over the box and eased the lid up a fraction. Then I felt inside, knowing the animal couldn't see me. I could feel the fur and shape of the rabbit. Once we knew it was harmless, we let it out of the box.'

King Philip looked at me narrowly. 'So why didn't you do this clever investigation in the first place? Why the charade, with priests and medical experts in attendance?'

I had been asking myself the same question, and wishing I'd thought of the cloak trick while we had the box in the castle grounds. Or even while we had it on the riverside. But everyone thought the gecko was inside. Barney had said it was, and it never occurred to me that it might be some other animal.

'I'm sorry, sire. I wish I'd thought of it at the time. The movements in the box didn't seem much like a lizard, but I didn't realise that until we'd ridden down to the Hurogol. It was only after I'd carried the box around for a while that I became aware the gecko might not be inside.' It sounded quite plausible, I thought.

Queen Julia smiled suddenly. 'You have done well, Lord

Rory. And it is good to know your castle and your household were never in danger after all. And Barney did show great courage, did he not?'

'Very great courage, ma'am,' I assured her, and it was true, too. The young prince had done well. So had Jonny, I reminded myself. He was a stalwart, from start to finish.

So that was done. And very soon, as I had known it would, word got around that the famed Box of Death had contained nothing but a rabbit. In a heartbeat, the mood in the castle changed. No longer were we harbouring a vile and malevolent beast, no longer were we in death's shadow. My household, in a typically extreme reaction to the news, found the whole situation hilarious. Pictures of rabbits have appeared in unlikely places – there's one drawn in the sand by the well, and another chalked on the buttery wall. But I caught my breath when, while walking past the dairy, I overheard two milkmaids giggling about their recent encounter with 'Prince Bunny'. *Prince Bunny.* Priceless.

As I moved around the castle during the rest of the morning, I assumed that today the royal party would be making their preparations to leave. The problem has been dealt with and there is no more Fiorello. Barney came through unscathed, and I could see no reason for them to stay. The royal palace in Hicrown is sumptuous compared with my fortress here in Hambrig. The wall hangings are magnificent, all the ceilings are vaulted, and they dine off gold and silver, not like us with our stale bread trenchers, our earthenware jugs and our dented pewter utensils. As for their bedchambers, they're richly decorated, lavishly furnished and comfortable beyond belief. Truly, it's like sleeping on a cloud! When I visited recently I was given a chamber with curtained hangings over the bed and colourful tapestries on the floor.

But as the dinner hour approached, I saw no sign of any preparations for departure. The royal chariots remained drawn up in my courtyard, the royal horses stayed comfortably in my livery, and nobody called for servants to wash and dress them for the journey home. I saw the King's youngest child making daisy chains in the grass outside the granary, and she looked *very* settled in.

I have no objection to the royal family staying here. But why would they want to?

It's my custom on Thursdays to go through the accounts with Sir Patrick. Patrick could easily handle them on his own, and I trust my steward implicitly, but I have a good head for figures and I like to know what is happening across my estate. With a feeling of some relief, I took the spiral steps two at a time to reach my eyrie on the ramparts. The feeling of relief stemmed from a heartfelt desire to return to normal castle life. All this business with Barney and the so-called Sacred Gecko, the disappearance of Sammy, and the Lady Joan's strange behaviour – all this has disrupted the rhythm of our affairs.

I relished the opportunity to go through the accounts, to see laid before me in Patrick's neat script the ordered plusses and minuses of our petty transactions, the day-to-day business of the lives of many people, all of whom are directly responsible to me, and I to them. Going through the

Joan and Anthony

books with Patrick, I feel that the estate comes to life, every event and transaction, no matter how small or insignificant-seeming, is set down for anyone to see. There is continuity, predictability even, in these records that stretch back to the time of my great-grandfather, the man who built this castle. Sometimes I imagine that the ledgers and account books, the parchments and scrolls are the actual beating heart of Hambrig.

Patrick and I passed a very pleasant and useful hour looking through the records and doing the sums, but once we had closed the ledgers and sat back to rest our eyes from gazing at all the minute figures, I asked Patrick if he knew where Joan was.

'She's with Anthony Merry in the town.'

Anthony Merry. Of yeoman stock, a scholar and a master jeweller – and better educated than many higher-born men – Merry has written two full-length books and a short pamphlet. His larger volumes, called *The Book of Truth* and *The Book of Wisdom,* are hard going. If you ever get the urge to read them, you will want to set aside a considerable amount of time. Not only is it quite a struggle to get to the end, but when you do, you may wonder why you bothered. The books are full of Latin and Greek sermons on how to behave and what to do. I read *Truth* all the way to the end; *Wisdom* I just glanced through. I didn't appreciate being lectured by Master Merry. Anthony Merry is unafraid to tell the truth, I'll say that for him, and the books do not flatter those they describe. In fact, many people are pilloried by him, and it's a miracle he's never been handed over to the sheriff.

His little pamphlet, *The People's Puzzle* is very different.

It's a strange work of indecipherable goobledygook, and to my knowledge nobody has ever read it. It's said Master

Merry has offered a substantial sum of money to anyone who works out what it means, but my view is that he's not taking any great risk with that offer. The man has not moved with the times. He adheres to the old ways, continuing to wear the slit tunic and the close-fitting separated hose that went out of fashion thirty years ago. People titter as he walks by, a foolish and ancient bonnet on his head, but he's impervious to their cackling.

Joan and Master Merry have known each other a long time, and they have always been good friends, even while Anthony's wife was still alive. Many people assume Joan and Merry are more than friends. You know what gossips are; they've nothing better to do than weave other people's stories for them.

I decided to ride into town to see Joan and Anthony.

7

I WOULD HAVE LOVED HIM

On my way to the gatehouse, I heard the hue and cry go up.

For heaven's sake, what now?

I raced back towards the castle keep and was met in the doorway by Rachel and Eliza, angry to the point of incoherence. I hustled the cook and the maid into the great hall and sat them down on a bench, but the women were almost too distraught to speak. Fortunately, Gael came hurrying by, and I grabbed him by the seat of his hose.

'What's amiss? Do you know?'

Gael gabbled something unintelligible, but I forced him to slow his speech, and calm himself enough to talk to me.

'It's those minstrels, lord,' he gasped. 'Those three you brought to the castle. They've gone! Vanished! And they've taken all our dishes! They've robbed us blind, they have, the swabs, the unmitigated swine!'

Where does he learn this stuff? But it was no wonder the servants were upset. If our pewter bowls had gone from the stores, how could they present food to the King and Queen?

'They took my pies too.' Rachel, usually unflappable, was red-faced. Eliza clucked and tutted around her.

I was mystified. 'What pies?'

'All of them,' Eliza answered sourly. 'We have spent the entire day making pies for supper tonight, lord, with that useless Amie supposed to be helping us, and now there are no pies. And we'd made a special rabbit pie to serve to Prince Bunny – er, Barney. But now there's nothing to serve them on, and no pies to serve! What are we going to do?'

'Can we not make more pies?' I suggested.

But the look on their faces told me we could not.

'Gael, why the hue and cry? Surely not for the castle pewter and a few pies?'

'No, lord. The hue and cry is for the horses. Branca says the minstrels have ridden away on our best thoroughbreds.'

'*What?* They have taken Guinevere?'

'Yes, lord. Not just Guinevere, but Prince Barney's Arab stallion and Sir Patrick's palfrey. They're all gone from the stables. Sir Patrick set the hue and cry going and then Branca jumped onto Sammy's little pony and galloped down the bailey and out over the drawbridge. Nobody knows where she's gone or how she can get our bloodstock back, not if it's just Branca against the three of them. Lord, what's going to happen to Amie? Is she to stay in the kitchen for ever?'

But I had no thought to spare for Amie. 'Get me . . .' I'd been about to say, *Get me Guinevere*. But there was no Guinevere. 'I guess we're all on foot now, until we find those bloody troubadours,' I said grimly.

It was nearly dinner time, and normally Rachel and her team would have had the trestle tables ready and food on dishes for serving. People would be waiting for the horn to summon them to the great hall to be fed. But the tables were

I would have loved him

folded away, the kitchen was silent, the maids were in tears, and the hue and cry was still sounding out, loud and clear. King Philip strode into the great hall, demanding to know if what he had heard was true. Naturally, he held me accountable.

I allowed the King's voice to thunder around me, the women to wail and Gael to plead tearfully for Amie's imminent release, and I paid no attention to any of it. I was wondering how we could possibly not have heard three horses being taken. I was wondering how Branca could have allowed it to happen when she guards the stables in person, day and night. And I was concerned at how this was all going on at the same time as Sammy's mysterious defection to the enemy, the Lady Joan's running off to her bolt-hole with Master Merry, and the Nahvitch's 'Box of Death' trick. *The Nahvitch*. They are the mysterious Swamp-People, the barbarians who live in the marshes. They are the enemy; cruel, and without mercy. They are not known for their practical jokes.

With an exclamation, I turned on my heel and walked away from the mewling, the raging and the rending of clothes. Missing pies, missing horses, missing boys. *What else was missing?* I ran to the gatehouse, to the dark corner where I had left the empty wooden box. And it was no longer there. I sank down onto the stone bench at the side of the archway. Afternoon sun slanted across the flagstones outside, but even though the day was a warm one, I was chilled to the bone. For why would anyone take an empty box? I reached into my jersey and pulled out the parchment Sammy had given Barney.

Fiorello is death to those he looks upon. Only a person of great courage and determination will open this box, but if such a one can be found, a great reward will be his. This message comes from Hope, Endurance and a New Beginning.

Was it all nonsense? Perhaps meant to throw us off some other scent? For there had been no great reward, and nobody knew what the last sentence could possibly mean. I read it and re-read it. At the river, I'd decided the message was meant to make us believe that Fiorello, if he even existed, was in the box, and so only a brave man would open it. But *would* a brave man open it, knowing it meant certain death? Surely that would be the action of a very stupid man, not a brave one. The *only* reason I had consented to opening the box was that I was convinced Fiorello was *not* inside. And yet, *great courage* was still required, the writer said, and a *great reward* would result. You would only open the box if you knew the lizard wasn't in it. Yet, knowing that, the opening of the box would not require courage at all. And when the box was open, and the rabbit jumped out, the box would be empty, so where was the reward? Surely the reward wasn't the *rabbit*.

I made for the stables. Guinevere had been taken, but the King's horse was still there. In haste, I readied the mare and rode across the bailey. From the corner of my eye, I saw folk gathering by the keep, and there was much waving and shouting. For some reason Davy was on his knees, while King Philip towered over everyone. He roared some command at me, which of course I ignored, and there was little Gael, hopping up and down at the very front of the crowd. Pulling hard on my right rein, I hauled the mare round and bellowed to the boy. He ran to me; I caught his outstretched hands and swung him up into the saddle. We turned, leaving everyone else behind, and crashed through the gatehouse and out of the castle.

I would have loved him

The mare was a fine mount, answering all my cues with ready intelligence. Once clear of the castle, we settled into an easy trot, heading for Hambrig Town.

'Lord, you have stolen the King's horse,' Gael said in wonder. 'The King's!'

'Yes,' I replied, but I felt light-hearted, and happier than I had for a long while. 'Yes, it's true, Gael. I have been very bad indeed. But we have things to do, you and I, and we cannot take the time to walk to Hambrig Town. This was the only way.'

'Will the King ever forgive you?'

'That I don't know. I suspect it will depend on the outcome of our mission.'

'What is our mission, lord?'

'To recover the Box of Death.'

Gael gave a great sigh of contentment, nestled back into my body, and allowed the rhythm of the ride to take over.

———◆———

If you are a single man in your thirties, and a noble one to boot, they are wont to ask you why you never married.

And what about an heir? they probe. How many times, I wonder, have I been asked this question? How many people, whose business it is decidedly none of, have wanted to know into whose hands my castle will pass when I die? *Because, Lord Rory, without an heir, you can be sure the castle and all your land will pass to someone not of your line. And how will you feel about that? And what of your tenants? You have a duty to them. You must provide a legitimate heir, Lord Rory. You must marry!*

As I gazed over Gael's fair young head, and between the

alert ears of the King's horse, whose name I didn't even know, I pondered on this matter. They asked why I never married. Well, I loved a lady once. She was fair, she was clever, and she could hold a conversation. She lived on our estate, and she was a high-ranking lady, the only daughter of a nobleman who was doing knight service for my father. Her name was Lady Kathryn. I loved her, and I would have died for her, but it was she who died.

I don't know what happened; it was all a long time ago, fifteen years, to be exact. I was a young man then, only eighteen, and she was just a girl. One Sunday before chapel, a stranger came to the gatehouse and asked to speak with my father. They had their meeting, and I was not allowed to be present. Afterwards, my father stood before me and told me that the stranger was Lady Kathryn's uncle, come to inform us she was dead. I remember the feeling of utter hopelessness and despair that washed over me. I remember facing my father, his face stern, while I tried hard not to show the dejection and misery I was feeling.

Later, the tears flowed, and I railed against God and the world. But my love was gone, and I never wanted another. I could not bear the thought that I might feel so abandoned, so alone, ever again.

But what if Kathryn and I had married? What if we had had a son? He would be Gael's age. He would be like Gael. And perhaps I would have ridden around my demesne, my son nestling into me on Guinevere's broad back, my arms wrapped tightly around him, shielding him from danger. I would have buried my face in his curly blond hair, smelt his little boy smell, and I would have loved him.

8

TAKE ME TO HIM

The townsfolk were responding to the hue and cry, searching the streets for the wrongdoers. They would be found, of course. Such an abuse of my hospitality left a bitter taste, and I intended to punish the minstrels hard. I made straight for the Merchants Quarter, a big square near the eastern wall of the town. Anthony Merry's house is one of several facing the Guildhall. Leaving Gael looking after the mare, I pushed open the door and went in.

I had never been in Merry's house before, though I'd heard much about it over the years. It was said to be all cobwebby and dirty, to have mice and rats running everywhere, and for huge numbers of books to be in your way wherever you turned. The books would block doorways and passages. They would be piled higgledy-piggledy on the floor and on the furniture, and Master Merry himself, in his decades-old clothing, would be buried somewhere underneath them. I didn't care what the house was like. I didn't mind stepping over vermin, furniture or mountains of books, and I was well prepared for all of it from the tales that were told.

What I was *not* prepared for was the immaculate, clean and tidy hall I found myself in, the books – and there were certainly plenty of them – arranged neatly on shelves that ran from wall to wall and from floor to ceiling. The furniture was old, to be sure, and well worn, but everything was in its place. I stood in the doorway, taking it all in, and at first there was no sign of anyone. And then I saw them. At the other end of the hall was the screens passage, and there they stood, holding hands: a white-haired man in his late sixties, and Joan, fair, curly-haired and buxom, a good fifteen years younger than her companion. I crossed the room.

'Master Merry, Lady Joan, I should like to speak with you both. Some serious things have happened and I need counsel.'

Merry made a stiff little bow, and then the three of us sat on wooden stools, facing each other. I explained about the theft of the horses and the kitchenware, the presence of the three troubadours and their subsequent disappearance. I didn't bother mentioning the pies. Of course, Anthony Merry had heard the hue and cry go up; indeed, we could still hear it reverberating around the town and out into the countryside beyond. I also told Joan and Master Merry about Branca chasing after the robbers, but I kept the strange disappearance of the empty Box of Death to myself.

'Lord Rory,' Master Merry said when I'd finished, his voice as dry and clipped as I remembered it. 'You made an assumption that the Box of Death contained the Sacred Gecko. Yet it did not. Now you make the assumption that the minstrels, who are gone, have taken the horses, which are also gone. But suppose there is some other explanation?'

I frowned. What other explanation could there be? Joan spoke. 'Where are the minstrels from, Rory?'

'I've no idea. I did ask, but Master Kit gave me some stuff and nonsense in a song he sang. I do remember a bit about *Over the mountains and onto the Downs*. And he also said they'd come from the south, which fits with coming over the Downs into Mallrovia, almost certainly through Westador. But there was also something about paddling and prancing, and he mentioned treetops. Treetops! I think it was just one of his peculiar troubadour songs. And all the time he sang it he was twirling a stick and dancing backwards!'

'It sounds like he was trying to confuse you. What did you think at the time?' Master Merry asked, blinking at me.

'I didn't think anything. I scarcely took it in. I was far more interested in the fact that they were musicians.'

I was angry with myself. We needed musicians now Amie was banned from singing, and that's all I'd thought about. I should have talked to them more, and I should definitely have made Master Kit answer my questions.

'From the south, then,' mused Master Merry, sitting very upright on his simple, homemade stool. 'Where could that be? Of course, it could be Westador. Or the south of England. Or even over the Narrow Sea into France. Have you ever been there, Lord Rory?'

'To France? I have indeed, Master Merry. Have you?'

'I am ashamed to say I have never left Mallrovia.'

'There's no shame in that, Anthony,' Joan said quietly, putting her hand over his. 'You mentioned paddling,' she went on, turning to me. 'That sounds like they came across the water in a boat.'

'There was water,' I said, remembering. 'Water, but not the sea, or something like that. Which water would that be do you think?'

'The Dorbney Flood in Westador?' suggested Master Merry. 'I believe it's quite possible to row or paddle across it.'

'What about the treetops?' asked Joan. 'Apart from the woodland on Baudry Hill, there's Hambrig Woods and Nightmolben Forest, but no one wants to go to *that* horrible, haunted place. Or there's the Wartsbaye Woods, way up north. Oh, and the King's Forest outside Hicrown! Plenty of treetops there!'

'Then they came through Wartsbaye or via Hicrown,' I said in some excitement.

'But either of those would be a very round about route,' Joan objected. 'Why travel through Wartsbaye or Hicrown if you're coming north to Hambrig?'

'Because they're troubadours, of course,' I said promptly. 'They perform everywhere they go, for board and lodging, or for money. They are just travelling around the country, Joan.'

'And stealing from everyone they lodge with?' Merry sounded doubtful. 'That doesn't seem likely. Word travels faster than people do, and they'd soon find they weren't welcome anywhere, no matter how well they dance and sing.'

'Well then, I don't know why they'd come through Wartsbaye at all.' Then I slammed my fist into my other hand. 'Wait, I *do* know! *That's* why my squire Davy was involved in the trip to Blurland! Davy comes from Wartsbaye, Master Merry. He is Baron Giles's son, don't you see?'

'But what has Blurland to do with your minstrels, Lord Rory?' Merry sounded perplexed.

'I don't know,' I admitted. 'But I intend to find out. Somehow, all of this is connected.'

Take me to him

On an impulse, I showed Master Merry the 'great reward' message that I always keep on me.

'I do not comprehend it,' he said with his old-fashioned turn of phrase. 'It is a puzzle, is it not?'

'It is. Perhaps one to rival your own *People's Puzzle.*'

He gave a slight smile.

As I left the house, I noticed a pile of Merry's pamphlets on a small table by the door. 'Do you get many coming for these?' I asked, picking one up. They were sombre-looking things, with much closely spaced writing.

'No,' Merry admitted, 'nobody calls. But I keep them there, just in case. Would you like to take that one? I would normally charge of course...' In the hopeful sentence that he left hanging, I stuffed the pamphlet down my jersey.

Outside in the daylight I had to blink and shade my eyes until they'd adjusted. And then I gave a start of surprise. For Gael, looking after the King's horse as instructed, was also chatting away to Branca, who stood next to him, holding Sammy's little pony by his halter. They saw me at once, and both bowed low.

'What has happened, Branca?' I demanded. 'Where are Guinevere and the other horses?'

'They are safe and back at the castle,' she said, her dark plaits swinging. 'It wasn't long after the hue and cry went up that Master Kit was apprehended.'

'Where was he found? And what of the other two thieves?'

'Master Christopher and Mistress Annis were not found, I'm sorry to say. Master Kit was arrested at the landing stage. There was a boatman there too, one of the Spiderboatmen.'

So it is as the King feared. His brilliant network of Spiderboatmen are corrupt and working for the enemy. Or perhaps just for themselves. This is a disaster.

'Where is Master Kit now?'

'With the sheriff. It was the hue and cry. The whole of Hambrig was out to get him.'

'Well done, Branca. You ride home now. Gael and I still have work to do here.'

'The pony has gone lame, lord. I'll have to lead him.'

It was bad luck, but it happens. I watched her walk the pony slowly up the track towards Baudry Hill, which loomed in the distance. Shading my eyes and looking southwards to the hill, I was struck afresh by how imposing the castle looked. Like it had always been there, its red and yellow sandstone walls, ramparts, towers and crenellations simply part of the landscape.

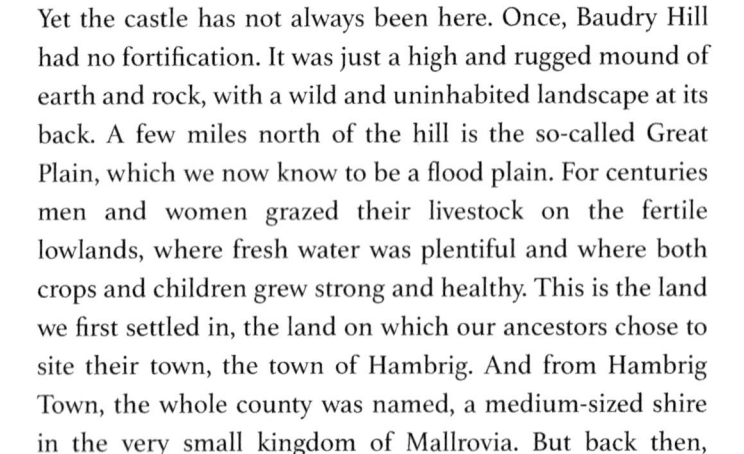

Yet the castle has not always been here. Once, Baudry Hill had no fortification. It was just a high and rugged mound of earth and rock, with a wild and uninhabited landscape at its back. A few miles north of the hill is the so-called Great Plain, which we now know to be a flood plain. For centuries men and women grazed their livestock on the fertile lowlands, where fresh water was plentiful and where both crops and children grew strong and healthy. This is the land we first settled in, the land on which our ancestors chose to site their town, the town of Hambrig. And from Hambrig Town, the whole county was named, a medium-sized shire in the very small kingdom of Mallrovia. But back then, everyone lived on the Plain.

Until the Great Flood. The Great Flood of 1159 was caused by torrents of rain and extremely strong winds, which forced a giant tidal wave up the River Hurogol. The river burst its banks, and the water rose high and surged over the land, drowning many people and animals, ruining farms and homesteads. It's said that people fled from the rising waters in many different directions. Some scrambled north, eventually taking ship across the North Sea. Others travelled south, heading for Westador and the southern counties of England. But there were many who simply climbed the hill, the hill they'd looked at every day of their lives, the hill that brooded over the Great Plain and the little town, where the shepherds liked to wander in the summertime, the coarse grass and sorrel being much appreciated by sheep.

And so people sought refuge from the water by climbing high above it, and eventually the waters receded and the river became tame again. But the people had come to enjoy living on a hill. They made a rough road out of the boulders that lie everywhere on Baudry, and they set about building a fortress. They found themselves a natural leader, a warrior named Rory. This Rory was my great-grandfather. The castle was built, and my great-grandfather became its lord.

My musings on how my castle came into being were interrupted by Gael. 'Where are we going now, lord?'

'To the sheriff. We shall be meeting Master Kit again.'

'Oh good! I *love* Master Kit! I wish I could do his drumming tricks.'

'We will get him to teach you,' I said easily, and enjoyed watching the boy's eyes grow round and his face pinken with pleasure. We rode back towards the centre of Hambrig Town and into the marketplace.

I found myself beginning to see the town through Gael's eyes: the colourful stalls with ribbons, fabrics and spun wool for sale, and the sweetmeats and bonbons displayed on trays and trestles, all very tempting to a small boy. And I'd learnt my horse's name! Gael, with some presence of mind, had asked Branca, and so I was told the King's horse was called Fanfarinette, affectionately known as Netty. In the short time I'd known her, I'd grown rather fond of Netty, although of course no mare could take the place of my Guinevere. As we rode along, I discovered that Gael was woefully ignorant of our society. As vassals and villeins, gentlemen, husbandmen and yeomen paid their respects to me, I found I was having to explain to my young companion who everyone was; who was free and who was not free; their positions and possessions, and to whom they owed obedience and why. It seemed that Gael had not understood even his own high birth and rank. And, oblivious to it as he was, he was still pleading with me for Amie's release from her punishment. By now we were on foot, having left Netty in stables nearby.

'Enough!' I cried eventually, rounding irritably on the child.

He cringed away, but still found the courage to say, 'But lord, she is my friend. For months she was the only person I could talk to.'

'That may have been so then, Gael. You were both children, and it didn't matter. As you grow, you have to understand the way we do things. You cannot be friends with Amie now.'

I felt him withdraw from me then, and was astonished to find it hurt. He clamoured to know why I would not let them stay friends, but I kept silent. I did not want to say that their friendship could not be. I did not want to tell him that Amie would never be free, while one day he, Gael, would be a knight, his brother Davy a lord. I did not want him to know that a boy and a girl, once they reach a certain age, cannot be 'friends'. In my cowardice, I spared his innocence.

We came to the sheriff's house. Gael looked wonderingly at the stocks outside, but I would not let him stay. We went to the courthouse door and knocked loudly.

The sheriff, Master John of Hambrig, is the tenant of a vast amount of land, not much less than I. It's said that he is fair in court, but that he abuses his own servants. Patrick, who comes to the town more often than I, has told me of the cries you can hear coming from the courthouse, and how the servants have their eyes permanently cast down for shame. It's said he abuses women, and forces himself on the young men and boys who work for him, and even the prisoners in the gaol. My flesh creeps at the thought, but no one reports him, no one denounces Master John; it's only rumour, and you can't act on that. Strangely, Patrick has also told me that the sheriff saves his harshest sentences for those found guilty of rape or sodomy.

John of Hambrig ushered us into the courthouse, and Gael gazed at the benches and the high throne where the sheriff sits when hearing his cases.

'Lord, I am honoured at your visit,' John said, though he didn't sound honoured. 'But you should know I have a tribunal at Nones. Will you require me for long?'

'Not long. You have a new prisoner, I believe. Master Kit.'

'The horse thief? Aye, he is in the gaol.'

'Take me to him.'

9
PIES OR NO PIES

John led the way to a long, low building behind his court, and we descended a narrow stairway to a stinking underground cell that was guarded by a heavy wooden door. An enormous key was produced from somewhere about John's person, and the door was unlocked. There were several prisoners inside: four or five men, and at least one woman. Gael gagged at the smell, and I pushed him behind me so he would not see what I was looking at. John stepped inside, and then dragged a prisoner out to us. Immediately, the door was slammed shut and locked again, and I found myself gazing into the insolent face of my one-time troubadour, Master Kit.

'Here is your horse thief,' sneered the sheriff. 'When you're done talking to him, throw him back.'

John thrust the key into my hand, pushed rudely past Gael, and stamped heavily up the stone steps. I handled the key with distaste, certain I'd seen Master John extract it from down the front of his undergarments. We listened to the sheriff's footsteps echoing in the tiny chamber where the three of us stood. Then I heard Gael vomiting behind me. I

Pies or no pies

swung round, just in time to catch him as he fainted. Flinging the boy over my shoulder, and signalling to Kit to follow, I climbed the stairs, strode along the passage and out into the fresh air. I knew Kit was behind me as we mounted the steps and walked the passage, but I did not know if he would try to run once we reached the open. As soon as I could, I turned, forcing him against the wall, while gently setting Gael down on the ground, where he slowly opened his eyes.

'Is that your son?' Kit asked me.

'He's my page.'

I took off my girdle and tied Kit's hands in front of him, keeping a strong hold on the other end, winding it round and round my fist.

'Did you think I was going to try to escape?' Kit asked, amused.

'Of course.'

He laughed. It was the laugh I remembered from the night before, the carefree sound that went with the merry eyes and the wide grin. It was, I knew, what had made Gael say 'I *love* Master Kit!' Gael wanted to do Kit's drumming tricks, but it wasn't the tricks that made Kit loveable and made my page admire him so. Gael, nervous, often tongue-tied, once so achingly homesick, longed to have Kit's charm, his easy-going bonhomie and his light-hearted banter.

I looked the lad over and judged him reasonably sound. Digging into my purse, I took out a handful of coins.

'Here's sixpence, Gael. Give the money to Master John and tell him it's Kit's bail. Hand over the key as well. Tell Master John I'm taking Kit with me, but he will have him back for trial later.' Gael ran off, clutching both key and coins. A few moments later Master John appeared, scratching lewdly at his testicles, Gael skipping ahead of him.

'A bit irregular, lord,' said John in his dour, northern-English voice. 'A bit irregular, this. You'll bring him back though? Bring him back by Wednesday next, if you will, Lord Rory, for I need to hang the miserable sod.'

'He'll be tried first, surely?' I asked, but he just sniffed, then turned and shuffled back to his courthouse, reappearing almost immediately with a length of stout rope.

'Take yon silky waistband off his wrists,' he said. 'That stuff's too nice for the likes of him.' And he replaced my girdle with his rope, which he knotted with practised ease around Kit's wrists, behind the man's back this time, and so tightly the minstrel winced in pain, his fingers and knuckles turning white.

When this was done, I pushed Gael in front of me, and we took our leave of the sheriff. I was glad to turn my back on the place. I did not like to think of those men and women in their underground prison, with only the perverted Master John to visit them each day, their freedom hidden in his nether garments. God knows what he forces them to do down there where no one can see and no one can tell.

I took Kit and Gael to the stables to fetch Netty, and I made my little group sit on a low wall at the entrance. There were things that needed to be said. I watched Kit easing himself uncomfortably onto the hard stones.

'I'm going to release you,' I said. 'But I want your word of honour first that you will not run. You will stay with me, and you will do as I ask.'

He looked up, his dark eyes full of passion. 'I will be nobody's bondman. I am a free man.'

'I did not mean that,' I said calmly. 'I meant, I will untie you, provided you give me your word that you will stay close

Pies or no pies

to me, not as villein, but because I want you to come back with me to the castle. My people liked your music last night. And I want to talk with you.'

After a moment he said, 'I give you my word.'

'Now tell me. Where's the Box of Death?'

'*The Box of Death*?' He sounded startled. 'I thought you'd thrown it in the river?'

'They told you that, did they?'

'Hmm. Yes, I think it was mentioned.'

'Yet I did not throw it in the river. I brought it back to the castle with me. In fact it was tied to the saddle of my horse as we walked to the castle together. And I think you know this already.'

'Why do you think that?'

'Because you were there when I took the Box down from Guinevere. Branca also saw me do it, so either she took it or you did. I trust Branca, I don't trust you.'

'Good thinking!' He smiled appreciatively, but I couldn't tell if it was praise or sarcasm.

'Well, where is it then?'

'The thing is, Rory,' he said, addressing me as no minstrel should, 'you're too late. The Box has been returned.'

'*Returned*?'

'Yes.'

I was infuriated by the man. He never said anything directly; it was always a riddle, always a game. Well, no matter. It's just an empty box, when all's said and done.

'Netty can't carry all three of us,' Gael said suddenly, staring at the King's horse.

'No, she cannot,' I agreed. 'Kit can walk.'

'It's a long way to walk,' Kit complained. 'Why don't we all ride? Perhaps you would like your own mare?'

'Guinevere? Isn't she back at the castle?'

'She is not back there. She is quite safe though, and I can take you to her.'

'But Branca said—'

'You've seen Branca? I didn't know that.'

'Branca told me the horses are all safe. They've been taken home.'

'Lord, she was lying.' Gael spoke a trifle breathlessly. 'I *knew* she was lying when she said it. I knew because the Lady Joan has taught us that when someone lies they touch their face and cover their nose or mouth. Branca was touching her nose and mouth all the time she was talking to us about our horses, but when she was talking to me about Netty she didn't touch her face at all!'

'The Lady Joan taught you that?'

He nodded, his eyes serious.

I turned back to Master Kit. 'Where is Guinevere?'

'Hidden close by,' he said casually. 'I'll show you.' So I had to trust him after all.

Kit led us to the market, where the stallholders and tradesmen were packing up and going home for the night. A big, brawny labourer, one of my poorer villeins, took us down a passage between two dilapidated houses, and we came out into a mews where a couple of hawks were pegged out. Under cover, clearly having been well cared for, stood my beautiful Guinevere. Her tack hung on the wall and I soon had her ready to go.

I made the decision that Kit would ride Netty, while Gael and I were on Guinevere. Another bloody great risk, I thought, as I hauled Gael up. If he wanted to, Kit could make a very quick escape. The man had given me his word, but what was that worth? Then again, Branca had made a fool of me. That would need dealing with.

Pies or no pies

As we came to the junction with the Wartsbaye Road, I saw the Great Plain directly ahead. Just the other side of the road is an ancient birch tree and some old tree stumps, the trees having fallen or been felled long since. The logs and stumps make a well-known meeting place for couples in the summertime, though no one was sitting there now. Guinevere turned left towards home, and Netty dutifully followed.

I was mostly silent on the ride back. Gael chattered across the gap to Kit, and Kit was pleasant to the boy in return. For my part, I felt mostly anger. I knew I'd been deceived, certainly by Branca and the three troubadours, probably by the Lady Joan, and definitely by Sammy, who wasn't even available for questioning.

My household is my family.

The idea that the people who live with me had betrayed my trust was unthinkable. There had been lies and deception. There had been theft, insurgency and considerable distress. And, thanks to Amie, there was nearly a riot.

I cast my mind back to my father's time. He was a good ruler, and I learnt much from him. But he was a severe man, unapproachable and implacable in his expectations. Any vassal who failed to deliver on a commitment was punished hard. *Fac Fiat* was his motto. *Make it happen.* And he always did, while any man, woman or child who let him down lived to regret it. I was not his only child; a sister died in infancy and a brother, younger than I, left Mallrovia to become a mercenary soldier as soon as he was old enough. As children, we were subjected to harsh discipline, but I never saw my father lose his temper. I also never heard him speak rudely to anyone, whatever their standing, and, though not loved, he was respected throughout the land. Would all this have happened in his day? Could the thefts, the lies and the deceptions have taken place? Would Amie, or any other bard for that matter, have had the temerity to sing the song she did if it had been my father at the high table rather than I? I scowled at my questions, and my persistent, corrosive self-doubt.

I twisted in the saddle to glare at Kit. 'Who are you? *What* are you? And where are your blasted companions?'

'My name is Kit, and I'm a travelling minstrel. My companions are Christopher and Annis, and I believe they are still in your castle. I apologise for stealing your horse. Unfortunately, there was a pressing matter I had to deal with.'

'Pressing matter be damned. What of the other two horses? I was told three were missing.'

'They are not missing. I don't know who told you that. They will be in the stables, as usual.'

Now I was beginning to doubt myself. Who had actually given me that information?

'What about the dishes and the pies that were stolen?'

'Dishes and pies?'

'Yes, damn you! Taken from the kitchens. My servants were distraught.'

'I know nothing about that.' His voice and face were deadpan. So much for the Lady Joan's intuition regarding liars.

Gael was singing a song to himself, and now here we were, crossing the drawbridge and ambling past the little track that leads to the *Egg*. Guinevere tossed her head and

Pies or no pies

whinnied a little, the way she does when she sees someone she knows, although no one was there. At the main gatehouse, I saw Sergeant Alex and Captain Kerry on patrol.

They reported that all was quiet, for the hue and cry had died down since the miscreants had been apprehended.

'Only one of them was,' I said sourly.

I told them to take charge of Master Kit and put him in the dungeon. Kit looked pained, and Gael cast me a reproachful look. I made a comical face at him, for first his best friend Amie was banned from seeing him, and now his new friend Kit would be locked up. Perhaps one of the things the Lady Joan should teach her apprentices is how to choose better friends. I'd expected tears, but to my surprise, Gael smiled gamely back, so perhaps he is growing up at last.

I stayed to watch while my two officers marched Kit away, and then Gael offered to take Netty to the stables for me.

'Yes, do that,' I agreed, 'and see if the palfrey and the grey are there. Branca told us they would be, but you didn't believe her. So let us find out. And after that, we must get some food. We've missed supper, I'm sorry to say, but there's bound to be *something* we can eat!'

Gael skipped away to the stables. He must be as ravenous as I was, I thought, making my way to the kitchen. Hopefully there would be food there, pies or no pies.

10

WE CALLED IT THE BOX OF DEATH

Today is Friday 11th May, and my squire came to me in my library in response to my summons. I sat in my carved oak chair while Davy stood before me, a gangling and awkward sixteen-year-old, worried and nervous, and rightly so. He shifted from foot to foot.

'Whose idea was it to take Sammy to the Nahvitch?'

'Lord,' he stammered, 'I think it may have been Branca, lord.'

I was not expecting to hear Branca's name. Indeed, I had decided in my own mind that the Lady Joan was behind this whole business, what with Sammy and his itchy feet. But Branca, who lied about the horses being stolen, who crashed out of the castle with the hue and cry but didn't apprehend anyone, and who is not, when all's said and done, from Mallrovia at all?

I thought back to when Branca first came to us. About fifteen years ago, I judged, remembering that she arrived almost at the same time I was sent off to fight under the banner of King Louis of France. Five years later I returned, and found Branca's knowledge and understanding of horses impressive. I was not surprised my father had instantly appointed her his marshal, for she came to Castle Rory seeking employment. But *why* had she come? And all the way from the Iberian Peninsula, too.

'If you have betrayed my trust,' I said softly to Davy, 'if you have caused me harm, or caused harm to anyone in my household, then you will face trial and execution as a traitor to Mallrovia. And if you are found guilty, I will take your head off myself.'

'Lord, I never intended to betray you! I didn't know Sammy would stay with the Nahvitch, truly I didn't! I thought he would return with Prince Barney. I thought it was one of Barney's adventures, and Sammy was... was...'

'Was what?'

'Was sort of required. For the Nahvitch to talk to him or something. I didn't think, lord.'

I dismissed the boy for now. Hurrying down the stairs, I almost bumped into Rachel.

'The King and Queen and their retinue are all going back to the palace, lord. They won't stay!' Rachel seemed genuinely upset.

'Well, that is their right,' I said, inwardly rejoicing at their departure.

'No, you don't understand; they're going because we didn't feed them well. It's a humiliation!'

'What do you mean, we didn't feed them well?'

'All our dishes and pies were taken. We had to start again, and it wasn't good enough. We could only give them scraps, and a milk pudding Amie had made, but unfortunately it had curdled. His Majesty was furious. He called the pudding 'shameful fare', and demanded to speak with you. When he discovered you had not returned to the castle, he was even more angry.'

Last night, when Gael and I got back from Hambrig Town too late for supper, we'd scrounged what we could from the kitchen. I'd enjoyed the remains of the milk pudding – it hadn't seemed 'shameful fare' to me. Perhaps I don't have the King's high standards.

I looked for Branca but couldn't find her, so I went to see the King. My audience with Philip was brief and stiffly courteous. He was displeased with every single outcome of his visit to Castle Rory.

The gecko has not been destroyed, so is undoubtedly still at large somewhere; Barney has been made a fool of – everyone has seen the smirks and heard his 'Prince Bunny' nickname; Davy is an undisciplined youth, whose indiscreet behaviour has resulted in the whole sorry mess.

Not only that, but the food last night was a disaster, and there was no entertainment of any sort; the chamber wherein the King and Queen slept was cold and draughty, and there should have been a private latrine. Word was circulating that I borrowed Netty without permission, not that Philip listens to gossip of course, but he wouldn't put it past me. I was further informed that the two princesses have been bored, and the Queen is displeased no jousting tournaments were laid on. Castle Rory has failed dismally, that was the clear message, but every indictment from the King was met with a respectful silence from me.

Then the King issued a royal command. 'Lord Rory, you are to find Fiorello, the Sacred Gecko of the Nahvitch tribe. You are to kill it, destroy it completely, and you are to burn the Box of Death.'

I turned to leave, but the King called me back testily. 'One other thing. Get yourself married and get an heir. Your land, your estate, is closer to the enemy than any other part of Mallrovia. When you die, and that can happen any time, Hambrig will be unstable. Unless you produce an heir to the estate, you will leave an open door for the Nahvitch. Once they're established on this side of the Hurogol, Mallrovia will be fighting for its very survival. Are you really going to leave a weakened and vulnerable land behind you?'

'I will not allow Hambrig to become weak, sire,' I said stiffly.

This matter of an heir is a sore point with me, especially as it is raised by all and sundry. However, I have to concede it actually *is* Philip's business, and he is rightly concerned for the safety of the kingdom.

'Then what are you going to do about it?' The King's tone was aggressive.

'I will marry.' For what else could I say?

And then I hurried away and found Sir Jonny in the bailey by the great hall. I instructed him to organise a search party.

'We're looking for Branca?' he asked.

'For Branca and for those two scoundrels, Christopher and Annis. *And* for the Box of Death. If you find any of 'em, bring them to me at once. And do not open the damned Box!'

Jonny gave me an odd look. For of course he knew there was nothing in the Box. I didn't tell him I wasn't so sure about that. For if it was empty, why had it been taken?

My next job was to talk again with Master Kit. Or so I thought, but as I was making my way towards the steps that lead down to the dungeon, Gael came hurtling towards me, his curly fair hair bouncing up and down, his tunic all askew. He more or less fell into my arms, and I frowned at him. This was no way for a page of mine to behave.

'Lord! In your library! It's the Lady Joan! And she's got someone with her, lord. They're waiting for you.'

I postponed my plan to interrogate Kit, and hastened up the winding stairs to my room in the high ramparts.

'Lady Joan!' I exclaimed. There she was, sitting in my beautiful carved oak chair.

'My lord.' She inclined her head. 'Sir Patrick kindly let me in.' Next to her stood a tall, handsome young man, suntanned and bearded, dressed like a sailor. 'Do you remember William?' Joan asked. 'Captain of the *Senjo*?'

I wouldn't have known the name of his ship, but I did remember the man. He visited Castle Rory a year or two ago when his ship docked in the River Hurogol. Irritated that Joan was sitting in my chair, I made some noise or other. William bowed to me. He looked an intelligent young man.

'Is the *Senjo* one of the King's warships?' I asked.

'No, Lord Rory. The *Senjo* is my own vessel.' His voice was deep and serious.

'Then you are a privateer.'

The Lady Joan took a deep breath. 'Rory, it is time for some plain talking, and that is why William and I are here. We have much to tell you.'

I went to the outer door, clicked my fingers, and the watchman disappeared to fetch a couple of canvas stools from the store in the buttress. The three of us sat in a group. I positioned myself so I could lean against the wainscotting, but William sat in the middle of the room, his back straight, his hands resting on his knees.

'Everyone knows that Sammy's mother was a Nahvitch woman,' began the Lady Joan, leaning forward slightly, her eyes bright.

Joan is a born story-teller, and in my father's day she would often entertain in the great hall. I know that seems strange, seeing that her title is that of a noblewoman. I've known the Lady Joan for many years, but I have never asked her about her early life. Privately, I believe she's not of noble birth at all. I am certain she and my father were close, if not very close indeed. I suspect that he gave her the title 'Lady Joan' so they'd both be above reproach. I'd forgotten about her gift to weave a tale, forgotten how compelling it could be. But now – now I remembered...

'Everyone knows that Sammy's mother was a Nahvitch woman. And everyone knows that a Hambrig fisherman found her in an old punt adrift on the River Hurogol. The fisherman's name was James, and he brought the woman back from the dead, as she was very ill and like to die. James and I cared for her, and between the two of us, we made her well again. We did not involve physicians or surgeons, because the woman had a secret, and only James and I knew what it was. James disguised the woman's secret by marrying her straight away. The ceremony was conducted in James's cottage, with the woman on her sickbed. Yes, they married in haste, and in time Sammy was born. But James was not Sammy's father. The woman had been pregnant when he rescued her, and that was her secret. But childbirth is difficult and dangerous, and James's wife did not survive. Sammy was premature, or so everyone thought, and he was very sick when he was born. James vowed to bring Sammy up as his own son. No one would know the truth.

'Then, when Sammy was just seven years old, the Nahvitch came in the night. They came for Sammy, but they did not find him. Sammy heard noises. He woke his father, and his father told him to run and hide. From his hiding place Sammy watched four of the Swamp-People come to his father's door and batter it down. He saw James dragged outside, and he saw also that it took all four of the Nahvitch to hold his father down. The child saw his father knifed to death, stabbed in the back with a cowardly Nahvitch dagger. The tribesmen then looked everywhere for Sammy. They tore the fisherman's dwelling to pieces and they smashed his boat. But they didn't find Sammy. They shouted and swore in their own language, while the little boy hid, shivering and terrified. But he remembered his father's words: *If the Nahvitch come, hide at once. Do not make a sound. No matter what happens, do not come out of hiding until after they have gone. Even if they kill me.*

'Sammy followed his father's instructions. He stayed holed up in the place they'd chosen together for when the attack came. James had known it would come, and he had prepared his young son. He knew there would be no warning, so they needed a place that was quick to get into and impossible to discover. James constructed it himself – a false back to the chicken coop. There was a clever sliding door at the back, and the space was just big enough for the child to squeeze into. Every few weeks, James made Sammy practise getting in and out, hiding away and staying silent, in preparation for the real thing. James made an eye-hole through the front of the chicken coop so his son would know when it was safe to come out. The day it happened, Sammy saw everything through that hole, but he could not scream or shout, he had to stay perfectly still and quiet while his father was butchered in front of him.

'Afterwards, he came to the castle, again as instructed by his father. James was not an educated man. He could neither read nor write, and his speech was rough. But he'd thought of everything to keep his son safe. He'd made sure Sammy knew exactly what to do. James did not die in vain, my friends, for Sammy survived, and survives still. Sammy's instructions were to make his way to Castle Rory. There he was to ask for the Lady Joan and seek her help. And that is exactly what the little boy did.

'However, Sammy's mother had another secret, an even bigger one than her pregnancy. You see, everyone assumed that Sammy's mother was a Nahvitch whore, cast out by her own people. But she was no whore. On the contrary, she was a princess, descended from the original Nahvitch kings. A few days before Sammy was born, his mother lay on her bed, ill and in pain. While I tried to comfort her, she told me something of her people's history, and from her story I don't believe the tribal name is Nahvitch at all. She said the tribe was once a powerful and prosperous civilisation in this land, living side by side with the Hambriggers. There was no enmity between us and them. But one winter, more than a hundred years ago, the rains and the winds were monstrous, and the River Hurogol burst its banks. The Great Flood was upon us, and the tribe had to run for their lives. Everything they had was destroyed. Buildings were washed away, streets and market squares under feet of water. Many, many people died, swept away, drowned and lost for ever. Some of the Nahvitch managed to get across to the other side of the river and find refuge in the swamps and the reedbeds there.

'The royal family was saved, but only just, and they made their way south, through Westador, through England, and eventually across the sea, south through France and westwards across Spain until they arrived in the Celtic land of Smander. But the Nahvitch were decimated. Only a tiny fraction of them remained here, and they were leaderless too. They now inhabited a bog of sodden ground on the other side of the river. Their king and queen were gone, and did not return to them. They elected a new leader, whom they called the Kyown-Kinnie, which, in their Celtic tongue, means "chief of the tribe". Their royal family heard about the Kyown-Kinnie and the swamp settlement, for visitors and traders brought them news. But by now they were comfortably settled in Smander. They had quarters in the royal palace there, and they were content. Later, they moved into a big palace of their own on the edge of the city. There was no swamp and no flood, and the weather was warm all year round. So they stayed in Smander. Their children grew up there, and eventually the eldest son became king, but he was king in name only. He had no kingdom to rule over.

'This went on for another couple of generations, until one day there was no son to be the next king, there was only a daughter. When her parents were both dead, this daughter thought she should return to her own people, for she had more guts and go about her than any of the previous male heirs. This girl was called the *bannafree-oonsa*, which means "princess" in the Nahvitch language, although she herself was fluent only in Smandego. This *bannafree-oonsa* decided to make the journey to the swamp-lands, which she had heard were now called Blurland. She took a woman companion with her, a woman whose name she would not reveal. It took them several months to make the journey, but eventually they arrived at the Nahvitch settlement. I told you that "Nahvitch" is not the real name of the tribe. The princess simply called them "my people", or "my father's people". She never used the name "Nahvitch", neither did she tell me their real name.

'There must have been something special about the princess, for the Kyown-Kinnie himself married her. Well, it wasn't long before the princess realised she was with child.

We called it the Box of Death

She told the Kyown-Kinnie, and a great celebration was organised in the settlement. Huge beacons of flame were lit, and there was singing and dancing and feasting. But a few days later, the princess fell ill. She had often been ill as a child, and the arduous journey from sunny Smander to the cold, wet swamps in the north had been very bad for her health. She worried that she would die before the baby was born. The medical men tried to help, but they were useless, with their chanting, their spells and their leering looks at her breasts. She despised them. She decided to write everything down before she died.

'But before she could write a single word, one beautiful, moonlit night the Kyown-Kinnie's hut was raided. Robbers came and forced their way in. They took the woman and dropped her into a boat, which they set adrift on the river. The princess had become *seriously* ill by now. She was in a fever and unconscious. She was unaware of James finding her and taking her home in his own fishing boat, coaxing her to drink the rich and nourishing milk he had from his goats, and wrapping her in love and tenderness in his own bed. She remembered little of all this, but slowly and gradually she grew well again. She came to love James, her fisherman rescuer, and when he asked her to marry him, she agreed. She did not tell him she was married already. But she did tell him she was with child. James treated her with love and compassion, and they were married the next day.

'The princess became stronger every day, and she and James had a good life together, although it was not a long one. She had recurring dreams, in which she gave birth to a healthy baby boy, but she herself died in childbirth. She told James her dreams, and he tried to tell her this was nonsense, but she knew it wasn't. Well, that is the gist of the princess's story. Of course, we know her dreams foretold the truth, for she survived only a few hours after Sammy was born, and James then had a babe to care for. Being the man he was, James did everything he could for the infant, and Sammy grew up respecting and loving him.

'James never told Sammy he was not his real father. Sammy only found that out when I told him myself. And that is the *bannafree-oonsa's* tale, which I have kept secret all these years.'

I exploded in fury. '*Why?* Why have you kept it secret? Why did you never tell me all this before? I didn't know Sammy was fully Nahvitch! I should have been told!' My stomach cramped painfully, as it so often does these days.

Joan answered me calmly. 'Sammy didn't want anyone at all to know, but *particularly* you. He was afraid you would throw him out, and he desperately wanted to stay here. He felt safe, and James had told him to come to me.'

But I would not have thrown Sammy out, and Joan should have told him so. 'Did the princess mention the gecko at all? Or the Box of Death?'

'Not exactly. But she spoke of something powerful which could be used to restore her people to the land they lost in the Great Flood. That could well be the lizard.'

'Did she say where it is?'

'She said that her people have it, and that they can use it against their enemies.'

'Then they still have it!' I exclaimed. 'They still have it, and it could still kill us.'

'You believe that tale?' asked William. 'You really believe the gecko can kill just by looking at you?'

But I was thinking of how it must have been, all those long years ago: the Nahvitch king and queen in a frenzy to get away from the surging waters, making sure to take the thing that mattered most to them, their symbolic, sacred lizard, cared for in a wooden box, the very box I'd seen with my own eyes, touched with my own hands. Was it ancient, that box? If it was made before the Flood it would be even older than the castle. *And we called it the Box of Death.*

11

THREE DAYS

'I know you're angry about Sammy,' Joan said. 'But you see, he knows his mother was a princess. He wants to claim the throne of his own people. I told him we would talk to you, and it would be properly arranged through you. I had no idea, no idea at all, that he would actually go off with Barney.'

'*Why*, though, Joan?' I tried to steady my voice. 'He was happy here, and he's a child, he still has much to learn. Why would you want him to go to the enemy?'

'To make them not the enemy.'

So Sammy was to be a peacemaker.

The Lady Joan was nodding. 'If Sammy were the Nahvitch king, Rory, the first king they have had in generations, he could bring peace between Blurland and Hambrig. He could start a new relationship between our two peoples, and bring an end to conflict here.'

No, I thought at once, no, no and no. *Nobody* would pay any attention to Sammy. He was barely educated, ridiculously young, and with precisely zero experience of leadership, kingship, absolutely bloody everything. But Joan was smiling. Her faith in her protégé was touching.

'Did he know you were sending him to do that?' I asked. 'He's had no training, Joan.' I was shaking my head. The more I spoke of it, the worse it seemed. What a bloody awful mess.

'Of course he knew,' Joan said calmly. 'Why do you think he spent time perfecting the pavonalilis colour? It is the colour of kingship. He has taken a robe, dyed in this regal shade, to prove himself to his people.'

A coloured robe. *That* was his claim to the throne? *That* was all the preparation he had?

Joan was still talking. 'Rory, you forget that the Swamp-People know who Sammy is. They know he is their own, their lord, their rightful king. They came for him once, but his father was too clever for them. And what have they done since then? Ravaged our land, attacked our villeins, burnt our crops, and shot flaming arrows into our barns. And now they are on a war footing. They are preparing for a full-scale attack. *That* is why William is here.'

I sat up suddenly. 'Who says they're on a war footing?'

William made an odd, seated bow in my direction. 'Lord Rory, I have been observing things. The enemy are making ready for war. They have raised an army.'

'An army? Or a fyrd?'

There is a difference. In comparison to our fighters here, a fyrd would be just a rabble. If the Nahvitch army were simply its people massed on the shores of the swamp, armed with trowels, sticks and bread knives, we would make short work of them.

'It's not just the Nahvitch,' William said in his deep voice. 'There is a professional army now.'

Joan gave me an odd look. She was moving things

around on my desk, a sign of nervousness. 'I hoped Sammy would go to his people to bring peace. I did not want to send him into danger. I knew the Nahvitch would welcome him home, and I hoped they would fête him as their king. But something has gone wrong. Terribly, terribly wrong.'

My insides contracted again. I knew we were coming now to the whole point of this long session in my library.

The Lady Joan's voice shook a little. 'Rory, you have been betrayed. There are Smanderinos in the Nahvitch territory, scores and scores of Smanderinos, perhaps hundreds of them. The Smanderish army is legendary. Their discipline and their weapons are second to none. William has seen them with his own eyes. The Smanderinos have been training the Nahvitch, turning them into warriors. Sammy may be too late after all. We are about to be attacked, and it is going to be bloody.' She looked close to tears.

'My ship – the *Senjo* – is being careened in Dorbney in the Hurogol estuary,' William said, taking over. 'I have an arrangement with a Dorian shipyard there. But while the ship has been out of the water, I've seen columns of spearmen and bowmen, men-at-arms and scores of well-trained cavalry too, all going north into the plains west of the Hurogol. I ventured upstream in one of my ship's boats, and I saw where they were all going. They were joining the Nahvitch beyond Blurland. I recognised them. They are Smanderish warriors. As soon as I was sure, I borrowed a fast horse and came to tell you.'

I stood up. 'Then we must prepare as best we can, and there is a great deal to do. Joan, I don't know how much of this is your doing, but my priority now is to defend my castle, my people and my land.'

William got to the door before me and blocked my way.

Three days

William is as tall as I am, and a similar build too. And I'd say he has ten years on me.

'Get out of my way, man,' I snarled.

Joan had presented me with a crisis. We had a mountain of work to do to prepare our defences, and I also had to think of how to rescue Sammy and bring him back. My priority was to talk with Jonny, get him up to date with the situation, and prepare the garrison for battle.

William saw the look on my face, but he did not back off. 'Lord Rory, there is one more thing.'

I swore at him. One more thing? More than out-and-out war with a well-trained army of thousands?

'It is this,' said Joan from behind me. 'William is my son. You can trust him absolutely. He has brought his ship, his crew and his experience for you to use as you will. He places himself under your command.'

'Your son?' I said stupidly, swinging round to face her.

The Lady Joan had never married.

'My son, yes,' she repeated gently. 'Do not judge me, Rory. I have a son, and I am proud of him.'

'But ...?' And then I knew. 'Anthony Merry.'

Joan's steady grey eyes held mine. But there was no time to think more about it. 'With me,' I said tersely to William, and the two of us raced down the stairs and into the courtyard. I knew now that we would not find Branca or the missing musicians. They, Smanderinos, Dorians, or whatever they were, would be in Blurland by now. But there was still Master Kit, and I intended to question him within an inch of his life.

I sent William to the river. I wanted the entire fleet of Spiderboats to come to the landing stage. There was a signal they used, a flag with King Philip's royal blazon. I gave one of these flags to William.

'Once you have one Spiderboat, you'll get them all. Word will spread quickly. Use this flag by the landing stage and—'

'I have a boat,' William interrupted. 'With a boat's crew. They've come up the river from Dorbney on my orders. I'll row downstream with this flag at the masthead. All the Spiderboats will see it then.'

'Good. Get to it.'

Jonny reported to me in the gatehouse. Of Branca, Christopher, Annis and the Box of Death there was no sign. He looked anxious. His search parties had been everywhere; they had turned the place upside down; they'd ridden into Hambrig Town and searched every dwelling, every shop, every corner of every street. No one knew anything, no one could help. Some of his men had trekked along the riverbank, parting the reeds, looking for signs of anyone having been there. These were trained scouts, knowing how to interpret trampled vegetation, newly turned earth and washed down banks. The scouts reported that there had been some damage to the riverbank near the landing stage, and it looked as if something heavy had been concealed. But there was nothing there now.

'They have all simply vanished,' Jonny told me in bewilderment.

'Far from it,' I rasped. 'They are the enemy, Jonny. *The enemy.* They have gone to the Nahvitch, where they belonged all along.'

Jonny's mouth dropped open. 'Oh my God! Are you sure? Branca has been with us for years! How can she be with the Nahvitch?'

He raised an important point. Branca has indeed been in my household for many years. I sent a servant to fetch the record books. These are huge ledgers where I record everything, and I mean *everything*, that happens on my estate. But I didn't have time to scrutinise the close handwriting on the many pages of each ledger, searching for Branca's name and the date she arrived, bringing treachery into our midst.

I sent for Master Peter, my Yorkshire alchemist with an eye for detail. He would find the entry. I set the pile of ledgers up on a table in the great hall, under a window so there was plenty of light. I told Eliza to make sure Peter had everything he needed, including a quantity of food and ale. He arrived with a bag of tools and instruments. I eyed them askance.

'Lord, I di'n't know what tha wanted me for,' he explained apologetically. 'I thought I'd best be prepared for owt.'

I sat him down at the little table and explained the task. His blue eyes lit up, which made me smile. I left him with the first ledger, and was interested to see him extract a long metal rule from his bag of instruments and place it on the page. He used it to line up the entries in the columns, so as not to muddle the lines or become confused by the densely packed script. I nodded, satisfied.

Crossing the courtyard and the bailey, I made my way back to Jonny's barracks and asked him to send Master Kit to me. Then I fetched my sword.

Against all logic, I like Master Kit. He kept his parole and did not try to run. And he was friendly with Gael, answering the lad's questions and good-naturedly putting up with his chatter. And I cannot forget the amazing displays of showmanship and wizardry the troubadours treated us to on the night they entertained us. There had been magic and sorcery; there had been songs to make you weep, and dancing to lift your spirits again – and

Christopher had even swallowed fire! Of course, I know now it was all a bluff, a way into my household, breaching our defences, knowing us from the inside and understanding the landscape of my fortress. I am angry more with myself than with anyone else. I took the minstrels at their word, and ran no checks on them. And we were all about to pay the price for that.

Kit was brought to the gatehouse, his hands once more tied, his eyes bloodshot, his face unshaven. The soldiers either side of him pushed his shoulders over, forcing him to bow to me. I dismissed them.

'So you are a spy,' I said flatly.

'Am I?'

'You, and your friends, came here to spy on my household, to infiltrate my castle, and then to attack us. Is that not so?'

He looked straight into my eyes. I could not use the Lady Joan's advice on how to spot liars, for Kit's hands were tied, but I was watching him carefully nonetheless. I saw a good-looking young man, lean and capable, his skin swarthy, his curly hair thick and black.

'You had the tribe's king,' he said with a shrug. 'They wanted him back, that's all.'

'That is *not* all, Master Kit. The Lady Joan has already sent Sammy back to the Nahvitch.'

'The Nahvitch? Oh yes, the enemy. I know why you call them that. Well, if the king has been returned, all is well. There is no need for further alarm.'

'Why did you steal my horse?'

'I had something important to do and riding was quicker than walking.'

It was so obviously the truth that I was taken aback. I remembered he'd mentioned a *pressing matter*. I had not

Three days

followed that up. 'What was this important thing you needed to do?'

'It doesn't matter now, it didn't get done anyway. Christopher and Annis stole some trivial things from the kitchen and made sure your cook and serving women discovered the theft. Then, while you were dealing with them, I rode your horse out of the castle. Unfortunately, your steward immediately discovered I'd taken her and he raised the hue and cry. Branca was furious – she didn't want the town out searching for us. Hambrig was in uproar, as everyone turned out to hunt the thieves down. Branca came to look for me, but she was too late. The hue and cry had done its work and I'd already been hauled off to the sheriff. So Branca turned round and came home again.'

'The pony went lame.'

'Not really. Branca made that up so as to account for being unable to find us.'

I digested this information, finding it bitter in taste and hard to swallow. 'And now Branca and your Smanderino friends are all on the other side of the river, ready to attack my castle, a place you were welcomed in as guests, and where Branca has worked with our horses for fifteen years. It's despicable.'

'It's not quite like that. We knew you'd go to the sheriff and get me out. It was easy really.'

I stared at him, suddenly hostile to this arrogant young man who had played me as effortlessly and as confidently as he played his musical instruments.

'Why are you and the others involved in this business?' I asked. 'Branca, even. This is not your fight and Sammy is not your king. You are Smanderinos, not Nahvitch!'

He didn't reply at first, but his eyes became distant, as if he were somewhere else.

'To answer that question,' he said eventually, his voice very quiet and even, 'you will have to go back many years. At least a hundred years, in fact. Back to *The Meridian*.'

'*The Meridian?* What the hell's that?'

'*The Meridian* is a book, somewhat like Domesday. I am not surprised you've not read it, but I'm astonished you haven't even heard of it.'

What was the man talking about? *The Meridian?* No, I had not heard of a book of that name. And I resented his tone. Kit never shows any respect, damn him.

'Tell me more about this book.'

'It was written more than a hundred years ago, and not twenty miles from here. A man in Hambrig Town wrote it. He's important to me, though I've never met him, but I am sure you know him.'

How would I know a man who lived in Hambrig more than a hundred years ago? This was arrant nonsense. I realised the minstrel was playing more tricks. This is his trade, after all – music, magic and mayhem. It's all one to him.

'How long do we have?' I asked, deliberately turning the subject from this fantastical talk. 'How long do we have before the Nahvitch and the Smanderinos attack the castle?'

'Three days.'

12

HIS PRETTY BOATS

If you control the castle you control the shire. Once the shire is yours, you'll have the kingdom too. Castle Rory is the country's first line of defence – it falls on *us* to hold Mallrovia.

Jonny has recalled his search parties. He's drilling the troops day and night. Archery practice, handling weapons, tactics and strategy, all are worked out in the courtyard and on the hillside. Jonny is hard on them; no one complains. Meanwhile, Patrick is poring over lists, organising and planning. Whatever you can think of, Patrick has it on a list. We have brought in plenty of food, both grain and livestock, and the kitchen is kept busy organising storage and prioritising what should be used first. The dairy, the pantry and the buttery are full to bursting. I've been in a siege before. You think you have enough. You never do.

And as the castle prepares for war, so do the people of Hambrig. They've been climbing the hill – at first just a family or two, a lone shepherd with his dogs, a handful of freemen and their wives. Now the rest are arriving, and we somehow have to cram everyone in. The bailey is full of makeshift tents and shelters, and the great hall has become a dormitory for all, just as it used to be in the old days.

I made Joan move out of the *Egg*. 'It won't be safe,' I told her. 'It's far too isolated.'

'We have lookouts posted,' she replied acerbically. 'They will inform us when we need to spread panic and flee.'

'I am not panicking, Joan, and nobody is fleeing, least of all you. This is just common sense.' And when she continued to look mutinous, I simply ordered her, as her lord, to move close to the keep. Eventually all were gathered in, and we raised the drawbridge on the rest of the world.

Peter has of course found the entry that detailed Branca's arrival with us. It was in early spring, fourteen years ago, while I was away fighting the infidel in Egypt. Peter has marked the entry in the appropriate ledger with a neat cross; I have it open beside me in my library this evening. My journal lies on the desk as well, and I'm making notes. Outside, the sky is golden and orange as the sun sets on a lovely spring day. My door to the ramparts is open at the top, and I can sit back and gaze at the vivid colours in the sky. I know what I have to do. I must look at the other entries in the ledger, the ones made just before and just after Branca. The ones that will, I hope, help me understand what her game is, why she came here, what she wants. But fourteen-year-old records of crops that were brought in, petty misdoings punished and stores ordered and delivered, while relevant at the time they were written, are of little use to me now.

His pretty boats

I almost give up looking, but then, in a record from the autumn of the previous year, I come across this:

Fisherman rescued dying woman in abandoned boat. Probably a Nahvitch prostitute, very likely poxed.

Two weeks later in the ledger is the following entry:

James, not a freeman, given permission to marry Nahvitch woman.

Then, at the expected times, the ledger notes Sammy's birth and his mother's death.

So. Branca came to Castle Rory a few weeks after Sammy was born, which meant that Branca didn't see Sammy's mother before she died. That poor woman had been abducted from her own hut. Who took her and why? Joan, in her narrative taken from the woman's own story, mentioned a female companion who escorted the young princess, the – what was it? – the *bannafree-oonsa,* from civilised, prosperous Smander to bleak and bleary Blurland. I think about Joan's words.

She took a woman companion with her, a woman whose name she would not reveal.

The more I think about it, the more convinced I become that the unnamed woman was Branca, who is the right age, and came from the same country. I envisage the two of them undertaking the perilous and challenging journey together, over the mountains, across whole countries, crossing the Narrow Sea that separates England from France, supporting and helping one another along the way.

Two women with no male protection. They arrive in Blurland, make contact with the Nahvitch and settle down amongst them. The princess marries the Kyown-Kinnie, but what does Branca do? Possibly she marries a Nahvitch man also. They are secure in their new lives until the unthinkable happens.

The princess, or the chieftain's wife as she now is, is abducted in the night. The alarm is raised of course, but she has gone for good. Months go by, and eventually the Nahvitch realise she is now in enemy hands, across the water in Hambrig. Branca vows to find her. She crosses the River Hurogol and finds work in the castle, since she has this amazing affinity with horses. By now, the princess is dead, and Sammy is being raised by James the fisherman.

I wonder if Branca has known all along that Sammy is the Kyown-Kinnie's son and not James's. I wish I had a name for Sammy's mother. It doesn't seem to be recorded anywhere; nobody bothered to write it down. And yet she had been a royal princess, and then a tribal chieftain's wife. Joan must know it.

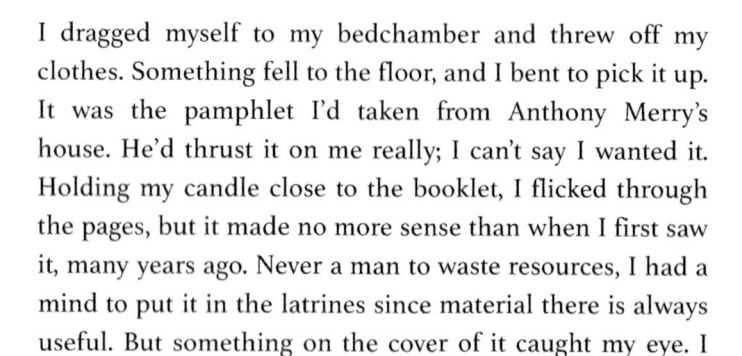

I dragged myself to my bedchamber and threw off my clothes. Something fell to the floor, and I bent to pick it up. It was the pamphlet I'd taken from Anthony Merry's house. He'd thrust it on me really; I can't say I wanted it. Holding my candle close to the booklet, I flicked through the pages, but it made no more sense than when I first saw it, many years ago. Never a man to waste resources, I had a mind to put it in the latrines since material there is always useful. But something on the cover of it caught my eye. I sank onto the bed and started reading. For the cover proclaimed that this small publication was in fact, *The People's Puzzle or The Meridian, a Columnar Approach*, by Anthony Merry.

Kit said I would find answers in a book called *The Meridian*, a book somewhat like Domesday, which had been written by a Hambrig man more than a hundred years ago. Well, that man had to be none other than Anthony Merry, though he'd not written it a hundred years ago – that must simply have been more Kittish nonsense.

I tried reading it properly, yet it seemed to be written in another language, and I could make no sense of it at all. There had to be meaning here *somewhere*, surely. Sometime between midnight and daybreak, and feeling I was no nearer to any kind of understanding, I padded down to the room Peter shares with Laurence, our chaplain. I shook Peter awake and beckoned him out of the room. With blankets over our shoulders, we sat together in my chamber, poring over the pamphlet.

'What dost tha know of this already, lord?' Peter asked.

'Not a lot. I know it was written by Master Merry, and that was some time ago, perhaps twenty? Thirty years since? And I know it's a puzzle, but I don't think anyone has ever solved it.'

This thought filled me with despair, for if no one had solved it in all the time it had been in existence, what hope did I have? I am not a great thinker, nor yet a scholar. I could only put my faith in Peter of Redmire. And perhaps the knowledge that we simply *had* to find the solution would make the difference. Well, that's what I told him. The answers to all our questions were somehow hidden in this small and insignificant looking booklet. Peter looked at me, his expression one of consternation.

'Three days, lord? Tha says we only have *three days*?' I nodded. But it is less than three days now.

As dawn flooded the sky, Peter and I sat side by side, our heads together, *The Meridian* between us.

'I wonder why it's called *The Meridian?*' I mused. 'I knew it was *The People's Puzzle*, but I've never seen the other title.'

'Oh, I can tell thee that,' Peter said at once. 'Tha canst see it here, in t' dedication.' His stubby finger pointed to the inscription inside the cover.

> *To Mistress Diane, the most beautiful and the cleverest of women. My adored wife.*

I couldn't see what he was getting at.

'D'n't tha see, lord? Mistress Diane. Diane Merry, her name would have been. Diane Merry becomes Merry Diane, an' then Meridian.'

I sat back in awe. 'You. Are. Clever.' Then I bent over the first page of the manuscript again. 'But what on earth are we to make of this? It's not even in English! Look at the first three sentences. There are a few proper words, like 'ale' and 'he' and 'son'. But most of it's rubbish.'

I stared at the words on the page.

> *iaeey hmautil gneen eaaf yop ihebrahr ale he yndpvlsy son luiastac wcmo ek nod iia ore of rmr tadppnrn.*

And there were pages and pages of this stuff.

''Tis a cipher,' Peter explained. 'Some sort o' code. We have to crack t' code to find out what it says. Those words that look like English ones, they probably don't even mean what they normally mean. They'll be part of t' cipher.'

'Can you do it? Can you crack the code?' I gazed

His pretty boats

searchingly at him. Peter's homely face, his competent spatulate fingers, his curly, springy grey hair and pale blue eyes were all achingly familiar to me, and I knew him as a meticulous man, whose attention to detail was sometimes agonising. But it is one thing to search through the ledgers for something we both knew would be there. It is quite another to have the fate of the kingdom in your hands.

And he will have to work quickly, to get the job done before the attack starts. Always, I reminded myself grimly, always assuming that Kit has been accurate with his 'three days'.

'Why don't we get Master Merry to tell us himself?' suggested Peter. 'He must be here, in t' castle. T' whole of Hambrig is here. Can we not find him and ask him to translate it for us?'

I jumped to my feet. Of course! We must ask Anthony Merry himself. Since by now it was fully daylight, I hurriedly dressed again and went in search of him. After two hours of looking, and getting both Davy and Gael to look too, we still hadn't found him, and it seemed no one else had either.

While we were searching in vain for Master Merry, the royal family took their leave of us. I dutifully saw them out through the gates, and then I went to ask the Lady Joan about her friend.

'He won't come to the castle,' she told me calmly. 'Anthony won't leave his books.'

Damn the man. That would mean sending someone for him, and if he wouldn't leave his books even then – must I arrest him? I explained why we needed him.

But the Lady Joan just shook her head. 'Rory, you don't understand Anthony. He won't tell you what the *Puzzle* means. Even if you dragged him to the castle, he still would not say. Do you think I haven't asked him myself? He says it is for Hambrig to work it out.'

'But the future, the *survival* of Hambrig is at stake!' I fumed. 'Surely he will help us? Surely he will not see us annihilated by the Nahvitch?'

Again, she shook her head. 'He will not care, Rory. He simply will not care.'

I looked away, frustrated and furious. Who was this man to hold us all to ransom? In a black mood I strode away from Joan's makeshift shelter in the bailey. I thought of my father. He would have sorted all this out with calm efficiency, while I was permanently on edge. Then again, I'd had no sleep, so perhaps it wasn't surprising. I began to make my way back to Peter to tell him the bad news, but I was waylaid, and it was William.

'I have come to report that my mission has been successful, and the Spiderboat fleet is by the landing stage as you wanted.'

'Well done. Yes, well done, William. And we shall be glad of your assistance in the days to come.'

He bowed. 'What would you have me do now, lord?'

'Are you any good with ciphers?'

'Ciphers?'

'Codes. Making sense of them, cracking them or whatever it's called.'

'Are you speaking of *The People's Puzzle*?'

'You know it?'

'My mother gave me a copy years ago. I didn't understand it at all. I always thought it must be in some foreign language, perhaps the Nahvitch language.'

'Why the Nahvitch language, William?'

'Because my father's wife was a Nahvitch woman. You didn't know that?'

His pretty boats

Diane had been Nahvitch? No, I hadn't known. But at least I now understood why Anthony Merry didn't care what happened to Hambrig. I told William to take Peter and *The People's Puzzle* to my library, and not to emerge until they had deduced something useful from it. Buckling on my sword, I made shift for the stables, got Guinevere ready myself, for there was no marshal to do it for me, and swung into the saddle. I called for Jonny, told him I was going to the river, and left him in charge. He suggested an armed escort, and I agreed.

Before long, I was joined by Captain Kerry and Sergeants Bess and Alex. These three are Jonny's best people, our Special Guard. They've seen serious combat, which most of our garrison have not, since we've only had a few minor raids from the Nahvitch recently. There have been no foreign campaigns since King Philip withdrew the budget for a war chest back in '59.

The four of us cantered over the hurriedly lowered drawbridge onto the track that leads down steep-sided Baudry Hill, to emerge onto the low-lying flatlands bordering the River Hurogol.

As we trotted through tiny hamlets, meadows and pastures, I reminded my three companions about the Spiderboat fleet. 'They are our communication system. But not only for us. They hear things and they see things. I want you to talk with the Spiderboatmen. Get them to relax and open up.'

The landing stage was spiky with masts and tossed oars. I did not dismount. From my seat on Guinevere I could see clearly, and I needed to count the boats. There are eight Spiderboats in the fleet. Only seven were present.

'Spiderboatmen!' I called to them. 'I thank you for

coming here in response to the signal. But there is one boat missing. Does anyone know where it is?'

Someone spoke up. 'Tha's Quinn's boat. An't bin seen since Thursday night. We bin lookin' for Quinn, we 'ave, but in't no sign of 'im.'

Thursday night. And now it was Saturday. Thursday was the day of the hue and cry, the day Branca, Christopher, Annis and the Box of Death all vanished from the castle. Well, I had my answer. I'd been wondering how they managed to get across the Hurogol. It seemed there was indeed a corrupt boatman, and King Philip was right to be worried.

A horrible feeling of fear lodged itself in my stomach. If the Spiderboatmen had turned their coats, then there was no barrier between us and the enemy. The River Hurugol, which had always kept us apart, would soon be swarming with Nahvitch and Smanderish forces. I desperately needed intelligence on how far this corruption had spread, but, whether it was one man or many, it would break King Philip's heart.

'I want to sail across the Hurogol to Blurland,' I called to them. 'Which boat will take me?'

There was a hurried conference among the boatmen and then one man volunteered. I dismounted and climbed down into his Spiderboat. The rowers slotted their oars into the crutches, the boatman muttered something to them, and we pulled smartly away from the landing.

It's a fact: the Spiderboats are the best kept, the best run and the fastest boats in the world. The hulls are always gleaming, the ropework is golden, the crews are well turned out and their boatmanship is second to none. I made a sour face. The Spiderboats are King Philip's pride and joy. This is

His pretty boats

why there's no money for a war chest – he spent a fortune on his pretty boats.

13

I JUST NEEDED TO SLEEP

There was no one on the river today. Hambrig has decamped to the top of Baudry Hill, and the fishing boats swung to their moorings, or lay upturned on the bank, unused. My Spiderboat was alone on the water. Her skipper was a veteran called Godric.

'How far we goin'?' he called to me, his Hambrig accent distorting the words.

'As far to the other side as possible. I want to see what's going on.'

'Beam reach, that work for us that do, but there's the tide. That push us upstream.'

Godric lowered the leeboard, laid our boat on the starboard tack and we made good progress across the current. I shaded my eyes. Misty Blurland became more defined as we approached, and I could make out sparse vegetation, a few withies, and a post or two sticking up out of the mud like abandoned limbs. We edged closer and closer.

I could see no sign of human life, no movement at all in that murky landscape. Around me, the crew was busy with

I just needed to sleep

halyards and sheets, and then it was suddenly quiet, the sail tamed, scandalised up to its yard, and the oars dipping and rising on each side. I sat in the sternsheets with Godric. We moved as quietly as we could, the oars making barely a sound, water dripping softly from the blades.

'You know the way in?' I asked in a low voice.

'I do.' Godric spoke seriously. 'But d'n't advise goin' in jis' now. Someone say the Nahvitch and the Smandermen 'ave joined forces. If they do take yer pris'ner, we shall 'ev noo chance.'

'We'll take the risk. Find the channel. Unstep the mast.'

Godric pursed his lips; he clearly didn't relish the thought of being the boatman who got the Lord of Hambrig captured by the enemy. But he followed my orders.

With the mast down we were low in the water, hidden mostly by reeds and rushes. We nosed into the channel and paddled our way along. Moorhens, coots and mallard swam to our sides, and I was afraid we would provoke a flight of them, all quacking and honking our presence in the marshes. Godric knew his business though. We came alongside a kind of muddy staithe, shored up by rough wooden planks. One of the crew scrambled up to the top of the rickety structure. We didn't make the boat fast, but simply passed a line round one of the supports and waited there while the crewman reconnoitred the lie of the land. Godric looked anxiously around. We were deep in enemy territory. We couldn't say for certain we hadn't been seen, for surely they would have scouts posted, and although the alarm hadn't been raised, I was pretty sure it was only a matter of time. A few curlew called plaintively over the swamps, and a bittern boomed twice in the reedbed, but apart from that it was eerily quiet. Godric kept his hand on the tiller, and the bowman was all set to slip our painter in a hurry. If the alarm sounded, we would make a quick getaway. The man ashore would just have to take his chances.

A scuffling sound from above. The man holding our mooring line prepared to throw it; the men with the paddles had them ready, leaning over the gunwales. I tightened my grip on my dagger. We all ducked as moss and clods of mud rained down on us, and then sighed in relief as we realised they were being kicked by our own scout. A sack was lowered into the boat, and then our crewman dropped down too.

'Not much ter report, sir. After 'alf mile or so I 'ear noises – men an' 'orses. I din't go far enough ter see 'em. But I find this sack, just lef' in a muddy puddle. There's suff'n 'eavy inside, so I bring it back 'ere.'

'Let's go.' Godric shoved off and we made our way back down the channel towards the river. About halfway down, we felt a sudden bump. The boat had hit something. Everyone stopped dead. The curlews called, but there were no other sounds. One of the crew leant over the gunwale, and we all watched, horrified, as a dead body rose out of the water. The crewman was holding the corpse's head.

'Oo my God,' whispered Godric beside me, and the rest all muttered something and crossed themselves.

'Who is it?' I whispered back.

'Quinn,' Godric said, shocked. 'Tha's Quinn.'

His throat had been slit.

It's the hell of a job, hauling a heavy, waterlogged body into an open boat, but then we got ourselves down the rest of the channel as fast as we could. Everyone was relieved when we were finally back in open waters. There is something very claustrophobic about poling through a muddy channel with waving reeds either side of it. I had the

I just needed to sleep

sack between my knees. Quinn's body lay on the bottom boards. Godric hoisted sail again and the Spiderboat leant over on her ear as the wind filled the sail. The corpse rolled in the boat's bilges, and the crew had to lean right out to windward to balance the boat.

My mind was occupied with the scout's report. The enemy had cavalry. William had reported it, and our scout had heard horses. To swim the animals across the Hurogol would take time, and would allow us to pick them off at our leisure. They couldn't use transports; there was no way of getting *those* up the narrow channels, nor could you embark horses from that ramshackle jetty. I wondered what their plan was. There *is* a ford, a way of crossing the Hurogol on foot, but it's far upstream, where the river is narrower and flows through a ravine, bordered on both sides by a forest. This offers cover. If the enemy rode upriver, crossed by means of the ford, or even the Wisbech Bridge, our most northerly crossing, and then rode down onto Hambrig, they'd have the advantage of surprise. We would never expect them to come on horseback from the north.

Would they try to attack the city first? They'd be nearer Hicrown than Hambrig, but Hicrown is well protected, with a fortress-style city wall all around it. My guess was that the Nahvitch and the Smanderinos, and it's the Smanderinos who have experience of cavalry charges, intend to ford the river high up, counting on nobody seeing them, pick their way through the trees and come out on the hills above Hicrown. It's about fifty miles from there to Hambrig Town, so they would need two days at least to get here, assuming they also have foot soldiers with them. More likely three days. And fear clutched at me then, for in my head I heard Master Kit ominously intoning his *three days*. Did that mean they were already here? Already on our side of the river?

Already travelling south? But the scout had heard them, so they were still, God willing, in Nahvitch country, making their preparations. And now I have to make mine. As for Quinn – I guess he went too far into the swamps and the Nahvitch didn't like it. We got away with it, thank God.

I stepped onto the landing stage, dragging the heavy sack with me, then lugged it onto the grassy riverbank. The other Spiderboats were still there, Alex, Kerry and Bess sprawling on board one of them, and there was much laughter and banter, exactly how I hoped it would be. But word about Quinn spread very quickly, and the mood became sombre. My two sergeants helped to get the dead man ashore, while Godric spoke quietly to Captain Kerry.

Everyone crowded round as I untied the sack's drawcord, then reached with both arms into the depths of the hessian. My hands closed on hard surfaces and rigid corners. I grasped the thing and pulled it out. With a gasp of horror, the crowd stepped away. I was holding the Box of Death.

On the ride back to the castle, I learnt that the Spiderboatmen are not corrupt. They are loyal to the King, but they'd been suspicious of Quinn for some time. Quinn, they said, was often away from the fleet. He wasn't 'one of them'. Kerry, Alex and Bess also learnt the truth of William's observations. The Smanderish army are indeed mustering on the other side of the river, and they are drilling those Nahvitch barbarians into disciplined warriors. They have infantry, they have horse, they have arms and they have fire in their bellies. They are coming for us.

Davy met us at the gatehouse, and was clearly doing the

job of marshal, as he took charge of the horses and spoke to them in Branca's voice.

Jonny tried to catch my eye. 'What's happened?' I asked, dreading some further calamity.

'Peter has cracked the code. He's solved *The People's Puzzle.*'

'Good. Let's hope it's of some use to us.'

In the great hall, supper was just about over. I was suddenly aware of how hungry I was, though I'd long since accepted my state of total and permanent exhaustion. Peter and William were talking with the Lady Joan. They turned happy smiles in my direction, but I was too tired and too hungry to smile back.

'What news?' It came out more roughly than I intended.

'Lord,' Peter said quickly, 't' cipher's solved. William an' I have read t' *Puzzle*, and I've a copy, translated for thee.' He held out a booklet, much the size of the original pamphlet. I saw it was filled with his meticulous, tiny writing.

'Just give me the gist.' I threw myself down on a bench seat in the alcove. My stomach rumbled loudly, but I ignored it.

Peter swallowed. 'I think tha should read it, lord,' he faltered.

'It tells of a people,' William said, taking over. 'The first sentence actually says, "The Toosanik are a proud and ancient people who lived peacefully in Hambrig for many years."'

'The Toosanik?' I was mystified.

'It is the Nahvitch's real name.'

'And they lived in peace with us? That's what it says? Exactly as the Lady Joan related?'

'That is what it says. They lived peacefully on this side of the River Hurogol, occupying most of the Great Plain. There was a treaty between us, a treaty which gave rights to each community and allowed trade and free movement between us all.'

'Then the Nahvitch, or whatever you called them, ended up on the other side of the river?'

'After the Great Flood. But they'd lost everything, and the flood water, which was salt, had ruined the land. They had to stay in the marshes and scratch a pitiful living there. Years later, when the land had mostly recovered, they wanted to invoke the treaty, so they would be allowed to live on this side of the river and have equal rights with Hambriggers. A party of Toosanik crossed the river. They were met by the King himself – it was King Harold II back then. Even though the treaty had been lost in the flood, the Toosanik warriors asked the King to respect it. They promised him men and weapons for his army, if he would grant them good land nearby.

'But the King of Mallrovia said no, they couldn't return. The Toosanik were angry and shouted in their own language. "*Sharn Nahvitch aha sheen*," they said. When they didn't get a response, just a lot of blank looks, they repeated the word, "*Nahvitch! Nahvitch!*" and pointed to themselves. After that, King Harold always called them the Nahvitch. He didn't realise it, but in their language, the word *Nahvitch* means "enemy". They were telling us that as we disregarded the treaty we were now enemies. *Sharn Nahvitch aha sheen* means "We are the enemy."'

'How the blazes did you work it all out?' I was as impressed by the work that must have gone into cracking the code as I was shocked by the story.

'Peter did it,' William said simply.

''Twere one of those column ciphers,' Peter explained,

I just needed to sleep

blinking at me from his place opposite. 'Dost tha know them, lord? How they work, I mean?'

I shook my head impatiently.

'Tha needs a keyword. Tha writes t' keyword along top, and then tha writes text to be encrypted underneath, so columns form under each letter of t' keyword. Then tha rearranges t' columns, so t' letters on top are in alphabetical order. And then tha reads t'encrypted message vertically down t' columns.'

I followed perhaps a third of what he was saying. 'How did you know the keyword?'

'Oh, that were easy, lord. I reckon Master Merry *wanted* us to decode it. He wanted people t' understand the story of t' Toosanik, so he made it dead easy.'

'If he wanted people to understand it, he should have written it in plain English,' I said irritably. 'Well? What *was* the keyword?'

'Sorry, lord. It's "The Meridian", of course. The clue's in t' title!'

'And "The Meridian" was his wife, Mistress Diane?'

'That's right. Mistress Diane were a Toosanik woman. In fact, she were the Kyown-Kinnie's daughter. She told her husband t' story of her people. When she died, he were heartbroken, and vowed to help her people get their land back. He wrote t' book in code because of t' sensitivity of lost treaty. No one knows where it is now. And that's why t' book is called *The People's Puzzle,* of course – it depends how tha says it, d'n't it? The very first sentence, as William has just told thee, says, "The Toosanik are a proud and ancient people." It's t' puzzle that belongs to a proud and ancient people, lord, a people who once had a treaty with us, but *we* broke it. We broke faith with them, and allowed them to suffer for generations.'

'But if we could find this treaty—'

'If we could *find* it, lord,' Peter broke in excitedly, 'we'd finally be able to make peace wi' t' Nahvitch. Wi' Toosanik, I mean.'

'Then where is it? Where can it possibly be? Does Merry give any clues?'

'He says just one thing – that t' Toosanik king had it. He mentions another document too, a document which is also called *The Meridian*. It's old, more than hundred year old even when Master Merry wrote his coded puzzle. He tells us that *The Meridian*, t' original one, is with Fiorello, t' Sacred Gecko.'

Not the damned gecko again. I remembered I'd brought the Box of Death home with me, though it was back in its sack now, so nobody in the castle had seen it. I'd left it with Jonny, but I didn't think it had any importance. At one time I thought it must hold the clue to the deadly weapon, Fiorello. But it was discarded in a scruffy old sack and left in the marshes. If the Box were truly an ancient relic, surely the Nahvitch would have guarded it, gecko or no gecko. I said some of this to Peter and William, and it was William who pointed out the flaw in my thinking.

'If the Box is worthless, why did your marshal go to the bother of taking it across the river?'

Why, indeed. Just one of many unanswered questions. Peter said Merry was 'heartbroken' when his wife died. But not so heartbroken that he didn't have a son, William himself, by another woman. I was angry with Merry. I was sure he must know the whereabouts of the treaty. And if the gecko really does exist, then it must have been removed from its box and replaced by the ridiculous rabbit before the foolish prince's arrival among the Nahvitch. That would make sense of Branca's reclaiming the Box, but not of the

I just needed to sleep

Box subsequently being abandoned in the mud. My head was starting to hurt. And the answers seemed as elusive as ever.

'We need to find that treaty, if it still exists,' I said. 'We also need to get a party of crack troops to the ford as quickly as possible.'

Jonny agreed. 'I'll see to it directly. If we get there in time – and that's a big *if* – we'll make sure they don't get over the ford alive. I'll put Captain Kerry in charge of the S.O.F.'

The Special Operations Force are our crack unit, our best people. While Jonny went off to brief them, I walked over to the keep. Master Kit was still in the dungeon. His rations would be basic, and he would be hungry. Perhaps nearly as hungry as I was, I thought savagely as I strode across the bailey, avoiding all the tents and the hundreds of people getting themselves ready for the night. I had the guard on duty release Kit from his bonds, and I led him out into the fresh twilight air of the bailey, where he breathed deep lungfuls.

'What do you know about the Toosanik and their treaty with us?' I asked him directly.

'Very little.'

'I'm going to get you some food, Master Kit, and some ale too. While you are eating and drinking, please think again about my question.'

I spied Gael lurking by the buttery wall and told him to see to it, and soon after that Eliza brought out a pewter jug of beer and a trencher of food, and set them down before Kit. I impressed on him that I wanted his information so we could end the warfare and the bloodshed, and so we could make peace with the Toosanik people. In the end, he told me much about the Toosanik and the treaty, but nothing new.

He doesn't know where the treaty is.

And Fiorello?

His answer was a sarcastic sneer. *Fiorello?* Surely I don't believe in *that* fairy tale? I finished the interrogation as frustrated as ever.

The S.O.F., led by Captain Kerry, thundered out of the gatehouse on horseback, their lightweight armour gleaming in the setting sun, their swords and bows slung from their waists. I watched them go, saluting their courage and their discipline. Then I went to the chapel and knelt before the altar. I prayed our troops would be in time to intercept the invading forces. I prayed also that my theory was correct, that I hadn't sent my best warriors on a wild goose chase, leaving us open to attack from some other direction. I finished by asking the Almighty for his help in finding the treaty and bringing peace to our country.

Finally, I clambered wearily up the stairs to my chamber and threw myself onto my bed. I'd had no sleep for thirty-six hours. I'd also had nothing to eat since breakfast, but I was too exhausted now to think about food. I just needed to sleep.

14

MY POET AND MY PAGE

On my orders, Gael is following me around the entire time. He is useful for fetching anything I need, or going to find people I want to talk to.

No one is idle. Even the children are kept busy, fetching and carrying, re-stacking the pantry, the buttery and the dairy, bringing in armfuls of fresh vegetables from the kitchen garden, chopping firewood, and helping with the animals. Fit and strong adults are drilled by Jonny. There aren't enough proper weapons for them, but there are pitchforks and shovels, stout sticks and old wagon axles. Just as important as the weapons, though, is the *attitude*. Jonny makes everyone chant and stamp and shout; he gets their blood racing so they'll be ready to fight for their lives.

I've given up on Kit for the time being. He's been put to work in the kitchen, chopping onions probably, and is both busy and out of harm's way. There's a team of people, preparing food all day long, bringing provisions out to the soldiers drilling in the courtyard and on the ramparts. And Eliza has found a number of folk who are good at sewing –

making and mending clothes, and checking there are enough blankets and wool fleeces put by for the wounded, for we are under no illusions: we are going to be hit, and hit hard.

I've always known that Bethan is a brilliant physician. As part of her preparations, she has recruited a workforce of assistants and nurses, and has commandeered the great hall to be her hospital. Whenever I am inside it now, I picture it full of the injured and the dying. Bethan has spent hours instructing and training her new medical team. She's issued them with white robes so we will all know who to go to. A gang of girls and boys has been detailed to tear up strips of linen to make bandages, which they've coiled up ready for use in large wicker baskets. Bethan's bag of tools has been checked over; the knives, augurs and scalpels oiled and sharpened; while the trestle tables we dine off are ready to be turned into makeshift hospital beds. We have all the villagers and practically the entire town within our walls, and though it's crowded and there is no privacy for anyone, it is a determined and purposeful gathering. As I look around at the activity, the teamwork and good spirits, I hope my father would have been proud.

———◆———

Today I woke before dawn, lit a couple of wax dips, and spent the first hour or so of this Sunday morning lying in bed, going through Peter's translation of *The People's Puzzle*. It makes very interesting reading, and I am beginning to understand why the Nahvitch are so angry with us, why time after time, year after year, they attack us and try to take

My poet and my page

our land, our livestock, the crops out of our barns, even our women.

As I read of the flood and the tribe's desperate attempts to save themselves, I can't understand why the Hambriggers of the time didn't help them. We, those long-ago Hambriggers, literally ran for the hills. Exactly as we are doing right now, the entire town congregated on Baudry Hill, safe from the tidal wave. Presumably from here they watched the Toosanik being swept away to their deaths. Did it *really* happen like that? My great-grandfather, who built this castle, is said to have been a wonderful man and a first-class leader. It is hard to reconcile that with the picture that has just formed in my head. Did the first Lord Rory not see the desperate plight of those hapless Celts?

Towards the end of the translation there are a couple of sentences that also make me wonder.

But there is still Hope. Hope is not dead.

———◆———

I let myself out through the postern at the back, into the chilly dawn. At this time of the year – and at this time of the morning – Baudry Hill is stunning. The wild flowers haven't yet opened, but you can make out their colours, and the birds are singing their hearts out. And the best thing is, there's nobody else about.

A lord's life is seldom his own. He's surrounded by people who want him all the time; they want him to do things, or they want decisions made, or they want a dispute settled or permission for something. There's hardly ever a peaceful moment when you can be by yourself. That's why I had my library constructed, and now, with Guinevere stepping gracefully down the lonely hillside, I relished the solitude of this early start to the day. I was bound for Hambrig Town, and one of its few remaining residents.

Naturally, Master Anthony Merry was still in bed when I called. The element of surprise should never be underestimated. He shambled to the door on my fourth or fifth knock, and let me in. I flourished the two pamphlets at him, one being the original, the other the translation.

'I've read it!' I announced. 'All of it, Master Merry. Finally, you have a reader!'

Owl-like, he blinked at me. After a moment, we both took seats, exactly as like the last time, except now there was no Lady Joan and my host was in his nightshirt, hair sticking up, glasses askew.

'So you've solved the puzzle.'

It was hard to tell if he was pleased or sorry.

'I didn't solve it, Master Merry, but one in my household did. It's an interesting history of the misfortunes of the Toosanik people.'

'It's their history, yes,' he acknowledged, 'but how interesting it is, I do not claim to know. You are the first to read it.'

I was annoyed at his tone, but tried not to show it. 'You have dedicated your *Puzzle* to your wife, Diane, haven't you. And she was a Toosanik woman?'

He looked at me through his owlish glasses, then nodded slowly.

'Did you and Mistress Merry have any children?' I asked.

'We have one daughter. But she died.'

'She died? What was her name?'

But I already knew. There was silence. I needed him to

confirm the name, though. 'Master Merry, what was your daughter's name?'

'If you want to know her name, do not use the word "was" when you speak of her.'

'I am sorry,' I said gently. 'Tell me, Master Merry, what is the name of your daughter?'

'Her name is Hope.'

There is still Hope. Hope is not dead.

'How old was your daughter when she died?' I asked.

'Ten years old. She is exactly your age, Lord Rory. Born on the same day in the same month of the same year.'

Somehow, that information shocked me. I pressed on with my questions. 'And your wife, Diane. She died soon after?'

'She died of a broken heart, a month after Hope.'

'Master Merry, how did your wife and daughter die?'

'It was sudden,' he said, distantly. 'That is all I can tell you.'

I left him sitting in his chair, staring sadly at the wall, his glasses misted right up.

I rode back, thinking I'd wasted my time, and not only that, I'd missed chapel. I'd discovered nothing of importance. Anthony Merry is a sad and lonely old man, though I thought he might have been able to help me, since his wife had been a Nahvitch, or rather Toosanik, woman. But he either couldn't help, or didn't want to. Joan would know.

I found her outside in the bailey, one of her vivid, multicoloured shawls draped over her shoulders, surrounded by children winding bobbins. When she saw me coming towards her, she shooed them away, and I dropped down onto the grass next to her wicker basket chair.

'Joan, tell me about Anthony Merry.'

'He is a scholar,' she said at once. 'Anthony's a very clever man. He speaks the classical languages, he reads the Bible in its original Greek and Hebrew, he studies astronomy and nature. He knows a great deal. And of course, he's a master jeweller.'

'But I want to know about the *man*. Who is he? What is he like? What about his family?'

'Ah. I see.' There was a pause while she picked some loose threads off her skirt. 'You want to know if we are lovers, he and I?'

'That too,' I conceded. 'But also the other things.'

'You know we have been lovers, for there is William. Yes, we are lovers still. Anthony is a private man, Rory, he does not give much away. He is law-abiding and honest, but he does not like being in a crowd and, knowing he is not popular, aware he's a laughing stock on account of his appearance, he does not venture out very much.'

'How old is William?'

'William is twenty-two.'

'Hope died when she was ten. And Merry says she would have been the same age as me, which means she died twenty-three years ago. Her mother died a month later. So if William is twenty-two, that means you and Merry got together very quickly after. Is that right, Joan?'

She laughed at me then. 'Rory, you know nothing of women, and very little of men, it seems to me. Anthony and I were lovers long before Hope and Diane died. Anthony is fifteen years older than I, and I have known him since I was a child. We had what you might call "an understanding". There was only one child from Anthony's marriage to Diane. Why do you think that was? I'll tell you. They did not sleep together, not after Hope was born. Hope was very

My poet and my page

poorly, and it took all Diane's strength to look after her. So, since I had always been his friend, I helped in that way too. It worked for both of us. For all of us.'

'Did Diane know?'

'I am sure she did. I never asked.'

I became aware that Jonny was hovering nearby.

'Lord,' he said formally, as I looked enquiringly up at him. 'Special Operations must have arrived at the ford. There is no word from anyone. I am anxious as to what has happened.'

'As am I.' I pushed myself up off the ground. 'Do you want to send a rider?'

'I was thinking I should go myself.'

'Very well, go now. But not all the way to the ford, there isn't time. See what you can find out and be back by sundown with your report.'

A little later, I saw him ride through the gatehouse.

Then Patrick arrived. 'Lord, there is a problem, and it is Amie.'

'Why, what has she done now?' I'd completely forgotten about Amie.

'Your page, Gael, has been with her a great deal.'

'But that's impossible! He's been with me the whole day.'

'No, lord, he has not. You send him on errands all the time. He completes those errands for you, but he also visits Amie, and they talk, and then they kiss, perhaps more. It has been happening a lot. And last night, he rose from his bed to meet her in secret. I saw them myself.'

This was intolerable, and I felt my anger building again. 'Then it must be stopped. He is only twelve years old, for God's sake! What is he thinking of?'

'He is a child, but Amie is a young woman. Whose idea do you think this is?'

That did it. 'Lock her up, Patrick. I won't have any more of it.'

'On what grounds?'

I closed my eyes. He was right. There were no grounds for imprisoning her. Blast the girl. I have more important things to think about than my poet and my page.

15

SHAME FOR THE REST OF HIS LIFE

There was a huge commotion on the ramparts, horns sounding raucously, and then a shout came from the gatehouse.

I squinted into the sun, and saw the guard pointing to the road that snakes down from Wartsbaye in the north to the border with Westador in the south. I ran to the watchtower, just in time to see Jonny and Captain Kerry hurtle across the drawbridge and come to a shuddering halt in the courtyard, Kerry slipping sideways from the saddle. She had a man behind her, an enemy warrior by the looks of him.

The rest of the S.O.F. followed, and I could see there had been casualties. So they *must* have met with the Smanderers, and my hunch must have been right. The bridge was being drawn up again almost as the last horse galloped across it. Burning with questions, I raced back down and found Jonny helping a limping Captain Kerry to the gatehouse. The Smanderino, his wrists tied behind him, was led away by two guardsmen. Jonny and I made a sling with our hands and carried Kerry up the gatehouse steps and into the barracks. We lowered her onto a bench, found a stool to support her injured leg, and then the physician arrived.

An hour later, Doctor Bethan had left, and Captain Kerry was resting. She had taken a spear wound to her left leg, and had lost blood. Gael brought us all wooden bowls of whatever stew was being served for dinner, and we four ate together in the barracks. While we were eating, the captain gave us her report.

'We arrived at the ford just after midnight. No one was there. We checked everywhere, then we hid among the trees and waited. An hour or so before dawn we heard the sound of horses arriving from across the stream. We positioned ourselves ready to attack, keeping out of sight. We heard them splashing through the shallow water, and we heard their armour clinking. They weren't trying to keep quiet, sir, they didn't expect a welcome party. When they were within range, we struck. We gave them everything we had. We expected to be greatly outnumbered. We thought it could be a full invasion force, but they were just a small cavalry unit, and we dealt with them easily. We left their officer alive though – and he had this on him.'

She handed a sealed and folded document to Jonny. Jonny gave it straight to me. A dispatch from the Nahvitch.

'No, they weren't Nahvitch,' Captain Kerry corrected me. 'The Nahvitch don't have cavalry. These were all Smanderers.'

'You killed them all? All but their officer?'

'Yes, lord. Some of the horses survived, and we turned them loose. They would have delayed our return and my report to you.'

'I'll want to interrogate that officer.' I was opening the dispatch as I spoke. It was in English.

Shame for the rest of his life

Honoured friend, make the rendezvous as arranged for Wednesday. Proceed to the castle the next night. Signal your contact inside to lower the bridge and open the gate. We judge the castle to be well defended but not impregnable. When all is secure, send word and we will join you.

There was no signature. I passed the parchment to Jonny.

He looked at me, appalled. 'There's a traitor in our midst.'

'There's a traitor in the castle, that's clear. Someone who is to open the gates for the enemy. But who *is* the enemy, Jonny? Who the hell are we fighting? Where did they intend to deliver this?'

'*Honoured friend,*' Jonny said with bitterness. 'Who the fuck is that?'

I went straight away to the prison cell at the top of the gatehouse. This leader of the Smanderish cavalry had to be made to talk.

He told me his name was Arkyn, and he was a lancer.

'You are from Smander?' His name wasn't Smanderish, and his appearance wasn't Mediterranean. But he was certainly the enemy.

Silence. He would answer no more questions.

I paced around the cell. It has bare walls, bare floor, no windows, and contains nothing but one small truckle bed. Arkyn held himself as a nobleman would, and I deduced that in civilian life we would be equals.

'I've read the letter,' I told him, suddenly wheeling round so we were eyeball to eyeball. 'I know you were planning to meet someone here in Mallrovia.'

No response.

'You don't have to answer me. We'll get the information

out of you one way or another. I'll have my guards get to work on you, Arkyn, and you'll talk then. You might as well save yourself the pain.'

I watched the sweat bead on his upper lip, but he remained silent.

I told Jonny and the rest of the company to leave Arkyn to his own thoughts for a couple of hours, and then to come and find me. In the meantime, I sought out Sergeants Bess and Alex and explained what I wanted them to do. And after *that*, I called a meeting in the great hall.

'Friends, vassals and villeins,' I began, standing on the edge of the dais. 'Five days ago I said I would tell you more about Fiorello, the Sacred Gecko. I have called you here so I can keep my promise.' Around the hall, excitement fizzed and crackled. 'You will remember that Amie, our bard, sang of the Nahvitch and their aggression towards us. She mentioned the night they came and attacked us here in this castle, killing our men and women, slaying the Lord of Hambrig too. That was my grandfather! He was cut down in front of his son, my father. Our marshal at the time, a man called Thomas, took over command, and our troops drove the enemy back, pinning them into Blurland and beyond. Even though this was fifty-five years ago, there may be a few here who remember it.'

I saw Patrick nodding. I was told the story many times by my father, and the poets all sang of it when I was a boy. In many ways it was Hambrig's finest hour; everyone rallying around Sir Thomas and, with great tenacity and courage, charging at the so-nearly victorious Nahvitch, creating panic and fear in their hearts, and driving them back to the river and across to their dismal swamps.

'They had no Sacred Gecko with them then!' I declared stridently. 'They acquired it later, didn't they?

Shame for the rest of his life

The legend of Fiorello began forty years ago, my friends! How long do geckos live? Not forty years! Master Peter, who knows about these things, told me that geckos live for five to ten years. So of this we can be confident – *Fiorello is dead!*'

A cheer went up, which was very heartening. I needed them to believe me. After the meeting I watched people trooping out of the great hall, chattering to each other, hurrying off to their various jobs and duties. And now I planned to investigate the infamous Box of Death more thoroughly.

Jonny and I knelt on the garrison floor and opened up the Box. In my heart I didn't believe I'd find the treaty inside, for how could we have missed it? But if not the treaty itself, perhaps there was some clue as to its whereabouts.

Because if we don't get hold of that treaty before the Nahvitch and the Smanderers attack, the whole damned lot of us are going to be slaughtered right here on Baudry Hill. I know it, and Jonny knows it.

So we opened the Box and examined every inch of it, inside and outside, both the Box and its lid. Empty, as before, and nothing engraved in the wood either. No clues at all. I sat back on my heels, puzzled and disappointed. What was the point of the rabbit in the Box then? And the message that came with it. I pulled it out of my shirt and read it for the umpteenth time.

> *Fiorello is death to those he looks upon. Only a person of great courage and determination will open the box, but if such a one*

can be found, a great reward will be his. This message comes from Hope, Endurance and a New Beginning.

Perhaps it was just a joke. I looked at Jonny, but he just shrugged. Frustrated, we returned the Box to its sack and left it in a corner of the gatehouse.

I ran down the steps and out into the courtyard, hopeful Bess and Alex would have something to report to me by now. They'd had an hour with Arkyn. I touched the dagger in my belt; Davy had sharpened it this morning. It was ready, and so was I. In his cell, Arkyn was alone. Bess stood outside the door, and came to attention as I approached.

'What news, sergeant?'

'The prisoner is unwilling to talk, lord.'

'Has he told you anything?'

'Nothing but his name and his rank in the cavalry.'

'Then move on to Plan B.'

'Alex has gone to fetch the things we need.'

'Let's make a start.' But I wasn't looking forward to it.

Bess unlocked the door and we entered. Arkyn was sitting on the floor, but scrambled up when he saw us. We shackled him to the wall.

'I want to know the invasion plans in every detail,' I said. 'If you lie, believe me I will know, and it will go badly for you. If you do not talk at all, it will be the same. If you tell me the truth, and answer my questions with complete honesty, you will remain a prisoner until this is all over, but you will not be harmed. The choice is yours.' I hoped he'd talk. I had no relish for the torture.

―――◆―――

Shame for the rest of his life

I wonder how I would hold up in similar circumstances. No man can know his limits until he reaches them. When I think about it, which, thankfully, is not often, my toes curl, my skin crawls and the foul bile fills my throat. What if I am a coward? I've proved I'm no coward in battle, but what if I cannot bear the pain? Will I betray my country, my King and my family? And if I do betray them, will I thereafter be unable to live with my shame? And if I am *not* a coward, what then? I will hold out, and hold out, and suffer indescribable agonies, only to find that eventually I give in and tell them everything.

Arkyn looked up at me. I watched him gather the spittle in his mouth and then launch it as far as he could in my direction. It hit my breeches below the knee. A pointless gesture of defiance.

I took my dagger from my belt and ran my thumb along the edge. Bess stood by the door, waiting for Alex.

He had raided the kitchen, and he brought in some fearsome looking objects. I couldn't help wondering what on earth they were used for normally. Alex made sure Arkyn could see the horrors in store for him. He also brought a small, folding trestle table, and this he set up at the side of the cell. Bess placed the kitchen instruments, one by one, on the table. Arkyn's eyes followed us as we silently made our preparations. Alex carefully sharpened something on a whetstone. The rhythmic rasping was the only sound in the cell. Arkyn had closed his eyes.

I nodded to Bess. She approached the prisoner with a sharp knife in her hand. With one slash, she slit his clothing from top to bottom, exposing his naked body. She ran the point of her knife down his chest, not pressing hard enough to draw blood, but scratching the skin nonetheless. Down went the knife, gliding over the man's taut stomach, down to his groin. Feeling the blade explore his genitals, Arkyn gave a howl of terror, but, unable to move, he could only wait for the slicing and hacking to begin. I watched Bess play with him, using the knife expertly, pricking at his thigh, his testicles and the backs of his knees. Blood coursed from the wounds now, though they were not serious. Meanwhile, Alex was busy with his implements, sharpening and honing, stacking and repositioning. To be honest, it was all taking longer than I had thought it would. Finally, the man broke. He started to sob, and Bess, hearing this, gave him an extra nick or two in the ribs.

'I'll tell you what you want to know,' Arkyn gasped. 'But dress my wounds and release me, I beg of you.'

The knife cuts had caused a lot of blood to flow, and they were painful, but the wounds were only surface ones. It was clear though that Arkyn was very scared of what would happen next, especially if Alex got to work on him. I didn't blame him, or think the worse of him for cracking. It was the only sensible thing to do. But sensible isn't always honourable, and Lancer Arkyn would bear the shame for the rest of his life.

16

HIS NAME IS QUINN

Eliza dressed Arkyn's cuts with turmeric and honey paste. While the woman was making the wretched prisoner comfortable, I met Gael in the great hall. I wanted to talk to him about his meetings with Amie, who was supposed to be keeping the company of women only. His reply astonished me.

'Lord, I talk to Amie because the Lady Joan asked me to. The Lady Joan told me that one day Amie will be a great bard, even as great as Taliesin of Wales, and I should be with her as much as possible and learn from her, because I might never be a knight, but one day I might be a musician. That's what the Lady Joan said. Amie has been teaching me to play the recorder, lord – and I can already play six different tunes!'

'And what about the kissing?'

Gael blushed. 'Whenever I play a tune right, or learn a new one, Amie says I can kiss her. It's my reward.'

'And do you like your reward?'

He nodded, his eyes on the floor.

What a ridiculous situation. I'd forbidden Amie any

male companionship, yet Joan has told Gael to take music lessons from her! But in a few days we will all likely be dead or seriously injured, so what do a few illicit kisses matter now?

I clapped my young page on the shoulder. 'Gael, you should keep practising the recorder. Soon, I will ask you to play to me.'

He looked up, his mouth open in amazement. 'Play to *you*, lord? Oh, I couldn't, I'm not ready!'

'Then you must tell Amie to double your lessons, for I shall hear you play, ready or not!' And I loved this exchange with Gael, for the simple reason that it assumed there was a future for us, a future in which my young page could play his recorder and I could be cross with him for kissing a girl. It lightened my heart to pretend it might even happen.

As I made my way back to the gatehouse, I couldn't stop thinking about the Lady Joan. She let Sammy go across to Blurland without my knowledge, and now it appeared she'd been talking to my page behind my back and setting him up with a girl four years his senior.

I stopped suddenly, as an appalling thought came into my head. What if Joan is the spy who will let the enemy in through our gates? Is that possible? Even with blocks and tackles giving a favourable mechanical advantage, would the Lady Joan have the strength to lower the drawbridge? And anyway, I thought sourly, she is no lady. No one has ever told me her story.

A married man is able to talk about everything that concerns him to his wife, but I have no wife. Over the years, Joan has become the person who relieves my loneliness as Lord of Hambrig, someone I can confide in without worrying about gossip or rumour, because I know she is discreet and trustworthy. I've known her all my life. For

God's sake, she *can't* be an enemy. I stood on the hall steps, my insides suddenly queasy. *Joan. It just can't be her.*

Eliza was leaving the gatehouse prison cell. Arkyn was ready, his wounds bandaged. Someone's robe had been found to cover his nakedness. Alex and Bess stood to attention as I entered, and they hauled the prisoner to his feet. I perched myself on the trestle table, and instructed Arkyn to begin talking.

And so we heard that the invasion has been in the planning for a year. The Smanderers had been communicating with the Toosanik. They'd talked about the Toosanik princess who left Smander and travelled to the swamplands, together with a high-born female friend.

'A high-born friend?' I queried. 'Who?'

'She was your marshal,' Arkyn said softly. 'And she was our spy, here in your castle.'

'Branca? But she's been here for many years.'

'Branca is good, and not just with horses.'

I digested this. I'd already deduced that Branca had been the princess's companion, and I also knew that she, a Smanderina herself, had gone across to the enemy, taking the minstrels with her. But spying and plotting these last fifteen years? My father hadn't known it, and nor had I. I thought back over the Nahvitch attacks we'd been subjected to, their uncanny knowledge of who was where and how to find us. My lip twisted in disgust as I thought of my marshal, the horsewoman I'd trusted with my beloved Guinevere, letting the enemy know about everything we did.

Well. So much for Branca. Right now I wanted to know about the dispatch Arkyn had been carrying. Who was it intended for? From whom was it sent? Did he know the contents of the letter? Who was the spy still in our midst, the person who would lower the drawbridge and open the gates? What was the signal?

It took quite a time, since Arkyn was still reluctant to lose his honour. Lose it he did, however, for Bess and Alex reminded him, whenever necessary, of the consequences of not cooperating. As I watched the wordless, but abundantly clear threats made by my veterans, and Arkyn's total, inevitable, and deeply humiliating surrender to them, I knew he would have died rather than talk. Unfortunately for him, death wasn't one of the options he was given. And so, four hours after our little game had started, I knew everything.

It's Monday 14th May, AD 1263, and at last I'm catching up with my journal.

Straight after Mass and a rudimentary breakfast I called Jonny and Patrick to my library. We had a very short meeting, and then Davy was sent, on the fastest mount in the stable, to deliver a message to the King in Hicrown. If all goes well, the King and Davy will return together. It has not slipped my mind that today is Day Three of the *three days* Kit gave us.

The tension here is almost unbearable. Jonny will not let up on the training for one moment, but our troops are tired and everyone is on edge. It's like the hours before a massive thunderstorm. You know it's coming and you just want to get it over with.

His name is Quinn

———————◆———————

Get it over with? It's two days later, and I have no idea how we have got through the last forty-eight hours without going totally mad. But today, the lookouts sighted our horsemen. Davy is returning, and he has brought with him the King and one other. It's easy to discern the King, riding beneath his red and silver royal banner. We can't yet identify the other rider.

So much for Master Kit's *three days*. The castle has been in a state of readiness since the moment William told me he'd seen the Smanderish army marching north. Friday, that was, and now it's Wednesday! No invasion, no siege, no attack at all by Smanderers or Nahvitch. Perhaps it's a deliberate tactic. If so, it seems to be working. Poor Gael keeps being sick. He can't cope with the waiting. Captain Kerry has seen the only action there's been, and even that was just a small party of Smanderish horse, nothing we couldn't easily have dealt with at any time. There was no need to send our Special Operations at all.

So what the hell is going on? Then, quite suddenly, I got it. Kit has been bluffing all along. Not just about the *three days*, but about the invasion itself. Either he knows nothing about it, or he knows everything and has deliberately tried to mislead me. My one advantage now is that Kit doesn't know we've taken the Smanderino lancer.

For the last few days, the minstrel has been kept busy working. I have seen him in passing, carrying heavy barrels from one place to another, labouring in the kitchen garden or servicing and repairing the wagons and carts. He never looks happy, and my guess is he misses his companions. But most of all he must miss his music.

I sent Gael to fetch Kit, and I showed him the enemy dispatch. 'Who is "Honoured friend"?'

He shrugged. 'I don't know anything about this. And you do know you're ruining my hands, don't you? I'm a musician. I shouldn't be dragging rough trees around, knocking the skin off my fingers and callousing my palms. I may never be able to play again.'

'You're lucky not to be in the cells,' I growled at him. 'Just answer my questions and be thankful you're not only alive but at liberty.'

I was not going to threaten this man as I threatened the other. Not because I thought Kit would be able to hold out any more than Arkyn, but because I knew there was a better way. After all, I had just sent for the King.

King Philip must have ridden fast and hard. The horses were led away to be rubbed down and given their nosebags. I bowed low to the King, and thanked him for coming so promptly. The other rider turned out to be Lady Lillian. What a surprise.

'Lady Lillian, I am happy to see you again,' I lied. 'Although I'm not sure it was wise for you to come. Perhaps we can arrange an escort back—'

'You did the right thing in sending your squire for us, Lord Rory,' the King interrupted loudly. 'It is good to see he has learnt courtesy and respect. We were not pleased with him before, as you know. I imagine you have been stricter with him since we spoke to you about that.'

His name is Quinn

So Davy has finally made a good impression on the King, and Philip thinks chastising me for leniency is responsible. I snorted to myself. The King does not yet know the truth about that young man. For it is Davy, I learnt from Arkyn, who is the spy in our midst. It is Davy who is to let the enemy cavalry ride freely into the castle. Davy, my squire, is to be the agent of the massacre of Hambrig.

I've treated him like a son. I thought I'd taught him loyalty and integrity. But there it is, the lad's a traitor. This is a black day for Castle Rory.

In a thoroughly bad mood, I got some maids to look after the princess and make ready a chamber for her, while I went in search of the Lady Joan and found her down at the *Egg*. I sat opposite her at the big table.

'How long have you known that Baron Giles is a traitor?'

Joan put down the fabric she was working on and stared at me. 'A traitor, Rory? What makes you say that?'

'Don't prevaricate. You knew about the letter a Smanderish officer was taking to him, didn't you? The letter that promises the use of Smanderish cavalry in return for breaching the castle defences. You knew Davy was corrupt. You knew he was working to destroy us. Maybe you knew about Branca too.'

All these years. I was bitter. Angry that I had been so betrayed by members of my own household, my own family as I thought of them. And devastated that Joan, such a special friend, had deceived me. This could surely *never* have happened in my father's day.

Joan leant forward in her chair and took my hands. 'Rory,' she said gently, 'I am your friend, not your enemy. If I knew of spies, I would tell you.'

I looked away, aware that too much emotion was showing in my face, that the sickness was rising in my gullet again. 'You did know. Don't deny it, Joan.' I had to clear my throat.

'I know nothing of any letter, nothing of traitors, nothing of cavalry. All I know is Davy was too helpful to Barney in contacting the Swamp-People. Davy made it all happen. And when Barney brought the Box of Death back across the Hurogol, what did Davy do?'

I turned to look at her. 'What? What did he do?'

'Nothing.' She spread her hands, palms upwards. 'He did nothing. Is that what you would expect from a young man who has just brought back a lethal enemy weapon?'

She was right, and I hadn't seen it. 'Why didn't you put these suspicions to me at the time then?'

'Because it was just a hunch, and I had no evidence at all.'

But she should have told me her suspicions, however tenuous.

'We've all known for a long time that Baron Giles has Nahvitch sympathies,' Joan went on. 'Smanderish ships frequently put in at Pevarile and their sailors roam the town on shore leave. There's talk and gossip between Smanderer crews and Wartsbaye people. Since Smander is heavily tied to the Toosanik, as we now know, it's no wonder that Giles leans towards their side.'

'Wartsbaye is in Mallrovia.'

'But Giles himself isn't from Mallrovia at all,' she pointed out.

I had forgotten that. 'You're right. Giles was born in Westador, wasn't he? He came here when his wife's father died. I don't really remember how it happened.'

'No, you were just a child. Giles married the daughter of Baron Simon of Wartsbaye. She was his only child. When the baron died, she inherited the estate, which is most of

His name is Quinn

Wartsbaye itself. She and Giles moved to Mallrovia then. Their two boys were both born in Wartsbaye, and Davy has grown up knowing his father is close to the Nahvitch.'

Joan is my father's generation. She always knows more than I do. 'Does he know about the flood and the treaty?' I asked her.

'I have no idea, Rory. Do you mean the ancient Hurogol Treaty?'

'Yes, of course. I believe you helped Merry write his *People's Puzzle.*'

'Do you? What makes you think that?'

'Joan, we don't have time for riddles. We have a crisis here. Did you help him write it or didn't you?'

'I didn't help him. You've met Anthony, he needs no help. He wanted to see if anyone had the determination to work it out. You see, there was once a much older manuscript. It was called *The Meridian*. It was a kind of chronicle of the Nahvitch tribe and their relationship with Hambrig and those who lived here. There was no treaty then, none was needed. The Nahvitch – I mean the Toosanik – were peaceable, and Hambrig was an open, welcoming shire. We don't know who wrote *The Meridian*, and it might well have been several people. It listed how much land belonged to each vassal, who had a fief from whom, how many cows your neighbour had and where he was allowed to graze them, that sort of thing. A Domesday Book of Hambrig.'

Kit had said much the same thing. His words were beginning to make sense now. There are two manuscripts: the original one, *The Meridian,* written long ago, and now *The People's Puzzle,* written about the fate of the Toosanik since the time of the Great Flood. Kit tricked me by joining the two together.

It was written more than a hundred years ago, and not twenty miles from here! A man in the town of Hambrig wrote it. He's important to me, though I've never met him, but I am sure you know him.

I asked Joan where the original manuscript was.

She raised her shoulders. 'Nobody knows, unfortunately. It is a very precious thing to the Nahvitch, though. It was written before the treaty was drawn up, of course, but *The Meridian* and the treaty together give them a powerful case to reclaim their land, their rights and their livelihoods on this side of the Hurogol.'

'Do you think the Toosanik have the treaty?'

'If they had it they would have waved it in our faces long ago. No, the treaty has not been seen for many years. That's why Anthony wrote his *Puzzle*. The treaty needs to be found. It was for Diane, you see.'

I was confused. 'I thought I understood the meaning of the word "meridian". Peter said it was a word-play on Diane Merry, Anthony's late wife. But the original chronicle was also called *The Meridian*. Why was that?'

'We're not sure, but Anthony has a theory about it. Diane was an educated woman and an avid reader. Her father was the Kyown-Kinnie of the time, and he was a wise and responsible chieftain. Not only did he allow his daughter to marry outside the tribe, but he made sure that before she left she knew the history of her people. Diane told Anthony that in ancient times the Toosanik people were great healers. They believe there are pathways inside the body along which life-giving fluids flow. If a pathway is damaged or interrupted, disease and illness occur. By moving their hands along the pathways, the Nahvitch can cure diseases. The pathways are known as meridians. The

His name is Quinn

chronicle they wrote is the ultimate pathway – the pathway of the people. But the tribe's meridian was damaged when the floods came, and it has never been repaired. That's why the tribe has sickened.

'Diane wanted Anthony to rediscover the treaty, and he tried to find out more about it through her. But she became ill, Rory, and she knew she was dying. She was convinced it was because her people were suffering so much. She said that if only the treaty could be found, if only the King of Mallrovia could see that the Nahvitch were entitled to resume their lives here, then all would be well, and the suffering would end.

'And after Diane died, Anthony was even more determined to find the treaty. He wrote his pamphlet in code, in the hope it would be intriguing, not just another history book. He said the code needed to be easy, so people wouldn't give up too quickly, but would want to sit down and solve the puzzle. Then, when they had read it properly, they would be inspired to hunt for the treaty. Anthony even offered a reward. Did you read that bit?'

I did read it. Anthony Merry, towards the end of his *Puzzle*, tells his readers that whoever finds the treaty must bring it to him. He gives his actual address in Hambrig Town, and promises a startlingly large sum of money. Had anyone actually known about it, I would not have been surprised to have found Anthony Merry murdered in his bed and all his money stolen. It is insanely stupid to declare in a public document that there are untold riches hidden in your house.

'But,' Joan said sadly, 'nobody read the manuscript. No one bought the pamphlet or bothered to decipher the code. Even *you* weren't going to do so, Rory. Anthony gave you a copy himself.'

True enough. I do feel sorry for the man, though. He lost his wife and was just trying to help her people, her family. And nobody cared.

'If we don't find this treaty,' I told Joan brusquely, 'the Toosanik are going to attack us and kill us. They wouldn't be able to do it on their own, but they have whole battalions of Smanderish warriors with them now. Crack troops. Your son, William, told you this himself.'

'Sammy and I have long wanted peace between the Nahvitch and Hambrig.' Joan spoke as if she hadn't heard me. 'Sammy is of age now, and has ideas of his own. By going to his own people and assuming the mantle of kingship, Sammy can work for peace between us all.'

I snorted. 'I don't think that plan is having much effect, Joan. Captain Kerry intercepted an enemy force on its way to Baron Giles in Wartsbaye. Giles is to lead an attack on the castle, and he promises to kill us all. Not only that, but Davy, my own squire, is to give the attackers entry!'

Joan looked up, shocked. 'I don't believe it. Sammy would not have allowed that.'

'Aren't you making the assumption that Sammy has been accepted as the Nahvitch's leader? What about the Kyown-Kinnie? What about the history of violence between us, the years of hatred and aggression? That's not all going to be washed away by the appearance of some fourteen-year-old boy!'

'Sammy is not "some fourteen-year-old boy"! He is their rightful king! Why do you think they wanted him back all those years ago? Why did they kill James?'

'But why did they wait so long? Why didn't they come and get Sammy long before that? In fact, why didn't they go and get their chief's wife back before Sammy was even born?'

'Well, firstly, they didn't know where she was. Then, when they found out what had happened to her, they tried to get her to return to them, but she wouldn't go, she wouldn't leave James. I don't know why they didn't just take her, but they didn't. Oh, I've already *told* you all this.' She sounded exasperated, and I think she knew then that her mission had failed.

What a tragedy. Joan sent Sammy to the Nahvitch to make peace, and the Smanderers have arrived to help them make war.

'How have you and Sammy been communicating?' I asked.

'A Spiderboatman takes messages between us. The same Spiderboatman who took the boys over to the Nahvitch, and brought back Barney and the Box of Death. He's James's brother, Rory, so he'll do anything to help Sammy. His name is Quinn.'

17

HOW COULD YOU EVER KNOW THE MAN?

Quinn. Murdered in Blurland, his throat slit, dumped in the channel. Joan didn't know. The other Spiderboatmen had been suspicious of him; they'd thought he wasn't one of them – and I'd thought he'd gone over to the enemy. But he hadn't. He'd wanted to help because he was James's brother, and James had loved a Nahvitch woman, and, like everyone else, Quinn would have thought Sammy was James's son. Joan hadn't trusted me enough to tell me about it; instead, she'd meddled again, high-handedly using one of the King's own Spiderboats, and very likely getting Quinn killed.

'I didn't know about Davy,' Joan was saying, shaking her head. 'Nor about the letter to his father. It is the Smanderers who've done this, not the Toosanik.'

'No, Joan. The Toosanik have always been hostile. They used their word "Nahvitch", calling themselves the enemy. Sammy has no influence on them. They mean us great harm, now they have the Smanderers with them. Joan, you need to understand. *We will not survive this.* They are the

How could you ever know the man?

best fighters, the most highly trained in Europe. Why do you think Smander is the only Iberian country to have resisted the Crown of Castile? The Smanderers are regular soldiers, skilled in hand-to-hand combat, proficient in every aspect of modern warfare. We have regulars too, but not enough of them. Other than that – a handful of the fyrd. Ordinary peasants, with no experience and very little training.'

'I've seen Jonny drilling them. He's very thorough—'

'He doesn't have enough *time!*' I broke in angrily, jumping up, my fists clenched, my insides churning. 'This is going to be a bloody disaster for all of us, Joan, you said so yourself in my library. And at the end of it, when the enemy takes the castle and Hambrig too, followed by all of Mallrovia, it won't be Sammy on the throne. He's being used. The Smanderers will raise up one of their own.' I realised I was shouting and stormed out.

How could Joan think an inexperienced youth could change the mind of the Kyown-Kinnie, and reverse everything the Nahvitch have stood for my entire life? They have *always* been our enemy. It won't be Sammy who can change that; it'll be finding this damned treaty. All the skirmishes, raids and petty stand-offs of the last forty years have now come to this. Little sorties of Nahvitch warriors we can deal with, but an entire force of highly trained Smanderish knights, lancers and dragoons?

My stomach and bowels griped, almost overwhelming me at the thought of my household doing its best to defend itself, my people fighting for their land, their lives and their children. And it will all be in vain. I have seen the Smanderish warriors, and now I know they will be strengthened, not only by a pack of screaming Nahvitch barbarians, but also by Baron Giles's well-armed garrison. We don't stand a chance.

I had the minstrel brought before me again. Rachel told me Kit is earning his keep in the kitchens now, since he's shown he can bake bread and roast meats with some skill. Sourly, I wondered what skills this man does not possess. He is a thorn in my side, but he has information and I need that. This time there was no friendly chat on the grassy slopes of Baudry under a setting sun. This time I made sure Kit stood in his bare feet in my library, while I sat comfortably in my carved oak chair. I have noted Kit can be insolent; I would have none of that today.

'Have you served in the military?'

'No.'

'No, *lord*,' the guard corrected him. Kit shot him a look of pure hatred.

'Why is the Smanderish army with the Nahvitch?'

'Well, *lord*, to frighten the pants off you.'

'Why would you want to do that?'

'Wait and see.' He ducked, but not in time to avoid the brutal swipe round the head he was given by the guard. He staggered, his hands to his face, a nasty gash opening in his temple.

I dismissed the guard, and then I ground out the questions. Why had Kit said there would be an invasion? What had he meant when he told me we had three days before the attack? Who was attacking and from where? How did he get his information? Where was he from? What were his parents' names? Did he have brothers or sisters? What languages did he speak? Had he ever met Anthony Merry? And on and on and on. He stayed silent throughout, though he had to keep wiping the blood from his face, and he had some trouble keeping his balance. Two or three times he nearly fell, but managed to save himself with a hand against the wall. He looked less and less able to cope as the

How could you ever know the man?

questions went on, but his grim and glowering expression showed his determination to stay upright throughout. When I judged I'd made my point, I called an end to it. It was a most uncomfortable interview for Master Kit, but an equally unproductive one for me.

As for Arkyn, he *seemed* to have given everything he had, but my officers thought otherwise. He said he knew nothing of the big picture, only his part in it. Under duress, he revealed that his group of riders had been heading for Wartsbaye to deliver their dispatch to a certain Sir Roger in the garrison. They were to provide an escort for him and two other high-ranking officers, bringing them to Hambrig Town. Once in the town, they were to liaise with two people, whose names Arkyn said he didn't know, but who were to rendezvous at the courthouse. What would happen then was in the hands of those two people, and Arkyn was adamant he had not been briefed on that. Sergeants Bess and Alex were equally convinced he was withholding the information. They were certain Arkyn had told us just enough to save himself from the torture, but had kept a great deal back.

I decided I would visit Arkyn after dinner. After the milk pudding fiasco, Rachel went to some trouble to serve a dinner fit for the King and his daughter. I sat at the high table with them, but I made it as quick a meal as I could, and I said as little as I could get away with.

I released Arkyn's shackles and helped him walk out of the cell and down to the gatehouse archway. He blinked in the light, and I let him sit on the bench there. And then I produced the sack containing the Box of Death. Slowly, I withdrew the Box from the sack, watching Arkyn intently as I did so. He made no sign of recognition. I told him that this was the famed Box of Death. The Box of Death contained a lethal weapon, an animal whose gaze would kill you. This time, Arkyn's eyes flickered, and he swallowed hard. I was banking on his having heard of Fiorello and his legendary powers. Just to make sure though, I referred to them frequently.

Fiorello wasn't in the Box. But a mouse was. The mouse scratched at the inside, and it slithered when I tilted the Box.

'Fiorello's in here,' I said. 'He's the Sacred Gecko of the Nahvitch. They don't normally let him out of their sight, but he was given to Prince Barney to bring here, so we would all die. D'you know how that works, Arkyn? The gecko is a powerful talisman. If it looks at you, you are a dead man. Only the Nahvitch are safe from its gaze. Just one look, and you're dead. It's not a pretty death, I'm told. They say you shrivel from the inside out. Your vital organs shrink and bleed inside you, and terrible pains convulse you. Your cock falls off, and your eyes sink inside your head. Your limbs wither and then you are paralysed. Eventually you are unidentifiable, a blob of skin and bone on the ground, no longer a man, but – *you are still alive!* Slowly, very slowly, the poison worms its way through your entire body, consuming and devouring it, until there is nothing left at all. You cannot even be buried. No consecrated ground for you. You are just – gone.

'The Nahvitch played a trick on us, Arkyn. They gave Fiorello to Prince Barney, but they told him the legend was untrue. Fiorello is harmless, they said. He won't kill you. Barney believed them, but I didn't, Arkyn. I knew it was a trick! What would you have done? Would you have opened the Box and let the lizard out? *Will you do it now?*'

I watched Arkyn shrink back from me and from the Box. Oh yes, he'd heard of the Sacred Gecko, but never such a

How could you ever know the man?

detailed description of what it could do to him. Well, of course not, I'd just made it up!

'What did you do?' he gasped. 'Did you open the Box?'

'We opened the Box!' My eyes bored into Arkyn's, my hands caressing the Box of Death. 'But we did it in the *dark*, you see. I felt the animal all over. I felt its reptilian skin, its sticky, splayed feet and its sinewy tail. I squeezed its pulpy body, and ran my hands along its disgusting underside, where it crawls on the ground. And then! I rubbed my fingers over its *eyes*! Arkyn, I am about to release the bolts on the Box of Death once again. While I hold the Box like this, I am safely behind the gecko. It cannot harm me. But it will look directly on you.'

'No! No, lord, please no! I will tell you more, more than I told you before, only do not open the Box!'

And he did. He told me the names of those who were to meet at the courthouse in Hambrig Town, and he told me the plan behind it. Lancer Arkyn was not the brain behind the plan, but he was considered a brave man, and therefore he had been his commanding officer's first choice to carry it out. Perhaps he had proved himself in battle, or maybe he had a good line in talking big about himself. But they were wrong about him: he was not brave at all.

I sent a fast rider to Wartsbaye with a dispatch for Baron Giles. Sir Roger will not be keeping his rendezvous, for he will never know of it, but *we* will keep it on his behalf. Up in my library, and in total secrecy, I informed the King that, thanks to Captain Kerry, we have a Smanderish knight here, and we've extracted vital information from him. If we don't act on that information, the consequences could be dire.

THE BOX OF DEATH

In interrogating Arkyn, I was only just in time. The courthouse rendezvous is scheduled for midnight tonight, and General Sir Jonny, Archer Sybil and Master Kit will ride with me into the town. King Philip is apprehensive, not so much about the expedition itself, but that both Jonny and I are putting ourselves in danger when the invasion is imminent. I admit it is extremely risky. Jonny, superb general and commander, will be desperately needed when the castle is attacked, and I am shortly to convene a War Cabinet to discuss strategy. If we are both cut down tonight, our defence, such as it is, will be weakened to the point of collapse. The King paced around my library, his face full of foreboding and doubt, but in the end he knew we had no choice. There is no one else to send, and the thing has to be done.

As I've noted before, Eliza has organised a group of tailors and seamstresses, all of whom have been busy making tents, shelters, blankets and clothing in readiness for the invasion. Now I needed something else from them. Just before supper, I called them to the great hall and briefed them. I told them they had just under four hours to come back to me with the finished garments. And this they did.

Later, much later, when Arkyn was back in his stinking cell with his shame and his cowardice, and the castle and its

How could you ever know the man?

many occupants were sleeping, Jonny, Sybil, Kit and I quietly left the castle, our horses' hooves and harnesses muffled. We opened the postern ourselves and closed it silently behind us. Apart from King Philip, the only other person who knew of our venture was Sir Patrick. I always let him know where I am.

Hambrig Town is about fifteen miles from Baudry, so it can take a couple of hours to get there. I calculated we'd arrive at midnight. Thanks to our sewing crew, Jonny, Sybil and I wore roughly fashioned tunics in gold and azure, the Wartsbaye colours. Kit wore his normal clothes, and his hands were bound. He jolted along next to me on a docile palfrey, and I held the leading rein. To the courthouse we went, for I wanted to talk to the spy and the traitor together. There was a moon, a bright semicircle, casting light down onto the path. In front of me, secured to the pommel of my saddle, was the Box of Death.

Even though I myself had tied Kit's hands and secured him to his horse's saddle, I'd be glad when we arrived, for I suspected Kit of having supernatural abilities. I half expected him to release himself magically from his bonds and knife me in the back.

To take my mind off that thought, as we rode along the moonlit track I pieced the various events together and tried to make sense of them. I could see now how the thing had been set up. The horse stealing must have been Kit's idea. He needed to do 'something important', though I still didn't know what. Branca didn't know about it either, but Patrick's hue and cry prevented whatever it was from happening anyway. *Music, Magic and Mayhem,* I once dubbed Master Kit, and so it is proving. I realised now that Christopher and Annis didn't go with Kit, and the other horses were near the stables all along, probably down by the *Egg,* where my own horse sensed them on our return. Only Guinevere was taken, only Kit was hunted. Once Branca knew Kit was in the town gaol, she returned to the castle, stopping along the way to talk to Gael outside Anthony Merry's house, spreading more rumours and lies.

Kit and the sheriff of Hambrig were to meet Giles's officers at midnight. *Tonight*, according to Arkyn, and according to the message he'd been carrying. Well, there would be no officers from Wartsbaye, but Kit would keep his rendezvous. After all, I did promise to return him to Master John by today, and now I knew why he had insisted on that.

And at last here we were, trotting softly through Baudry Gate into the town itself. The main road took us past dark and abandoned houses, past the church and along to the courthouse. Candles glowed dimly in the sheriff's windows. John, like Anthony Merry, was one of the few people who had not come to the castle for protection. He had no need of it, of course. I knew that the purpose of this meeting was to let the Wartsbaye men know the layout of my castle. They would enter by stealth, murder us all in our beds, and, once that was done, Davy would lower the bridge for the Smanderish cavalry. Arkyn had been clear about his own role; his men were to provide an escort for Sir Roger's party. He didn't know what part the sheriff was to play. I hoped to find out. Masquerading as the three Wartsbaye men, Jonny, Sybil and I accompanied Kit, the spy, to rendezvous with John, the traitor.

I released Kit from his ropes and we all dismounted. I pushed Kit towards the door, my dagger pressed into the small of his back. We all walked forward, the silvery moon picking out the path for us, and showing our fake uniforms off nicely. In the daylight they wouldn't have fooled anyone, but by moonlight they were as convincing as they needed to

How could you ever know the man?

be. And there was the sheriff, waiting by the door. He was fully dressed, expecting visitors. We walked confidently up to Master John, who saw, of course, what he expected to see: three Wartsbaye officers and Master Kit, the Smanderish troubadour.

'Greetings,' John said softly, as we approached. I pushed slightly harder with my dagger.

'Greetings, Master John,' Kit said, and though he appeared to be following my orders, I'd no doubt he had a plan of his own.

'You're from the Wartsbaye garrison?' queried Master John nervously, and we three imposters nodded, our faces in shadow.

'There will be a detachment of Smanderish horse here shortly,' Master John said, licking his lips. 'They will escort you to the castle. And this uncouth minstrel will show you where to go from there.'

At that, the uncouth minstrel made a strange noise. The point of my dagger pushed a little more firmly into his ribs, and the sheriff stepped backwards in alarm. Kit mouthed something to him, I couldn't tell what, but in that moment Master John realised something was wrong. He flung himself round, seeking safety inside his house but Jonny floored him easily. The others slipped inside to reconnoitre the house. Of course, I was right about Master Kit; he did have a plan up his sleeve. The moment Jonny and Sybil had gone inside, Kit whipped round to face me. He was very quick, but I was quicker. I had my dagger point to his neck in a heartbeat, and the man's head had to tip back uncomfortably to avoid being stabbed in the throat.

Before he could speak, I said, 'What is this rendezvous for? Why were you meeting the sheriff here tonight? Why bring men from Wartsbaye?'

'Why should I tell you anything?' Kit croaked, my dagger still tickling his throat. 'I only sell information at a price. Or you can kill me, and you won't be any the wiser.'

Briefly, I thought of using the Fiorello trick again, but I knew instinctively that Kit would see through it. 'I don't need your information,' I growled at him. 'I already know enough. If you don't answer my questions, it won't make any difference.'

Kit's eyes were rolling in his head, which had tilted back even more as I applied a little more pressure to the dagger. He wetted his lips with his tongue, and then his croak came again: 'I thought you wanted to know where the treaty is.'

The treaty! The one thing I wanted more than anything. It was at this moment that Jonny and Sybil returned. They'd found nothing; the house was clean.

I gave my orders. 'Take that disgusting traitor and lock him up in his own dungeon. The other prisoners will eat him alive.'

It was Sybil who was given the highly unpleasant job of fishing the key out of John's underwear, after which she hurried off to wash her hands in the horse trough. My soldiers have to do some grim things in their time, but clearly *that* was one of the most disgusting. Then Jonny and Sybil carried the sheriff's inert body down the winding stairs. They locked him away, and the filthy key was thrown into the courthouse. I turned again to Kit. Jonny knew about the treaty, but Sybil didn't. The garrison had been told very little.

Kit had gone purple in the face; I was in danger of strangling him to death. I loosened my grip and demanded to know what he meant.

'Read the message,' he said with a sneer, massaging his

How could you ever know the man?

throat. 'And if you've damaged my singing voice I won't tell you anything.'

'You haven't told me anything anyway. Do you know where the treaty is or not?'

He turned away, still furious at my treatment of him. Grimly, I tied Kit's hands again and the four of us mounted our horses and set off for Castle Rory once more.

I didn't know whether or not to believe Kit; I never know if he is telling the truth. The mockery behind his eyes, the insolent looks – how could you ever know the man?

18

THEY WANTED THEIR REVENGE

From the top of Baudry Hill, you can see a great distance – in good weather, right across the river to Blurland. But if you climb up to the battlements, your view extends into the murky swamps and reedbeds, and sometimes you can even make out the smoke from the Nahvitch cooking fires.

As Sir Jonny, Archer Sybil, Master Kit, the Box of Death and I returned to the castle, the dawn pinkening the sky in the east, and the sun starting to show promise of a fair day to come, we heard the alarm raised on the ramparts, and we knew it had started.

Everyone had a job, and all had practised ready for this day: Jonny immediately mustered his troops, issuing weapons and equipment, briefing his officers; the kitchen swung into action, preparing a mountain of easy-to-carry, easy-to-eat food; the stables were secured, the palfreys blinkered and shut away so the noise and commotion would trouble them less; the number of lookouts and snipers on the battlements had been doubled, and everywhere – absolutely everywhere – was the King.

They wanted their revenge

Philip strode around the bailey, organising and giving orders. His experience on the battlefield surpassed everyone else's, even mine and Jonny's. Today he came into his own as a warrior-king. Between us, we had a wealth of experience, and we had organised our workforce to the last detail. So we had water on hand to put out fires. We had slings, which even the children had been taught to use, and piles of ammunition strategically placed. We had duty rosters for lookouts, for mealtimes, for sleeping and waking, for fetching and carrying and for taking messages. Everyone knew what to do and when to do it. We would be a highly efficient machine today.

My squire thinks he is going to let the enemy in. As yet, he's not aware we know that. He is not in disgrace; he hasn't even been questioned, far less punished. I've taken care to tell as few people as possible of his treachery. He's been going about his business as usual, except I no longer take him with me when I leave the castle. Does he wonder why? I don't know.

When the shout came, I was ready. I took the stairs at the double. The watchman was pointing towards the River Hurogol. Far away, gliding towards us on the shimmering water, were three flat-bottomed landing craft, and they were packed with warriors, high-ranking ones by their dress. But the leading craft, the one spearheading the delegation, contained only a few people, and the person we all saw, the person the watchman was pointing at, while shouting incredulously, 'Look! Look, everybody, look!' was our boy Sammy, mounted on a tall grey stallion, regal and motionless, looking every inch a king. Above his head flew two flags – a blue flag emblazoned with seven silver crosses, and a white flag of truce. As the flotilla drew nearer to our side of the river, we on the wall-walk saw that there were three Nahvitch and three Smanderish warriors with Sammy, who was resplendent in a cloak of vivid pavonalilis blue – yes, I even remembered the name – turned back at the throat to reveal a silver-white fur lining. And on his left collar bone was a beautiful, shining brooch. Someone beside me began to clap, applauding the spectacle. I turned, and found it was the Lady Joan.

'You made the cloak for him?' But I was making a statement really.

She smiled broadly. 'I *knew* he would be king. I knew his parentage, Rory. It was just a matter of waiting for the right moment.' Her proud, happy voice was telling me I'd been wrong to question her and stupid to doubt Sammy could pull it off.

'And the attack? The invasion?'

'Does this look like an attack to you?' She laughed gaily. 'No, of course it doesn't! This is what we wanted, Rory, it's what Sammy and I wanted all along. Peace between our two peoples. See the flag of truce? I *knew* he could do it!'

'And the Smanderers? The message to Wartsbaye? How do you account for those?'

'That may have been the plan once, and yes, we were convinced there would be war, but Sammy has turned it round. Look at him! He is so splendid, up there on that great stallion. The King of the Nahvitch!' And she was pointing and waving to her protégé the whole time.

'I shall go down. King Philip and I will receive his Majesty,' I said, with a heavy heart. I believed not one word of Joan's effusive speech. Sammy, however splendid he looked, could never have changed the Kyown-Kinnie's mind. And this little deputation could only be a formal declaration of war, or why would the Smanderers be here at all?

King Philip was waiting for me in the great hall and, to my disapproval, Lady Lillian was with him. She saw my expression.

'Lord Rory, I *know* Sammy. We played together as children. I may be able to talk some sense into him.'

'Probably not necessary,' I told her dourly. 'He's here under a flag of truce.'

Lillian flushed. 'Well, I might be of some help.'

I suggested to the King that we meet the delegation formally outside the castle walls. Jonny was in the gatehouse with three or four of our crack shots. Should any of the enemy breach the truce, they wouldn't live long to enjoy it. Our soldiers were all leaning over the parapet, not just to keep an eye on things, but to make sure the visitors knew they were there. The three of us went out through the gatehouse and crossed the drawbridge. It felt very strange to be thinking of parleying with Sammy, so-called King of the Nahvitch, who only a month ago had been just one of my household, and an insignificant one at that.

Sammy dismounted, which may have been a mistake for him, for up on his charger he had the advantage of height and power. Once standing on the ground, and being only fourteen years old, he was considerably shorter than either Philip or myself, and as for kingly bearing – well, none of us actually laughed, but all the authority lay with that mighty warrior, King Philip.

'We have come under a flag of truce,' Sammy began in a haughty voice, 'to ask you and all Hambrig to invoke and recognise the ancient Hurogol Treaty that was drawn up and signed by ancestors from both our kingdoms, and which recognises the right of my people to live on this side of the river.'

It sounded like a well-rehearsed speech. But the boy's voice hasn't even broken yet, and King Philip was unimpressed. I had never heard Sammy speak in that high-and-mighty way before, and it didn't suit him at all.

'Show me the treaty,' Philip said.

'We do not have it,' Sammy admitted. 'Nevertheless, we ask you to recognise it and uphold it.'

'How can we do that when it doesn't exist?' scoffed Philip. 'This is a ridiculous claim, Sammy, and you know it. Stop playing at soldiers and come home like a good boy.'

The Smanderers stepped forward. Clearly, they did not like Philip's tone.

Sammy was undeterred. 'Your Majesty, unless you agree to uphold the ancient Hurogol Treaty we will declare war on you. We have been joined by the Smanderish army, and they are ready and willing to fight with us for our rights.'

It was a bold and brave speech, and you had to admit the lad was giving this his best shot. Sammy, who'd been nothing but an orphaned fisherman's boy from the age of seven, really believed he was King of the Nahvitch – or rather the Toosanik. In years to come, he might play the part well, I thought, always assuming he lives long enough.

'There is no Hurogol Treaty,' Philip declared flatly. 'I do not believe this treaty exists. The Nahvitch are settled in the

They wanted their revenge

swamplands, and we are settled here. Let us each keep to our own territory.'

Sammy's eyes flashed with anger, and then, for some reason, I looked more closely at the huge clasp holding his cloak together. It was iridescent in gold, blue and green, and very beautiful. But what caught my eye and made my heart lurch was its shape. With a gasp, I pointed to the brooch. 'My God! It's the gecko!'

'Yes, it is.' Sammy's mouth twisted unpleasantly. 'This, my lords, is *Fiorello,* the Sacred Gecko of the Nahvitch. Fiorello only has to look at you, and you are a dead man. You will have heard the rumours. Well, they're true! Behind Fiorello's jewelled eyes are capsules of poison, and in front of his eyes there are golden spikes. Touch the spikes and the capsules will spring open and cover your hands with a lethal fluid. You will never, ever recover, but will die an agonising death. How can I wear this poisoned clasp? It is because I know the secret way to hold it, the way to prevent the capsules from opening. Don't come too close, or the gecko will get you!'

The large golden lizard appeared to be climbing up Sammy's shoulder. The eyes were the brightest part of it, and seemed to shine out of its head. There was a ring of gold spikes around each eye, and I assumed that touching or pressing on these would trigger the opening of the poison-filled capsules. The rest of the gecko's body was amazing. Panels of blue, green and gold decorated it, and its striped tail curled to the left, while its splayed feet appeared to be hauling it bodily up towards Sammy's neck. The enormous brooch pinned the two sides of the splendid pavonalilis cloak together.

'The gecko clasp is always worn by the king,' Sammy

announced proudly. 'Fiorello crowned me King of the Nahvitch. Oh, and just so you know – there's no antidote.'

'What about the Box,' the King asked suddenly, looking from Sammy to me and back again. 'The Box you gave to my son. And the message too. What did they mean?'

'It was a trick. We never said Fiorello was in the Box. We put a rabbit in the Box to make you all think it was Fiorello. We found the Box somewhere.' He pouted childishly, trying to remember. '*Someone* found it, anyway. It seemed the right size box for a lizard to live in, and the rabbit just fitted, so we used it. It was funny about the message 'cos it was already in the Box when we found it.' He shrugged.

King Philip spoke again. 'Sammy, you are an ungrateful upstart, but we are willing to forgive and forget if you will give up this folly. Come home, and we will not hold it against you, on account of your youth. But if you leave this place, you will have the might and fighting force of all Mallrovia to contend with.'

All Mallrovia? Up until now, King Philip has made it clear to me that the skirmishes and raids carried out by the Nahvitch on this small part of his kingdom are unimportant to him. He usually refers to them as *little local difficulties*. Now he is contemplating the superbly trained Smanderish warriors descending on the whole country, wiping him out. Not so little. Not so local.

But instead of answering the King, Sammy turned to me. 'Lord Rory, I will always be grateful you accepted me into your household. And I thank the Lady Joan for the kindness she showed to my mother and then to me, and for teaching me nearly everything I know. I will love her forever. But I am Nahvitch! My father is the chief and my mother was a princess. I must be with my people, and I must lead them, for I am a descendant of the ancient kings and queens.'

They wanted their revenge

I watched as the descendant of the ancient kings and queens mounted his horse and wheeled round, signalling to his escort. They began the long walk back down Baudry Hill. My heart was full of dread and sorrow. Sorrow that Sammy has turned on us, that the Smanderers are about to launch all-out war on us, and that we are all, therefore, doomed. Treaty or no treaty, the Nahvitch will get their lands back, and the hill and the castle to boot.

But they had only gone a couple of hundred yards when one of the Smanderers turned suddenly and loosed an arrow. I heard it scream past my face, and then a cry of terrible pain split the air.

Treachery! The flag of truce meant they should all have been unarmed! I turned and stared up at the gatehouse parapet. The guards and Jonny himself had all disappeared. I raced to the stone steps, and there, at the bottom, was one of my garrison, an arrow between his eyes. Jonny and the others looked at me, their faces full of horrified questions.

'It's war,' I told them grimly. 'Get to your posts.'

Of course, nothing more will happen today. It will take time for Sammy to return and make his report to the Kyown-Kinnie and for them to put their battle plan into action.

I called everyone to the great hall and told them the bad news. King Philip sent a fast rider to the palace, summoning his household troops, the King's Squad. They'll be good soldiers, but there won't be enough of them to turn the tide in our favour. Philip made it clear he was angry I hadn't told him Sammy's father was the Kyown-Kinnie. I retorted that there hadn't been much time for history lessons. As a precaution, I had Davy locked in the dungeon. I couldn't risk him being free to let the drawbridge down and open the main gate to an invasion force.

'We have a massive advantage, being high on the hill,' Jonny pointed out at our first War Cabinet meeting, held just before dinner. King Philip was there, and so was Sir Patrick. I had half a mind to co-opt the Lady Joan, as she knows Sammy better than any of us, but I am still not altogether sure of Joan's loyalty, and anyway we all know the enemy battle plan will not be drawn up by Sammy. The Smanderish commander will take charge as soon as the deputation returns. All that blue and silver, all the banners and the fancy horse, the beautiful cloak, even the death-dealing gecko brooch, they were all just for show. The real business lies with the professionals, the hardened veterans of many campaigns, the only army to resist the combined all-conquering forces of Castile and León under the indomitable Alfonso X. *The Smanderers.*

'Why are they even *here*?' Patrick asked. 'Why are they *involved*? It's not their fight.'

'They've made it their fight,' I said tersely. 'Remember, the king and queen of the Toosanik fled this land, pursued by a massive tidal wave. Where did they go? Smander. And that's where they stayed for generations. Each new prince or princess married a Smanderino. Their children are mixed race. The Smanderers and the Toosanik are joined now.'

'The Toosanik should all just go and live in Smander then,' Jonny said sourly.

'Maybe they haven't thought of doing that, Jonny,' I said with a laugh. But I knew that wasn't the reason. The Toosanik were still aggrieved at what happened to them. They wanted their revenge.

19

AND THEN SUPPER WAS SERVED

A shout from the ramparts and a commotion outside the great hall. My pulse racing, I ran to find out what was happening. Were they here already? Had the lookouts sighted the massed ranks of Smanderers marching towards us? But it was a different army that approached. Golden banners with bright blue waves flew above dozens of horsemen, while a hundred or so foot soldiers and spearmen tramped behind. Behind *them* came a fyrd similar to ours, men and women from the countryside and the coast, pitchforks, fishing spears and fence posts in their hands. Word flew around the castle, the lookouts and watchmen passing it onwards and downwards, until all had been made aware, and a mighty barrage of cheering went up. My entire company flocked to the gatehouse and lined the way into the courtyard, much as they'd done for the King himself. For this was Baron Giles of Wartsbaye, whom I had thought a traitor, come to join us.

It had been some time since I'd seen Giles, and I thought he looked tired, pale and considerably older. He told me of his distress and rage when he discovered how he'd been betrayed. Three of his most trusted knights had turned their coats. When he got to the bottom of it, he found they'd been dealing privately with the Nahvitch.

Giles told me that his knights, two of them brothers and the third a harum-scarum friend, found it would take exactly one duty and two off-watches for them to paddle a coracle up the River Ruthen as far as Weyburn, a village about ten miles north of the Great Plain, and be back again by roll-call next morning. Two would take the coracle, while the third covered their duty, and by taking turns in this way, they went undiscovered for months. So, what was the attraction of a night trip by boat to Weyburn? The answer is *sex*. Weyburn has an unfortunate reputation, and these young men tested it to the full. Of course, there are whores in Wartsbaye too, but apparently they're tame by comparison, and Giles's men were in search of wicked adventure and fun.

On one such trip to Weyburn they encountered a Nahvitch tribesman. He had crept up the River Hurogol by boat, then trekked across to Weyburn in the secret dead of night. The Wartsbaye knights and the Celt, all four in Weyburn without permission from their respective commanders, fell to talking, and, somehow finding a way through the language barrier, they discovered they had much in common. After a while, and with careful negotiating, they found they could trade with each other. Trinkets, sweets and liquor exchanged hands at first. But it wasn't long before their Nahvitch friend offered the Wartsbaye men a strange plant in the form of dried flowers, which he pushed into a clay bowl, finally lighting the flakes so they burned, and then inhaling the smoke. The Wartsbaye officers were intrigued by this, and paid money to be able to try it for themselves. Soon, they had a habit

And then supper was served

they could not break, and acquiring this herb became all they could think of. In the end of course, the Celtic dealer had them over a barrel, and could ask anything he wanted of them. It wasn't long before he knew every detail of the Wartsbaye garrison, its armaments, fire power and state of readiness. It seems he put that knowledge to good use, and by the time Branca had chased the hue and cry all over Hambrig, the Smanderish army had arrived, and a Smander-Nahvitch plan was in place to gut Mallrovia from the inside out.

Master John, sheriff of Hambrig, was recruited in a similar way, although there was no need for the flowery flakes this time. John is a sexual deviant, with needs few of us would understand or want to have anything to do with. Predictably, it seems that John would also make his way to Weyburn from time to time, and eventually he found the Nahvitch gentleman himself. Or the Nahvitch found him, which is more likely. Copious amounts of money and information were extracted, in exchange for which John was allowed to release his sexual tension in various disgusting ways with the Nahvitch. My stomach turned as I listened to Giles's low voice describing this supreme humiliation; a respected member of my town, in my demesne, selling our secrets and laying himself open to blackmail, in return for debauchery and sex with the enemy.

And of course, blackmail ensued, as anyone with a grain of sense would have predicted. The three hot-heads from Wartsbaye and the middle-aged pervert from Hambrig were all given their orders. Unless they obeyed every word, their wrong-doing would be exposed for all to know, and one of these days, though they'd never know which, they wouldn't make it back from Weyburn. So the plan was devised and – *almost* – carried out. Sheriff John, the three Wartsbaye men and Master Kit were to meet at the courthouse in Hambrig Town. There, the plan would be put into action. Keys and access to my home would be handed over, together with many details of strategic points of attack and defence, not only in relation to Castle Rory, but Wartsbaye and Nightmolben Castles, and the palace in Hicrown as well. This information would be relayed to the Smanderish commander by means of dispatches carried by a certain cavalry officer named Arkyn.

As Giles told of his discoveries, it became clear this was to be an invasion on a grand scale; nothing less, in fact, than the conquest of Mallrovia. Once the information had been received, the massive invasion force would be mobilised. The attack would begin with Davy letting the enemy over the drawbridge, through the gates and into my home. We'd not have known what was happening, for it would all have been over so quickly. The Smanderers would have met no resistance, and most of us would have been murdered in our beds, or perhaps the castle would have been fired. They would then ride the length and breadth of the country, rampaging as they went, occupying or destroying manors, demesnes, estates and even farms, for they would have known every weak point, every hastily gathered defence. Within a week, the country would have been theirs.

It was a long story, and told with many pauses and great heartache, for Giles had been betrayed by men he had himself commissioned.

———◆———

I've never really hit it off with Baron Giles. We meet twice a year at the King's court, a fancy affair in itself, which I

And then supper was served

endure rather than enjoy. Oh, the feasting and the drinking, the jousting and the tournaments, and all that fuss and ceremony, none of it to my taste, which is much more austere. Much as I dislike it all though, I've been looking forward to presenting Davy at a royal occasion in a few years' time, and to dubbing him knight there.

———◆———

Davy! I'd grown very fond of the boy over the years. And now his father was sitting opposite me, miserable as hell. A good ten years older than I, Baron Giles is portly and rather going to seed. But I felt for the man. Bad enough his knights had betrayed him, but his own son too? No wonder he looked so harrowed.

And it was clear now that 'Honoured friend' was not Baron Giles after all. The dispatches were for Sir Roger, the leader of the trio of traitors. Thanks to Captain Kerry, those dispatches never reached Wartsbaye, while thanks to the legend of the Sacred Gecko, Lancer Arkyn caved in completely and gave me his part of the story. From Giles I've now heard the other part, and the sorry tale is complete.

'So what has happened to Roger and his friends?' I asked.

'Hanged.'

After a few moments' silence, Giles heaved himself up from his chair. 'I'm going down to your dungeon.'

An hour later, he was back.

'I would like to bring my son before you. I will understand if you do not want to see him. However, he has things to say to you, and I would be indebted to you if you'll consent to hear him.'

A guard brought the boy in. His hands were still tied and his face and clothes were filthy. There are rats in the dungeon, after all.

We all waited in silence. 'Go on, Davy,' Giles urged. 'Tell Lord Rory what you told me.'

'Lord,' began Davy, in a desperate, broken voice, 'I wish to be your man again. I wish to fight for you, for the castle and for Hambrig. I am abject with misery at what I have done. I crave your forgiveness, but even if you cannot forgive me, I ask of you the opportunity to redeem myself by fighting the enemy alongside you, and if necessary dying to defend you.'

'You wish to be my man?' I asked incredulously, because that is a powerful and binding phrase.

'Yes, lord. I humbly and heartily wish it.'

'Why did you agree to let the enemy in?'

'I – I didn't know they were the enemy, lord. Roger is a friend of mine, and he told me he was coming to join us, to help us defend ourselves. He said he'd bring reinforcements, so I thought he was on our side.'

'Why didn't you tell me about this?'

'He didn't tell you,' – Giles was unable to keep quiet any longer – 'because Roger said it was by no means certain they could come, and it would be best not to mention it until it was definite. Davy did not intend any treachery, Lord Rory. The boy thought he was being helpful. But he has been a gullible fool, and he knows it. He knows that his stupid and thoughtless actions could have cost everyone here their lives and might have lost us the kingdom itself, had it not been for your quick thinking.'

Gullible. I sighed. Davy had been taken in before, hadn't he. Of course, he would know Sir Roger of Wartsbaye, the two other knights as well. They were all

And then supper was served

probably good friends. When Sir Roger said they were coming here to help, Davy simply believed him. I could imagine Giles explaining the real facts, in words of one syllable.

Davy dropped to his knees, his head bowed, while Giles stood very upright to the side. He did not look at his son. I saw that he took a great deal of Davy's shame on himself, and for that I respected him.

'Look up at me,' I commanded Davy.

The boy looked up, and I saw what I'd hoped to see. No tears and no self-pity – instead, I saw humility.

We were on the eve of a great battle. The enemy would attack tomorrow. We were as ready as we could be, but perhaps there was one more thing we could do this evening.

I called the guard. 'Take my squire away and get him cleaned up. Dress him in my heraldic colours, and bring him to the great hall. Assemble the company there too. We're going to have a great Commendation Ceremony before supper!'

And so it was. I stood on the dais at the high end of the great hall, in my finest regalia. Davy was brought in, his father on one side of him and Sir Jonny on the other, both in ceremonial dress. Davy, bare-headed and weaponless, knelt before me, his hands clasped. I took his hands between my own, claiming superiority over him.

'Who are you?' I asked him, using the time-honoured words and ensuring my voice thundered into the far corners of the great hall.

'Lord, I would be your man,' answered Davy, equally strong and clear.

'I accept your homage, and now you must swear the oath of fealty.'

Baron Giles stepped forward with the Bible and placed it

in my hands. I held it towards Davy and he also put his hands on it.

'Repeat these words after me,' Jonny said. And, phrase by phrase, Davy swore the ancient oath of fealty: *I swear before God that I will be faithful to Lord Rory and never cause him harm, and that I will observe my homage to him completely against all persons in good faith and without deceit.*

There were cheers from the company, and Davy rose to his feet, flushed and breathless, but a freeman and my confirmed vassal.

And then supper was served.

20

WE COMMAND THE HILL FOR NOW

It was an uneasy night. King Philip retired very late to bed, after talking more tactics with me and Sir Jonny, though the War Cabinet had thrashed most of it out already. The Watch was doubled, and I slept fitfully in my clothes in the great hall, with Gael curled up on a rug nearby. His face was tear-streaked in his sleep, and I wondered what would become of him. He's in love with Amie, that's clear enough.

That girl. She used to be our bard, and now we have none. If ever we needed a bard to give us a song of heroism, a reminder of our greatness and our ability to win the fight, it was now. So, in the middle of the night, I rose from my bench, checked with the Watch that all was well, woke Rachel and asked her to fetch Amie. The girl came to me in the great hall, wearing just her shift, full of trepidation and shivering in the cold. I threw a rug around her shoulders and she huddled into it.

'I want a song.'

'Now, lord?'

'Not now. At breakfast. I want a song that will rouse our people to fight for their lives. A song everyone will remember, that'll be chanted around campfires by our children and our grandchildren when they remember the fierce warriors who fought and died at the Battle of Baudry Hill. *That* is what I want. You have less than four hours.'

Amie, pale, thin and freezing, did not look at all like she could deliver, but she nodded vigorously. 'I am grateful you're giving me another chance, lord. I won't fail you.'

Amie padded away, and I looked out at the dark, deserted courtyard. It would be light in two hours. Rachel and Eliza would be urging their team to get breakfast out quickly. Everyone would need a hot meal, for who knew when it would be safe to light the fires again?

And then a very strange idea came into my head, and I could not get rid of it. After a brief moment of indecision, I reached out with my foot and poked Gael awake. He jumped up instantly.

'Gael, go to Amie. She needs you, and she needs your help.'

He stared at me in astonishment. I nearly laughed aloud, for the boy clearly thought I'd gone mad. But I was completely sane. I remembered myself at Gael's age. I would not have known what to do with a girl. I was probably incapable of doing anything at all, and I certainly never had the opportunity. But Gael isn't me, and there is something between him and Amie that's hard to pin down. Patrick knows it, and he tried to warn me. Gael scampered off.

I've done all I can, and soon will come the day, the battle, and the reckoning. Having updated my journal, I stretched out on my bench, and pulled a couple of rugs over me.

We command the hill for now

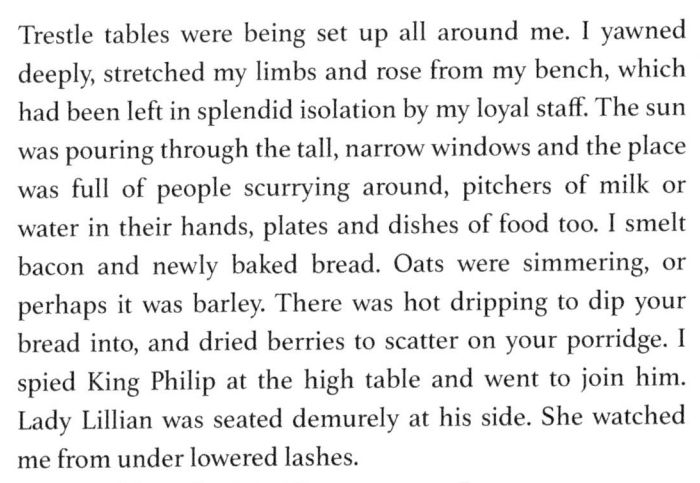

Trestle tables were being set up all around me. I yawned deeply, stretched my limbs and rose from my bench, which had been left in splendid isolation by my loyal staff. The sun was pouring through the tall, narrow windows and the place was full of people scurrying around, pitchers of milk or water in their hands, plates and dishes of food too. I smelt bacon and newly baked bread. Oats were simmering, or perhaps it was barley. There was hot dripping to dip your bread into, and dried berries to scatter on your porridge. I spied King Philip at the high table and went to join him. Lady Lillian was seated demurely at his side. She watched me from under lowered lashes.

'It will be today,' the King announced.

'Yes, your Majesty, it will be today.'

'Well, I won't tell you your business or get in your way. My horsemen and foot soldiers will be arriving, and we must pray they get here in time.'

I didn't think his household forces would make a lot of difference, in all honesty, and without some sort of miracle we were all doomed to die today. Even with Baron Giles and King Philip lending their support, we were simply outnumbered. We had two strengths – the hill and the castle. Jonny's garrison is well trained, but they are just a small troop, much like the King's Squad. As for the rest – oh aye, I know Jonny has been training them as best he can, and they've drilled their little socks off, but they've never fought before. Jonny knows well enough the line won't hold, not once the enemy attacks. We have a plan, discussed and honed by my War Cabinet. It won't give us victory, but it will give us honourable deaths.

As the great hall filled up with Hambriggers from all walks of life, and as I looked round at them with enormous affection, and with sorrow for the end of it all, I saw Amie out of the corner of my eye. She came in with her harp and made her way purposefully to her stool by the hearth. There was no fire burning this morning, for the sun shone and the day was fair. She tuned the harp quickly and deftly. Then I saw Gael. He walked up to Amie, stood to the side of her, and held his hands in the air. Of course, everyone was watching, for Amie hadn't been seen in her place by the hearth since the infamous *Ballad of Fiorello,* ten days ago. When Gael raised his arms, there was a howl of derisive laughter, for Gael is only my page, and therefore not to be heeded. He had no right whatsoever to call people to order, or try to get anyone's attention. The eyes of the entire hall flickered between me and my page. Why was I not calling him to order and smacking his brazen little bottom? And what about Amie? How come she was back as the bard?

Suddenly Gael snapped his fingers down onto his palms, and an extraordinary noise was heard, something like a clap and a high-pitched click in one sound. *Clacketty-clacketty-clack. Clacketty-clacketty-clack.* Dead silence fell instantly upon the hall. Gael slowly turned himself round in a circle, his knees slightly bent, his arms still held high, clacking his hands in this preposterous way all the time. I have since learnt that he was holding a small pair of wooden discs in each hand, and clapping them together very cleverly. I'm told these discs are very popular in Smander. I didn't know that at the time though, and could only marvel with everyone else at the extraordinary sounds Gael was making, seemingly just with his fingers.

Then Amie started to attack her harp, harshly and with aggression. Gael danced around her, his feet tapping a rhythm on the flagstones, his fingers clacking. He reminded me of Master Kit. And where the blazes *was* Master Kit? I found him at a table in the corner, a table also occupied by Captain Kerry and Sergeants Bess and Alex. I relaxed; he couldn't do much harm with them at his elbow. But it was uncanny how like him Gael was, with his dancer's moves and his rhythmic tapping and clicking. Then suddenly, it stopped dead. Gael had frozen in a strangely war-like position, arms raised to shoulder height as if shooting an arrow, legs bent, crouching forward. A single detuned harp string twanged raucously, and was left jangling.

The song started in a whisper. Gael's untuned, almost-breaking voice hissed around the hall, but the song grew and grew. Louder. Faster. It became aggressive. The harping had started up again without any of us noticing. As the song moved on, the strings twanged and thrummed, and Gael's voice became strident, while – from God knows where – he produced a drum. I recognised it: Kit's drum, decorated with all manner of beasts around the side. The drum was banged hard twice at the end of each verse, and after the first verse the audience got the message and joined in. The rhythm of the strange clacking discs was echoed and copied with knife handles thumped down hard on every table in the hall, and the insistent double-tap of the drum thundered from every stamp, clap and shouted 'Boom!' until the great hall in Castle Rory echoed to the rafters, and Amie's *Battle Morning Song* careered into history.

Breath is bated,
Soldiers waited,
Castle gated,

THE BOX OF DEATH

Orders stated.
Men from Smander
Understand a
Goose and gander
Propaganda
Better than they ever did before!
Boom! Boom!

Are we ready?
Bold and steady?
Weapons deadly?
What a medley!
Marshal daily
In the bailey,
There's a shady
Little lady!
Runs away and makes us go to war!
Boom! Boom!

Here come Nahvitch
Bringing carnage,
Rome and Carthage,
Load of garbage!
When we sight them,
Fuck and flght them,
Bugger-bite them,
Expedite them,
Blame it on the laddie from Wartsbaye!
Boom! Boom!

Send the bastard
Home, unmastered,

Buttocks plastered
Balls disastered!
Not impartial,
Squire and marshal,
Controversial
Bitch and rascal,
Off they ran to fight another day!
Boom! Boom!

We are Hambrig!
Hearts are damn big!
Leave them stranded,
Where they landed,
Go and screw them,
And subdue them,
Stick it to them,
Then pursue them!
Every Hambrigger will do his best!
Boom! Boom!

I listened in a kind of fascinated horror as Gael shopped his older brother, and Branca's treachery was laid bare before the entire company. We'd been trying to keep these things under wraps, but it was all out in the open now. There'd be no hiding place for Davy, freeman and oath of fealty notwithstanding. Hambrig loved it, so much so that an encore was demanded, and the entire vulgar song was run again. And then again, and *again,* the BOOM BOOMs louder and more strident every time.

The King leant over and spoke to me. 'I thought you'd have got rid of that girl by now, Rory. After her last effort.' He looked as shocked as I was.

'She has not been allowed to entertain us since then, sire,' I answered truthfully. 'But today – *today* we need all the help we can get.'

'And you seriously think that will do it?'

'Actually, yes. I do.'

For it was true. The chant, the rhythms, the drum beat and the castanets, the language of fucking and fighting, buggery and biting, were pitched exactly right. These people weren't soldiers. They were ordinary men and women, and today they were going to be expected to be extraordinary. This piece of flagrant propaganda was just about bloody perfect, in my opinion.

Davy sat next to his father, his head in his hands. Cheering and applause at his ceremony last night, and now this. The entire castle knew of his treachery and stupidity. Baron Giles stared furiously straight ahead, but what could he do? His younger boy had spoken the truth. All the same – castrating his brother in public? No wonder Giles's fists were clenched, his knuckles white, his eyes full of despair.

I looked across the hall at Kit, managed to catch his eye and beckoned him to me.

'Did you teach Gael to play and sing?'

'He didn't need much teaching. He's a natural.'

'But you started him off? Why?'

'I like him. And he's got a gift.'

'Tell me about Smander. Is it true you have flying horses there?'

'Flying—? Oh! Flying horses. Sure, it's true.'

But I could tell it wasn't. Not because of Joan's Idiot's-Guide-To-Liars, but because it was Kit, and he was always trying to deceive me.

'But what is Smander really like, Kit?' And it was as I asked the question, observing him standing insolently before me, slouching a little, his thumbs through his girdle, that I realised what I had to do. I indicated the seat beside mine, and Kit sat down. King Philip eyed me with distaste. What was this hostile and dangerous enemy spy doing, seated at the high table? But Kit, who never calls me 'lord' except in sarcasm, would not talk otherwise.

'Why do you want to know?' Kit asked.

I've always disliked prevaricators. Either answer the question, or say you won't. Don't ask another bloody question. I took a long drink of ale, throwing my head back, letting the liquid slide down my throat. I'd had nothing to eat, though I'd made sure everyone else was well fed. The kitchen team were on the go the whole time, but they also ate their fill. I wanted no hungry bellies at the Battle of Baudry Hill.

'It's exciting,' Kit said suddenly. 'There are red, craggy mountains to the north, but lush plains in the south. It's medium sized – small compared with Castile, but three times the size of Mallrovia. The climate's warm and sunny all year round, and wonderful fruits grow there. You can pick oranges straight off the bushes! Also, there are animals you don't find here.'

'The ones decorating your drum!'

'And others besides. As for your flying horses, I don't know who started that idea. They're bloody fast, but they don't actually fly!'

I grinned. It was good to know Smander wasn't some place of mythical beasts. A real country, with real people – that I could deal with. 'I should lock you up during the battle,' I said.

'Are you going to?'

The truth was, I didn't want to. I instinctively felt he would be good in battle, good to have by my side, in the same way that Jonny was. On Crusade, Jonny and I were the perfect team. In a fight, we got through because we had each other.

'Are you in the Smanderish army?' I asked Kit.

'I have never been in anyone's army.'

'But you were sent here to spy on us? Who sent you?'

'If that were true, I would hardly tell you the answer. If it is not true, then there's no answer anyway.'

'Just give me the damned answer. Are you a spy?'

'I didn't come here to spy, Rory. And neither did Christopher and Annis. We are genuine troubadours, we travel around with our music, our plays, our acts of entertainment. You want to know why I came to Hambrig? My mother sent me. When I turned twenty-one, my mother said I must come here. It was Branca who set up the meeting between me and Master John at the courthouse, using Arkyn to deliver the message so we had armed backup from Wartsbaye. But I wouldn't have helped them. I was going to help – I have my own reasons, though you won't know anything about that – but as it turned out I wouldn't have lifted a finger. Not after being called an "uncouth minstrel". Those men, they've all been such fools. Davy trusted Roger, just as he trusted Barney. Some people never learn. Amie and Gael were spot on, you know. This entire campaign was masterminded by Branca, and Davy stupidly bought into it.'

'Aren't you forgetting Sammy's part in it?'

'Sammy's a pawn, a figurehead. They don't need him, except to look like a king and be a rallying point.'

This was so clearly true I was inclined to believe everything else Kit had said.

'Where are Christopher and Annis?'

'I don't know. I don't think they went with Branca. And if

We command the hill for now

you're wondering how *she* managed, a boatman called Quinn rowed her across the Hurogol.'

But I'd already worked that out.

In the end, I did lock Kit up. There was too much at stake to have such an unpredictable force in the castle. He submitted with good grace and one of his enigmatic smiles. I did not bind him or shackle him, but simply ushered him in with Arkyn and turned the dungeon key on them.

———◆———

We heard the enemy before ever we saw them. The ground seemed to shake, and a massive rumbling filled the air. Everyone tumbled up onto the ramparts, and Jonny, Patrick and I had to work hard to restore order. By then, the enemy horde had been sighted.

I gazed at it, transfixed. I could not think how they had done it. Carts and wagons, cavalry and infantry, all under the blazing blue flag with its seven silver crosses; rumbling, prancing and marching in tight formation, advancing towards Baudry Hill, with battle-axes, spears, halberds, lances, longswords and broadswords, daggers and knives glinting in the sun, while bows and crossbows lay piled in the carts which travelled slowly but inexorably; bowmen, spearmen and horsed men-at-arms tramping in steady time, all so well disciplined and trained to kill.

Soon after breakfast, the King's Squad arrived, having beaten their way along the wild and untended track that is a back way here from Hambrig Town. They're a well-trained and highly disciplined troop under the command of Sir Allan of Hicrown. King Philip moved quickly, forming his men up in the courtyard, then moving on to Baron Giles's company of soldiers.

We have horse, but not enough. We have soldiers, but they are ill-assorted. We have weapons and we have ammunition, but we do not have the fighting power of this army on the move. We do have the castle, and we command the hill. For now.

21

AND NOW HE'S DEAD

It took two hours from first sighting the enemy to engaging them. We watched them tramp down the road, then wheel to the left and begin climbing the hill. During that time, kitchen and campfires were doused and more buckets of water made ready. I held one last War Cabinet meeting, and we went over our plan for the final time. Jonny, Patrick and I reported to King Philip.

'All is well. Everything has been done that can be done,' Patrick said calmly, in that way he has of reducing each sentence to a pithy saying.

'Who will carry the day?' asked the King. A stupid question.

'We will!' shouted Jonny, suddenly leaping about like one of his recruits. 'We will carry the day! *We are Hambrig! Boom! Boom!*' And Jonny threw his head back and yelled the line again and again, until the entire castle had taken it up and was shouting and chanting and stamping and circling in a communal war-dance, the like of which I had never seen before. Even King Philip joined in. The *boom-booms* were deafening, spears crashing as one on shield bosses. And as the war-chant swelled to a mighty crescendo, the final *Boom! Boom!* making a great wall of sound, I saw the enemy horde falter in its tracks. Not for long, mind you. But they had heard us.

We had the huge boulders ready and waiting. As the enemy slogged up the hill, we shoved the boulders hard down it, and, gathering speed as they rolled, they clove through the Nahvitch ranks and sent their men sprawling. It was an intense onslaught, part of the War Plan, and something I'd learned in Egypt: *When you're defending your position, attack first.*

Some of the boulders broke up as they rolled, hurling rocky shrapnel into the Nahvitch lines. The Nahvitch made up the front line. Perhaps the Smanderish commander decided to use them as battle fodder, saving his own troops for the real fight. Or maybe the Kyown- Kinnie had insisted on being first through the gatehouse. After all, it was supposed to be so easy for them: Davy would let down the drawbridge and open the gates, and the blue-and-silver conquerors would enter the courtyard in dazzling array. King Philip would kneel before them and proffer his sword; then it would be my turn, and the castle would be theirs.

The Nahvitch front line was smashed to pieces, but there were row upon row of warriors, who merely stepped over the writhing or inert bodies of their fellows, and came on, even through the hail of arrows from the parapet. As yet, the enemy could not use their weapons. But in their great numbers they came towards us, and we had nowhere to go. The Nahvitch were brave fighters. So many dead and wounded, so many lying in the coarse grass and meadow flowers that carpeted the hill. And yet they did not stop.

And behind them, the Smanderers.

And now he's dead

The Smanderers were clever. Not for them the vivid blues, reds and golds most warriors wear. Their garb was drab and dull. They wore brown and olive green in swirly patterns of dirty, muddy hues. They smeared their faces with earth. *You could not see them coming.*

It was uncanny. The Nahvitch were everywhere, jostling for position, nearer and nearer, and we were shooting and killing them, our boulders crashing through their lines, our arrows bringing them to their knees. But did we kill any Smanderers? We couldn't tell. With twigs and briars in their hair and their dark, mud-brown clothes, they looked like parts of the hill itself. We looked for them; we tried to get them in our sights, but it was impossible.

King Philip was beside himself. 'Why can't they show themselves like warriors do?' he fumed. 'The arrant cowards! Hiding behind masks, looking like trees and bushes! How are we meant to *see* the bastards?'

'I think that's the point, your Majesty,' Jonny said. 'They don't want us to see them. Then they have the advantage.'

'Bloody cowardly advantage,' growled the King, who was dressed in his full war regalia, banners flying overhead. And I realised the folly of that. Once he was in range of their sharp shooters...

'Sire, please stay out of sight,' I said suddenly. 'You are too visible. Your flags, your banners, your surcoat – they all reveal who you are. You will be picked off!'

'They're *supposed* to reveal who I am, damn you,' snapped the King, but he moved away from the parapet all the same.

Jonny looked at me. We were also in heraldic colours. 'Before they get here?' he asked.

I nodded, and we ran full tilt for our chambers. Changing at top speed into my hunting gear, I thought how arrogant and self-obsessed we all are, calling attention to ourselves with our bright colours and our lofty banners flying. On a hunt we don't bother, knowing that no stag or boar will be impressed with our finery. Out hunting, we try to merge into the forest, to see without being seen. And what is the difference between a hunt and a battle? Very little, I thought with sudden fierce clarity, tugging my belt round so my scabbard slid into place. Jonny and I arrived back on the parapet at the same time. His claret-coloured hose and dark brown tunic merged with the castle's stonework behind him. We grinned at each other. It was a token gesture, a nothing, and yet it was everything. Victory could not be ours today, no matter how many nobles donned peasant dress. But so far, the plan had succeeded: the attack had been delayed and the enemy forces dented.

'On to Phase Two,' I said in Jonny's ear.

Phase Two was to be a charge, a bold and futile attack on the enemy, outside the castle walls, the drawbridge up, our people still protected inside. Jonny's corps of veterans had been briefed, their pay doubled, and they were ready. The plan was for Davy to lower the bridge (ah, sweet irony!) and we brave few, the Forlorn Hope as they will call us one day, would charge across and into the fray. Davy would raise the bridge at once, cutting off any possibility of retreat. We had, each of us, marked targets. We knew who we were taking out; it had been planned to the last detail.

My target was the Smanderish commander. I even knew his name, for Arkyn had told me. With Arkyn's unwilling co-operation, 'Fiorello' scratching helpfully inside his box, we had names and descriptions of all the top Smanderish and Nahvitch captains and commanders. Jonny and I had pinpointed one man for each member of our small force, and the Kyown-Kinnie had also been marked for the kill.

And now he's dead

We mustered in the courtyard. Davy had wanted to be part of the raid, but his duties were inside the castle.

'You *have* to raise the bridge after we've crossed the moat, Davy. *You have to do it!*'

My hand was on his shoulder, and I looked steadily into his grey, troubled eyes. When Davy is a knight... But I will never see that day. It is hard to imagine things going on – days dawning, nights falling, people cooking, eating, travelling, singing – when you know that today will be your last on this earth. So, I didn't linger. Davy knew his duty, and his oath of fealty to me, taken so poignantly last night, would see him through. I sprang into my saddle, waved the others to me, and the enormous bridge began to move. We galloped towards it, and I, thankfully, judged it exactly right. As the huge platform fell into place, the twelve of us charged furiously across it, and I could hear Jonny yelling out his new battle cry, '*We are Hambrig, Boom! Boom!*' Once again, the others took it up, and there we were, standing in our stirrups, spurring our horses to gallop as never before, shields held to our chests, lances at the ready.

It was Captain Kerry who engaged first, her Smanderish captain being the nearest, and thank God Kerry's leg had healed well. I saw only the first part of their hand-to-hand combat, for I was soon in the thick of it myself. I had my sights set on the enemy commander, but that didn't stop other warriors hurling spears and axes at me, trying to pull me down, shooting their arrows. We'd succeeded in drawing their fire, so that was something. I saw Sergeant Alex find his man, and plunge a dagger into him, then pull out the reddened blade and stab again and again. And there was my target, sitting on his horse, proud as a peacock. I hurled a spear, then charged, lance thrusting forward, my eyes fixed on the man who had already taken my spear in his stomach. Guinevere galloped forward; battle-hardened as she was, nothing scared her. I swear she had also picked out our target and was thundering down onto him. Was I riding her? Or was she in charge, bearing me along in her own fearless, glorious onslaught? I do not know the answer, just that we were one, and we were warriors.

My lance knocked the commander off his horse, and I jumped down and finished him with my dagger in his heart. I looked round, tried to see what was happening. In the thick of a battle, with so much hand-to-hand fighting, you have no idea what's going on. You are so far from seeing the bigger picture, you don't even know there is one. All you see is what is directly in front of you; all you can focus on is staying alive, and trying to kill the enemy in your way. My hope was that, without their commanding officer, the Smanderish army would crumble. But all around me were shouts and yells and the clash of weapons, and there were the Smanderish forces, still pushing upwards towards my castle, unaware their general was dead. I mounted Guinevere, wheeled her round, and tried to spot Jonny somewhere in the mêlée. I couldn't see him.

I glanced back, and my heart nearly stopped in shock. For the drawbridge was stuck, half up, half down. I spurred Guinevere back up the hill towards the moat, and as I got closer I saw Smanderish and Nahvitch soldiers swinging themselves up and over the broad planks of the bridge, gaining entry to my home. With a roar of fury, I charged towards them. And then, with a thunderous crash, the bridge dropped down onto the bank, the impact making its timbers crack and fly through the air, the enemy soldiers who'd been clinging to it hurled far and wide, or smashed to pulp underneath. Someone must have chopped through the chains holding the bridge, and now it was a free-for-all.

And now he's dead

There was a yell in my ear, and I turned and gasped, for there, on his splendid grey stallion, was Sammy, King of the Nahvitch, still wearing his blue-and-silver cloak, clasped at the throat with the huge golden lizard.

'I don't want to kill you, Lord Rory,' he shouted to me, trying to control his horse, which was threatening to dump him in the moat. 'Don't make me kill you! Get out of my way and let me cross the bridge.'

It was only then I realised I had stationed Guinevere across the entrance. My warhorse was pacing from side to side, threatening to kick any enemy to the death, her nostrils flaring in aggression. Sammy stared haughtily at me, and then, unbelievably, he drew his sword. I had no chance of defending myself; I was at entirely the wrong angle to use a weapon against him. Sammy twisted in the saddle, and he swung his blade.

He's going to take my head off.

But at that very moment a red-and-gold caparisoned horse came thundering over the wrecked drawbridge, knocking me flying. The rider was Davy.

'Davy, no!' I yelled, but he never heard me. In horror, I saw my squire launch himself directly at Sammy, and the two of them crashed to the ground together. Davy, the bigger boy, was on top of Sammy, the beautiful blue cloak catching between his legs, his hands around Sammy's neck, throttling the young king. Everyone fell back to give the combatants space, and, slowly, an eerie silence veiled the battle ground. But before he could finish the job, Davy's hands suddenly flew away from Sammy and clutched at his own throat. He rolled in agony on the ground, his body in convulsions, head lolling, tongue protruding. His screams filled the air. Everyone watched as the writhing went on and the screams increased. And then, after far too long, the eerie stillness of death.

Sammy jumped to his feet. 'He pulled the gecko off me!' he shouted in triumph, whirling round on the spot, his arms spread wide. 'He touched Fiorello, the Sacred Gecko! *And now he's dead!*'

22

AFTER THE BATTLE

The silence didn't last long. From somewhere in the distance came a swelling, skirling sound, like nothing I'd heard before in my life. And round the shoulder of the hill came a new battalion of Smanderers, led by a female warrior. Some were playing strange instruments, while others had drums, thundering out an insistent rolling tattoo. They made the whole hill shake, and the enormous, raucous sound got right inside your head, so you couldn't think, you could only tremble in fear and trepidation. These warriors had bags under their left arms, with a pipe protruding from the bags and sloping over their left shoulders, another pointing downwards. And from the pipes came that strange, strident sound, loud as thunder, with a beat you could not ignore.

The battalion's leader was Branca, who had been *our* marshal, and they marched and marched to the beat of the drum and their skirling, shrieking war cries. I bellowed for whoever was left of our small raiding force to come to me, and together we ran like the blazes, over the ruined bridge and into the bailey. The scattered remnants of the enemy's original attacking force gathered themselves together and fell in alongside Branca's terrifying reinforcements, until the whole mass of them stood, a sea of military might, pipes and drums, ranged before the drawbridge, which should have been closed to them but was not.

Many of the enemy were in the bailey already, and our people had engaged them in hand-to-hand fighting, while our snipers on the ramparts tried to pick them off. Swords clashed, shields thudded and banged, spears and daggers flashed their blades, and the courtyard flagstones ran with blood. The King was fighting two Nahvitch at once, beating them to a pulp with his massive war hammer. Philip is a man of great height and strength. Taking out the enemy one by one was only part of the contribution he made that day; far more telling, he gave our people *heart*. They saw their King standing tall, felling the Nahvitch with blow after blow, swinging the mighty hammer with his great muscled arms, and roaring out his own war cry, '*Deus Vult! Deus Vult!*'

I sprang into the fray, placing myself at the King's back. Adopting my combat stance, my fighting sword in one hand, buckler in the other, I hacked into the enemy, knowing the King had my back, as I had his. Jonny and Kerry were doing the same, circling back to back, taking on all comers, and the rest of our core troops were operating well under attack. There were scores of casualties, though. Far too many Hambrig men and women lay dead on the grass and in the courtyard. I spotted children lying motionless on the ground, and didn't dare wonder what had become of Gael. The noise was deafening. I couldn't hear myself think. In a battle you don't know what is happening until it stops. You are acting purely on instinct, an instinct born of a cross between disciplined training and a response to the needs of the moment.

After the battle

Ducking under the flashing blade of a Smanderish warrior is part of that instinct. Leaping to plunge my dagger into the side of an enemy sharpshooter, who I see aiming at Sir Jonny, is another. So is throwing my short sword to Alex, who's lost his, so he can defend himself against a baying mob of the Nahvitch fyrd. But screaming in horror when I see Guinevere cut down, her proud body on the ground, dying a brave warhorse's death? No, that was not part of my soldier's instinct. That was me, the man, crying for my friend.

And still the drawbridge remained down, the gates gaping wide, inviting the enemy to slaughter us. For Branca's forces had reached the moat, and we could not hold on any longer. Still fighting, Philip and I, back to back, somehow edged our way to the castle keep. Hurling a dagger at my nearest assailant, and having the satisfaction of seeing it pierce him between the eyes, I ran up the stairs to the ramparts, the King hot on my heels. There were no enemy invaders there, just our own marksmen, doing the best they could but rapidly running out of ammunition.

'Can we not raise the drawbridge?' Philip panted as we ducked down below the battlements for a quick breather.

'I don't think so,' I gasped. 'I'm guessing the chains were cut.'

'But why? Who would have done that?'

'Davy,' I said, my voice low. I had no wish for anyone else to hear. 'No, not because he broke his oath, but because he was bound by it. He saw what was happening. He saw Sammy was about to kill me, and he *would* have, Philip. Davy knew it would take too long to lower the drawbridge – he knew he didn't have the time. He took an axe to the chains so it would crash. And then he saved my life.'

'And endangered everyone else's,' said Philip bitterly.

'Would this carnage be happening if Davy had followed your orders? No.'

It was true. Davy had made the wrong decision. He should have let me die out there on the hill in the summer sunshine, while keeping the rest of the castle safe. Instead, he chose to save my life and let the invaders in.

The war pipes grew louder and louder, terrifying in their aggression and their assumption of total victory. It was as if the pipers were so confident they could hack us to pieces, they could afford to play music as they did so. The music itself, at once haunting and militant, was unforgettable. I had *never* heard such a thing before.

But the fearsome pipers were themselves eclipsed. Our signalman, high up on the watchtower, began to blow his horn, the highest note he could reach on his instrument, screaming it out above the battle's noise and chaos. On and on and on it went, only stopping for a tiny moment as the man drew breath and then blew again, that one single shrieking note filling the air with its insistent demand to be heeded. It was a siren, a desperate, attention-seeking howl, far above the raging battle. We raised our eyes, all of us, Nahvitch, Smanderer and Hambrigger alike. We gazed, transfixed, at the signalman, his free arm outstretched, his finger pointing to the river, while he blew his single note to infinity.

Every person turned to look: a large ship, her sails set and hardened to the wind, her spars golden, a dragon at her prow. The sun blazed low in the sky behind her, making carapaces of her sails, and majestically she came until she was level with Baudry Hill, where she hove to. A puff of smoke billowed out, and a lump of iron crashed into the hillside. I saw small figures moving on the deck. The next time, the sailors found their mark and an enormous ball

After the battle

tore through the pipers and drummers. Fire broke out on the hillside, and fragments of iron ripped through the enemy spearmen and archers and destroyed their wagons full of ammunition. The music was stilled. Where there had been military might and discipline, there was now chaos, confusion and wholesale slaughter. Suddenly the Lady Joan was among us on the ramparts, leaning far out over the parapet, cheering and waving.

'It's the *Senjo!*' she shouted wildly. 'The *Senjo!* William's ship!'

The *Senjo* continued to scatter the enemy far and wide with scything balls of flame that tore through their ranks. What deadly weapon did the ship possess that it could wipe out the entire Smanderish army in so short a time? I was awestruck at the wholesale slaughter. Within moments a white flag was raised among the surviving Smanderers, someone's ragged shirt waving desperately from the top of a bloodied battleaxe. The murderous fire ceased, and cheering broke out in the castle. It was over.

There are moments sometimes when you cannot move. You just stand and wait for the news to sink in, to accept that the impossible has just happened. The Battle of Baudry Hill was over, and we were victorious. The enemy could not fight a ship, and they had surrendered. The King, Jonny and I were still alive. Joan too, beside me, her tasselled shawl billowing in the breeze. But who else? I gazed grimly down upon the dead and dying in my own castle grounds. I'd already seen Doctor Bethan deploying her fledgling team of assistants, hurrying from one desperate case to the next, applying poultices to wounds, removing limbs with her surgeon's saw, or consigning bodies for burial. I stayed long enough on the ramparts to watch Captain William come ashore and receive the official surrender from the enemy commanders, Branca among them. So she also had survived. I had a feeling Branca was a survivor.

Down in the courtyard, Jonny and Patrick took over. Bodies lay in a mounting pile by the keep, while the great hall became the makeshift hospital Bethan had been planning for weeks. I saw young Amie helping, and I admired her courage. It was not a job for the squeamish. Gael, I hadn't seen at all.

Baron Giles had turned out to be a rock. Standing firm in the gatehouse for the duration of the battle, he had fired arrow after arrow into the oncoming horde. He must have killed dozens of the Nahvitch in the first wave of the attack. He never faltered, even when he himself took an arrow in his arm. They're barbed; you can't just pull them out, but he carried on in great pain, with the damn thing sticking out at right angles, blood pouring down his arm and pooling at his feet. I felt a rush of affection for him. He must have seen with his own eyes the rash charge of his elder son, and must have watched him die in agony. Davy's death will haunt us all.

I left Patrick and Jonny to tidy up the mess. The hillside was strangely silent, people standing by themselves or huddled in small knots as they took in what had happened. There was grief for the fallen and there were the cries of the injured. I couldn't wait to thank William from the bottom of my heart, though I didn't know what had motivated him to up anchor and sail his privateer up the Hurogol, and I could not conceive of how he had managed to get to us in time. The river bends and turns on its way to the sea, and to sail a large ship such a distance, against the current, often against a headwind, would have taken many days. And yet William had arrived. How this miracle had been achieved I had no idea. Perhaps God had heeded our prayers in the chapel this

After the battle

morning. No doubt Laurence would confirm this was so. I would praise and give thanks to God, but later.

Whether or not God had sent her, it was the *Senjo* and her crew that had won the battle. One ship, with a contraption that could propel huge ball of metal into the enemy, and with its unassailable position on the wide waters of the Hurogol, had turned everything round. Slowly, I descended to the courtyard to help clear up after the battle.

23

SAFE FOR THE NIGHT

'Has anyone seen Gael?'

After three hours of hosing down, sweeping away, bundling up and carrying in and out, I still hadn't seen my page anywhere.

Amie looked up from the patient she was tending. 'He's with Davy. He said Davy would need his help.'

Perhaps Davy had wanted Gael's help with the drawbridge. I hurried off to the gatehouse. Our dead lay strewn on the floor, but Gael was not among them. As I made to go, I heard a quiet moan. One of the fallen was alive.

Sergeant Bess lay in a corner, blood seeping from many wounds. I lifted her onto my shoulders and raced to the great hall, searching out Bethan as I entered. I laid Bess on a trestle table, and pulled at Bethan's arm, but she shook me off.

'I have an injured warrior,' I told her urgently. 'I think she's dying. She needs you now.'

Bethan did not look up. 'Lord Rory, all these men and women need me now. I'm seeing to this one, and then there is a long queue of those I must attend. Your soldier will simply have to join the queue.'

'But...'

But she was right. Long lines of trestle tables, the ones we use at mealtimes, all bore injured men and women. Some had enemy soldiers lying on them. All were wounded, all were desperate for medical attention. Up and down these lines passed people in long white robes, Bethan's team of medical assistants. I saw that their job was to assess each person's needs and bring them forward or send them back in the line. That way, Bethan would tend the most grievously injured first.

Before the battle, Bethan had spent hours training and instructing her nurses in what to do, what to look for, how to assess their patients. And it was paying off. After Bethan had patched them up or operated on them, other people in her team carried them to the dais, and there they were left, hopefully to recover, or if not, to die. Bethan would then move to the next in the line. There were even wheeled trolleys for moving the patients around. I remembered Bethan ordering these from our carpenters, with strict instructions on exactly what was required.

Bess's injuries were very serious, and I thought she would most likely die from them. I beckoned one of the white-clad nurses over, and he bent over Bess, placed two fingers at the side of her neck, then felt her limbs for injuries. He nodded to two others, and between them they moved Bess to the next table along from where Bethan was working. I sighed with relief. I watched the physician's practised hands moving expertly over her patients, untwisting their limbs, sewing up the holes in their sides, rubbing soothing ointments on their skin. And once or twice I saw her sit back, wipe her bloodied hand over her forehead and half close her eyes in a desperate fatigue. But the next moment she was hard at work again, looking for the next injury, the next person to attend to.

Amie's job seemed to be to talk to the wounded who'd been carried to the dais.

'What do you talk about?'

'I tell them about my harp, and about my music, and about me and Gael.'

'You and Gael?'

'Yes, lord. After this is all over, we want to be married.'

'Married! He's not old enough to marry you, he's just a child.'

She gave me a strange look, and then turned back to her patient. I walked away, perturbed by her words, the cries of the injured clanging in my ears.

Near the gatehouse, this clanging was amplified by the noise from the hill. There were even more injured and dying outside the castle, and their groaning and crying was pitiful. I passed by the body of my wonderful horse, Guinevere. Silently, I promised to come back for her. And now I ran out onto the hill, because I'd just figured out what Amie's words meant. *He said Davy would need his help.* It wasn't anything to do with the drawbridge. Gael had meant now; now that Davy was dead. It didn't take me long to find him. Crouched over his brother's body, Gael was engaged in doing something intricate. His movements were slow, his hands steady.

I stood a slight distance away, careful not to startle the boy. I could see what he was doing, but at first I had no idea why. Gael took off his tunic and wrapped it around Davy's right hand. I watched him drape it over his brother's clenched fist, ensuring that it was pulled down to make a scarlet and gold covering for Davy's hand. But then he

Safe for the night

inserted his own right hand into the wrapping, and with his left he grasped the edges of the tunic and pulled everything as tight as he could. As he clung on to the gathered hem with his left hand, I heard small half-sobs breaking out of him. And I saw that the hand inside the tunic was moving. Under the cloth covering, Gael was slowly prising open Davy's fingers. After what seemed a very long time, and with much sobbing and sighing, eventually all five digits were unfolded, stretching the bound cloth into a spread hand shape.

Then Gael began to wriggle slowly backwards, and, inch by painstaking inch, the cloth was withdrawn from Davy's hand. I realised I was holding my breath. At last, the boy had moved back far enough to uncover his brother's hand completely, and I saw that I'd been right. The fingers were stiffly open now. But the red and gold tunic was still wrapped around Gael's own hand. Then my page moved to the side, and I nearly gasped aloud, for underneath him was the Box of Death. With his left hand, Gael drew the bolts, and lifted the lid of the box just enough to slide his right hand inside, still covered in the cloth of his tunic. I heard a thud, as something solid fell into the Box, and then watched Gael stuff the entire tunic on top of whatever it was and finally close the lid again and bolt it securely. The boy stood up, the Box in his arms. My heart leapt to see him alive, and looking just fine, his curly hair all mussed up and his face covered in dirt and sweat from his exertions.

'L – Lord!' he stammered, shocked that I was right there in front of him.

'What's this, Gael?' I asked.

'It's the Box of Death, lord.'

'What's inside the Box of Death, Gael?'

I watched him try to decide what to tell me.

'Lord, it's Fiorello. My brother pulled Fiorello right off Sammy's cloak, and had him in his hand when he died. I have reclaimed Fiorello for Hambrig, lord, and for you!' He held out the Box and I took it.

'And you were careful not to let the gecko look at you?' I said, thinking it was a bloody miracle Gael hadn't pierced himself with the poisoned spikes.

'Oh yes, lord,' he said fervently. 'I was very, very careful about that.'

I put my hand on his shoulder and steered him away from that terrible place, now peopled only by the dead and the soon-to-be-dead. Together we walked back to the castle, the Box of Death once more in my arms.

As it turned out, we were followed by a procession: William, riding Sammy's beautiful stallion, but with all the banners struck; Sammy, head bowed, walking between two tall, muscular sailors; Branca and several other Smanderers, mostly high ranking, trudging behind, also with an armed escort. The Box of Death and I led the way, Gael trotted behind me, and the sombre procession followed him. We crossed the bailey and assembled in the courtyard. The Lady Joan was waiting. She cast an appraising eye over her son.

'Why were you so late?' she asked him.

So late?

'It wasn't anyone's fault,' William replied. 'They came as fast as they could. But we had the tide *and* the current against us, and they had to tow the *Senjo* most of the way upriver.'

'The Spiderboats!' I exclaimed. I looked in amazement at the Lady Joan. 'You sent the Spiderboats for William!'

'I did indeed,' she said, 'and a good thing too.'

Safe for the night

It was nothing short of inspired. 'Where are the Spiderboats now?'

'We've left them moored downriver,' William said. 'We had a fair wind on the last reach, and it was quicker to hoist the sails. But all the crews came aboard, so we had enough manpower to handle the ship *and* use the artillery.'

Artillery. It's a new development in naval warfare, something William discovered on a voyage to the Far East, he tells me, but it's expensive, dangerous and difficult. The decks have to be reinforced to take the weight of the cannon, and you need a trained gun crew. William has clearly invested some serious money in the *Senjo* and I am profoundly grateful for it.

I cast my eye over the vanquished. Some of the Nahvitch stood beside Sammy, their blue-and-silver surcoats torn, dirty and stained with blood. The Kyown-Kinnie was dead of course, his body trodden into the mud.

A fanfare sounded from the door to the great hall, and King Philip, clad in splendid royal vestments, made an entrance into the courtyard. Everyone bowed. A second fanfare sounded, the King's herald still standing to attention at his post by the door. Lady Lillian, in a beautiful red-and-gold velvet gown, appeared at the doorway. The colours she wore were in my honour. I went to her and kissed her hand formally. Then I walked her into the courtyard, where we joined the King.

Jonny instructed the armed sailors to march the prisoners off to the garrison, but there was a sudden commotion: young Sammy was on his knees, his hands clasped together.

'Lord Rory! Lord Rory, please listen!' he begged, even as the guards hauled him to his feet.

'I'm listening,' I said. 'What do you have to say, Sammy?'

I was conscious of Joan, just across the yard from me. This boy had been hers, but he had turned against us.

'Lord, we just want to live in the land we used to own! We want our old territory back.'

I heard the King exclaim in disgust and saw him turn away. And he was right. The Nahvitch have no claim on the 'old territory'. They left it long ago.

'Please, lord,' begged Sammy. 'There's a treaty. The Hurogol Treaty. It sets out the lands we had, the lands that Hambrig *agreed* we could have!'

King Philip wheeled round in anger. 'There is no treaty!' he thundered. 'There is *no* Hurogol Treaty! I have never seen such a document.'

But Branca stepped forward. 'I have seen the treaty.' Her voice was clear and confident. The guards were getting jittery. They had their orders from Sir Jonny, and their prisoners were trying to make trouble. They drew their daggers from their belts.

'When did you see it?' I asked.

'Princess Eefa of the Toosanik had the treaty. When she and I travelled here from Smander, she was carrying it. She kept it always on her person. Many, many years ago, after the Toosanik were forced from their homes and their lands by an enormous flood, the royal family fled to Smander, taking just a few precious things with them. The Hurogol Treaty was one of the things they saved from the flood. Generations passed, and each new king or queen must have looked after the treaty, so that if ever they returned, they would be able to claim back their rightful territory.

'But the old king died in Smander, and never returned to his people. His daughter decided the exile had lasted long enough. Together we set out to return here. Eefa showed me

Safe for the night

the Hurogol Treaty, and we read it. It was because of the treaty that we came back.'

'Why did the princess choose you as her travelling companion?' I was glad that at last I knew the princess's name.

'I am the Duchess of Santiago das Cunchas in Smander.' And despite her battle-scarred appearance, and her roped hands, Branca suddenly looked like a noblewoman. 'I was a great friend to Princess Eefa. We grew up together. We travelled together, a long and perilous journey over the Red Mountains and then through Castile and Navarre; over the Pyrenees, north through Aquitaine, Brittany and Normandy, and across the sea to England. It took us many months. Eefa was frail, but she was determined to make the journey, to find her people, and to get them to invoke the treaty here in Hambrig. It was the treaty that drove her to the limits of her endurance, to find the Toosanik and restore their country to them.'

'What happened? Did you reach the Nahvitch swamps?' King Philip was interested now.

'Eventually we did. We were welcomed as royalty, and we were honoured by the clan. We showed the Kyown-Kinnie the treaty. He wanted Eefa to marry him and bear his child before invoking it over here; that way, the royal succession would be safe. But one night, when Eefa was newly pregnant and lying in her bed, someone came and stole her away. We looked everywhere, but we could not find her. Much later we discovered she had been kidnapped by a Hambrig fisherman. But the child was not his! The child was the son of a royal princess and the clan chief, who now lies dead on the field of battle.'

The clan chief? I'd not heard that term before.

'Eefa died in childbirth,' Branca went on. 'We were

heartbroken. But there was the child, a boy. I spoke with the Kyown-Kinnie, and we decided I would come to Hambrig and find a way of returning the boy to his people. A boatman brought me here in the middle of the night, and in the morning I found myself at Castle Rory. The Lord of Hambrig saw me handling my horse, a horse I had stolen in the night. He was impressed with my skill, and he offered me employment as his marshal. This was better than I could ever have hoped! I accepted at once. It was strange to hear everybody speak of the Nahvitch – the word "Nahvitch" means "enemy" in the Toosanik tongue. It's not their clan name, though all of you thought it was, and Eefa and I decided not to say anything.'

'You found me, too, Branca,' whispered Sammy, and everyone's eyes swivelled to stare at him. He was back on his knees, holding his clasped hands towards us. The beautiful pavonalilis cloak was in tatters. 'You found me, and you told me to come here. You told me the Lady Joan would take care of me.'

'I *did* take care of you!' Joan stepped forward, her eyes blazing. 'I took you in, I taught you everything. Branca, you came to Hambrig to find Sammy and return him to his people. But you didn't do that. Why not?'

'Lady, I could not. When Eefa was abducted from her hut and from her husband, she had the treaty somewhere on her person. It was never anywhere else. If I had stolen Sammy away, perhaps the fisherman he lived with would have found the treaty and destroyed it. Only by leaving Sammy with him could we keep James's link to Eefa, and the hope that he would keep the document safe. When Sammy reached the age of seven, the age when he should start being taught his duties as a clansman, a Toosanik party raided the fisherman's cottage, hoping to bring both Sammy

Safe for the night

and the treaty back with them. They found neither. Sammy had hidden himself away very cleverly, thanks to the fisherman's instructions.

'Sammy came here after that, but he didn't know where the treaty was. I questioned him, but he was only a little boy then and he knew nothing. I searched the fisherman's cottage myself, but didn't find the treaty. I was happy for Sammy to be with the Lady Joan, since she had taken such care of Princess Eefa when she was unwell. The Lady Joan has been a true friend to the Toosanik, and even though I know you all think I was a spy and Sammy betrayed you, we would never do anything to harm the Lady Joan. And because Sammy was with the Lady Joan, and he was happy and he was learning, the Toosanik elders decided he and I should both stay here in the castle, until he reached the age of fourteen. We didn't know how we were going to get him back across the Hurogol then, but it was easy. Prince Barney wanted to go adventuring into the swamps, and so I set the whole thing up and Sammy went too.'

'But how were you and the Kyown-Kinnie able to communicate with each other?' asked the King.

'James, the fisherman who married Princess Eefa, had a brother called Quinn, one of your trusted Spiderboatmen, sire. It was Quinn who ferried messages between the Kyown-Kinnie and me. Quinn only wanted to help Sammy, whom he thought was his brother's son.'

Quinn. Of course.

But the man was dead.

I've known for a while now that Quinn wasn't the spearhead of a catastrophic defection of Spiderboatmen to the enemy. But Quinn put family loyalty before his country. Similar to Davy, who put his loyalty to me before everything else. Can you condemn them for that? Yes, for there was too much at stake. Both made bad choices, and both paid with their lives.

The cook, God bless her, served a very late supper for the weary troops, although most of us were too tired to eat. We were victorious, in spite of all the odds, but we were bone-weary, there was much to do, and we had all lost friends or family or both. Hands were shaken and shoulders wordlessly punched; comrades were embraced; tears were shed; fallen loved ones were looked for, found and grieved over.

Triumphant celebrations and feasting will have to wait. For now, the clear-up continues, food is available to any who want it, although people are mostly just dragging themselves off to bed. But Jonny and I stayed up very late, ensuring the prisoners were held securely in the bailey and the castle was safe for the night.

24

I WHISPERED MY OWN GOODBYES

It's Saturday 19th May. Around mid-morning I retrieved both Kit and Arkyn from the dungeon. Kit, so Branca told me, is actually a Smanderino duke, highly skilled in many arts. That last I'd observed for myself, but I would never have guessed at his noble birth. We have discovered the other two wretched minstrels. They were locked in one of the horse boxes. Patrick told them they were free to go if they so wished. They were strangely attached to Master Kit though, whom I must now remember to call his Grace, since he is no lowly troubadour. The Duke of Casuel is what he is! Casuel, I'm told, is a territory in the Red Mountains of Smander. We are keeping him busy. He is a strong young man, and we've lost plenty of those on Baudry Hill. There is a lot of work to do, and the Duke of Casuel is listed on pretty much every roster Patrick has posted on the door to the great hall.

As for Arkyn, in his own eyes he has shamed himself beyond redemption. He genuinely wants to die. He was denied the chance to be a warrior, and had to wait out the battle in a dungeon cell. Not only that, but someone told him he'd been tricked: there was no gecko in the Box of Death, only a harmless mouse. Arkyn has been made a fool of. In a low and earnest voice, he begged me to kill him, and to let him die with his sword in his hand. This used to be a Viking tradition; if a warrior died holding his sword, he would enter Valhalla, which was their word for heaven, and he would be with his gods forever. If not, his body would be cut into pieces and fed to vultures, or something like that. I've never properly understood it.

Many centuries ago, this country saw the light and became part of Christendom, and we no longer know the old ways. But Arkyn described it as something glorious, something worthwhile. In Valhalla, he said, you fight battles for all eternity, each one followed by a magnificent feast. He called it Ragnarök. *Ragnarök!* I can picture it: the gods, the giants and the magnificent long-dead Viking warriors, fighting and triumphing, feasting and singing, until they come to the final fight, the mother of all battles that will destroy everything. But then, Arkyn told me, the world will start all over again, fresh and new. I was enthralled, Arkyn's voice whispering in my ear, entreating me to grant him this perfect afterlife. Our saintly Laurence would have a fit if he heard Arkyn talking, but whenever I think of Laurence it makes me more sympathetic to the barbarians.

'Are you a Viking?' I asked Arkyn, curiously. He has the look of one.

'There are no more Vikings,' he replied cryptically.

But his pleadings exasperated me. I had much to do, and more important people to see, people who had distinguished themselves in battle. There was also the business of burying the dead – and burying Guinevere, who was uppermost in my mind. I dismissed Arkyn's request and returned him to his dungeon cell.

Branca had not told the whole truth. She'd described her relationship with Princess Eefa and their journey north to Blurland. She'd told us how the Toosanik lost their princess: someone abducted her in the night. Well, I thought, they must know who it was by now, but she'd said nothing of that. Nor, to my mind, had she adequately explained why the princess wasn't fetched home as soon as they found out where she was. As for the precious treaty – if Branca knew the princess had it on her person at all times, and the Kyown-Kinnie knew it too, why didn't they rescue that at least? It was the most important thing in the world to them. There were too many unanswered questions, too many loose ends.

Just before dinner, I sent for the woman, and a guard brought her to me in my library. Most of the interrogations were taking place in the great hall, but for this one I wanted privacy. I wanted Branca to tell me everything.

She'd been the marshal on my estate for fourteen years, and I have known her for ten of them. In that long time I felt I'd got to know her well. It had given me a bigger jolt than I realised to find out that every day of those fourteen years, she was deceiving first my father, and then me.

'Leave us,' I said to the armed soldiers who had brought Branca to me. And then to Branca: 'I want you to help me bury Guinevere. At sunset.'

'Guinevere? She's dead?' I saw the tears start in Branca's

eyes. This fierce Smanderina warrior would have carried the day had it not been for William and the *Senjo*. Yet she was filled with sorrow for the death of my horse.

I began my questions. 'Why didn't you fetch the princess home as soon as you knew where she was?'

'We tried to. Some of the Toosanik and I rowed across the Hurogol during the night. We stayed hidden in the reeds until the fisherman went out in his boat at dawn. Then we made our way to his cottage. Eefa was there, lying on some rugs. James had tried to make her comfortable. I told the others to wait outside, to warn me if anyone came. But really, I wanted to talk to Eefa by myself. She told me James had found her drifting in a boat. She had no idea how she'd got there, but she hadn't been hurt. James took her home and cared for her, but he didn't know she was a royal princess. She told him that later – and that she was pregnant. And do you know? He was prepared to take her back to the Toosanik. He was a good man.'

'But she didn't want to go back?'

'No. The Kyown-Kinnie only married her because she had royal blood. He pushed her around and treated her roughly. He didn't care how frail she was.'

'Had she always been frail?'

'As a child she was often ill. I became her friend because she was lonely just lying in bed by herself all the time. I used to wrap her up warmly and take her out riding with me. Or we'd sit by the fire, just us two girls, and we'd talk and make up stories together. Don't you see how brave it was for her to come all this way from Smander? She knew it would take all her strength, but she had more guts than all the kings and queens before her. *They* didn't bother to go back to their people, did they. They stayed in Santiago das Cunchas, with servants to look after them, and warm sunshine every day. No muddy swamps and drizzly rain for them!' Branca's voice rose derisively, and I could see her point. It had taken a sickly girl to do what her robust ancestors hadn't even thought of.

I liked what I was hearing. Branca had stood by her friend and had supported her. Eefa had been a courageous young woman who had tried to help her people. I told Branca to continue.

'The first Eefa knew of the treaty was just after her father died. She found it when she was going through his things. We were both shocked. To think such a treaty had existed all these years, and nobody had used it, *nobody* had returned to claim their legal rights. But it was as I said, they were far too comfortable in warm and sunny Smander. Eefa cried to think her people could have been helped years and years ago. She said no more time must be wasted, she would go to Mallrovia and invoke the treaty. So of course I had to go with her. I never had any intention of being a spy. I just looked after Eefa. That was my job.'

'But you *are* a soldier,' I said. 'I watched you. Out there in the battle. You fought well, Branca. You led your troops like a pro. And those *bloody* pipes! They turned our bowels to water!'

She grinned. 'They're meant to! It is the *Gaita Smandega*, the bagpipes of Smander. As for soldiering, that is not something the women in our country can do. But I grew up in a garrison; my father was the Duke of Santiago das Cunchas, and he was a fighting man. In our palace, there's a mighty garrison, a hundred times bigger than the one here. The soldiers are drilled and trained as professionals. My father would have no mercenaries, he didn't trust them. He wanted only professional fighting men, and he paid them double what anyone else paid. As a result, he got the best. I watched and I learned.'

'Astonishing,' I murmured, thinking of our makeshift fyrds and tiny garrisons here in Mallrovia. 'Tell me why Princess Eefa didn't invoke the treaty as soon as she got to the Toosanik.'

'We had planned to do that, but we reckoned without the Kyown-Kinnie. *He* said we must secure an heir to the throne first. He said Eefa must marry him, and there must be a son. He said, "What if the Hambriggers don't recognise the treaty? What if they put up a fight? What if I'm killed? There will be no king of the Toosanik, and we'll be pushed right back across the river again. We do not have the might, the training or the weaponry to fight Hambrig." He was right about that last bit. The Toosanik could do nothing without my troops.

'But do you know what I think? I think that when Eefa arrived, the Kyown-Kinnie was frightened. He was frightened he'd lose control, that the princess would take his power away from him. I'm not sure he wanted royalty to return, and maybe that's why he treated her so badly. He thought a princess would undermine his position as chieftain. So he married her and got her pregnant at once. I said all this to Eefa at the time, but she had to obey the Kyown-Kinnie.

'I wasn't surprised she didn't want to go back to him once James had found her. After she fell pregnant, her health starting failing again. I wanted to protect Eefa, but the Kyown-Kinnie wouldn't let me near her. He had some servant woman sleeping just outside the door of his hut. The night the princess was kidnapped, that woman was tied up and gagged, and so was the perimeter guard. Whoever took the princess knew what they were doing. They knew

I whispered my own goodbyes

how to overcome the guard and they knew how to enter and leave the camp without making a sound. It was a professional operation.'

'But you still don't know who it was?'

'There were no clues. We did eventually find a drifting punt, but it was disregarded. It was only much later that Eefa told me she had been taken out of it by James. She loved James. He was kind to her. He knew she was having another man's child, but he said he would be the father. She told him it would be a boy, though how she knew that, I do not know. The Lady Joan went to their hut every single week that year, and she kept Eefa alive all through the pregnancy, but even she couldn't save her at the end.'

'You mean when Sammy was born? Were you there?'

'No, I was with the Toosanik. When I next crossed the river, Eefa was already dead. James told me what had happened, how the Lady Joan fought hard for Eefa's life, how she at least saved Sammy, who was just a little scrap and should by rights have died as well. James was in tears telling me about it. He begged me not to take Sammy away from him. I said I wouldn't, but that when Sammy was seven, the Toosanik would come for him. They would think he was theirs then.'

'It's the same here,' I told her. 'Seven-year-old boys can become pages to a nobleman. At the age of fourteen, they can become his squire.'

'It is the same the world over.' Branca sighed sadly. 'Well, James knew what would happen. He prepared Sammy. He made him promise to hide away when the enemy came for him. He built him a special hiding place. I was over here by then; after Eefa died, I didn't want to stay with the Toosanik. I didn't like the Kyown-Kinnie, and the rest of them are just marsh-dwelling barbarians. For Eefa's sake I wanted to keep an eye on Sammy, so I looked for a way to live over here. And then I found your father.'

'Yes, indeed,' I said drily. 'But why didn't you tell my father this whole story at the time?'

'You all thought of the Toosanik as the enemy. How would your father have reacted if I'd told him? Would he have let me stay?'

'I don't know. You know what they say – better to be in the tent pissing out...'

She laughed. 'You think I'd have pissed into your tent if you'd sent me packing?'

'Of course. Unless you consider yourself a friend to Mallrovia now.'

'I consider myself neutral,' she said.

'Some would call that sitting on the fence.'

'What do you want of me, Lord Rory? Am I a prisoner? Or am I now to spy for you? Would you trust my intelligence anyway?'

'Tell me about the flying horses.'

She was only momentarily disconcerted. 'Our Smanderino horses are so fast they *appear* to fly. People who come to our country are amazed at their speed. From travellers' tales grow tall tales, and from tall tales come impossible rumours. Those rumours give substance to the myth. Nobody knows the truth, and everyone wants to believe.'

I was pleased with her answer. She'd wanted to know if I would trust her intelligence, and she had just laid some foundations for that trust. 'I want you to get me one.'

'Lord?'

'Get me a Smanderino horse to replace Guinevere. I want to ride a horse that feels as if it's flying.'

I whispered my own goodbyes

Her eyes widened. 'I didn't say you can *ride* them. They're *wild* horses.'

'Then break one in for me.' I leant forward. 'I'm serious, Branca. Can it be done?'

'I don't know,' she said slowly. 'Maybe. Would you want to come to Smander to choose the animal?'

'No, I leave that to you. You knew Guinevere for ten years. You know how I ride, what I'd be looking for.'

She nodded, her eyes fixed on mine.

I drew a deep breath. It was risky, so very risky. But I'm a risk taker and I made my decision. 'I'm sending you to Smander.' I saw the disbelief on her face. 'I'm sending you home. You will find me the horse that will replace Guinevere. You will break the horse, bring it back here and then remain here as my marshal.'

I could already see the frown of disapproval I'd get from Jonny, and I could hear the tut-tutting and fuss-fussing I'd receive from Patrick, and as for the King – he would be beside himself. But this Branca was something. She had given up her luxurious life as a duchess to look after her childhood friend. She had stayed in hostile country, working for an enemy lord and doing the job well, in order to see Sammy right. She had engineered a very clever trick to get Kit, the sheriff and Arkyn together, and finally, she'd led into battle a regiment of the most ferocious warriors I'd ever seen, playing those awesome, deafening *gaitas*. She had fought well, with bravery and skill. Why would I let this woman out of my sight?

Because I want a Smanderish horse, and *she* can bring me one. And because for some crazy reason, I trust her. Is she the *shady little lady* of Amie's *Battle Morning Song*? I would say so. But there's a lot more to Branca than that, as

I've already seen for myself, and when it comes to horses, there's no one to touch her.

'Another mare?' Branca asked, stretching tired arms towards the ceiling. 'Or a stallion this time?'

'I don't mind.'

On my instructions, Jonny has been digging a pit for my warhorse outside the curtain wall. Gael wanted to help, so Jonny kindly found him jobs he can do. Guinevere is lying on her side on the grassy bank. Stoutly braided ropes have been passed under her body, and these will be used to lower her into the pit. Not many of us will attend the ceremony. Laurence and Bethan are busy with the injured and the dying. Bodies are now being taken to the chapel, and a burial team has been detailed. William is back on the *Senjo*. Jonny has put Captain Kerry in temporary charge of the garrison. There are many prisoners of war to be dealt with, and Patrick has been sorting out the mass of documents. Names have to be logged, together with some idea of where the people came from. It all takes time. The kitchen staff are busy, as always, and our very own Duke of Casuel is still baking bread, making girdle scones and doing a great deal of fetching and carrying.

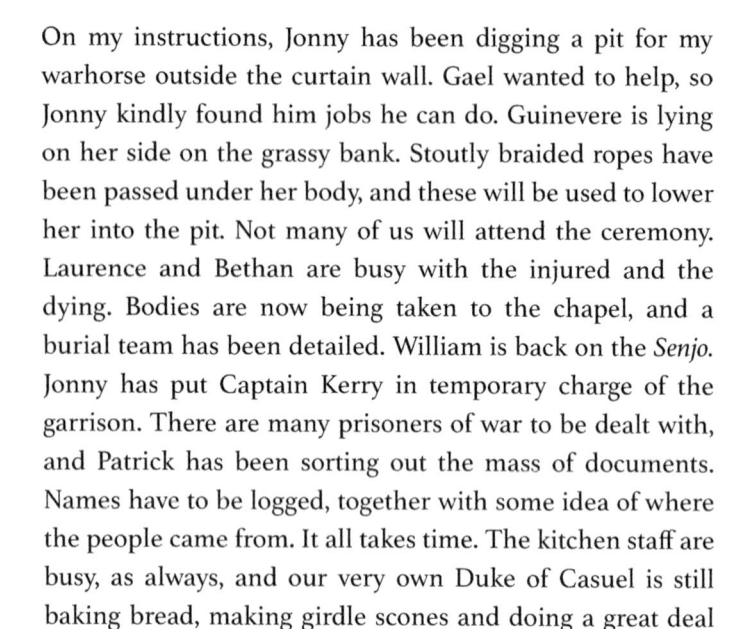

Then there's the matter of the town. Hambrig Town is in my demesne, and not every inhabitant came to the castle for protection. I am concerned for them all, but I am particularly worried about the prisoners in the courthouse cells. Someone will have to see to them, and to Master John too, if he is still alive. Jonny has sent a small unit into the town. They are due to report back by tomorrow morning.

I whispered my own goodbyes

And now it's nearly sunset, and I must change into my best regalia to do honour to Guinevere.

I looked up at the high tower, where my red-and-gold flag flew. The sun, low in the western sky, lit the grassy bank and my dead horse, but did not find my flag, flying so high above us all. How close I came to having my colours struck and a blue and silver-crossed ensign raised there instead. But it was my own blazon that whipped out dully in the darkening sky, and, as a heavy shroud seemed to settle on me, my thoughts darkened too: Sammy, betraying his fisherman father and all of us, flouting everything we have taught him, agonising death pinned to his shoulder; Davy, dead on the battlefield, but not gloriously so, for he let the enemy into the castle, a monumental error that could have cost us everything; Kit, a man I had liked and hoped to employ here, deceiving us, *using* us; Arkyn, weak and wasted, a would-be Viking but with neither the courage nor the honour.

But there was another side to the equation: Branca, object of my unwilling but heartfelt admiration; Jonny, steadfast, brave and true, always at my side, taking difficult decisions and standing by them; Kerry, courageously ignoring her wounded leg to be part of the Forlorn Hope; Amie, a bard with a difference, tending to the suffering, anxious to make amends; Gael, musical, impulsive and loyal; the Lady Joan, who did things her own way, and who kept vital information from me, but who sent the Spiderboats to fetch the big ship; Baron Giles, a man I'd had no time for, but who turned out to be a fearless and true ally; and the entire household – men, women and children – who fought and won the Battle of Baudry Hill.

Finally of course, William, saviour of us all.

A trumpeter, high on the ramparts, sounded the Retreat.

Jonny stepped forward. 'Guinevere, for ten years you were Lord Rory's warhorse. You carried him into battle, you fought with him and for him, you trusted him and he you. There never was and there never will be a better horse for any warrior, and you died as you would have wanted, fighting courageously on the field of battle. We who are left salute you.'

A drummer began a long roll; I stood to attention, and the salute was taken. I had decided my lance would be buried with Guinevere. She had charged at the enemy with that lance over her shoulder more times than I can remember. She knew her job so well, she never faltered or flinched from it. The lance was hers more than it was mine. I had cleaned and polished it so it gleamed like burnished bronze, and now I laid it on the grass beside her. Six sailors from the *Senjo* stepped forward. They took up the slack in the thick hawsers, moved carefully to stand either side of the big hole in the ground, and slowly, very slowly, lowered Guinevere into it.

A gulping sob came from somewhere near my elbow. I looked down at Gael. He had done his best not to cry, but it was too much for him. Gael had ridden with me on Guinevere so many times. Maybe my sorrow was communicating itself to him, for I felt almost consumed by it. I knew it would not last, I would be caught up in the tasks I had to perform, in the hurly-burly of castle life, and I would not dwell on Guinevere's death. But just now, at this funeral with full military honours, I allowed myself to

I whispered my own goodbyes

grieve, to feel sad and to say goodbye. I squeezed my page's shoulder, and he buried his head in my surcoat.

The horn sounded again and a group of archers sent a flight of arrows soaring across the grave. The arrows flew and the drums beat their insistent rhythm, as Guinevere sank from view into the dark, dank ground. I stepped forward, and lowered her saddle and harness into the grave. My final act was to place my lance reverently by her side. As I stepped back from the grave, the sailors began their task of shovelling the earth on top, filling up the hole, burying my treasured companion forever.

And at that moment a haunting melody began behind me, filling the air with a tune so beautiful, so poignant, I thought my heart would break. I whirled round to see Branca with her pipes. She stood to attention, night falling around her, the ruffled silver cords that dangled from the drone swinging in the slight breeze. The evocative music drifted effortlessly over us all, over the castle itself, lifting to the sky to reach the red-and-gold pennant high above the ramparts, and floating into the bailey and through the castle walls. Everything was stilled and silenced, all other sound and movement ceased. No stirring military anthem this time, no frightening call to arms; instead, the pipes played a slow and sorrowful lament, and then a heart-rending and desolate retreat, slow-marching us back to the gatehouse, silent and hatless in the dark.

Later, in total darkness, Giles and I ventured onto the hill and together we retrieved Davy's body. We wrapped him in a blanket, covering his terrible, contorted features and his twisted limbs, and we laid him across Giles's horse. The surviving Wartsbaye troops mustered quietly in the courtyard, their banners furled, their numbers vastly depleted. They had fought so well and so bravely. Desperate to find honour again, Giles had *needed* to bring his troops to us; hanging the cowards who'd betrayed him was nowhere near enough. No fanfares sounded, no cheering servants lined the way, as Giles led the shattered remnants of his army out through the gate, down the steep rocky track and onto the road north to Wartsbaye. He would bury his son himself.

But Davy had been in my household since he was seven years old, and as the sad little procession moved off, I whispered my own goodbyes.

25

MY DRAUGHTY GREAT HALL

King Philip was seated in an upholstered chair near to the great canopied bed in the solar. Next to him, on a stool that must have been brought in specially, was Lady Lillian. She was dressed in a lacy white gown with wide, flared sleeves. Her long throat was encircled with a narrow gold band. The King had sent for me, and I wondered why.

I bowed to them both and was kept standing.

'You have won a great battle,' Philip said. 'We congratulate you. You have saved Hambrlg and all Mallrovia from the Nahvitch, and you have kept your castle, your estate and your people safe.'

I bowed again.

'Your heroic deeds and this triumph deserve a reward. We are therefore offering you our daughter's hand in marriage.'

I took a step back. I had not expected this.

'Your Majesty.' I paused. 'I am honoured, but I am not sure I deserve—'

'If ever a man deserves it, it is you, lord!' the King said

emphatically. 'And we have chosen you for many reasons. We believe you should be married, and as soon as possible.'

'Sire, I do not wish to get married just yet.' *And if I ever do so wish*, I said to myself, *I will choose my own bride.*

The King looked as though he had not understood me. 'Lord Rory, we command you to marry our daughter. She will give you sons.'

'I do not wish to marry. I have said it plainly enough, I think.'

'Too plainly for your own good,' Philip growled. 'You do not have this choice, Rory. You *will* marry. You have not saved the castle only to have it founder through lack of an heir.'

'I can name an heir.'

'Is that what you want? The end of your line? What would your father have thought of that?'

I was getting angry. The King had no right. Except that he did. I am the King's tenant, a mere vassal. Hambrig is my fief, land held on behalf of the King. He could, indeed, instruct me to marry. I looked again at the princess in her white bridal gown. She was very lovely. She would bear my children, she would manage the castle in my absence, and I would become part of the royal family. My fortune would increase a hundredfold with the dowry Lillian would bring, and I would be able to fortify the castle in ways I'd always dreamt of but never been able to afford.

I'd be able to buy more livestock, and even – something I'd *always* wanted to do – build a watermill on the banks of the River Eray, which flows fast enough to make such a thing work. My dream watermill could become a reality. Lillian would bring me everything a man could desire: sons and daughters, honour, status and wealth. And I would never again be lonely in bed. What would my father have

My draughty great hall

thought of that, Philip wanted to know? My father would expect me to accept the King's offer, he would think me a fool to refuse it. He would want a legitimate heir for the demesne and the castle. That was, in the end, the thing that mattered most of all, and it was my one great failure.

Lillian stood up, and her bearing made it clear: she was a royal princess, but she was giving herself to me. She held out her hand, and I knelt before her and kissed it. Then I stood. 'Sire, I will consider. I will let you have my answer by sundown tomorrow.'

I strode from the room before he could say another word.

I slammed into my library and threw myself into my chair, then rested my head on my great-grandfather's desk and gave myself up to forbidden thoughts, thoughts I had not allowed myself to have for the last fifteen years, images that had been banished from my mind. But now they crowded in on me with heart-aching clarity, and in solitude and darkness I dwelt on memories of my Lady Kathryn. Kathryn, fair and beautiful, the only woman I had ever loved, the woman I would have married, had she lived.

I couldn't indulge myself for long, for there was Sammy to deal with. I knew he was in a bad way, the boy was only fourteen years old. He'd been a pawn in a bigger game than he had the wits to understand. Putting my thoughts of Kathryn to one side, I set off for the gatehouse.

Sammy had been given a peasant's rough tunic to wear, and the pavonalilis cloak lay across his mattress, mocking the boy's ambitions. I did feel a pang when I saw him. He looked so like the Sammy we all knew. But he had left that behind when he went over to Blurland. I reminded myself of the murderous look on his face as he drew his sword to kill me. In the middle of turning Guinevere around, I could not have defended myself. In the boy's brain I had become the enemy and he wanted me dead.

I already had a kind of plan. Much as I'd asked Branca to break a wild Smanderish horse, to tame it, make it biddable, gain its trust and create a bond, so would I have to do with this boy, who had thought himself man enough to be a king.

'You have let me down,' I said heavily, standing in the doorway. 'You have disappointed both me and the Lady Joan.' It sounded as if he'd failed a spelling test. Sammy flushed. I had just reduced his kingship and an entire bloody battle to a 'disappointment'.

'Lord, I had to do it! I had a duty to my people!'

'Your duty was to *us*. *We* are your people, Sammy. You were brought up from your very birth by a Mallrovian fisherman. You were looked after from the age of seven by the Lady Joan, a Mallrovian noblewoman. You were taken in, clothed, fed and protected by me, a Mallrovian lord. What other "people" do you have, you silly child?'

He glowered at me. He didn't care to be called a silly child, nor to have his heritage discredited and thrown in his face. I stared right back at him, not angry, just a disappointed adult, whose child had done something foolish.

'The Toosanik *are* my people,' Sammy said sulkily. 'They *are*. My father was the Kyown-Kinnie! My mother was a princess! How can you say I don't belong with them?'

'I didn't say that. I said you should not have been our enemy, fighting us in battle, prepared to kill those who have defended and protected you all your life. When you are a man you will have the right to make your own choices. You may want to live with the Toosanik. You may try to earn their respect, and perhaps they will want you to lead them, if you show you are trustworthy and bold. What have you

My draughty great hall

shown the Toosanik so far, Sammy? You have shown them you care nothing for loyalty. You have shown them you are easily persuaded to change sides. Do you think they will want you as their king, knowing you have already betrayed the people who love you?

'The Toosanik saw you as a puppet,' I went on relentlessly. 'They used you. They dressed you in a fine robe and sat you on a splendid horse, and then they sent you out as a figurehead to torment your *real* family. They didn't care what happened to you. Was the Kyown-Kinnie by your side? No, he was not. You have no standing with the Toosanik, nor will you have until it is earned. It is your *real* family, here in Hambrig, who value you for who you are, not requiring great deeds or proof of kingship. We *know* you, Sammy.'

His head was bowed. I could not see his eyes. I put a finger under his chin and tilted his head up. Tears glistened on his cheeks.

'Before the battle, Amie sang a song,' I told him sternly. 'Amie sang of Fiorello, the Sacred Gecko of the Nahvitch. But the song was all wrong. There was no living gecko. The legend was based on a lie. The idea that it could talk, that it ripped our soldiers to shreds, none of it was true. And yet everybody here believed in it. Why? Because they wanted to. They wanted to think the Nahvitch had a weapon we couldn't fight. It made them feel better about being beaten. When Prince Barney brought the Box of Death into the castle, there was panic and pandemonium. And what was in the Box? A harmless rabbit. Do you understand? Things are not so just because you want them to be, or because someone has told you they are. You will be a king when you are ready. Not before, just because you wish it, or because someone has put you up to it.'

'The Kyown-Kinnie said he was my father,' whispered

Sammy. 'He said I was the rightful king of the Toosanik, and that I was born to lead them.'

'Of course he said that. That's exactly what I've just told you, isn't it? You have no idea of leadership, Sammy. Not yet. But the Kyown-Kinnie wanted you to think you could take charge. They pushed you to the front, didn't they? They put fine, bright colours on you to make you stand out. They made you a target.'

'Did they want me to be killed then?'

'They didn't want it, but they wouldn't have cared if you had been. They don't care about you, Sammy. The Lady Joan does, though. She was with your mother when she was ill. She cared for you after James died. James wasn't your father, but he was more of a father to you than the Kyown-Kinnie ever was. James taught you, he looked after you and he loved you. And what happened to him, Sammy? You know the answer to that. He was killed by the Toosanik, in front of your eyes, on the Kyown-Kinnie's orders. Your "people" killed James, the man who had loved your mother and who loved you as his own son.'

Now the tears were flowing, unstoppable. Sammy sobbed and sobbed, and if I'd been Joan I'd have taken him in my arms, but I'm not and I didn't.

I stood up. 'I'll leave you to think about it. Think about what you've done. Think about who you want to be. Think about your mother, and about James, whom she loved, and the Kyown-Kinnie, whom she didn't. And then think about the Lady Joan. You can let Sir Jonny know when you're done thinking, boy.'

My draughty great hall

The Lady Joan had moved back to the *Egg* as soon as she could be spared from the kitchen and the hospital. I walked down to the little workshop.

'Joan, Sammy is going to ask you to take him back. But you will refuse to have him.'

Joan nodded slowly. 'What's your plan, Rory?'

'He needs to know what he's done. I am going to ensure he never makes the same mistake again.'

'But eventually? Is he coming back to me eventually?'

'If all goes well.'

'Oh good,' Joan said happily. 'I have put a pavonalilis cover on his bed!'

'Have you now.' I sighed. 'Not really suitable, Joan, given the circumstances. Give him a plain brown blanket, like the soldiers have.'

'Is he to be a soldier then?'

I laughed. 'I didn't mean that. Although it's not a bad idea. A spell under Jonny's command would do Sammy a power of good. But take the bright blue away, Joan.' And I decided to ask her something I've been wondering for some time. 'Why did you make him the cloak in the first place? Didn't you realise they were using him? He was a puppet king, nothing more.'

'The Toosanik wanted Sammy as soon as he turned seven years old. They recognised him as the son of Princess Eefa and the Kyown-Kinnie.'

'But you *wanted* him to go. You made the cloak for him.'

'It wasn't like that. Sammy was working in my House of Colours, he was learning a useful trade. Dyers are skilled, and he has an eye for design. He produced this amazing colour, a colour I'd never seen before. He and I named it: Pavonalilis Blue. But he got really excited about it. He said it was the colour of kingship, and he was the true king of the

Nahvitch. He used the word "Nahvitch", he really didn't know much about the clan. It was much, much later I discovered he'd been talking a lot with Davy. Sammy had shown Davy the new colour and Davy told Sammy it was splendid, and just right for a king to wear. He told him to get a cloak in that colour, and put in it a silver lining. Davy told Sammy that a cloak in those colours would mark him as the king of the Nahvitch, which he was by rights, because of his parents. Anyway, Sammy begged me to make a cloak for him, just like Davy had described. Of course, the next thing I knew, Sammy had gone with Davy and Prince Barney. You're thinking I was naive, aren't you?'

She was right – I was.

———◆———

The detachment Jonny sent to survey the situation in Hambrig returned just after breakfast this morning, and their report told us what had happened in the town. Some of the Nahvitch, fleeing from the *Senjo's* devastating attack, had slipped round the shoulder of Baudry Hill and raced along the muddy track that exists on that side, which can be a back way into Hambrig Town if you don't mind clambering through nettles and brambles. The soldiers reported that quite a few of the enemy had scrambled along this track and had attempted a rudimentary sort of sacking of the town, but it got nowhere, since those Hambriggers who'd remained there, by definition a hardy and self-sufficient lot, made short work of them.

The only cause for alarm was that one Hambrigger in particular had had his house ransacked and his books burnt before his eyes, and that man was Anthony Merry. The

My draughty great hall

soldiers described Master Merry as being 'extremely upset'. Having met the man and seen the vast number of books he possessed, I thought this was probably an understatement.

As for the courthouse, and its rank and stinking gaol, the prisoners inside have been rehoused in a secure but empty warehouse, and people from our garrison have been assigned to look after them. Strangely, there is no news of the sheriff.

So, after dinner, I took a palfrey from the stable and rode into town, taking Captain Kerry with me. We were on the lookout for two people: Anthony Merry and Master John the sheriff. Kerry trotted along beside me and, the afternoon being bright and fair, it was a pleasant ride into Hambrig Town.

'How is Sergent Bess?' I asked.

'Making good progress. But she's fed up she can't do anything much.'

'That will pass,' I said. 'She must follow Doctor Bethan's orders, you know.'

Kerry nodded.

'How long have you known each other?'

'Since we joined,' Kerry said at once. 'Me and Bess and Alex together. About fifteen years ago now.'

Everything seems to date back to sometime around then. I let the palfrey carry me along; it knows the way as well as I do. I was thinking hard. Fifteen years ago I was eighteen and in love with Kathryn. A year later, Kathryn died, or so her uncle told my father, but I never knew any details. I just never saw her again. At around the same time, Eefa was snatched from her marital bed in the Kyown-Kinnie's hut, found by James the fisherman and brought to Hambrig. Then Sammy was born and Eefa died. I shook my head. Perhaps I should run it all by Peter sometime. He might be able to make sense of it; it couldn't be any harder than *The People's Puzzle,* surely.

I snapped out of my thoughts to find Kerry staring at me. 'What?' I asked.

'Nothing, lord.' She looked hastily away. But it couldn't have been nothing. She'd seen something, or thought something. After that, we kept silence until we reached Hambrig Town. We made straight for Master Merry's house, tied the horses up outside, and, with a perfunctory knock on the door, we entered. Everything looked different. The furniture was gone, the books were gone, the walls were blackened and the place smelled of smoke and burning. It was foul, and I was appalled.

'Master Merry?' I called out, for there was no sign of the man.

He appeared then, shuffling into the hall from somewhere.

'Lord Rory?' His voice was high-pitched and quavery. His hair was thinner and wispier than before, and his body looked emaciated, the grimy clothes hanging off him.

Impulsively, I went up to him and took his shaking hands in mine. 'Are you all right, Master Merry? What has happened here? What have they done to you?'

Merry was on the verge of collapse. Captain Kerry caught him just in time, and lowered him carefully to the floor, so he was sitting with his back against a wall. Then she and I squatted down beside him.

'Oh, Lord Rory,' Merry gasped, 'they came. The Toosanik rebels came here. These were not the brave fighters, but the cowards, the ones that ran away, the looters and the pillagers. Do you know what they did? They came into my house and they flung my books onto the floor. Then they set fire to them. They burnt my books! My furniture they set alight too, and would have burnt my whole house down if my neighbours had not chased them away. I have good neighbours, but they are old men like me. And these Toosanik are not worth fighting, they are scum, just scum. My wife was Toosanik, did you know that? She was a good Toosanik woman, the Kyown-Kinnie's daughter, and she would have despised those cowards, those *bastards*...' He couldn't carry on, but finished with a terrible coughing fit that left red-flecked spittle running down his chin and the man gasping for breath.

Captain Kerry looked at me with concern. 'I think smoke must have got into him, lord. He can't breathe or speak properly.'

'Do you think they targeted you and your house deliberately?' I asked him.

'I don't know,' he managed to whisper. 'How can people burn books? Books have done them no wrong. They are our knowledge, they are what makes us people and not animals. It is the knowledge we have written down over centuries that has shaped us and our land. They wouldn't understand that though. They were vermin, illiterate vermin.' He clutched at his chest and coughed again.

'We'll take him to Doctor Dethan,' I said. 'Make the arrangements, captain.'

As for the sheriff, he was easily found. He lay face down in his own horse trough, his gaol keys halfway down his throat. Someone must have found the keys and decided the sheriff could choke on them, but whether that was before or after they drowned him, I couldn't tell. I did think, though, that it wasn't Merry's verminous Nahvitch that had done it. Far more likely it was someone from the town, someone who had been used badly by Master John. The evidence for that was clear: he wore neither breeches nor undergarments, and his penis and scrotum floated beside him in the trough. Poetic justice.

Kerry and I commandeered a flat-bottomed cart equipped with a pair of shafts, lined it with a couple of horse blankets and laid Master Merry down carefully. I found traces, hitched the cart to the palfrey and Kerry drove it home, being more used to such things than I.

So much for the visit to my town, more a ghost town now, I thought wryly. Well, that would take care of itself. People were already starting to drift back. After all, who wouldn't prefer their own house or hovel to a blanket on the floor of my draughty great hall!

26

IT DOESN'T MAKE ANY SENSE

The cook was waiting for me. She wanted to know when I planned to hold the Victory Banquet.

I've never been one for feasting. Overeating, drinking oneself under the table? Why even would you? But a Victory Banquet is expected, and my household bloody well deserves one. As Rachel hurried back to her kitchen to prepare for her own moment of triumph, I walked back to the House of Colours, also known as the *Egg*.

Anthony Merry was in the *Egg*, and Doctor Bethan was tending him there. There were poultices for his chest, some kind of mixture he must drink to help his throat, and a prescription for rest, rest and more rest. Joan will see to that. And now it was time to deal properly with Sammy.

William stood up respectfully as I entered the House of Colours, and soon after that Sammy arrived, escorted by Sir Jonny and Captain Kerry. We all squeezed into the *Egg* and sat down.

'Sammy.' I opened the meeting by looking squarely at the chastened young man facing me. He looked like he'd barely slept. The silence became oppressive.

'All *right!*' he shouted suddenly, half standing, but Jonny shoved him back in his place. Sammy burst into noisy tears. Still I waited.

'Please, please, somebody say something,' Sammy cried. 'Please just tell me what's going to happen to me.'

Still nothing.

'*Please!* I can't bear it any longer!' He began to scream. He would have smashed and thrown things too, as his control left him, but Jonny had him in an iron grip. Sammy fought uselessly against the big man's hold on him. I sat and watched impassively while he wept and struggled and railed. Nobody moved, even when he suddenly clawed at the front of his breeches and then ostentatiously and vulgarly pissed himself, all the while shouting filthy, blasphemous insults at us all. Finally, totally hysterical, he flung himself down and banged his head again and again on the table, until Kerry got a fistful of his hair and yanked his head up painfully, and Sammy shrieked again, spittle, tears and snot mingling in a noxious mixture down his front and on the table. And still I waited.

Merry fell asleep at some point, and then woke again later. Jonny and Kerry kept Sammy pinned to his chair, but, when it was quite dark outside and Joan had lit candles on the mantlepiece and a fire in the hearth, very gradually, Sammy quietened. In the candlelight, I saw the boy's eyes start to close, his head drooping onto the table. He had worn himself out completely. It was time.

I stood up, leant over, grabbed the back of his tunic and jerked him upright in his chair. He shouted out in shock.

'You don't go to sleep,' I growled.

He blinked, but found it hard to keep his eyes open. He began to sob, but this time the sobs were quiet, desperate ones.

It doesn't make any sense

'You have betrayed and disgraced us,' I told him. 'You are not fit to be one of us anymore. You will spend tonight back in the gatehouse, and tomorrow I shall tell you what I intend to do with you.'

The boy's tear-stained face was horror-struck. If he could, he would have thrown himself at my feet. 'No! Please, lord! Please tell me now!'

I nodded to Captain Kerry, and she marched the boy away.

'What *are* you going to do with him?' Anthony Merry asked from his sickbed.

'I'm going to build him back up again. In time, he will be stronger, fitter and more of a man. He will also be a Hambrigger.'

Joan was looking strangely at me. 'I had no idea you could be so cruel.'

Cruel? Perhaps. But also necessary. The boy had had to be broken, all the arrogance beaten out of him, and in front of his family too. It was how my father had treated me on occasion. The only discipline I knew.

There was silence in the cabin for a few moments while Jonny and William cleaned up Sammy's disgusting mess. Eventually William declared the place shipshape again.

'Well,' said Joan decisively, 'I think I'll make some tea!'

Joan has this curious predilection for tea. She loves the taste of the strange infusion of flaky leaves in hot water. Making the tea is an interesting and rather lengthy ritual. Joan's workshop is right beside the River Eray so she can use the water to dye her fabrics, and of course the little stream is also useful for filling the exotic samovar. William, Jonny, Merry and I watched as she took it down from the shelf and then shovelled up a few burning sea-coals from the fireplace. These she fed down the samovar's chimney, and

241

followed them with some pinecones and cinnamon sticks. The water in the samovar was heated by the burning coals. Soon the little workshop was filled with the sweet, spicy aroma of pine and cinnamon and the sound of water bubbling as it boiled. Now Joan damped the fire in the samovar's chimney, then took a teapot down from the shelf. From a brass jar, she scooped out some of the black, flaky leaves she loves so much, and dropped them into the teapot. She peeled a small orange fruit, cut the peel into very small pieces and added them to the teapot. The oranges come from Portugal, Joan told us, and they're expensive. Finally, she added a few small brown kibbles: cloves, apparently.

Then the pot went onto a metal tray, on which the samovar also rested. I could see that everything was made to fit, the tray holding both the samovar and the teapot exactly. Not only that, but the teapot was now in position under a small tap that protruded from the samovar, which could be turned to pour boiling water directly into it. This was done, and Joan told us that the strong black tea would have to infuse for a short time. With its lid back on, and to my surprise, the teapot was now placed on the top of the samovar. Joan saw my expression, and explained that the steam from the samovar would keep the tea hot.

'Why does it have to infuse for so long?' Merry's thin voice came from the far end of the cabin, where he was resting on Joan's bed.

'To give it flavour,' Joan answered. 'But it depends on how strong you like your tea, and what sort of tea you're using. I'm using black tea, called *Karavanserai*. It's hard to get hold of. I can't tell you how useful it is having a deep-water sailor for a son!'

William grinned.

'What happens next?' asked Jonny.

It doesn't make any sense

'You have to judge the time,' Joan said, 'and it's hard to do here, because you can't hear any bells. It was much easier when I lived in Hambrig Town. When the tea has infused in the teapot it will be really strong. Much too strong to drink. So we will pour some of the infusion into a teacup, and place the cup on the tray. We can then add hot water from the samovar until the tea is the strength we want it to be.'

'And then you drink it!' I said, triumphantly.

'And then we drink it,' Joan laughed. 'But don't worry, I have more than one teacup. There will be enough for everyone.'

I shook my head. I've tried the strange stuff before, and it isn't to my taste. But Jonny looked interested, and Master Merry, I thought, will have no choice in the matter. If Joan thinks her *Karavanserai* will do him good, he'll be drinking it morning, noon and night.

'Where did this samovar come from, Joan?' I asked. 'I've never seen anything like it in Hambrig – or the whole of Mallrovia, come to that.'

'A sailor gave it to me,' Joan said, dreamily. 'I knew him long, long ago, before you were born, Rory, and before I got to know you, Anthony. He was young and handsome, with long black hair and kind, twinkling eyes. But I only saw him from time to time, when his ship docked in Pevarile and he made the trip south to Hambrig Town. He always brought me something wonderful and exotic. He'd stay a month or so, and then he'd have to go back to sea.'

'What happened to your sailor boy?' William asked, his arm around his mother.

'He died,' Joan said, matter-of-factly. 'Well, he stopped coming, and eventually I made some enquiries and was told his ship had been sunk by pirates in the Baltic. They didn't think anyone survived.'

'What was your sailor's name?' I asked her gently.

'Jack. He was called Jack. But then, aren't they all?' She laughed, and it was a sign to change the subject.

William said, 'The black tea has medicinal properties. They say it's calming and helps you relax. Oh yes, and it can cure your sore throat and your stomach problems!'

'Is that so?' I was interested. 'Has that worked, Joan? I mean, has it cured any ailments you've been suffering from?'

'Not mine,' Joan said. 'I am not often ill, thank the Lord. But when I knew of James's wife being so unwell, I took the samovar and the black tea to his cottage, and I showed him how to make tea for her. I honestly believe it was the *Karavanserai* that kept her going until Sammy was born.'

But I'd been wondering something. 'What made you visit them in the first place, Joan? How did you know anything about James and Eefa?'

'It was talked about in the town – how James found a poxed Nahvitch woman in a wrecked old punt and brought her home to live with him. There was a lot of gossip, not that James cared. I decided to go and see for myself.'

'Did you know she was a princess?' Jonny asked curiously.

'Not at first. James wouldn't tell me anything about her to start with. He was frightened, you see. Frightened of losing her, frightened she would die – and frightened that if anyone found out she was already married, *and* pregnant, her marriage to James would be annulled. But as time went on, and as she rallied a bit, getting stronger, he realised I just wanted to help. I wasn't judging anyone. I went to their dwelling every week to see how she was, how they both were, really. In the end, James trusted me, and he told me everything he knew about Eefa. And *she* told me a few things too, things she hadn't even said to James. And the tea really did help her get stronger, you know. As William says, it's a powerful medicine.'

It's quiet outside the *Egg*. I sit back in my chair, feeling my body relax at last, and, by candlelight, I scribble some notes in my journal.

In the castle, things are slowly getting back to normal. The prisoners of war have mostly been put to work repairing and rebuilding the damage, including the wrecked drawbridge. Eventually they will be allowed to return to Blurland. The slightly injured and the walking wounded, whether ours or theirs, have been given light duties and sent back to the garrison. The seriously injured are being moved to the barn by the eastern wall. Many of our own wounded from the fyrd, mostly peasants and the poorer townsfolk, have returned to their own homes where their families will care for them.

There are more deaths each day, but it's tailing off. Laurence has been kept busy with Last Rites, prayers for the bereaved, and funerals. The man is in his element, in constant demand. A fussy man is Laurence, and a deliverer of boring sermons, but he knows his business at a time like this. He's even seeing to all the many records that need to be updated, liaising with Patrick where necessary, and taking on more responsibility than he really needs to. In truth, he's saving me a lot of trouble.

I'd been listening to Joan talking quietly about the tea and her visits to James and Eefa, while thinking my own thoughts, but then Merry spoke up.

'I remember you telling me about the tea years ago, Joan. I was having trouble sleeping, and you said it would help me. You told me about the samovar then. Do you remember I suggested you bring it to my house and show it to me? But you never did. You told me you'd lent it to someone, but you didn't say who. It was Eefa, wasn't it? You'd lent it to Eefa.'

'That's right, Anthony. I couldn't tell even you where it was, but I did tell you the truth. I gave the samovar and a supply of *Karavanserai* tea to James and Eefa. She was a wonderful girl. So brave. She just wanted to live until her baby was born. I think she knew she wouldn't survive the birth, but she asked me to promise to look after her baby. James and I both promised.'

Joan's voice was full of tears. William squeezed her in a hug. 'You did your best,' he whispered. 'No one could have done more.'

There was great anticipation when Joan declared the tea was ready. She produced two teacups and a small goblet, apologising, as she handed the goblet to William, that she didn't have enough cups for everyone. I watched with interest as a cup was placed on the tray under the samovar's tap. Then Joan reverently removed the teapot from the 'crown' of the samovar, as she called it, and poured a very small amount of the strong black liquid into the cup. She topped this up with hot water from the samovar. Jonny and Merry were given proper cups, while William had the goblet and Joan made do with a saucer. Jonny and Merry sipped cautiously. William had obviously tried the tea many times before, but even he sipped it. I could see it was hot enough to scald you if you weren't careful.

It doesn't make any sense

'Where do the samovar and the *Karavanserai* come from?' Merry asked William.

'A strange land, Anthony,' he answered, setting his goblet down on the table. 'It used to be known as Rus, but the Mongols have been there many years now. They're calling the place "Mongolia". I have been trading with them for some time. It's a cold country. People wear furs all year round.'

'Mongolia.' I tried the name out on my tongue. 'There were Mongols in Egypt, fighting us in the Holy War. Fierce, deadly warriors. How long does it take you to sail there?'

'I couldn't really say. I don't sail directly there, you see. I have my trading routes, and they take me all over the place. I was in Mongolia eighteen months ago, and it's taken me that long to get back here.'

He was being rather coy, but I remembered that the *Senjo* is a privateer. Who knows what antics she gets up to on the high seas? Still, I now had my cue to tell William my plan for Sammy. 'I want Sammy to sail with you when you leave. I want him to experience the discipline and hardships of life at sea. I know you'll treat him well, seeing as your mother worked so hard to bring him into the world!'

Joan looked shocked. 'Oh, no, Rory! Sammy can't sail with William, he's too young, too small. He'll never survive.'

'Joan, we have boys much younger than Sammy on board,' William said mildly, but he was looking at me.

'Sammy sails with you,' I repeated. 'Joan will pack him a big, fat duffel bag, full of warm clothing, treats to eat, and all her love. And then he will leave. And when he returns he will be a man, and, God willing, a good one.'

Joan was clearly unhappy, but she stopped protesting.

There was silence for some time as everyone drank the black brew. Merry made a bit of a face, but continued sipping from his cup. Jonny seemed to be enjoying it, and as for Joan, she leant back in her chair with a sigh, cradling the warm saucer in her hands.

After a while, Jonny yawned and stretched in his chair.

It certainly was late, and time for the two of us to make a move back to the keep and leave Merry and Joan to get some rest. Joan stood up and picked up the samovar – but put it down again suddenly, with an exclamation.

Jonny, in the act of removing his cloak from its hook on the back of the door, turned in surprise.

'What is it?' I asked, my gauntlets only half on.

'It's very odd,' she said. 'There is something inside the samovar.'

'There may be some water left in it.'

'No, it's not that. It's the first time I've made tea for so many people, and normally there *is* water left in the samovar, but this evening I actually had to empty it to make the last cup. So there's definitely no water left. But I heard and felt something move inside when I picked it up!'

I stepped forward and lifted the samovar. I tilted it to the side slightly, then to the other side. We all heard it. A faint thud as something moved. I took the cover off the samovar and tried to peer inside, but could see absolutely nothing; the light in the *Egg* was too dim.

'Feel inside it,' urged Joan. 'There's definitely something there.'

I tried to put my hand into the urn, but the chimney pipe runs through the middle of it, and there wasn't a lot of space either side. Joan has the smallest hands of all of us, and she managed to get her fingers down to the bottom of the samovar.

'I can feel it,' she announced in great excitement. 'I wonder how long this has been in here!' She withdrew her hand, and between her fingertips was a small cylindrical object. We all crowded round the table. Joan gave the cylinder to me, and I turned it over in my hands. You couldn't possibly tell what it was. It was tightly wrapped in oilcloth, presumably to keep it from being spoilt by the water in the urn. The oilcloth wrapping was sealed with something black and sticky, which looked and smelled like tar.

William sniffed at it. 'Caulking pitch,' he said knowledgeably. 'It's used to seal boat decks and planks. You stuff the holes with oakum and then cover it over with tar. Keeps them watertight.'

'What's the best way to undo it without damaging it?' I asked William.

'The tar can be melted, but that would risk burning whatever's inside. Try just teasing it apart. Here, use this.' He held out his sailor's knife.

I slipped the blade between the folds of oilcloth and gently cracked through the tar covering. William was right, teasing the material, bit by patient bit, was the way to do it.

'Go carefully with the knife, Lord Rory,' Merry warned anxiously. 'We don't know what's inside. It might be fragile.'

Gradually the cloth began to fall away. It had been wrapped many times round, and the further I got, the more we realised how careful the person who did this had been. No water could have got inside this package. Several times I had to put William's knife down, and bend and stretch my fingers to uncramp them. Nobody offered to continue the job for me; I imagine they wanted it to be entirely my fault if something got damaged. But none of us thought of going to bed now. As I finally broke through the last bit of tarry coating, a swathe of cloth fell onto the table, and in my hand I held a small bronze conical tube with a hook on one side of it. One end of it was completely closed off, coming to a point. The wide end of it was sealed just as William had described – tightly packed fibres of oakum onto which molten tar had been poured. Whatever was inside the tube was very precious indeed. I turned suddenly to Jonny.

'Get Peter. Get him here now.'

'Rory, it's the middle of the night!'

But I gave him a look that said *just do it,* and he sped off into the dark.

William was examining the cone. 'It's the end of a boathook. Usually attached to a wooden pole, and then this end is used to hook the boat on to a line, or grab something in the water.'

I nodded. I've sailed to Cyprus and Egypt, and I recognised the boathook as soon as the covering was off.

'So,' mused Merry, 'a sailor's boathook, sealed with sailor's tar, and wrapped in sailcloth. What do we make of that?' He looked pointedly at William. '*You're* a sailor. And you bring the tea for your mother. Seems to me you put this thing inside the samovar.'

'I did not.' William looked directly at Merry. 'I know you're my father, Anthony, but you know absolutely nothing about me. I don't know why this boathook has been sealed, wrapped in cloth and placed in a tea urn. It doesn't make any sense.'

27

CHALK LINES ON A DEERSKIN

I waited for Jonny to return with Peter. Peter of Redmire is a scholar and an alchemist. Whatever was inside the cone would be of interest to him.

Eventually there were seven of us, all crowded around the hooked metal cone: Peter, Jonny, Joan, Merry – who'd risen from his blankets and tottered over to the table – William, Kerry and I. Kerry said she'd been relieved by Sergeant Alex and had hastened back to the *Egg* to see if she could be of assistance. Jonny would have filled her in on the way. While waiting, I'd been whittling away at the solid tar coating, and the saucer Joan had used for her tea was now filled with black shavings. I showed everyone I'd managed to make a sizeable hole in the caulking at the top of the cone.

Merry was introduced to Peter. 'You're the man who solved *The People's Puzzle?*' he asked.

Peter confirmed he not only solved it, but made a translation, which I had read. Merry looked with an unfathomable expression at both of us. 'Then you know about it,' he said, dully. 'You know why Hambriggers call the

Toosanik the Nahvitch, and you know about the loss of Hope.'

'We'll come to all that later,' I said impatiently. 'We need to find out what's in this metal cone, and why it was sealed away and put into Joan's samovar.'

'Surely tha's worked that out by now,' Peter exclaimed, rather forgetting his manners.

'Oh, I think I have,' I replied. 'But let's see.'

With the point of William's marline spike, I cleared away the rest of the tar and scraped the oakum fibres out. At first glance, the cone seemed to be empty.

'Put thy finger inside,' Peter suggested.

My finger touched on something. Something smooth, but with an edge to it. Sliding my finger slowly up the tube, I gradually drew out of the hollow boathook a very thin parchment. It had been rolled up tightly and inserted into the boathook, where it had clung to the metal sides. Peter let out the breath he had been holding.

'T' treaty,' he whispered. 'It *has* to be.'

I lifted my eyes from the parchment and saw through the small window that dawn was breaking and the sky to the east was rosy. I looked around the assembled company. Joan had her hand to her mouth. Merry was perspiring. Jonny stood by the door, as if on duty, and perhaps he felt he was. William was doing as I was – gazing around the room, assessing everyone's reactions. William, I reminded myself, was a sea captain, and used to being in command. But he was not in command here. Kerry was fingering the boathook, and Peter was stammering something under his breath. The man could barely contain his excitement.

I unrolled the parchment. It lay in the palm of my hand. 'We will sit down,' I said, and everyone moved at once.

I spread the document out on the table and looked at it

carefully. It had been divided half and half, with English on one side and a different language on the other. I presumed the two columns were the same, translations of each other. I began to read from the English side.

'*The Treaty of the Hurogol.*' I looked up at everyone. For this was momentous. I carried on reading aloud:

The Treaty of the Hurogol, made this day between King George of Mallrovia and King Donnakug of the people who live by the banks of the River Hurogol in Hambrig, Mallrovia, in the Year of our Lord 1084.

'My God, that's nearly two hundred years ago!' I looked up again, amazed. Merry was nodding. William's eyes were boring into me.

'Only a generation after the Normans invaded England,' Merry said. 'Domesday!'

There was more.

Having agreed that the River Hurogol is a natural boundary to Hambrig and having further agreed that the River Shamet, a tributary to the said River Hurogol, makes another natural boundary within the Shire of Hambrig in the Country of Mallrovia, both parties being willing to divide an area in the Shire of Hambrig between the indigenous people of that place and the diverse Celtic peoples, hereinafter known as the Clan, it is agreed that the Clan be granted tenancy of all the land between the River Hurogol and the Wartsbaye Road from Baudry Hill to the River Shamet, south-west along the course of the Shamet to the confluence of the Rivers Shamet and Hurogol, and south-east along the course of the Hurogol to the border between the country of Mallrovia and the principality of Westador, this land being part of the area known as the Great

Plain, but with the exception of Baudry Hill itself; and it is further agreed that, together with this tenancy, the Clan be granted all living, grazing and farming rights to that land, in return for which the elders of the Clan will pay the Hambrig tenant of this demesne the sum of five hundred pounds on the first day of every year and in addition will guarantee to provide whatever men and equipment may be needed to form a fyrd to be placed at the disposal of the said tenant should there be war between Mallrovia and any other country; this agreement to come into force with immediate effect.

I looked up, stunned.

'But we'd be isolated!' Jonny exclaimed. 'Apart from the Downs, Baudry Hill would be the only part of Hambrig not owned by the Toosanik!'

'No, no, no,' Merry said. 'It doesn't mean that at all, any idiot can see that.'

'It doesn't say they would *own* the land, Jonny,' I broke in hastily. 'They'd have tenants' rights. This is basically a tenant-in-chief agreement, with scutage replacing knight service.'

'Scutage? What's that?' Joan asked.

'Scutage is a type of tax. A vassal can pay scutage instead of owing his lord military service. The treaty only binds villeins to military service – they would be the ones making the lord's fyrd. But the freemen and knights would pay a tax instead. That's the five hundred pounds each year. It's called scutage.'

I scanned the document again. 'You think it's a bad deal for Hambrig?' I asked Jonny.

'Yes, I do. Like I said, it isolates us here on Baudry Hill. We'd be surrounded by the enemy.'

'They only became the enemy because this treaty got

disregarded,' I pointed out. 'They weren't the enemy to start with, and certainly not at the time this thing was written.'

'And actually,' Peter broke in excitedly, 'it would've been most beneficial to us. *Most* beneficial!'

'How so?' asked William.

'Well, d'n't tha see? Five hundred pound a year is a lot of money. And then tha knows, thy tenants are farming the land for thee, they're lookin' after it. They're bringin' their skills to the country, whether as farmers, doctors, sailors, scholars, whatever. They enhance our land and our culture by bein' here and livin' peacefully wi' us. Of course, they'd owe allegiance to Lord Rory, and ultimately to t' King. In time, there'd be marriages and births, and eventually no one'd know or remember who was Toosanik and who was Hambrig. We would all be one!' He sat back, beaming.

'Right,' I said decisively. 'You are all sworn to secrecy. You are to tell no one about our discovery here tonight. There is much to decide. I will call a meeting when I'm ready.'

'Just one thing though, Lord Rory,' called Anthony Merry, who'd retreated to his sickbed and his blankets again. 'Why was the document in the samovar, and who put it there?'

I sighed. I thought I knew the answers, but hadn't wanted to air them just now.

However, it was Joan's low, clear voice that spoke up. 'I think it's obvious what happened. Princess Eefa put the treaty in the samovar. I'd lent the urn to her so James could make her infusions of black tea, and that's what kept her alive all those months. She had the treaty with her when she was kidnapped, but then, when she knew she was dying, she made plans to keep it safe. She must have asked James to package it up, using his fisherman's knowledge of how to make something secure and waterproof. Eefa knew I would come back to the cottage, and take my samovar home. I expect she thought I'd find the package straight away.'

'But you didn't,' William said. 'Because there was always some water left inside. So you never realised it was there, and the boathook, being metal, had sunk to the bottom and just stayed there.'

'Then it's been there these fifteen years,' Joan said sadly. 'All this time, and we could have avoided so much fighting, so much bloodshed.'

I had not wanted our talk to go down this road. I remembered Branca's words when she spoke to me in my library not long after the battle: *To think such a treaty had existed all these years, and nobody had used it, nobody had come to claim their legal rights.*

Out of the corner of my eye I saw Captain Kerry shaking her head. I was sure she was thinking of her crippled friend, Bess, who will never fight another battle.

I dismissed the meeting, reminding everyone of their secrecy vows. Peter bobbed his goodbyes to everyone and hurried back to his quarters. Jonny, Kerry and I walked more slowly, talking quietly in the growing daylight. Jonny wanted to know why I'd sent for Peter.

'I was pretty sure it was the long-lost treaty inside that boathook,' I explained. 'I thought we might need Peter to translate it or decode it. Of course, I should have realised it was bound to be in English as well. Anyway, wasn't he delighted to be there at the unveiling!'

I long for sleep, but the day stretches ahead of me, full of commitments to and clamourings from my household.

Chalk lines on a deerskin

I washed my face, hands and hair at the well outside the kitchen, hoping the cold water would wake me up. Then I went up to my library to have another look at Peter's translation of *The People's Puzzle*. The treaty is safely back in its boathook hiding place, and I have it with me, feeling rather like Princess Eefa, keeping the thing on my person at all times. She was a resourceful young woman, though, hiding it the way she did. The Toosanik raiding party would never have thought to search there, and in any case, Joan had taken back her samovar by the time they came looking.

What puzzled me was why Eefa hid it at all. Hadn't she wanted it out in the open, so her people could use it to reclaim their land? After all, wasn't that why she'd made the long, arduous journey from Smander in the first place? But something Branca said gave me the answer to that. Eefa was mistreated by the Nahvitch, and by the Kyown-Kinnie in particular. She found peace and affection with James, a humble Hambrig fisherman. She may have decided to leave well alone. The Toosanik were away in Blurland, and they couldn't touch her now. Or perhaps she was thinking of her child, moving in her womb, waiting to be born. James would be its father, and maybe she wanted that. Poor Eefa. All the trouble she took to get the treaty to her people, and then she didn't want them to have it after all.

I sat in my library re-reading *The People's Puzzle*. I took the treaty out of the boathook and laid the two documents side by side on my desk.

And I have not forgotten that somewhere there is an even older manuscript, the original *Meridian*. Joan said the Toosanik still have this document, but she doesn't know where they keep it. *The People's Puzzle* describes the flood pretty well, but it's the treaty that gives the details of land that was promised to the Clan – a new word to me. The other thing I am trying to bear in mind is that Merry's history of the flood and his descriptions of the plight of the Toosanik are not first hand. His late wife gave him the information, and it all happened well before her time, so she would have passed it on as she heard it from someone else. No telling how accurate or otherwise the account might be. Then again, Anthony, a scholar and an historian, would probably not have written it down unless he'd verified it first.

I went to the drawer in my chest where we keep all the estate documents and records, and I drew out a rolled-up map of my Hambrig estate.

I unrolled the deerskin and spread it out on my desk. I'd not looked at it for some time, and I was astonished afresh at its glory. It truly is a wonderful depiction of my estate. I walked round my desk to view the thing from all sides.

There's Baudry Hill, with a little turreted castle drawn on top. You can even see my red and gold banners flying above the tower! And down at the bottom of the hill, the blue Hurogol snakes its way along the wide edge of the deerhide. The artist has even painted the farms and smallholdings of the tiny hamlets of Baudry and Toldesdane along its banks. You can see the broad plain where nothing grew for a long time after the flood, as the land had become as salt as the water. I sucked in my breath as I saw, more clearly than ever before, how a gigantic tidal surge could have wiped out the Celtic settlers. In my mind's eye I could see the river. Not the narrow, blue-painted strip, but the real, living, breathing watercourse, rising up like a huge wild animal and pouring itself over the land, devouring it, crushing everything it touched, sweeping away the rickety dwellings, the animals, the trees and the people,

Chalk lines on a deerskin

so that when it finally withdrew, its huge appetite satisfied, nothing was left, nothing at all.

This was the story so graphically told by Anthony Merry in *The People's Puzzle,* but the Hurogol Treaty tells another story. I got myself a piece of chalk, and began to draw lines on the deerskin map, tentatively at first, but then more boldly, checking with the treaty all the time as I drew.

Here, inside my chalk lines, were the old Toosanik territories. And this square I was roughly hatching in showed where their king lived. These small chalky circles were his farms, his homesteads and the fiefs he could grant to his vassals. There, right by the big birch tree I know so well, was the Toosanik Meeting Place, and I drew a few turrets on my outlined hut to show its importance. Finally, along the painted brown pathway, I drew a straight chalk line, running between Baudry Hill and the River Shamet, west of Hambrig Town. It would be the boundary between the Clan and the Hambriggers, a natural boundary that all could respect.

I sat back and looked at my work. I was struck by its clarity. The treaty was so specific and so detailed that it was possible, nearly two hundred years later, to see exactly what was agreed and why. And what did I discover? *It all makes sense.* The Toosanik had enough land for their needs, but no major towns, for they prefer a simpler life. Hambrig was secure, and Baudry Hill provided a bastion for everyone. There was no castle on Baudry then. But the hill had been there forever, and had looked down on Toosanik and Hambrigger with equal favour. Peter was right, and he saw it at once, even without chalk lines on a deerskin.

28

WHO DUG IT UP?

A gong sounded in the courtyard far below. I must have spent hours chalking in my lines, examining the treaty, trying to work it all out in my head.

And now it was dinnertime, and I suddenly remembered that today we were to have the Victory Banquet.

I stretched my limbs, hearing them crack with tiredness. I would not have chosen this day for the feast if I'd realised I'd be up all night in the *Egg*. Levering myself up from my chair, I rolled up the deerskin map and put it carefully back in the chest.

Everyone was gathering, and when I say everyone, I mean my household proper, since by now most of the townspeople have returned to Hambrig, and the villagers and villeins have traipsed back to their farms and cottages. They've animals to look after and fields to tend; the work has to go on, their livelihoods depend on it. So we are, more or less, back to normal now, although there are still injured soldiers and civilians being cared for in the big barn that Bethan has requisitioned, and of course our numbers are

Who dug it up?

sadly depleted. But at least the hall is back in use for meals and meetings, and the trestle tables will have food on them rather than dead and dying bodies.

Word went round very quickly that this was our Victory Feast. Amie was expected to sing again, and many people gleefully anticipated a reprise of the 'Boom Boom' chorus. Discussions and predictions were aired at great volume, as everyone crowded into the hall and found their places on the benches set out for them. Discussions and predictions be damned though, for what actually happened confounded us all.

The kitchen was serving the best the castle had to offer – wild venison, goose and swan, vegetables and fruits from the garden, loaves of plain bread, sweet bread, nutty bread and even bread made with ale and figs and cheese. Dishes and trenchers were brought to the tables; benches scraped the floor as everyone found somewhere to sit, and then decided it wasn't where they wanted to be after all. The level of excitement exceeded anything I've ever known. *This* was the meal we never thought we'd have. The King and the princess, in their royal regalia, sat by my side at the high table, and Sir Jonny was there too.

The Lady Joan was absent: William was keen to eat dinner quietly with his parents in the *Egg,* which was a shame since he was the hero of the hour. But he wanted to put to sea in the morning, and this was the only time he could spend quietly with his mother and father. Patrick wasn't with us either; he was in his little den, writing up the reckoning. He doesn't like festivities and celebrations, he tells me.

The feasting had just begun when we heard a great shout, running footsteps and scuffling, then thudding sounds from just outside the door. The door flung wide and, unbelievably, Lancer bloody *Arkyn* erupted into our midst, a broken chain dangling from his left wrist. He leapt over tables and benches and hurled them out of his way, as he crashed through the hall, gasping and swerving from side to side. Everyone froze, fistfuls of food in mid-air, mouths wide open. King Philip rose from his seat, but I pulled him down again. I must protect my king, no matter what. The dungeon guard charged through the door, a large club in his hand.

No one is allowed to bring a weapon into the great hall, so we were all unarmed. At first, I couldn't see what Arkyn was aiming for, but it obviously wasn't me or the King. He cast about wildly, and finally flung himself at the long wall behind the fireplace. Leaping up, and he was a tall man, he managed to snatch, from its mount high on the wall, an Arab scimitar. Seizing the sword with both hands and falling back down onto the hearth, Arkyn began to swing it rhythmically through the air like a scythe through hay. He jumped round to face the company, whose mouths gaped open in horror, and whose terrified eyes were riveted on the man standing tall and proud on the hearth, armed with that savage and heathen weapon. At the high table, Jonny, Philip, Lillian and I could do nothing but stare at the Smanderer, our hearts in our mouths.

I stood up and faced him. 'How did you get out of the dungeon?'

'Not too difficult,' Arkyn sneered across the distance between us. 'Master Kit showed me how. We had an entire battle to live through together, shut away in a locked cell, not knowing what was happening, who would win, who would lose. Kit said the Smanderers were bound to win, as they had greater numbers, better weapons and were much better trained. Kit said Hambrig had no chance at all. I was

Who dug it up?

shit-scared. I was scared no one would know I was there. I would starve to death in a fucking dungeon cell!

'So we made a plan, Kit and I. He showed me how to get out of my chains! And how to force open the door of the prison! I'll tell you something, something you, in all your glorious victory and clever planning, know nothing about. While you were all fighting for your lives, Master Kit escaped from the dungeon. He was away for a long time, but he came back! He came back to *me,* so that when the Smanderino army had smashed you all to pieces, the two of us would stay together, we would escape from our chains and *we* would be the victors! You didn't know that, did you, Rory, Lord of fucking Hambrig! Master Kit is a magician – he can do *anything!* He is a Smanderino. *He* should be on the winning side!'

Arkyn's blue eyes were hostile, and all the while he was speaking, the Arab blade arced menacingly through the air. I was dumbfounded. Even if it were possible to escape from the dungeon, why would you return once you'd got out? I myself had released Kit two days ago, and he hadn't said a word about an escape. I was not inclined to believe the furious Arkyn.

And anyway – 'You're also a Smanderino, Arkyn. You too would have been on the winning side.'

'No!' he screamed, swinging the sword again, making the very air shriek. 'I am from Orkneyar in the north. I trained in Smander because I am born to be a Viking warrior, and because the Smanderino army is the best in the world!'

From Orkneyar. The man was from the seal islands, inside the Norse country. I stared at the tall, blond man with new understanding. He really did believe he was a Viking, then. It hadn't been just talk.

'Put down the scimitar, Arkyn.' I was acutely aware of

the danger to the entire company. This one man, violent, resentful and with nothing to lose, could finish what the Toosanik had started, turning our Victory Banquet into a bloodbath. I had no idea how to play it, so I felt my way, conscious of Jonny beside me, his feet on springs, itching to get after the intruder. Gael hovered by the high table too, his bright eyes darting everywhere. And on my left sat the King, tense and outraged, about to witness a massacre.

The Norseman did not obey me. He swung the sword again.

'What do you want, Arkyn?' I asked softly.

'*Ragnarök!*' he screamed back at once, his voice cracking. 'I want a Viking's death, Valhalla, a seat in the sky with the gods I love!'

The King stirred beside me in unconcealed anger. 'Who is this heathen?' he growled through clenched teeth. 'And what the devil is *Ragnarök?*'

'It is the Twilight of the Gods,' I answered quietly. 'It's the Norseman's destiny, a new beginning for the world.'

A new beginning? A Viking legend – was that Fiorello's message? Surely not.

'Arkyn,' I called, and the man stilled the sword, and turned his furious eyes on me. 'Listen to me, Arkyn. I know what you want, and you shall have it. But not here, not in this hall, where fighting and the use of weapons is forbidden.'

Arkyn stood very still, and the entire hall held its breath.

I carried on talking to him, as if there were nobody else there. 'We'll go outside, you and I. And when it is over, you will be at the high table with Odin, Thor and Loki. I give you my word of honour.'

I stepped down from the dais. My household, silent and edgy, followed me with their eyes. Without looking at

Who dug it up?

Arkyn, but praying he was behind me, I walked purposefully to the door, down the steps and into the courtyard. And then I turned. Arkyn stared straight at me, a wordless appeal in his eyes. The scimitar dangled from his right hand.

'Is this your sword of choice?'

He nodded.

'Give it to me.'

He hesitated.

'You have my word of honour that you will die with this sword in your hand. Now give it to me.'

I saw fear change to acceptance, and then to trust. He offered me the sword, hilt first.

'Now kneel.'

Arkyn knelt on the cobbles in front of me, his head bowed, his hands clasped to his chin. There was nobody to see, no one to witness his death, as he tried so desperately to turn shame into glory. I gave him time to say prayers to his gods. And as I ran him through with that wicked Damascus steel, I called down those gods by name, and he fell forward onto his face. Quickly, while he still breathed, I found his right hand, and thrust the sword's hilt into it, curling his fingers around it, holding them tight within my own hand, knowing beyond any possible doubt that this man, the last Viking on earth, died as he'd begged me he might.

Whether it was an honourable death, I will never know. I am a follower of Christ, and have no interest in pagan gods and ritual. But it was important for this one man, and it cost me nothing. The King would not have approved; I doubt anyone in my household would have. But I'm the lord here, and Arkyn was beyond caring.

We never had the feast. After Arkyn's death, people drifted away from the hall, back to their work in the bailey, the buttery or the battlements, and the King and his daughter went up to their quarters without a word to anyone. It was as if no banquet had ever been planned or thought of, and in no time at all the great hall was totally empty, the food cleared away, the tables folded up. There will be no celebration, for what happened here was hideous and shocking.

I buried Arkyn in a clearing in the woods on the far, shadowed side of the hill. I put no cross at his head and I said no prayers for him. I cleaned the scimitar, and it's back on its mount. It has a bloody history, that sword.

I was sent on Crusade soon after my nineteenth birthday, travelling first to Cyprus and then to Egypt. This was when I first met Jonny, and we formed our close friendship during the long and tedious ocean passage. We learnt a lot about each other; our boyhoods, our parents, our homes and families. We couldn't have been more different, yet we somehow hit it off. By the time we arrived in Limassol we could practically read each other's minds.

We were told we'd be fighting for God and for Christ. The French knights took the town of Damietta in Egypt with no trouble at all, since the Saracens all ran from them before they even arrived. We tried to take Mansurah then, where the enemy was under the command of that legendary Mamluk hero, Baibars. Baibars, known to us as 'The Panther', let us charge into the town as if no one was there, the same as in Damietta. But it *wasn't* the same as Damietta, because this time it was a trick. Baibars trapped us in Mansurah, and there we were holed up for months, sick,

Who dug it up?

starving, beaten and demoralised. Our French leaders were killed, and so were most of the brave Templars who'd come with us.

I heard from someone that the plan was to retreat to Damietta, probably under cover of darkness. We didn't like the sound of it, so Jonny and I quickly made a plan of our own. We decided to take our lives in our own hands, and thank God we did, for the next battle the Crusaders fought was their last. We heard later that it was a disaster, our forces wiped out.

We spent the next couple of years helping King Louis in his desperate attempt to keep his campaign alive, but it was a lost cause. At Caesarea Philippi, Jonny and I disguised ourselves as Arab fighters, stole a couple of horses and rode confidently through the enemy lines. Our luck held and we weren't challenged until we'd crossed the Levantine Sea to Cyprus.

But at Limassol, where we looked desperately for a ship to take us across the Mediterranean, we aroused the suspicions of a pair of Mamluk horsemen. I'm not sure even now what it was that made them attack us. Perhaps, so close to success, we let our guard down. Or maybe they were more perceptive than the Ayyubids had been. At any rate, they challenged us in Arabic, and we couldn't answer. We didn't hesitate. We charged those Mamluks, taking them by surprise. They rallied quickly, and galloped full tilt back at us. One of them had a scimitar, and with it he cut away the legs of Jonny's horse. Jonny fell to the ground, his horse bleeding to death by his side.

With a roar of fury, I attacked both the Mamluks at once, and struck lucky, as one of them tripped over the body of Jonny's horse and nearly fell. Jonny had his dagger ready and thrust it upwards into the Mamluk horse's belly. The horse staggered, the Mamluk crashed to the ground, his enormous javelin rolling harmlessly to the side, and Jonny threw himself on top of his man. I had fiercely engaged the other Arab in hand-to-hand combat. Finally, hot, panting and grinning with success, for we were only young, the two of us kicked the dead Mamluks into a ditch, and made it down to the harbour at last.

I flaunted my new scimitar, Jonny his javelin prize. We found a galley willing to take us to England, provided we worked our passage. Then we headed north to Mallrovia. Jonny comes originally from somewhere in the south-west of England, but he had no wish to return there. When I found I'd inherited the Hambrig estate, I asked Jonny to come with me to Castle Rory. We brought our spoils of war, and my scimitar has hung on the wall of the great hall ever since.

I remember showing the scimitar to Master Adam, our best swordsmith at the time. He whistled in admiration, and told me the sword was made in Damascus from *watered steel*. That's what they call it, because it has wavy, watery patterns along the blade. It was, and is, a murderous weapon. And now it can add one more victim to its tally.

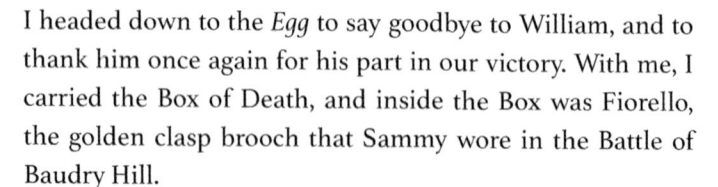

I headed down to the *Egg* to say goodbye to William, and to thank him once again for his part in our victory. With me, I carried the Box of Death, and inside the Box was Fiorello, the golden clasp brooch that Sammy wore in the Battle of Baudry Hill.

Joan has expressed an interest in Sammy's gecko brooch. I've already shown it to our physician, as I thought she might be able to identify the poison. She looked warily at it, and shook her head.

'The thing is,' I said thoughtfully to Bethan, 'Davy didn't *drink* the poison. It didn't go anywhere near his mouth. I thought you had to drink poison for it to kill you?'

'This is a very powerful toxin,' Bethan told me, keeping her distance from the brooch. 'It works by getting under your skin. Those sharp little needles, fixed all around the gecko's eyes, they prick your skin and then the toxin gets into your body. But I don't know how it works, Lord Rory. And I didn't see Davy die.'

The poison, or *toxin* as Bethan called it, was still there, swimming under the gecko's eyes, making them bright and luminous. The brooch itself is a work of art, beautiful yet deadly. I have examined it carefully, wearing thick gauntlets and keeping my fingers well clear of the needles. The body is solid gold, inlaid with rubies, sapphires and emeralds. The tail is also bejewelled, while the splayed feet are pure burnished gold with diamonds encrusted into the toes. The whole thing must be worth a fortune. But I'm struggling to understand the legend of the gecko.

Way back, the Nahvitch trumpeted their acquisition of a powerful and lethal weapon, a monstrous lizard with a deadly gaze. Our ancestors here in Hambrig all believed in this, because the Nahvitch gave it a name: Fiorello, the Sacred Gecko. We believed they worshipped it, pagans that they are, and that one day they would bring it across the Hurogol and use it to destroy us. No wonder there was panic when Barney returned from the swamplands with his big wooden box. Until that point though, we'd never given any thought to where the gecko was kept, or how it was housed or looked after. But when Barney told us Fiorello was inside his wooden crate, the 'Box of Death' it became, taking on a powerful symbolism of its own.

I've been keeping the gecko brooch inside the Box ever since Gael removed it from his dead brother's hand, but I can't forget that the Nahvitch discarded the Box as if it meant nothing to them. We found it in Blurland, abandoned in a marshy puddle in an old sack. Presumably the Kyown-Kinnie knew we thought their deadly lizard was real. Wanting to frighten Barney and everyone in the palace, he must have found a box, or else had one made. Then he put his rabbit inside and sent Barney off with it to wreak havoc. He told Barney the lizard was harmless, but he would have known we wouldn't trust him. We would think it a trick. A well-wreaked piece of havoc, in my opinion.

William had packed his dunnage and was enjoying a last cup of *Karavanserai* before leaving for his anchorage. Joan and Anthony were sitting at the table, and I saw that Joan had made some new garments for Anthony, good serge breeches and an ochre-coloured tunic, open at the neck. I nodded my approval. For far too long the man has gone about the town in ancient and outdated garb. He was a figure of fun to the children, while older people shook their heads in pity. The Nahvitch rebels burnt his books and they used his pathetic old clothes to start the fire. He'd nothing left. He too is getting a new start.

The three of them greeted me warmly as I entered the little cabin. I put the Box down on the table, and was totally unprepared for Merry's reaction. He flung himself backwards, sending his chair flying, crashing into Joan's loom, and upsetting his cup. He turned as white as a sheet, his hand flying to his mouth in shock.

'What's up? What's wrong, man?' I barked at him.

Who dug it up?

'The Box,' he quavered, scarcely able to talk at all. 'Where did you find it?'

William was mopping up the tea with some cloths. Joan had risen and put her arm around Merry. She tried to coax him to sit back down, but he wasn't having it. The man was shaking. I couldn't understand it. Everyone now knew the Box of Death had not contained a lizard with superpowers. So what was there to be frightened of?

'I didn't *find* it, Anthony. Surely you know about it? The Kyown-Kinnie sent it with Barney after he went "adventuring". We opened the Box and it had a harmless rabbit in it. There's nothing to be frightened of.' I admit I spoke rather roughly. I was completely taken aback by his reaction.

'The Kyown-Kinnie?' he repeated dazedly. 'The Kyown-Kinnie had it? No, no, that's not possible. It's Hope's. I mean it's Diane's. The Kyown-Kinnie couldn't have it, of course he couldn't. No, no, no, I buried it myself.' He was rambling.

I looked at Joan with concern. None of what he said made any sense. Joan was patting Anthony's arm, and William had picked up the chair. Between the two of them they managed to get Merry into it.

'Anthony, explain what you mean about the Box.' Joan held Merry's hands in her own and spoke very gently to him.

'Hope had it,' Merry said, and I was shocked to see tears in his eyes. 'She kept special things in it, things she wanted us to have. I didn't like it. It was macabre, wasn't it, but Diane said it was helping her. After Hope died, Diane took the Box and did the same thing. But they both died, so what was the point? I hated the Box, but it meant so much to my girl. I wanted her to have it always.'

I tried to make sense of this. 'What did Hope keep in the Box?'

'Parchments,' he whispered. 'She kept precious parchments in there. Do you know she wrote everything down? That's how I made the *Puzzle*, you see. From her parchments.'

'Hope's parchments?'

'No, not Hope's. Diane's. She wrote it all down so it would never be forgotten. That's what she said. It must never be forgotten. It must endure. Hope will endure forever.' The old man seemed confused, muddling up his wife and his daughter.

'How does Hope endure forever, Anthony?' This was William asking. He always calls his parents by their Christian names, perhaps because he didn't grow up with them.

'Ah, that's the irony,' his father said with a sigh. 'If Hope endures, then the promise cannot be fulfilled. But when the promise is fulfilled, there is no more need for Hope. And that would be unbearable. She was your sister, you know.' He really looked as if he were going to cry. Joan was patting his hand again.

'The promise?' I was trying to latch on to some part of this rambling nonsense. 'What promise?'

'The promise we made to them, of course. The promise in the treaty. Haven't you read it yet?'

'So this is all about the treaty?'

'Of course it is! Diane was a high-born Toosanik maiden, the daughter of the Kyown-Kinnie! Did you know that? Of course not, there's so much ignorance, so much waste of knowledge. Diane was proud of where she came from. She knew the history inside out. She wrote everything down so it wouldn't be forgotten, so that Hope would endure forever. I've already told you.'

Who dug it up?

'Then what happened to the parchments in the Box?' asked William.

'I took them. I wrote the *Puzzle* from them. It was an easy cipher, wasn't it? It was columnar, just as I said on the first page. Anyone could solve it.'

But nobody had tried. Nobody had bothered to work it out and read the words Anthony Merry had written from his dead wife's history of her 'proud and ancient people'.

'But what happened to the parchments?' persisted William. 'Did you keep them?'

'Of course I kept them. Hope wanted me to keep everything. That's why I buried it all. Do you know what she called it? Because she knew she was dying? She called it "the Box of Death".'

The Box of Death! That little girl, Hope Merry, had called it that?

'Anthony,' I asked rather breathlessly, 'did anyone else know it was called the Box of Death? Apart from you, Diane and Hope, of course?'

'Well, I don't know. Hardly anyone knew about it. Only Eefa, I suppose.'

'Eefa? You mean Princess Eefa?'

'She was a royal Toosanik princess, but she married that stupid, illiterate fisherman! He kept her in his hovel! I offered her shelter with me, but she wanted to stay with that ignorant lout. I could not understand it. I told her Diane was Toosanik, the Kyown-Kinnie's daughter. I told her I had written the *Book of Truth* and the *Book of Wisdom,* and I lent copies to her. I asked for her help with a sequel to *The People's Puzzle.* I wanted to write about the Toosanik royal family, their journey south and their exile in Smander. She wouldn't help me! She wasn't interested in my books, and she didn't want to live in my house.'

Joan withdrew her hands from Merry's and sat back. 'You wanted Princess Eefa to live with you, Anthony? You wanted to sleep with her, is that right? Is that what you're saying?'

'She was Toosanik, you see.' Merry wiped his eyes with the sopping wet cloth William had used to mop up the tea. 'She reminded me so much of Diane. Her colouring, her manner, her speech. I only met her once or twice, in the market when she was buying food. As soon as I saw her, I knew. I knew she was Toosanik, and my heart jumped for joy. Diane has come back to me, I thought! Hope is not dead but endures forever! I spoke to her in her own language and she was so pleased to hear it. Diane taught me some phrases, you remember, Joan? She loved to hear me use the Okkam.'

'And then you suggested she move in with you?' Joan's voice was icy, and no wonder.

Anthony looked up sharply. It was as if he had just realised what he'd said, what it meant. 'You don't understand,' he whimpered, but it was too late, the damage was done.

'Oh, I understand all right.' Joan was angry. 'I know you, Anthony Merry. I shared your bed while Diane was still alive, remember? After she died, I stood by you, no matter what anyone said or thought. I watched you write *The People's Puzzle*. And all the while you were lusting after Eefa!'

'She was so like Diane,' he whispered.

'She was *not* Diane, though, was she. She was Eefa, and Diane was dead.'

Merry flinched. I stepped in. 'What about the Box, Master Merry? Where did you bury it?'

He looked sullen now; he didn't want to tell me. I pushed the Box of Death towards him, and he recoiled.

Who dug it up?

'Tell me where you buried this,' I said again, and William moved to stand behind his father. I didn't know whether that was to protect him from me, or to stop him getting away. It didn't matter.

'With them. I buried it with them.' Merry's voice was barely audible.

'You buried the Box of Death with your dead wife and daughter? Is that right? So, in the churchyard?'

'No, no! They are not in the churchyard! They were not welcome there. Diane is not a Christian believer, she is Toosanik, and they have different gods. I buried them both myself, and then I buried the Box of Death next to them.'

I drew a deep breath. Of course it would have been like that. No unbelievers could be buried in consecrated ground. 'Where, Merry? Where are they buried?'

He started to cry gently, rocking back and forth in his chair.

'They're buried under the birch tree on the Great Plain,' Joan said, her voice muffled. She had her head in her hands.

I know the place, of course, and only this morning I'd been chalking in the Toosanik Meeting Place by that very tree. It was designated so on the treaty, although there must have been a different birch there then. Birches don't live forever, but they do regenerate. They – what's the word? – *endure*. That's it. Birch trees, symbols of hope and endurance. I began to understand.

'Right,' I said slowly. 'So the Box of Death was buried under the birch on the Great Plain. Then how did it get into the Kyown-Kinnie's hands? For it was he who gave it to Prince Barney, implying that Fiorello was inside. So now tell me, Merry. Who dug it up?'

29

I'LL HANG THE BASTARD MYSELF

Captain Kerry put her head round the door. 'All set, lord?' she asked cheerfully.

I felt a rush of affection for her, together with a welcome release of tension. Obviously, Kerry wasn't going to let Arkyn and his wretched *Ragnarök* spoil her habitual good humour. 'Sammy's ready,' she announced, 'and we've ponies saddled and waiting.'

William looked around our tense little group in the *Egg*. 'I'll be going then.' He sounded relieved. 'Don't worry about Sammy, Joan. I'll look after him. You'll see us both again in a year or two.' He gave his mother a great bearhug, picked up his duffel bag and walked out into the afternoon sunshine.

I followed. Sammy was standing beside his pony. Gone were his delusions of grandeur. His hair was brushed and tied back neatly with a piece of twine, his blue tunic and loose calico leggings were threadbare but serviceable, and he finally looked relaxed and content.

And so Sammy left Castle Rory for his new life, and William went back to sea. Captain Kerry was to escort them to the anchorage, and would then return to the castle. I went with them as far as the gatehouse, standing in the porch to watch the three of them ride away, down the hillside and out onto the Wartsbaye Road, westward to the river. The *Senjo* would then slip south towards Westador and the sea.

In my mind was the map of my demesne. I began to see the country as a map-maker might see it, with graphic representations of towns and villages, rivers and roads. It was a fascinating new way to think of my land, and perhaps the whole of Mallrovia. Perhaps even, and I gasped in amazement at the thought, the whole, wide world! Could there be such a thing? A map of the world? How big would it have to be? To draw the world, would you have to stitch a hundred deerskins together and spread them out over the land? How else would you fit the whole world onto a map? I decided I would speak to Peter about it. Perhaps he would have some good ideas about how it could be done. Anthony Merry, whose scholarship perhaps surpassed even Peter's, would know too. But Anthony Merry had lusted after Eefa, and had very stupidly said so in front of the Lady Joan.

Realising I'd left them alone together far too long, I raced back to the *Egg*. As I ran, I remembered something else I'd left there – the Box of Death. But it was still there, on the table. Merry was fingering the carvings on the lid.

'Do you know what these represent, these runes?' he asked me without looking up. Runes? I didn't know the word, but I remembered having decided long ago that the carved lines probably represented a crude letter F, meaning Fiorello. But – perhaps not.

'Tell me.'

'These are the signs for *croov-bayha,* the birch tree,' Merry said dreamily. 'The Toosanik language is based on tree names.'

'Didn't you call it "Okkam"?'

'Okkam, yes. Look at the rune. A long vertical mark with a base and a shorter mark sticking out to the right near the top.'

Merry grabbed my hand and pushed my fingers into the carved wood. He scraped my index finger along the sign he'd just described. 'See? That's the rune. It's the letter B.'

B, not F.

'But you said "croov"?'

'You're thinking of *croov-bayha*. *Croov* just means "tree". It's the *bayha* part that means birch and that's the letter B. I should've thought it was obvious.'

'Did you carve it?' I asked. 'And why is the letter B all over the lid?'

'No, no,' Merry said testily. 'And I've already explained about the birch, weren't you listening? It's the tree of hope and new life. Hope and new life.'

'You buried your daughter under the birch tree because her name was Hope?' I was still trying to understand.

'*Is, is, is!* Her name *is* Hope! Why doesn't anyone understand this! *Hope and new life!* I've just told you.'

I had overlooked his disrespectful way of talking to me for some time now, but this was too much.

'You should say "lord" when you speak to me, Master Merry.' Privately, I thought he was mad.

Merry subsided onto a chair, and rather belatedly I asked him where the Lady Joan was.

'She had to go out,' he said sulkily. 'She left in a hurry.' But there was an odd look on his face, and my stomach flipped in alarm.

'Did you open the Box of Death while I was out?' I asked him. But he had, I knew he had. I shot the bolts and pushed the lid off. The Box was empty.

'Where is it? *Where's fucking Fiorello?*' I pushed Merry

back in his chair, my hand loosely around his throat, my face close up to his.

'You'll never know if you throttle me.'

'I'm not throttling you yet, you pathetic, miserable bastard. But I will if you don't tell me what you've done with the gecko.'

'I have the gecko safe, lord,' he said in his thin whine. 'He doesn't hurt you if you know how to hold him.'

So I searched him. I ripped his nice new clothes off him, turned them inside out and shook them hard. I felt in his hair and I forced his mouth open. I even looked in his ears and nose. I know it sounds absurd, but I was desperate. Something evil and deadly like that shouldn't be just lying around somewhere. It is my responsibility, my *duty* to keep everyone safe from harm, so where the hell was the damned gecko? I drew my dagger from my belt.

He was an old man and he'd been very ill, possibly still was, but I cared nothing for that when I thought Fiorello was on the loose. The old fool capitulated instantly, squealing, 'Lord Rory! Please don't hurt me!'

I told him I wouldn't just hurt him, I'd hack him into little pieces unless he produced Fiorello that very instant. With trembling hands, he felt inside the Box of Death. Stunned, I watched as a panel at the bottom hinged upwards, revealing a second compartment underneath. As Merry withdrew his hand, I saw that the golden gecko squatted malevolently atop a small wad of parchments.

'Pick him up and put him on the table,' I commanded. I know I should have said 'it', not 'him'. But the gecko looked so real, and he looked so nasty. I saw past his beautiful colours, his precious jewels and his intricate design. I saw the evil expression on his prehistoric face, and the poison swimming behind his opalescent eyes. Merry lifted the gecko out, holding him by his tail.

'Always lift him by his tail,' the old man said softly. 'Then the poison drops down into his nose, and the needles fold flat. He cannot hurt you.' He held the gecko out to me. I wrapped my fingers around the golden tail and kept the lizard swinging face down, as Merry had done. Then I placed it on the table. I reached into the Box to take out the small pile of parchments.

'Don't take them,' Merry begged. 'Please, please leave them there. They're for Hope.'

Hope again. He certainly had a fixation with his dead daughter's name. I ignored him and pulled out the parchments. Instantly, I understood the message that had come with the Box of Death. It was clear at last. A person of great courage was needed because he or she would have to open the Box knowing the poisoned brooch was inside. And the reward was the bundle of documents I was holding in my hand. I looked at the bundle then, and realised it was actually a small booklet. *A Veehan Loinya* was inscribed in faded ink on the soft vellum cover.

'What does this mean?' I demanded.

'*A Veehan Loinya*. It means *The Middle Line*. Do you understand? No, of course you don't, nobody does. The middle line is the meridian. It is the first *Meridian*. It is Okkam, the language of the Toosanik. My coded pamphlet, *The People's Puzzle,* that is the second Meridian.'

'So this booklet is the original *Meridian*?' I asked, wanting to be sure. 'The Domesday Book of Hambrig in the time of – when? When was this written down?'

He gave a short, barking laugh. 'You have been fooled, Lord Rory, though you're not the first. It looks old, doesn't it? Do you know how to make a document look really ancient?

I'll hang the bastard myself

You spill tea on it! And who has the best tea in Mallrovia? The Lady Joan does! How does she get it? Her son brings it for her. But who is the father of her son? Ask yourself that, Lord Rory. Is it Anthony Merry? What if only part of this chronicle is ancient? What if some of it has been deliberately made to look very old and important? How does that change things? Does it make the Toosanik less entitled to live in Hambrig? Does it even matter?'

'You ask a great many questions, old man,' I growled at him. 'Now give me some answers. *Where is Joan?*' I was now seriously worried about her.

'Use your eyes, Lord Rory. Did Fiorello use his? Did the Lady Joan touch those lethal needles, I wonder?'

My heart dropped like a stone at the thought that Merry might have forced Joan to touch the gecko because she'd found out about his sexual desire for Eefa, and I steeled myself to search for her body. But at that moment, thank God, Joan walked into the *Egg*. With her were Sir Jonny and two of his men. As Sergeant Alex bound Merry's arms behind his back, Jonny formally arrested him for the murder of Princess Eefa in April 1249.

Since I had no idea what had happened, I grasped Joan by the arm and ushered her outside. She was in a bad way, shocked and upset.

'He confessed,' she declared wildly. 'He said he'd killed her! You went to see William and Sammy off, and as soon as you left, Rory, Anthony opened the Box of Death. Inside was that awful lizard ornament Sammy wore on his cloak. Anthony took it out and waved it at me. I thought he was going to attack me with it, I really did. He told me about the stuff behind its eyes, and the needles that inject it into you.

'It was absolutely horrible. I was terrified. I asked him about Eefa. Had he slept with her? Had he wanted to? I didn't want to hear all the details, but he told me anyway. But she wouldn't leave James. Anthony called James some horrible names, just because he wasn't an educated man. But Eefa didn't *care* that James couldn't read! She really loved him. I can't understand why Eefa never said anything to me. She knew I was living with Anthony.'

'That's why, then,' I said, drily.

'Anyway, he couldn't take the rejection. Just before Sammy was born, Eefa asked to see Anthony. He was hopeful she had changed her mind, but of course she hadn't. Even back then he was in his fifties, and she was a young woman, only twenty years old. Well, he told me he offered her gold, half his fortune. You do know he's a very rich man? She refused. He made ever more extravagant offers, and she refused them all. Then James sent for me because the baby was coming. James was in a panic. As I got near to the cottage, I saw Anthony coming out of it; he told me he'd been reading to Eefa from his *Book of Wisdom*.'

Joan sighed, shaking her head in disbelief. 'But he'd injected her with poison. She didn't notice; I think she probably fell asleep while he was reading. He used a little tiny needle, Rory. Just a little needle, so small you can barely see it, with a tiny amount of deadly poison on its tip. I remember how shocked I was when I saw how ill Eefa looked, and how sick her new baby was. Eefa hadn't looked anything like as bad the day before. I tried so hard to save her, I did everything I could, but it wasn't enough. Of course it wasn't enough!'

Her voice rose in a wail of despair. 'Anthony says there's no antidote to the poison! Naturally, James and I thought Eefa was worse because she'd just given birth. But we should have realised. Oh, I wish we had realised! Her death was dreadful, Rory, she was in such pain and she couldn't breathe, she kept clutching at her throat.'

Joan finished with a great sob, and I could picture it only too well, having seen Davy die in exactly the same way only three days ago.

'He told you all this? He said that was how it happened, the needle, the poison – everything?'

'Everything. But I doubt he'd ever intended to tell me what he did. It was seeing the Box of Death and that awful lizard thing. I think it unhinged his mind.'

'How did his wife and daughter die?' I asked grimly.

Joan's eyes widened. 'You don't think... oh no, Rory! He loved Hope and Diane. He would never have hurt them.'

'He was in love with Eefa, but still he killed her,' I pointed out. 'He'll hang for it, Joan. I'll hang the bastard myself.'

30

AN EVIL THING

Just before sundown I had my second audience with King Philip on the subject of my betrothal to his daughter, Lady Lillian. This time the princess was not present. I told the King I would marry Lillian, but I would not be formally engaged to her yet. He wasn't pleased.

'You realise what this means, Rory? With no formal engagement, she is not committed to marrying you. I may offer her to somebody else. Someone more appreciative.'

I acknowledged this was a possibility. I knew King Philip would want my reasons for a delay in the betrothal, and I had them ready.

'Sire, I would wish to celebrate my engagement to your beautiful daughter in a grand style, with a banquet and with festivities. But I cannot ask my household to organise a formal celebration, inviting lords and barons from across the land, until I know my home is once more secure, loyal and true. I'm sure you will agree *that* should be my priority.'

I suppose he reluctantly accepted my argument. We cannot endanger the lives of other Mallrovian noblemen

An evil thing

and women. Castle Rory must be made safe. But the truth is, I have no wish to become engaged to Lillian until I have made some enquiries, enquiries I should have made years ago. What actually happened to Kathryn?

I remember the day as if it were yesterday. Kathryn's uncle coming to the castle, talking to my father in private, then leaving, sitting very upright on a tall bay. Then my father calling me into the great hall, telling me my love was dead. No details, no explanation, no further discussion. *She's dead. Accept it boy, you'll never see her again. And now you're going to fight a war against the infidel, so sharpen your sword and be off with you.*

But I'd never seen the uncle before, and Kathryn had never mentioned him. At first, I was not able to accept Kathryn's death, and I convinced myself that the uncle was an evil man who had taken Kathryn away from me. I promised myself I would find out the truth; but away, far from home, there were battles to fight, honours to win and women to make love to – paradise for a young man. Five years later I returned to find my father dead and Castle Rory mine. I had much to do, much to learn as well. I was lord of a sizeable estate, and one that was on the front line. I didn't forget Kathryn, but I put all my memories, my love for her and my pain at her loss into a part of my mind that is never visited.

But now the King is forcing me to go there. I have to get at the truth before I can commit to a marriage with Lillian.

Before I dragged my exhausted body off to bed, I spoke briefly with Patrick, and of course he remembered Kathryn's uncle's visit. But he couldn't shed much light on it. He did not hear the uncle speak with my father. Everyone else was too young. Except – ah, of course. Except the Lady Joan. Why does everything come back to Joan, I wonder?

Unable to think straight any longer, I plodded wearily to my chamber and fell asleep on my bed, too tired even to remove my clothes.

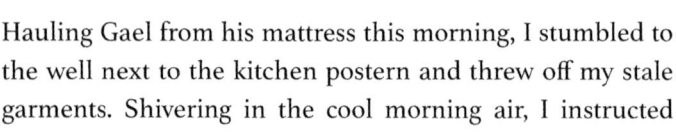

Hauling Gael from his mattress this morning, I stumbled to the well next to the kitchen postern and threw off my stale garments. Shivering in the cool morning air, I instructed Gael to throw bucket after bucket of cold water all over my body. Finally, clean and refreshed, I felt able to face this new day. Anthony Merry had to be interrogated and then executed. That was one of the first things to do.

But Kathryn was there, a ghost in my head. I knew she wouldn't go away this time; there was nowhere to hide until I found out what happened to her. And then – the gecko. I was sure now there must be a connection between the gecko brooch and Anthony Merry, and I was convinced the needles around the gecko's eyes, and the poison behind them, must be the same as those he used on Princess Eefa.

So where did the gecko brooch come from, and how had the Nahvitch acquired it? One of Joan's sentences echoed in my mind: *You do know he's a very rich man.* I hadn't known it, but the clues had been there. After all, Merry had offered a huge amount of money to the first person to solve his wretched *People's Puzzle*. I'd thought it a rash offer. But if the man had great wealth, where was it? Merry's house had been shabby rather than elegant, and there had been no signs of riches.

I dressed in clean braies, hose and shirt, and went straightaway to talk to Merry in the castle dungeon. With no sheriff, a trial would have been a farce, and summary

An evil thing

execution was what I had in mind. But it was not to be. I neither questioned nor hanged Master Anthony Merry. When the jailer let me into the room, we found the old man dead on the floor, a small gold needle near his hand. He had taken his own poison.

Joan took the news of Merry's death calmly. 'He was devious to the end then. Poor Eefa.'

'Poor Joan,' I replied softly.

We buried the man immediately. Only Joan and I were present, and of course Laurence, who intoned a dreary prayer, mercifully short, though I'd had to practically frog-march him there, the wretched priest bleating that no prayer could save a suicide's soul. Afterwards, I checked on Fiorello. He was safely locked up in the Box of Death in my library.

I invited Joan to join me in my library and offered her the oak chair, while I sat cross-legged on my great-grandfather's old desk. We kept silence for a moment or two, mainly because I didn't know how to start. Joan had had so much to deal with recently, with Sammy and Merry both betraying her so badly, and I wasn't sure how to broach the subject of my long-ago love. Finally, I simply asked her if she remembered Kathryn.

'Of course,' she said readily. 'She was one of my regular customers.'

'What happened to her?'

'I thought you knew. Kathryn died.'

'How did she die?'

No answer, so I asked again. 'How did Kathryn die?'

'Rory,' Joan said gently, 'why do you need to know? In all these years you've never asked this question. Why ask it now?'

So. There *was* some mystery about Kathryn's death.

'I'm not nineteen years old now,' I said evenly. 'I am thirty-three and the lord of this castle. Please answer my question, Joan. How did Kathryn die?'

And so Joan told me the story, and it began, of course, with her.

———◆———

Years ago, Joan was living in my father's demesne in the town of Hambrig. I was right that she'd never been a noblewoman. She was Mistress Joan then, the daughter of a merchant in the rag trade, but since his death she'd been living by herself. She had many suitors in her time, but the only one she truly loved was Jack, her sailor boy. After she found out Jack was never coming back, she took over her father's workshop in their house and began to experiment with fabrics and dyes, selling her coloured shawls and cloaks, blankets and hats. People would come to buy from her, knowing they were getting something different, something unique.

A gentleman walking down the street in a peacock-green hat would be the envy of the town, and soon there would be dozens of peacock-green hats and bonnets adorning the townsfolk – until, that is, a lady was seen in a shawl of a particularly beautiful pumpkin-orange. Then the Hambrig ladies would flock to Joan's house to acquire something in *this* latest trendy shade. Part of the allure, I learnt, was that Joan cleverly named all her colours. You didn't just get a choice between dark blue or light blue; you could hum and haw between 'indigo', 'cornflower', 'tiffany', 'seaspray' and so on. Tiny differences were noticed and remarked on, and sometimes Joan would

An evil thing

combine colours to create an even more special hue, such as 'cherry with flecks of fire', or 'moss-and-dandelion'. Garments made with these colour combinations were more expensive, and you were seen as a successful and prominent person if you were wearing one of these cloaks or hats. But it was hard to keep up with demand, and sometimes Joan's customers went away disappointed, unable to buy the latest fashionable colour because it was sold out.

One day, Sir Patrick visited Joan in the town and found her packing up her dyes and fabrics.

'For good,' she told him sadly, because people were angry when they couldn't get what they wanted, and Joan's reputation was suffering.

Patrick spoke with my father, and he offered to build her a specially equipped workshop in the castle, on the site of an existing rough outbuilding, which would be pulled down to make way for a new House of Colours. It was on the banks of the Eray, so there would be a constant supply of running water, and my father would ensure that Joan's finished garments and textiles were taken to the Hambrig Town market each week. He conferred a mysterious title on her too, 'the Lady Joan', which gave respectability to a woman living by herself in the castle grounds.

As usual, my father lived up to our family motto of *Fac Fiat. Make it happen.* But it was a good arrangement, and it worked out well for everyone, including my father, since he got commission from Joan's sales in return for her rent-free accommodation. Hambriggers also loved it, waiting each week for the colourful bales of cloth to arrive in the marketplace, together with finished hats and bonnets, shawls and tunics. The new colours and their provocative names were written on specially designed labels, so everyone could boast about their new fur-lined 'cobalt' cape, or their capacious 'butterscotch' bag.

Kathryn, as Joan said, had been a regular customer, first at the Hambrig Town house and then at the new workshop in the castle. After choosing what she wanted to buy, she became used to staying for a little while to talk with Joan. Soon she began to confide in Joan, and she mentioned her love for me, and our plans to marry. She often asked for Joan's advice, for Kathryn's mother had died when she was young, and she was living with her father, a busy man with little time for his daughter.

One summer's afternoon, the summer I turned nineteen, Kathryn came to see Joan, not to buy anything, but to seek advice. Kathryn told Joan she was expecting a baby.

'You must tell your father,' said Joan.

'I cannot. He'll either lock me up or kill me,' Kathryn whispered back. 'I'm too scared to tell him. I don't know what to do.'

'Did she have the baby?' I asked, my heart racing.

'I don't know if she had the baby. Kathryn asked me to tell her father she was pregnant. After that, I never saw Kathryn again.'

'But what happened to her? You must know *something!*'

Joan sighed. 'I don't know much more. I don't think Kathryn died. That was the story that was put about. Possibly she was sent to the Poor Clares. If so, they would have taken her baby and found a home for it. She would then be shut away from the world.'

'But why didn't she tell me?' I cried. A child! I had a child I knew nothing of. And my love, my Kathryn, *shut away from the world*? I couldn't bear it. 'She should have told me. I would have looked after her. I would have wanted to know my child.' I was almost in tears.

An evil thing

Then, after a pause, Joan said gently, 'Rory, the child wasn't yours.'

I stared at her. What the hell could she mean?

Joan sighed. 'It's hard to tell you this. Kathryn was unfaithful to you.'

I didn't believe it. 'I gave her a ring,' I whispered. 'My mother's ring. It was for us, for us to be together, a symbol of our love. Kathryn said she would wear it forever. Why would she say that if…if…'

Joan sighed again. 'Maybe she meant it when she spoke with you. Or maybe she was pretending, leading you on. We'll never know now.'

'How can you be so sure it wasn't my child?' I remembered the passion and the desperation as if it were yesterday.

'Kathryn herself told me. It was a young man in her father's household, one of the stable boys. It was a rough-and-tumble-in-the-hay relationship, she didn't love the boy.'

Why had Kathryn slept with a stable boy? We'd spoken of marriage. We'd been young and hopelessly in love. Or perhaps that had just been me. I felt as if someone had shot an arrow in my heart. I didn't want to ask, but I had to.

'What's his name? Who's the father of Kathryn's baby?'

'We don't even know she had the baby,' Joan said carefully. 'She might never have had it. There are – ways.'

Ways to stop a baby. 'You still haven't told me his name.'

'It's too long ago now, Rory. His name doesn't matter.'

But common sense told me his name *must* matter, or why withhold it? So I pressed her. Joan can be very obstinate. It took me a long time to get it out of her, and in the end it wasn't so much that I persuaded or forced her to tell me, but that she realised I had every right to know.

'It was Alex,' she said finally.

'Alex? You mean – you mean Sergeant Alex in the Special Guard? *That* Alex?'

It was.

For a moment I experienced complete calm, as if time had stopped. Then I took my dagger from my belt and placed it carefully on the desk. I went to the corner of the room and picked up the Box of Death. I was aware of Joan's eyes following me, her expression showing increasing alarm as she began to rise from the chair, her arms outstretched, thinking to stop me. Seeing this, the calm deserted me. With the Box clasped in my arms and a red mist before my eyes, I slipped past Joan, hurled myself down the steps and across the yard, racing towards the gatehouse. I knew what to expect. I had experienced the red mist before, and it is an evil thing.

31

NO RESIGNATIONS

I flung the Box under the stone bench, then pounded up the gatehouse steps. Through the open door I could see that Alex and several others were off-duty. I didn't see Jonny anywhere. Alex was playing chess with Bess, Kerry languidly watching them. I exploded into the room and everyone jumped to attention. I jerked my head to Alex. He hurried over and stood in front of me.

I stared at him. I've known Alex for years, and didn't have to wonder what he looked like, but I wanted to see him through Kathryn's eyes. I needed to see what it was that had made her want him. I saw a good-looking man, mature now because he's much the same age as I am. Thick brown hair, cut short in the military style, high cheekbones, clean-shaven chin, since that's one of Jonny's rules, and steady, light brown eyes. His clothes were clean, and he was well turned out.

'Were you ever a stable boy?' Even to me, the question sounded aggressive.

'I was, lord. Many years ago.'

'Why did you join the army?'

'I thought it'd be a good life, lord.'

'Or were you *made* to join?'

'Made to join?'

'Perhaps you had done something foolish and been found out. Perhaps you had been given some choices? Or was there no choice at all?' By now the room was in hushed silence. No one was playing chess. All eyes were on Alex and me.

'What was it you did, sergeant? Did you get into a fight, perhaps? Or did you steal something from the buttery? Or perhaps it was a worse crime.' I watched the fear growing in his eyes, the nervous tic starting in his temple.

And then Jonny appeared. I'd known it was only a matter of time; Joan would have sent Gael to find him.

'Lord.' Jonny spoke loudly and formally. His commanding officer's voice.

'Not now, Sir Jonny. Not even if the King wants me. I have business with your sergeant.'

'Business with any of my soldiers should be discussed with me first.'

'Are you forgetting I'm the lord here?' I rounded on him, my eyes blazing. 'I won't argue with you in front of your troops. I'm taking Sergeant Alex away for questioning.' And I made to leave, but Jonny blocked the doorway.

'What is the problem?' he asked. 'I need to know.'

I eyed Jonny's frame. I could probably take him out. Fortunately, something stopped me from engaging in an undignified brawl. Instead I said, 'Well then. You'd better come too.'

Jonny nodded grimly, but there was hostility in his eyes. The three of us went down the stairs to the enormous gatehouse arch. Neither Jonny nor Alex noticed the Box of Death under the bench.

No resignations

Jonny sat down. 'What's this all about?'

'Sergeant Alex is guilty of gross misconduct,' I said. 'However, this was fifteen years ago, when he wasn't in the army, and that is why I do not need to consult you first. He was a stable hand, working for his master. This really does not concern you, *General.*' I never use his rank when I speak to him.

Jonny stood up again. 'I'll be just at hand, then.' He moved out of the archway and into the breezy bailey where he began to sweep the cobbles. I turned my back on him.

Reaching down, I drew out the Box of Death and set it on the bench. Alex followed its movements with his eyes.

'You know what's in here, Sergeant Alex?'

'Yes, lord.'

'Tell me.'

'That's the Box of Death, and inside it is Fiorello, the Sacred Gecko of the Nahvitch.' His voice was deadpan, and he continued to stand to attention, his gaze now fixed on the yellow sandstone wall of the porch.

'If I open the Box, sergeant, what will happen?'

'If you open the Box, I will see the gecko. It isn't a real animal. We know that now. It's a clasp that holds your clothing.'

'Is it dangerous?'

'It's only dangerous if you touch it. It doesn't hurt you just by looking at you. You have to touch it.'

'So you're saying I could open the Box, and that's fine, but if you or I touch the gecko brooch then we will die? Is that right, sergeant?'

His eyes flickered. He knew he was being tricked. 'I think that's right, yes lord.'

'You think?'

'Your squire died after touching it. But Sammy was

wearing it and he was all right. So I reckon it only hurts you if you touch it.'

'Then how did Sammy fasten the brooch onto his cloak? How could he do that without touching it?'

'I don't know, lord. Perhaps he wore gloves.'

I was bored with the teasing, so I began to open the Box. The sound of a broom sweeping on cobbles grew louder. Nearer. Nearer still.

Jonny's right behind me.

I opened the Box slowly, and Alex began to tremble slightly. The sweeping noises slowed and became intermittent. The lid came right off the Box. Sweat ran down Alex's face, but he didn't move. Behind me, the sweeping stopped altogether. I told Alex to look into the Box. Breathing heavily, he glanced inside, and recoiled at the sight of the ornament, its wicked face staring at him, the liquid eyes so lifelike. I reached in, and Alex gasped as I seized the gecko by its tail, swinging it face down as Merry had shown me.

'The gecko doesn't kill you, Alex. It doesn't even hurt you. It *could,* but it doesn't. You had a choice, fifteen years ago. You could have kept your hands off my woman. You could have kept your filthy, disgusting prick in your breeches. But you chose differently. You fucked my Kathryn. You shouldn't have done that.'

With a cry of rage, I flung Fiorello backwards out of the porch, heard a shout from Jonny, and threw myself onto Alex, who was totally unprepared for my assault. We are the same height, but I'm a touch heavier. Alex fell face down on the ground with me on top of him. I smashed his face into the dirt, then I pulled his head up by his hair and at the same time I jumped hard onto the small of his back and pushed down on it with my whole weight. Finally, I grabbed

No resignations

one of his arms and bent it painfully up his back until I heard bones cracking. That really was 'finally', because at that moment, hands seized me and pulled me bodily off Alex. Livid, I turned to find Jonny, Patrick and Captain Kerry, who were all trying to get me away from the man on the ground. Half-pleased to find it took all three of them to manhandle me, I was still incandescent with fury.

'What the *fuck* do you think you're doing?' I bellowed. The red mist had intensified, crimson now, and very bloody.

Patrick was shushing and soothing like an old woman. I shouted at him to go back to the keep, I'd deal with him later, and then I'd sack the fucking lot of them. Captain Kerry knelt down by her friend. She turned him onto his side, and he vomited blood onto the cobbles.

'You have nearly killed him, lord,' she said to me, shocked. Then she called for Gael. The word was passed quickly, and Gael was sent at top speed for a bucket of water from the well. He gaped at us all when he returned, but no one spoke to him, and Kerry immediately began to sponge Alex's face and neck with water. Alex was moaning in pain and kept passing out.

Kerry exclaimed in horror as she gently removed his shirt and saw the extent of his injuries. Even I was taken aback at the damage I'd done. I thought I might have cracked a few of his ribs, but it looked more as if his back were broken. Jonny stood solidly in front of me, his legs apart, his shoulders squared. My back to the wall, I was trapped. My chest was heaving and my fists kept clenching and unclenching all by themselves. Jonny said nothing, but he was white-faced, and a pulse throbbed in his temple. He had an ugly, red weal on his cheek, and in his hand was Fiorello.

Fiorello was not swinging by his tail. The poison had not

pooled in his nose. Instead, the lizard squatted in the palm of Jonny's hand. It was facing me, and I could see the inky black stuff behind its eyes and the minute spikes that would prick my skin and let the poison in. Once again, time seemed to stand still, and I was suddenly acutely aware of everything around me.

Alex, sobbing, 'I can't feel my legs, I can't move, I can't move.'

Kerry, tending his wounds, but not really looking at him, for her eyes were huge, and fixed on Jonny and me.

Gael, standing to the side and hoping nobody would notice he was still there and send him packing. He was edging ever closer to me, but so slowly and silently only I realised he was moving.

And, of course, Jonny. Dependable, precise, drill-insistent, no-nonsense, hard-core Jonny. Together, we had fought the Mamluks and the Ayyubids. We had an unbreakable bond, Jonny and I, the bond you only get when you've fought alongside someone against monumental odds and come through together. We knew each other inside out.

'How did you get that cut?' I panted, pointing to the weal on his face. It was turning purple now, and his eye was puffing up too.

'You threw the gecko at me.'

'How is it you're still alive then?'

'It's your bad aim.'

Considering I'd thrown the gecko backwards behind me, I thought my aim had been rather good.

'So what now?' I asked viciously. 'Your turn is it? You going to throw it at me?'

Something touched my left hand. I looked down, and found that Gael had managed to sidle right up beside me. He slipped his hand into mine.

No resignations

Jonny noticed him for the first time. 'Get away, Gael. This could be unpleasant, and I don't want you here.'

Gael spoke up bravely. 'I don't care what Lord Rory's done. He's my lord and I'm his page. I stick by him.' And he squeezed my hand.

Kerry stood up. 'I'm getting Doctor Bethan,' she announced, 'and we'll need a stretcher. I think Alex's back is broken.'

'Jonny,' I said, controlling my breathing, trying to sound more normal. 'I'll explain it all to you. Let's go and sit down somewhere, all right?'

'Not all right. Not only have you attacked a defenceless man and half-killed him, but you recklessly threw the poisoned darts in my face. There is no way we are having talks.'

'What then? How long are we going to stand here?'

'I'm sending for the guard. You'll be locked up for now.'

I laughed. 'The guard? Who the hell are you sending? Gael, will you get the guard to lock your lord up?' I looked down at him, and he shook his head. 'See, Jonny? Gael won't go.'

'Oh, there will be someone to send. Or I'll take you myself.'

'Well,' I replied sarcastically, 'you can try, I suppose. Good luck with that.'

'*I* won't let you take him,' Gael said suddenly. 'Step away, Sir Jonny!'

Something in his tone made me look down again, and I saw the boy had a dagger in his hand. My God, it was *my* dagger.

'Gael, no,' I said, alarmed. 'You don't know what you're doing. Put the dagger down on the bench.'

'I'm going to use it to defend us against Sir Jonny and

anyone else who threatens us. I'm your page, and I'm going to protect you from harm.'

Jonny sighed. 'All right, all right. I can fight Lord Rory, but I can't fight you, Gael. Put the dagger down, and look, I'll put the gecko back in its box.'

Something inside me bubbled up, some sort of insane laughter at the thought of General Sir Jonny, old trooper that he is, negotiating a peace deal with a child. But it worked. Gael placed my dagger on the bench, and at exactly the same moment Jonny put Fiorello in the Box of Death and replaced the lid. They both stood up and looked at me. I was slowly regaining my self-control, and it was Gael who'd done that. He was just a boy. He deserved better from his master.

'Thank you, Gael,' I said seriously. 'You were very brave and very loyal. I won't forget it. How did you get hold of my dagger?'

'The Lady Joan gave it to me, lord. When Captain Kerry sent me for water, I met the Lady Joan near the well, and I told her what had happened. She had your dagger, and she put it through my belt. Then she told me to take the water to Captain Kerry.'

At that, my self-control gave way. I collapsed on the bench and broke down. It was all just too much, and in many ways it still is. I'd learnt that Kathryn cheated on me with a stable boy, and that she didn't die but was forced into a convent. I'd discovered that the stable boy joined the army, and for the last fifteen years has been part of the Special Guard in my own castle.

I've attacked him and I've severely hurt him. I don't know if Alex will ever recover.

But it was the fact that Jonny and I nearly killed each other that caused me the most anguish. That was the very worst part of all. I put my head in my hands in deep, black despair.

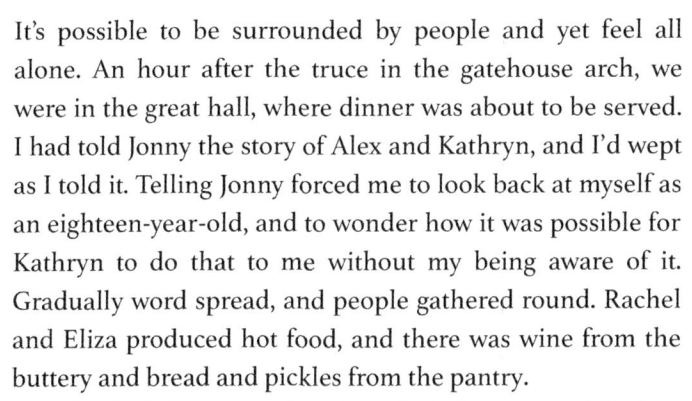

It's possible to be surrounded by people and yet feel all alone. An hour after the truce in the gatehouse arch, we were in the great hall, where dinner was about to be served. I had told Jonny the story of Alex and Kathryn, and I'd wept as I told it. Telling Jonny forced me to look back at myself as an eighteen-year-old, and to wonder how it was possible for Kathryn to do that to me without my being aware of it. Gradually word spread, and people gathered round. Rachel and Eliza produced hot food, and there was wine from the buttery and bread and pickles from the pantry.

Alex had been stretchered to the infirmary, and Bethan was watching him there.

She's pretty sure he'll never walk again.

Mired in my own thoughts, I felt totally alone. People settled at their tables, eating, drinking, talking. There was only one thing they were talking about.

Did you hear about Lord Rory's attack on Sergeant Alex, absolutely out of the blue and without any provocation at all? He must have gone mad. And General Sir Jonny had to try to control him, which wasn't easy because Lord Rory had the Sacred Gecko!

Oh. My. God. What happened? Did you actually see it?

Well, no, but I heard about it from the scullery maid, and she knows exactly what happened because the pot-boy overheard three soldiers up in the garrison talking about it afterwards. Absolutely frightful! They say poor Sergeant Alex might die from his wounds. He didn't defend himself, you see, and Lord Rory doesn't know his own strength.

What do you think is going to happen? Will the general have to arrest him? Can he even do that?

Doctor Bethan was weaving her way through the crowd. She signalled to me.

I followed her to the infirmary by the curtain wall. Alex was lying on a mattress. Bethan had tied wooden shafts to his body – splints, she called them. They were, she explained, to help the bones repair themselves correctly. She had applied ointment to the cuts and bruises on his body. His face was mashed and his chest looked deformed; because of the broken ribs, I supposed.

'Will he be all right?'

'Depends what you mean by "all right",' she said shortly. 'He'll live. He won't walk, though.'

'So he'll never be a soldier again?'

'No.'

I'd ruined this man's life, as he had ruined mine, but it gave me no pleasure. Alex was awake, his eyes on me.

'Lord,' he managed to croak. 'Lord, can I talk to you?'

Bethan nodded at me and left the room. I approached Alex's bedside, staying in his line of sight.

He moistened his lips. 'I never touched your woman.'

'Don't lie to me.'

'When you attacked me, I had no idea what I'd done wrong. Doctor Bethan told me it was to do with Lady Kathryn.'

'Lady Kathryn *was* my woman, Alex. We were going to marry. I was told she'd died, but I found out today, only *today,* that I was lied to. She didn't die, but was taken away from her home and sent to a religious order because she was going to have a baby.'

Alex's eyes moved frantically from side to side. 'A baby?'

'Yes, Alex. Yours perhaps. Or mine. We'll never know.'

No resignations

'No, lord. Not mine, I swear it!'

'We'll never know, will we, Alex.'

'I'm sorry, lord.'

'Bit late for that. Still, you'll know better next time you think of shafting another man's woman.'

'There won't be a next time, lord. I can't feel anything below my waist.'

So I had destroyed him. But it was no victory.

Jonny came to me and tendered his resignation as general of my army.

Something fundamental has shifted between Jonny and me. Still, I looked straight at him and I shook my head. 'No resignations.'

32

THIS NEW KYOWN-KINNIE

King Philip sent for me.

'You realise you won a tremendous victory, and then single-handedly destabilised your estate again?' His warrior's instincts were outraged.

'Your Majesty, the matter is finished. My castle is strong.'

He looked unconvinced.

I held my head high. I attacked Alex, and that was personal. The castle reacted, but I dealt with it. There was no need for the King to get involved.

'It is time for us to return to Hicrown,' he said at last. 'We will begin making preparations for your marriage to my daughter, which I intend to be a magnificent occasion. And there must be no more upset in Hambrig. We have beaten the enemy, Lord Rory. Let us make sure it stays that way. *And I do not just mean the Nahvitch.*'

I bowed my head. He was right, of course. The enemy was within our walls. He was unrest, he was mass hysteria, he was malicious gossip. 'You are very wise, sire,' I said with humility, and I meant it.

This new Kyown-Kinnie

An hour later, I mustered my household in the great hall. The King and his daughter, both in their riding gear, made a grand entrance and walked, arm in arm, to the dais.

There was spontaneous applause. We will never forget the way Philip threw himself into the Battle of Baudry Hill, hacking and slashing with his sword, and crashing his warhammer onto countless enemy skulls. He was a giant of a man, and it was his fearless fighting and his indomitable personality that held the castle.

The King and Lady Lillian were on the dais, facing the company.

'Lord Rory, Ladies, Gentlemen and others,' Philip said in a loud voice. 'We thank you for your hospitality towards us. We are leaving for the palace today. As you will know, your lord has pledged to marry Lady Lillian, with which we are delighted, and there is now much to be done to prepare for the grand ceremony. Any who wish to see us off will be most welcome. We shall leave within the hour.'

He got a standing ovation.

In the late afternoon a large group of servants and freemen mustered in the bailey. Eliza led the horses out; they were ready for the long ride back to the palace. Bits and harness chinked and the animals whinnied, anxious to be off. I looked with affection at Netty, the King's mare. She knows me now, and nuzzled her soft nose into my hand. The King mounted and took the reins.

Before the princess stepped onto the mounting block, she turned huge eyes on me. 'My father says we will marry soon, and it cannot be soon enough! I am full of excitement, but also full of sadness that we must be parted until the day of our wedding.' It sounded like a prepared speech, and no doubt Lillian had been coached by the Queen.

THE BOX OF DEATH

I took her hand and kissed it, wishing her godspeed back to Hicrown. *Godspeed to Hicrown, and then stay there, for I have no wish to marry you.* But the King has decreed I shall marry, and I have no choice. And Lillian, when you come to think about it, is the best possible bride for me. A beautiful, young princess who will provide me with a rich dowry and an heir. That's how I must look at it, I told myself.

After vespers, I retrieved the Box of Death and locked it up again in my library. This time, thank God, it had not resulted in a death. And then, having put it off far too long, I sent for Master Kit.

'You're a spy,' I said to him bluntly.

'I was a spy,' he corrected me. 'I have done nothing to endanger you or your household since the night you took me to Hambrig Town to keep my rendezvous with the sheriff. Quite the opposite, in fact. I've cooked for you, chopped firewood for you, run errands for you. I've been nothing but a lowly servant.'

'And yet you are the Duke of Casuel.'

He looked at me in surprise.

'Branca told me. You are a high-born Smanderer. What are you doing in the service of the lord of a small demesne in a country a third the size of yours?'

Kit made a face. 'Yes, I'm a duke. Casuel is a small territory in Smander, so you and I have similar standing in our own countries. You have kept me here, though you sent Branca home. But, apart from during the battle itself, you did not lock me up again. You allowed me my freedom within the castle. Baking bread, chopping wood, fetching butts of wine – I'm repaying a debt.'

Repaying a debt. So he was an honourable spy. 'Do you consider the debt sufficiently repaid?' I asked him.

This new Kyown-Kinnie

'No,' was his surprising reply. 'It is a large debt that I owe you. You will not be aware of the extent of it.'

'Tell me the extent of it.'

'Not yet. But here's some advice: you should show the Hurogol Treaty, *The People's Puzzle* and your map to Peter. He will understand the connection between the three documents.'

I frowned. 'I have already understood it. The treaty explains the boundaries of the Toosanik fiefdoms, I drew them myself on the map. The *People's Puzzle* relates the story of the Great Flood, and laments the loss of those fiefdoms and the loss of the treaty itself.'

'Yes,' Kit said, patiently. 'Look. Because I *do* owe you a great debt, which I will explain to you one day, I'll tell you exactly what I mean. There's more to connect these three documents than you realise. It's good you've drawn the lines on the map. You can see that the Toosanik fiefdoms benefit not just the Toosanik, but yourself and the shire too. The Toosanik will bring their culture, their wealth and their skills to this country. They'll enrich it. It's a tragedy that your King Harold was blind to that. He saw the Toosanik as barbarians, and as a threat. He wouldn't honour the treaty. But others understood what had been lost, and *The Meridian* explains it clearly. The Toosanik need these lands, Rory. We need to reinstate that treaty. You are the only man who can do it.'

I was nonplussed. Why did he care so much? And why would my alchemist understand this deeper connection between the documents?

'Peter will understand because he will read them more carefully than you.' Kit sounded impatient. 'He has a greater eye for detail. Give him all the documents and see what he makes of them.'

'Or you could just tell me yourself,' I suggested drily.

He smiled disarmingly. 'No, Rory, I could not. You will understand once Peter has deciphered the message. As for why I care so much – well, that will also become clear. But do it soon. Peter will need time, and then you will need to act fast.'

It was so cryptic and peculiar that I was inclined to dismiss it as part of his trickery. This was Master Kit all over, making you question yourself, throwing hints here and there, speaking in riddles.

So I said, 'Before I do any of that, you can tell me what you did during the couple of hours when you escaped from the dungeon. If, indeed, you did. And *if* you did, how was it achieved?'

'I went to your chamber and found your keys to the library. I then went up to your library and opened the door, there was nobody guarding it. Inside, I found the Box of Death, and I opened that too. I had a good look inside, and then I locked everything up and left it so you would never know I'd been there. After that I skirted round the curtain wall until I came to the *Egg*. I checked everything there, but I didn't take anything. You have nothing to worry about. I have not damaged or stolen a single thing. I then left the *Egg*, ran back around the curtain wall to the keep and let myself into the dungeon again. Arkyn was very pleased to see me.'

'And you're saying you did all this and no one saw you? Not even the prison guard?'

'Weren't you in the battle? Don't you know what it was like?'

He was right. No one would have been bothering with two insignificant prisoners who were presumed to be securely locked up and out of harm's way.

'But why? And why did you come back? Why not escape properly?'

'That's a lot of questions,' he said reprovingly. 'But I will do you the courtesy of answering them. Why did I escape? Partly to show Arkyn that I could, but mostly to carry out part of my mission. No, I know you don't know what that is. You will, later. Why did I come back? I told you just now. I intend to repay my debt to you before I leave.'

More riddles. His mission, I assume, is to spy on us. 'When you looked in the Box,' I asked him, trying one more time to understand, 'did you see Fiorello? The golden gecko brooch?'

'Yes, of course. Fiorello belongs in the Box of Death.'

I waited, but he said no more. I went on to the real reason I'd sent for him. 'I wanted to see you because I have a job for you, Kit. I want you to find something out for me. No doubt you know why I assaulted Sergeant Alex.'

'You were seeking revenge,' he said promptly. 'Revenge for a wrong he did you many years ago.'

'That's correct. The wrong was grievous.'

'He slept with your wife?'

'She was not my wife, but she would have been. She became pregnant and her family removed her from here and sent her to a convent. I need you to find her.'

'She may be dead. It's been a long time.'

'Find out.' I was watching his face.

'I'll do my best. But I can't do it from here. You'll have to let me leave the castle and travel.'

Well, of course.

'Do you wish to return to Casuel?' I asked finally.

'Not until this is finished.'

I let him go off to make preparations for his journey. He will travel through Mallrovia and beyond, and with my permission he'll take Christopher and Annis with him. As troubadours, they'll find a welcome in every village and hamlet they pass through. It is a good guise, as it was before, and hopefully he'll be able to garner some information about Kathryn. I have given him a month. I also took Kit's advice and immediately gathered together the map, the treaty, *The People's Puzzle* and the ancient document called *A Veehan Loinya*, which Merry had translated as *The Meridian*.

I told Peter what Master Kit had suggested. And I mentioned Merry's peculiar rhetorical questions: *What if only part of this chronicle is ancient? What if some of it has been deliberately made to look very old and important?* The man must have been mad, I decided, and then to take his own life, knowing that would mean eternal damnation? What a bloody waste of scholarship and learning. But Peter's eyes shone at the challenge of discovering a new message, so I piled all the parchments into his arms and he hurried off to his chamber.

After he left, I stayed in my library, just thinking. For it occurred to me then that the hallowed manuscripts must bear a charmed life. Though it took so many years, the ancient treaty and *The Meridian* clearly wanted to be found.

Pretty things hide but they want to be found. Now where did that come from?

———◆———

Having failed in their attempt to take Hambrig and Castle Rory, the surviving Toosanik had fallen back to their camp in Blurland.

But on this Wednesday morning, 23rd May, three Toosanik men sailed across the Hurogol. They were intercepted by a Spiderboat and challenged. They hoisted a white flag and declared they had a message for me. The Spiderboat escorted them to the landing stage; then the whole party set off up the hill to the castle. The Watch reported the sequence of events to Sir Jonny and me, so we were there, waiting for them in the gatehouse arch as they arrived. The Spiderboat crew saluted us and announced the Toosanik men as envoys from the clan.

One man stepped forward and bowed. I bowed to him in return.

'My lord, I have the honour to be the new Kyown-Kinnie of the Toosanik. I hope that henceforward we can have a good relationship with you, and with Hambrig.'

There was more dignified bowing.

I spoke to Gael, hovering by my side. 'Run and let Rachel know we have guests.'

This was a new situation, one I'd never before experienced, and I was unsure what the protocol was. The Toosanik – *the Nahvitch* – had *always* been the enemy. We met only in combat. This sending of envoys, this courteous bowing and formal introducing of dignitaries, made me nervous. I couldn't tell if it was some kind of trick. Even if it were not, I had no idea what they were up to. After all, they were a defeated nation. I'd experienced defeat myself, and the action that Jonny and I took was to get out and get home. Still. Times change. I decided I was prepared to find out how this worked.

So I introduced General Sir Jonny to the Toosanik deputation, and then we all made our stately way across the bailey, into the courtyard and over to the great hall. Wine and sweetmeats awaited us there, and Rachel and her team, all spruced up, were on hand to serve our visitors.

'Are you going to tell them about the treaty?' Jonny asked in an undertone as we walked up to the high table.

'Yes. But not yet.'

He looked to be an intelligent man, but he would need careful handling, this new Kyown-Kinnie.

33

DIPLOMACY

We talked, the elders, Sir Jonny and I. The Kyown-Kinnie began, his diction precise, his delivery slow and careful. 'We know you were defending your land, your castle and your people. We understand you had to fight the Smanderish army and our clansmen, and that to win the fight you had to bring the big ship from the sea to launch flaming missiles at us.'

'That was the *Senjo*,' I explained. 'She is a privateer in my service.'

'She is not a naval vessel?'

'No. But her captain has my letter of marque.'

'She fired her murderous weapon under your orders?'

'That is correct, Kyown-Kinnie.'

He pressed his hands together and seemed to be thinking. This new Kyown-Kinnie is very different from the old one. He's tall and dignified, with ruler-straight, iron-grey hair and aquiline features. He looks like one of the ancient Roman emperors. He sat silently by my side, sipping mead, for quite a while.

Finally, he said, 'Where is the *Senjo* now?'

'She has gone back to sea.'

'And where is Branca, your former marshal?'

That was unexpected. But I was truthful. 'She's gone to Smander to find me a horse.'

The Kyown-Kinnie raised his eyebrows at that. 'A horse! Well, you are a Hambrig warlord, of course you must have a horse. Celtic people do not ride much.'

'No?' I said politely.

'We walk. We walk for miles. Walking keeps us fit and strong.' He certainly looked fit and strong.

I spoke carefully to him. 'I am delighted to receive you at Castle Rory. But, Kyown-Kinnie, I am wondering why you have come.'

His face became serious. 'We are the proud and ancient Toosanik. We are the Swamp-People, but we need better land for farming and raising livestock. There was a treaty between your people and mine once, but it has been lost. This treaty explained where the Toosanik were allowed to live. In return, our warriors swore oaths of fealty to the Lord of Hambrig.'

'Not the Lord of Hambrig,' I broke in. 'There was no castle then, and no lord. The oaths were sworn to a knight whose fief this was.'

'I thought so. The treaty has been found and you have seen it. Is it in the castle?'

'It is in the castle, Kyown-Kinnie. But one of my scholars is looking at it even as we speak. He is searching for meaning.'

'The meaning is clear enough,' said the Kyown-Kinnie sharply.

'There are other documents. Documents that need to be examined in full. They have only just come to light.'

Diplomacy

The Kyown-Kinnie looked at his henchmen, and there was a whispered conversation between them.

'Which documents are these, my lord?' The Kyown-Kinnie turned back to me, leaning his elbow on the table, something we in the castle would never do. 'Could you possibly be speaking of *A Veehan Loinya, The Meridian*?'

'Yes. It has just been found.' The statement sounded too bald, and I knew it even as I said it.

'Found? Where, exactly, was it found?'

'It was found in a box.'

But they wanted to know what box it was in, how we found it, every detail – and the only thing I wanted to tell them was this: *You threw the box away. We came upon it in a puddle in the swamp. You did not want the box, yet it had a secret compartment which held your special historical document. Oh, the Toosanik are a proud and ancient people! But they snap their fingers at the proud and ancient document that details their history!*

Of course, I said none of this out loud.

The Kyown-Kinnie and his elders looked angrily at me. My disdain must have shown in my face. Perhaps I hadn't learnt the art of diplomacy after all. But when the Kyown-Kinnie spoke, his tone was mild. 'The document is very precious to us. It was made here in Hambrig, did you know that?'

I leant forward. 'What do you actually know about it, Kyown-Kinnie? Do you know who wrote it and why? Do you know anything about the box it was found in?'

Again, the three looked at each other, as if wondering how much they should reveal. Words in their strange language of Okkam passed between them, the conversation flowing like water, words merging, blurring, sounds that could drug you to sleep. I tried to work out if they were disagreeing with each other, but couldn't be sure. Finally, the Kyown-Kinnie turned to me again.

'I apologise, my lord, but we needed to confer. We do know about this document, *The Meridian*, but before we can speak of it, we should like to talk with a man who lives in your town of Hambrig. His name is Master Anthony Merry. Can you arrange a meeting?'

I shook my head. 'I am sorry, Kyown-Kinnie, but that won't be possible. Master Merry is dead. He took his own life.'

At that, there was consternation among the Toosanik. There were gestures, expressions of shock, and a torrent of Okkam flowed rapidly around the three of them. I waited patiently.

'This is distressing news for us,' the Kyown-Kinnie said at last. 'It is going to force us to trust you with further information. Can we go somewhere more private?'

I took them up to my library, and sent for extra seats for my guests. We sat in a circle, just the four of us. I had dismissed Gael long since, and Jonny had gone to see Alex.

'We know the treaty gives us land on this side of the River Hurogol,' the Kyown-Kinnie began, and I was pleased he got straight to the point. 'And we know you have the treaty. But we did not know it until just now, and that is why we asked to see Master Merry.'

'You thought Merry had the treaty?' I could think of no other reason for their wanting to speak with him.

'No, we thought the treaty was lost forever, but we have been told that Master Merry knew the terms of the treaty, and that he wrote them down in a coded document. Our intention was to ask him to show us the document.'

'Let me get this straight,' I said. 'You want to invoke the

treaty, but before you do that, you want to know what it says. Is that right?'

'We know what it says.' The Kyown-Kinnie corrected me patiently. 'We have always known. But we thought we would have to prove it to you. If you already have the treaty, then you also know its terms.'

The Toosanik chief put his hands together against his lips, sat back in his chair and regarded me over the tips of his fingers.

'I've seen and read the treaty, Kyown-Kinnie,' I conceded. 'I've also seen and read Master Merry's coded document. It describes the Great Flood. I have seen *The Meridian* too. But I do not have the Okkam, so I did not understand it.'

'We should like to see these three important documents,' the Kyown-Kinnie said, predictably.

'I've already told you that one of my household, a very well educated and talented man, is currently perusing them. You will have to wait until he has finished.'

'We will wait.'

'How do you know of Master Merry and his codes?' I asked.

He gave me a strange look. 'How do I know? Master Merry is – no, *was* – married to a clanswoman. Her name was Diane. Before she died, many years ago, she told us of her husband's work. He was very sympathetic to our plight at the time of the Great Flood and afterwards. He wrote the history of our people, and he had the treaty and this history in his possession. I cannot understand why he would want to kill himself. Do you know the answer to that, my lord?'

But there was much to unpick here. 'First of all, Kyown-Kinnie, the treaty was never in Merry's possession. It was held at all times by your royal family, the latest member of which was Princess Eefa. She had it on her person when she was abducted from your predecessor's hut. It was found later. Secondly, Merry killed himself to avoid being hanged for the murder of your princess.'

'Princess Eefa was *murdered*?' The three Toosanik stood up in agitation. I told them the sad story of how Eefa had rejected Merry's advances, and how he had poisoned her, just as her son was about to be born. They were appalled.

'If it hadn't been for the Lady Joan of Hambrig, Sammy would also have died,' I stressed to them.

'We watched Prince Sammy ride away with the captain of the *Senjo*,' one of the elders said sourly. 'You have sent him to sea, yet he belongs to us.'

'Captain William is the son of Master Merry and the Lady Joan,' I explained. 'Captain William will look after Sammy and will bring him back safely in a few years' time. When Sammy returns, he will be fit to be your prince.'

The Kyown-Kinnie nodded, and there was warmth in his eyes for the first time. 'I see you are a wise leader, my lord. It was a good decision to send Sammy with William.'

'Tell me about *The Meridian*,' I said again. 'Why was it written, and by whom?'

'Do you understand why it is called *The Meridian*?' asked the Kyown-Kinnie.

I tried to recall what the Lady Joan had told me. 'Something to do with pathways for diseases?'

'Our medicine men tell us that both good health and diseases travel along lines that run through the body,' the Kyown-Kinnie explained. 'And these lines are called meridians. When you are sick, it is because a meridian has been interrupted or damaged in some way. So the disease takes hold. *A Veehan Loinya* is a chronicle of our people and their collective pathway, which has never been free from interruption and damage, but which has somehow survived and recovered itself time after time, much as an individual will do after healing hands have passed over the corrupted meridian.

'It was written by an unknown scribe around the time of your King Harold I, about one hundred and thirty years ago. It is a precious manuscript, firstly because it is so old and it tells our history, and secondly because it works with the Hurogol Treaty to describe the territories we once occupied in Hambrig. It is not unlike the English Domesday Book.'

'I see,' I said. '*The Meridian* was found in a special box which Master Merry made for his daughter. I don't know how the Box made its way from Merry's house to your side of the river, but it came back with Prince Barney. Somehow it got back to the swamps again though, because we found it abandoned there.'

And Merry had shown me the secret compartment, which housed both *The Meridian* and Fiorello, but I didn't mention that to the Toosanik elders.

I was still puzzling over the strange way the Box seemed to move from one side of the River Hurogol to the other without anyone knowing anything about it, when there was a sudden hammering on the door and Peter burst into the library. He was waving a clutch of parchments, and he hastily bowed to me, but he was already speaking as he straightened up again.

'Lord Rory! I've done it! I know what t' secrets are, I know t' cipher, I've done what tha wanted!' I think he scarcely noticed the other three men in the room.

With trembling hands, Peter laid his documents out on my desk. 'This one is t' treaty,' he said reverently, his hand resting lovingly on its surface.

The Toosanik had moved near and were crowded

around the desk. We all jostled for position, trying to see what Peter was showing us.

'This one is *The People's Puzzle.*' He put his other hand flat on top of the *Puzzle,* almost as if he owned it. 'This third one is *The Meridian,* and it appears to be a very old document. Finally, here we have a drawing or map of Hambrig, on which Lord Rory has added chalk lines to show t' boundaries of t' Toosanik territories as defined by t' treaty. And now,' he added, in the manner of a magician about to do some extraordinary trick, '*now* I have some scraps of parchment on which I've worked everything out!' And he dived into the breast of his tunic and pulled out another great wad of documents, covered in scrawl. 'Permit me to show you how it all fits together!'

At that moment, outside and below us, someone blew the horn for dinner. People would be trooping into the great hall, and the kitchen servants would be busy passing food around, serving ale and wine and keeping everybody fed and watered. But up in my library, with the door shut against the cold and the wind, the only things that mattered were the manuscripts that lay enticingly on my old oak desk. There were five of us in the room, and it felt crowded. I briefly introduced everyone and suggested we all sit. Peter could then show us the documents in the manner of a presentation, explaining his findings to all of us at once.

'That way,' I said persuasively, 'you, the Toosanik, hear everything at the same time as I do. We will all have the answers together.'

The Toosanik, agreeing, sat down. And *that*, I decided, was diplomacy.

34

I KNOW WHERE IT'S BURIED

'My Lord Rory, honoured Kyown-Kinnie and gentlemen, I present a history of t' Toosanik, a proud an' ancient people!'

Peter flourished *The Meridian* at us.

'This chronicle were written more than hundred year ago. 'Tis t' year 1129, and t' first King Henry is on t' throne of England. Here in Mallrovia, King Harold t' First rules t' land. T' Toosanik clan live on t' shores of t' River Hurogol. Their territory is part of t' country of Mallrovia, in t' shire of Hambrig, but they have a long-standin' workin' agreement with t' lord of the estate, a knight who lives in t' Manor House in Hambrig Town. This wonderful book, *The Meridian*, were created to give detailed information about t' Toosanik land. It tells us who's livin' where, and exactly how many cows and sheep he owns, an' how much land he can take care of, for you see, crofters don't own their land, they rent it from t' landowner, Sir Rory of Hambrig.

'Now, we must jump exactly one hundred year on. 'Tis t' year 1229. *The Meridian* is in t' possession of a notable Hambrigger by t' name of Master Anthony Merry. Merry is a renowned scholar in his mid-thirties. He reads Latin and Greek fluently, and he's obsessed with collectin' original historical manuscripts. Anthony is married to a Toosanik woman. Her name is Diane, an' she's t' daughter of t' then Kyown-Kinnie. They have been married for five year, and Diane is expectin' their first child. To celebrate both the imminent arrival of his child, an' t' centenary of *The Meridian*, Anthony decides to write some more of it. He tries to blend his new narrative in with the original by colourin' the parchment. He wants his additional pages to look t' same as those that are hundred year old.

'First, Master Merry comments on t' title of t' book, observing that t' word "meridian" is a significant one to t' Toosanik. In the Okkam language, the expression is *A Veehan Loinya*. This literally means "The Middle Line", but Anthony, who writes in English, translates it as "The Meridian". You may be wonderin' how I've managed to read t' book at all, since originally it were entirely in t' Okkam. Well, Master Merry provides a direct translation! Merry explains that t' Toosanik use a form of "Meridian Healing", in which they believe there are twelve pathways running through t' body, an' these pathways, or meridians, carry life an' energy. The energy needs to flow freely. When inhibited in any way, t' person becomes ill. But you can heal them by treating t' correct meridian.

'Merry observes that you can see the whole Toosanik history as a giant meridian, whose energy were cut off by a terrible happenin' in t' year 1159. In that year an enormous tidal wave surged up t' River Hurogol an' engulfed t' Toosanik, their land, their crops, their animals – everythin'. Nay, not quite everythin'! For some of t' Toosanik, includin' their king and queen, managed to escape t' flood. They scrambled onto higher ground and somehow made it across t' border into Westador, thence to t' south of England, across the sea into France and Spain an' finally into Smander, whence many of them had originated. Meanwhile, says Merry, the Hambriggers were also fleeing for their lives, an' *they* climbed to t' top of Baudry Hill. They were only just in time, for soon t' water were lappin' at t' bottom of t' hill, an' there could be no escape now until it receded.

'On top o' the hill, one man took control: Rory, lord of t' manor. Of course this weren't the same Rory who's mentioned in *The Meridian* itself. This were his son, who had t' same name. He organised the Hambriggers into work parties, an' they made shelters in t' woodland on the eastern slopes of the hill. Gradually, t' flood waters went down, an' eventually t' survivin' Hambriggers could return to t' town.

'But t' town had been devastated! A huge amount o' repair work were needed, and of t' Toosanik, there were no sign. It were as if they had never been. Over a period of time, it became clear that many of t' Toosanik did survive t' Great Flood, but they were swept into t' river, and though many drowned, others were washed up in t' swamplands called Blurland. Eventually, they tried to return. The lord of t' manor wanted to welcome them back, but there were a new king o' Mallrovia, an' King Harold the Second decreed that t' Toosanik were *not* to return.

'A rough path were constructed, leading to t' top o' Baudry Hill, an' a castle were built there. This castle would withstand attack, provide vital lookout posts, an' be a safe haven for t' people of Hambrig, if ever one should be needed again. It would be Sir Rory's home, and now he would be known as Lord Rory of Hambrig. It took eight year to build t' castle, an' it were finished in t' year 1168.

'Now, t' Toosanik, desperate to regain their territory, sent more envoys to King Harold, but all were turned away, for the ancient treaty had been lost in t' flood. T' King would not agree to drawin' up a new treaty, and so t' Toosanik declared war on Hambrig. They renamed themselves "the enemy" – t' *Nahvitch*. Soon people forgot they were ever called t' Toosanik.

'All this is explained clearly in the additional notes to *The Meridian*, meticulously penned by Anthony Merry. He gets his information from various sources. He already has histories, written by scholarly Hambriggers of the day. He has no Toosanik perspective, though, until Diane comes into his life. As t' daughter of t' Kyown-Kinnie, she has been brought up on Toosanik history. From early childhood, she listened to t' storytellers and t' bards lamenting the exile of t' Toosanik, telling o' t' Great Flood, wondering at t' fate o' the Hurogol Treaty. She knows t' royal family decamped to Smander. But, like everyone else, she wonders why they never returned to rule their people once t' danger were over. But t' king and queen were never heard of again, an' t' Toosanik learnt to live without a ruling dynasty. The Kyown-Kinnie became all-powerful, an' he took on the role of king.'

The Toosanik elders sat impassively through all this. I hoped they weren't too bamboozled by Peter's Yorkshire accent, and perhaps they knew everything already, but much of it was new to me, and I was spellbound. I found myself wishing that Hambrig had a document like Domesday or *The Meridian*, but as far as I know, there is none. I got up, asking Peter to pause until I'd lit some candles.

The candlelight brightened the room, and Peter continued with his story. 'Now we must move forward again, my lord, Kyown-Kinnie an' gentlemen. 'Tis t' year 1234, a year which some of us can even remember! Our present lord is only five year old, still being nannied by t' women of t' castle. His father, t' third Lord Rory, runs t' shire. Down in the town, Anthony Merry is writing another book. He has already written two enormous volumes – *The Book of Truth* and *The Book of Wisdom*. These weighty tomes have not been well received, an' few have read them. They aren't easy to read, being full of Latin exhortations an' lectures in ancient Greek. He decides to write something more accessible to t' common man and woman. He makes this plain in t' title he gives his new work: *The People's Puzzle*. It's for t' *people* you see, *ordinary* people. At least, Merry hopes everyone will understand t' title in that way. But t' truth is, t' title d'n't mean that at all. Merry enjoys codes an' riddles, and his booklet is called *The People's Puzzle* because it is t' puzzle *of* a people. Remember t' line? *The Toosanik are a proud and ancient people.* T' Toosanik are t' people whose puzzle Merry sets out. It's not one puzzle, but many puzzles. There is t' fact that t' pamphlet is in code. So that's t' first puzzle. But within t' code is a second code, and this second code has only just been unlocked. 'Tis a code which accesses a hiding place, an' tells a fascinating story, an' I'll reveal more about that later. So that is t' second puzzle. Then, there is t' whereabouts of the Hurogol Treaty to be determined, and also that of *The Meridian,* the original Domesday Book of t' Toosanik clan.

'To understand all this, you have to get inside Anthony Merry's mind. 'Tisn't just our Lord Rory who is a five-year-old at this time. You see, Merry an' his wife, Diane, now have their little girl. She were born at the same time as Lord Rory, even to t' day, an' so she is also just five year old when her father begins to write *The People's Puzzle*. Merry adores his daughter. She is his whole world. But she is sickly. When she were born it were thought she would not live. She somehow manages to survive infancy, but she dies at the age o' ten. T' child's name is Hope, an Merry buries his daughter in a special place. Diane is heartbroken at Hope's death, an' she has also become very ill.

'Merry finishes writing *The People's Puzzle*, in which he continues the history of t' Toosanik, using Diane's memories and storytelling to guide him. He describes t' flood and what happens to t' Toosanik, very similar to his additional narrative in *The Meridian*. T' full name of t' booklet is *The People's Puzzle or The Meridian, a Columnar Approach*. Merry explains his play on words using his wife's name: Diane Merry becomes Merry Diane, and from there Meridian. It seems that before Diane became seriously ill, she were a playful, fun person to be with, truly a Merry Diane. Not only does he use these two names for his booklet, but he gives his readers a colossal clue as to t' code he's using to write it. Well, if you know owt about ciphers you'll have heard of t' column cipher. 'Tis an extremely simple one, an' even a child can decode it. But that's t' point, you see. Merry wants his readers to decode t' puzzle and try to understand what happened to t' Toosanik. He even offers a great reward to whoever manages t' decodin'. I think Merry assumes his little booklets will fly off t' shelf an Hambriggers everywhere will spend t' long winter evenings enjoyin' the challenge he's set them.'

Peter stood up a little straighter, and I sensed he was about to make his great declamation, the climax of the whole sorry tale. I glanced sidelong at the Kyown-Kinnie, but his face gave nothing away.

'Lord Rory, Kyown-Kinnie an' gentlemen,' Peter announced, 'sadly for Master Merry t' plan fails at t' very start, for absolutely nobody buys t' book. Merry is angry. He d'n't understand that people di'n't like his other books, so they won't be flockin' to read this one. He's furious no one cares enough to even *try* to solve his puzzle. In the meantime, Diane is becoming sicker and sicker, an' it's clear she won't recover. She knows this to be t' case, an' she tells Merry he must do something for her, for *them*. They have a servant woman in their household, a Toosanik woman that Diane brought with her when she crossed t' river to marry Anthony. Diane tells her husband he must sleep with t' servant and he must get her pregnant. Diane wants Merry to have another child. She tells him it will be a new beginning. This child must be strong an' healthy, an' half Hambrigger, half Toosanik, as Hope was. Diane tells Merry that Hambrig must welcome t' Toosanik back, an' a child who is half an' half will be the symbol of this new beginnin' for everybody.'

Peter's voice dropped in volume, and he put his scrappy parchments down on my desk. He didn't need them – he knew what was coming. The Toosanik didn't know, though. They were leaning forwards, their eyes fixed on Peter's face. I wondered at Merry having a child with Diane, a child with the Lady Joan, and now a child with this Toosanik servant. He hadn't managed to seduce Eefa, though.

'Merry is terrified,' Peter told us, his Yorkshire voice hushed now. 'He's terrified this child will also sicken an' die, an' then there will be no new beginnin', and he will have failed his beloved Diane. T' servant woman tells him that her people were originally from Smander, far away in north-western Iberia. Smander has a warm climate an' people thrive there. Merry decides to send the pregnant girl to Smander. She may find some of her family, an' she's to have her baby there. But t' journey to Smander is long an' difficult. Merry is now in his mid-forties an' he is a scholar, not a fit or active man. He is not used to askin' for help, but he's desperate, so he climbs Baudry Hill to t' castle and approaches his lord. Our Lord Rory is now eleven year old and he's been sent to be a pageboy in t' palace in Hicrown, so he will have no memory of this.'

The Toosanik all looked at me and I shook my head; my father never mentioned any of this to me. I motioned to Peter to continue.

'Merry swallows his pride. He begs for a military escort for t' Toosanik girl. He is truthful an' explains everythin'. Lord Rory is sympathetic, perhaps because Merry has been honest, an' he arranges for an armed escort to travel to Smander with t' pregnant woman. A year later, t' escort returns, havin' successfully delivered t' girl to Santiago das Cunchas, t' capital city o' Smander. Merry never sees his child, although word gets through to him eventually that he has a healthy son. He also finds out that t' Toosanik woman has gained employment, in t' royal palace, no less, and her baby will be brought up with the little Smanderish princesses. He is content. He may never see his son, but he knows he has one, and that t' lad is growin' and thriving. T' servant woman knows t' terms of t' deal. When her son is old enough, he is to carry out a set of instructions, devised by Diane before she died. This new beginnin', so carefully crafted, *has* to come to fruition. Here, in Hambrig, Merry waits for his son to grow to manhood an' come home.

'All of this is in t' sub-code, t' one that's hidden. Merry intends his readers to make rapid sense of his clumsy columnar cipher, but he does not want them to understand t' second code. I will tell you that it has taken me many long hours to work it out. T' cipher is called *tabula recta*. 'Tis a simple enough encryption, apart from t' fact that you need a particular keyword. To decode t' text, you need to know what keyword were used when t' text were originally encrypted. That were my problem. At first, I had no idea

I know where it's buried

which cipher were being used, although 'twas clear there *were* a second coded message.

'To be honest, I mostly used guesswork at this stage. I tried one cipher after another, an' you very quickly know if what you're doin' is makin' any sense, but t' problem is there's so many to try. And not only that, *many* ciphers require a keyword. Even t' columnar cipher needed a keyword, but that were easy, because Merry were careful to point t' way. So t' keyword for t' columnar cipher were simply "The Meridian". Obviously, I tried using t' same keyword in t' *tabula recta,* but that yielded no results. I tried Merry's name, and then various place names. I will tell you the keyword 'e used, because it is significant.

'You may be thinkin' that t' first keyword I mentioned, "The Meridian", is not one word but two. You're right o' course, but encoders don't care about that. You simply remove t' spaces between words in t' phrase and it all runs together as one word. And that is what I also had to do for t' keyword in t' *tabula recta*. After many, many failed attempts, I finally tried using "Box of Death", an' bingo! T' letters fell into place, an' I had a plain text story in front of me, the story I have just related to you all.'

Had it been necessary to give so much detail of this decoding? Probably not, but the man had got into his stride, and the Toosanik were hanging on his words. I shifted slightly to get more comfortable in my chair, and Peter, who'd noticed nothing, carried on.

'Now, that set me thinking. Why would Merry use "Box of Death" as t' keyword for his cipher? I was under the impression that we here in t' castle coined t' phrase when t' young prince brought t' Box back from Blurland. We thought there were a live an' dangerous lizard inside it, and so we called it t' "Box of Death". But I were wrong. This Box

THE BOX OF DEATH

has been in existence for some time. In fact, it were constructed for little Hope Merry, when she were a small child. She kept things inside it, as bairns do, and when she knew she were dyin', she made a collection of her favourite toys an' books an' stored them in t' box. *She* made up the expression "Box of Death"; she thought it were funny! Merry explains all this in *The Meridian's* additional pages, so his readers will understand why t' Box were buried, and what was to be found inside it.'

'Hope asked her father to bury t' Box with her after her death. An' that is exactly what he did. An' part of t' double-encrypted text I managed to work out, were t' clue to where Hope Merry is buried, along with her Box. But that's not all. Merry had made t' Box himself, an' into it he built a secret compartment, which is under a false bottom. I don't believe he told Hope about t' secret space, I think that were just for him. When he buried his daughter, he put *The Meridian,* the original chronicle, into that secret compartment.

'An' then, he buried yet a *third* thing. He buried his treasure. Anthony Merry accumulated a great deal of wealth in his life. He di'n't spend much, preferring a simple lifestyle to a grand one. His fortune came partly from his wife's magnificent dowry, for after all, she were t' Kyown-Kinnie's daughter, but mostly from dealin' in gold, silver and precious jewels. He were a jeweller by trade, t' same as his father, an' he bought an' sold in quantity. Aye, Anthony Merry were rich, though he had no need of his wealth. This, then, were the reward tha would get if tha decoded t' text, went to t' burial site that's described in *The People's Puzzle* and dug up t' Box of Death. If tha then opened t' special compartment tha'd find *The Meridian,* and in the additional pages of *this* document tha'd know exactly where to look for

I know where it's buried

Anthony Merry's great hoard of treasure. But first tha had to read *The People's Puzzle*. An' nobody did.'

Peter fell silent, blinking at us. He'd reached the end of his presentation. The Toosanik all sat back with a collective sigh. I thought Peter had done a magnificent job, and I knew I could never have worked all that out. But, for me, one thing stood out above everything else.

I looked at the Yorkshireman. 'You know where the treasure is buried?'

'Aye, lord. I know where it's buried.'

35

I INTEND TO FIND TREASURE

The *great reward*. It really existed.

'What an astonishing story,' I declared to the room in general. I felt Peter should have at the very least a round of applause, but the Toosanik elders were sitting still, seemingly waiting for more. I ploughed on. 'Peter, you've dealt with the Hurogol Treaty, *The Meridian* and *The People's Puzzle,* but what about the fourth document? The map.'

''Tis a fine drawing, an' a good representation of the estate. With t' treaty beside thee, tha was able to mark in the old Toosanik territory.' Peter stopped there.

'And?' I asked.

'An' what, lord? That's it.'

'Fiorello is death to those he looks upon,' I said pointedly. 'Only a person of great courage will open the box, but if such a one can be found, a great reward will be his. This message comes from Hope, Endurance and a New Beginning.'

Peter looked at me askance. 'Why art tha quotin' that message from t' Toosanik, lord?'

I intend to find treasure

'Because it's clearly *not* from the Toosanik. Merry must have written it himself. Don't you see? *This message comes from Hope, Endurance and a New Beginning.* His wife said the new baby would *be* a new beginning. Hope was his first child. And Diane herself symbolised Endurance, clinging on to life until she knew there was going to be another mixed-race baby.'

The Kyown-Kinnie stood up. 'In the Okkam language, which is *our* language, we use trees to stand for letters of the alphabet. The first letter in the Okkam alphabet is *bayha,* which means the birch tree. Each tree has a meaning according to our Moon Calendar, in which there are thirteen months. *Bayha* is the first month of this calendar. This tree is the Guardian of New Beginnings, the Bringer of Hope and the Stronghold of Endurance. That is the meaning of *bayha*, the letter B in the Okkam. The birch tree symbolises all three: hope, endurance and new beginnings. This will be the hiding place of which Master Peter spoke. This is where you will find Master Merry's gold!'

'And it's where the Toosanik Meeting Place was in the old days,' I said slowly, seeing the map in my mind's eye and picturing my rough chalk outlines.

The Kyown-Kinnie turned to me. 'That is why we chose that place, my lord. Hope, endurance and new beginnings – do you not see the significance for our people?'

I saw it. What's more, judging by their faces, so did everyone else.

'*Croov-Bayha,*' continued the Kyown-Kinnie. '*Croov-Bayha.* It means birch tree. For us, it means everything. For our clan, it is the *Crann Tara*, the Fiery Cross. When you hear the cry of *Croov-Bayha,* you must respond. It is our call to arms. There is a rune for it, and it is this.' The Kyown-Kinnie dipped a hazel twig in the ash of the fire and drew a huge sign on the stone wall. I recognised it at once: a long, straight vertical line with a small horizontal line at the bottom for its base, a little cap at the top, and a short, straight horizontal line projecting just below the cap. The rune for the birch tree, carved many times into the lid of the Box of Death. And it represented, not death by poison, but new life.

'Wherever you see this sign,' the Kyown-Kinnie declared, looking round at everyone as he spoke, 'if ever you see this rune, you will know that either you are on our land or that we have been there before you. If you hear the call to arms, the cry of *Croov-Bayha,* you will know that the clan is running with spears and knives, running to the Meeting Place and to the birch tree, for there is a battle to be fought.'

'And what of Fiorello?' I asked suddenly. '*Fiorello is death to those he looks upon.* Who made the poisoned brooch? And why? Do we know that, Peter?'

Peter scanned through his notes, frantically turning pages, and quite a few floated to the floor. 'There is a mention of t' gecko, lord,' he muttered, and then triumphantly drew one page out and waved it at me.

'Aye! I *knew* 'twas here! This is from *The Meridian*, and it's from the original part of t' book, not the additional pages Merry put in later.'

He traced some lines of his own tiny writing with one finger, and then began to read aloud. '"We have in this month found a thing that is most unusual and could be of great use in time of war. Under the hedgerow that forms the northern border of the Great Plain we found a poisonous reptile. This reptile, or speckled lizard, was living there, unbeknownst to anyone, Toosanik or Hambrigger. We have taken the lizard and we will take care of it until we need to use both it and its venom on our enemies. Fiorello!" That

I intend to find treasure

entry were apparently made by a person calling himself Fyoonlak the Wise, although Master Merry's translation is somewhat confused at this point.'

'Let me see this,' the Kyown-Kinnie said to Peter.

Peter glanced at me, and I nodded.

The Kyown-Kinnie looked, not at Merry's translation, but at the original Okkam written down more than one hundred and thirty years ago. The other elders crowded round, but the Kyown-Kinnie waved them away. He made them sit, and then he read to them from the original. There was much nodding of heads and pursing of lips among the three of them, and then, unexpectedly, a roar of laughter.

'What is it?' I asked impatiently. 'What is so funny?'

'It is Anthony Merry's translation,' explained the Kyown-Kinnie. 'Look at this word, my lord.'

I looked, but to me it was just a few sticks and lines, totally meaningless.

'This word says *jairthk*. *Jairthk* has more than one meaning. It can mean a speckled lizard or other reptile. It can also mean a berry. Here, it means that berries were found growing in the northern hedgerow. Fyoonlak, the scribe, was intrigued. One, because these berries had not been seen here before; and two, because he discovered they were poisonous. He makes a fanciful suggestion that they could become a weapon of war, but after that he adds the word *Fiorello!*'

'Which means?'

'Well, the word *fior* can mean 'extremely', but then there's usually another word following it. For example, *fior-vla* means "extremely warm", and *fior-gleek* means "extremely wise". But the word *fior* on its own just means "true". Our scribe is trying to be witty. He fancies himself as a comedian, so he writes *Fiorello!* He's put a silly, Latin-sounding ending on the word *fior*. So first he says these berries will make a great weapon if ever we are at war. And then he says, "It's the truth!" or, "As if!" He knows no one fights a war with berries, however poisonous they may be. He's having a laugh.'

I sat back in my chair with a bump. A mis-translation, that's all it was. Berries. Berries in the hedge. And *Fiorello*? Just some long-dead scribe trying to be funny. I wondered at Merry's command of the Okkam. 'Do you think Merry translated *jairthk* as "lizard" because he didn't know the word also meant "berry"? Or do you think he was having a laugh of his own, Kyown-Kinnie?'

The Kyown-Kinnie shook his head. 'We shall never know, my lord. The man is dead by his own hand. But either is possible. You knew him, and I did not. What do *you* think?'

I thought about it, and found I could not honestly say that I *did* know the man.

The Kyown-Kinnie was speaking again. 'Do not look so crestfallen, Peter of Redmire. You did your best, and you could only go by the translation, not having the Okkam yourself.'

It was true, but Peter looked gutted. I started the applause then. I had the fullest admiration for him and his patient, meticulous combing of the documents, working out the ciphers and doing his best to understand the man behind the puzzle. Getting to my feet, I told him so, as everyone joined in with genuine praise, and Peter blinked in astonishment.

But for now, all I could think was – *there it is, crystal clear at last*. I deduced that Merry created the gecko brooch himself, using the mis-translation, whether accidental or deliberate, as inspiration. He found the poison to put

I intend to find treasure

behind the eyes of the ornament, and he hid it in his daughter's Box of Death, so now it would really live up to the name Hope had given it. Merry was a master jeweller. He worked daily with precious metals and beautiful stones. He would have made his *Fiorello* as beautiful and as deadly as he knew how. Whether this was some kind of private joke against the long-ago man who wrote *The Meridian,* or whether it was a genuine attempt to fulfil a prophecy he thought had been made, we will never know. It is odd to think that Anthony Merry, that shy oddball, was at the bottom of everything. He created the *Sacred Gecko of the Nahvitch*, a creature that never actually existed. A legend started because of him, a fire that was fuelled by the previous Kyown-Kinnie giving the Box of Death, with its strange notification, to Prince Barney.

Peter was thinking about that too. He was saying, 'So 'twere Anthony Merry who wrote t' letter that t' Kyown-Kinnie gave to t' prince, the one that said Fiorello is death if he looks upon thee. How did the old Kyown-Kinnie have the letter in t' first place?'

'*That* isn't the question, Peter of Redmire,' the new Kyown-Kinnie told him. 'No, what we need to ask ourselves is this: how did my people acquire the Box of Death? The Box of Death was buried with Merry's daughter, Hope. It was buried under the birch tree on the Great Plain. Inside the Box were many things Hope had loved and that she had wanted to keep with her for always. But she did not know about the secret compartment her father had made in the Box. He had placed *The Meridian* in there. But what of the gecko ornament he had made, complete with the liquid poison behind its eyes? That would have been placed in the *main* compartment. After his daughter's death, Anthony Merry wrote the cryptic note, intended to be read by the person who dug up the Box. And that person would only do so if they had solved *The People's Puzzle.*'

I caught my breath. He had hit the nail on the head, this tall man with the intelligent face. The note would have been inside the Box of Death, buried with Hope under the birch tree, and would be found, so Merry assumed, by the first person to decode the *Puzzle*. When that person read the note, he would realise that the gecko's eyes were dangerous, but that there was great wealth to be found if he had the determination to look for the booklet that was hidden, a booklet written in 1129, but added to by Anthony Merry exactly one hundred years later to celebrate the birth of his daughter.

This information lay on the table in front of me. I had only to open *The Meridian* and read Merry's extra pages. Then I would know exactly where the treasure was buried. But too many people surrounded me, so I left the parchments untouched.

'Peter of Redmire, you have decoded and understood everything,' the Kyown-Kinnie was saying. 'It is for you to dig up Master Merry's treasure. You will be a very rich man.'

'Oh nay, nay.' Peter was flustered. 'Nay, Kyown-Kinnie, sir, I have no wish to be a rich man. I want nowt more than my books an' my work here at t' castle, an' Lord Rory has been so kind to me, so generous. I wish to continue to serve him in any way I can.'

I needed to act fast, and I remembered Kit telling me so. Everyone had heard that Merry's treasure was buried, probably under the birch tree as the Kyown-Kinnie had said, although only Peter knew for sure. I stood up abruptly, gathered up all four documents in one sweep of my arms, an indication to the Toosanik that our meeting was at an end.

'Master Peter, I fear we have missed dinner,' I said, 'and

I intend to find treasure

our guests will be hungry. Please escort them to the hall and ask Rachel to serve them a meal. I will join you there shortly.'

The three Toosanik men preceded Peter out of my library. I listened to their feet echoing on the stone steps that lead down to the courtyard. Then I dumped the bundle of parchments on my ancient desk again and threw myself back into my chair. It was all very hard to take in. In particular, I was trying to get my head around the fact that Anthony Merry deliberately created *Fiorello, the Sacred Gecko of the Nahvitch*, that mythical creature which terrorised us for nearly forty years. And it had never existed. This man had held our entire country to ransom.

But he had severely overestimated the average Hambrigger. He laid his careful trail to his treasure, crafting his wooden box with its runic decorations and its false bottom, and attempting to lead his readers to it via a coded pamphlet. He must have thought the entire town would be fascinated, motivated by the money to give it their best shot. So why didn't they? I guessed it was Merry himself who put them off, together with the boring, lecturing books he'd already written. Add to that the fact the pamphlets weren't given away – you had to *buy* your copy. Presumably, Hambriggers didn't want to part with their cash unless they were sure of finding the gold. I sympathised. We're not all scholarly types like Merry.

I locked up the documents in the bottom drawer of my chest. But before I did so, I checked in *The Meridian* to find the location of the treasure, and was greatly surprised by what I read. After that, I went down to the hall where a hot meal was being enthusiastically consumed by the Toosanik. The servants were all off-duty by now, but Peter was helping out and the atmosphere was friendly. This must have been the first time anyone from the Nahvitch tribe, as we used to call them, had eaten a meal in the great hall in Castle Rory. An historic occasion, and I knew I must let Patrick know to record it properly.

Afterwards, the Kyown-Kinnie and his two elders bowed to me in the courtyard, and I bowed to them. They were about to go back across the river. It was a formal leave-taking, our heralds sounding their trumpets in a fanfare of courtly tribute to guests from another country. I asked the Kyown-Kinnie if he felt our meeting had been successful.

He smiled. 'It is better than fighting each other, that is for sure. Yes, it is a start.'

I watched them depart, going from the castle in peace. *The Nahvitch.* The dreaded Nahvitch, and their lethal weapon. This was the narrative of my days as page and squire, when I learnt to fight with a spear, a lance, a dagger and a sword, not just for crusading, but in case the Nahvitch came in the night and we had to defend ourselves.

Look at us now! We talk, we discuss, we negotiate. We consult treaties and we make speeches. Perhaps it is better this way; it certainly saves a lot of young lives. But it lacks something also. Most likely, I am just not used to it and I need to adapt. The Kyown-Kinnie will come again to Hambrig, and although he has said nothing about it yet, I know he will want to invoke the Hurogol Treaty. My chalk lines will become real, solid Toosanik territory. They will build a new Meeting Place near the beautiful birch tree, and they will pay me their rent and their taxes. We will all shake down in the end, but, after all the warring and armed raids of the last hundred years, it will take a while for Hambrig to accept 'the Nahvitch' living among them.

That, however, is for the distant future. Tomorrow, I intend to find treasure.

36

COULD ANYONE BE SO SCRUPULOUSLY HONEST?

In the bright and early spring sunshine, Jonny, Peter, Gael, the Lady Joan and I walked out of the castle, down the stony track and onto the Wartsbaye Road, which runs north and south through Hambrig, parallel with the River Hurogol. It takes around two and a half hours to walk to the Great Plain, and it's on this plain that the birch tree stands, visible on the skyline for miles. We made our unhurried way to the tree.

Gael and Jonny had the tools we needed, and they chatted quietly as they strolled along. Ever since Gael faced up to Jonny in the gatehouse arch, forcing him to back off, there has been a new understanding between them. Peter brought rolls of parchment and a brand-new quill, and he walked silently, deep in thought. I walked slowly, with the Lady Joan on my arm. She looked wan and unwell, and I wasn't surprised.

And so we came to the foot of the tree. At first glance there was nothing to show that the ground had been disturbed, but after Gael had poked about for some time in the grasses and the sorrel, he found a short wooden stake. A bit more poking exposed two others. Gael stood back, and I got down on my knees to look more closely. There were inscriptions on the stakes, and I vainly twisted my body and my head to try to read them. I beckoned to Peter, who joined me in the long grass, but neither of us could make any sense of the markings. Eventually, Jonny used his knife to cut some short twigs from the tree. He pulled up each stake in turn and replaced it with a twig, so we would be able to return the stakes to their exact places afterwards.

And then we took ourselves off to an old pile of logs and tree stumps, and everyone found somewhere to sit. I was holding the three straight sticks in my hand, and I saw they were actually quite large, made from oak which had been carefully sawn to a length and then shaped with an adze. One end was tapered to a point so it would go smoothly into the ground. The other end was rounded, and there were no sharp edges anywhere. At one time a resinous varnish or glaze had been used to protect the wood and its inscriptions, but this had mostly flaked off. The stakes had been evenly spaced around the base of the tree, and I decided to examine them each in turn, in the order in which Gael had uncovered them.

The first one seemed to be the oldest, the wood the most weathered, the varnish almost completely gone. The inscription had been carefully etched into the oak lath, but, apart from the name and the last three words, it appeared to be in the Okkam, using runes rather than letters. The name was in normal lettering though, and clearly spelled the word 'HOPE'. As for the last three words, they were Latin: *Requiescat in Pace,* so it wasn't hard to guess what the Okkam runes would be telling us. But I handed the wooden marker to Peter, who had gained a passing knowledge of the Okkam runes by now.

Could anyone be so scrupulously honest?

'But why just this wooden stake in the ground?' Jonny was asking. 'I mean, Hope meant the world to him.'

Joan turned to face Jonny. 'Neither Diane nor Anthony wanted people to know where their daughter lay. Diane told Anthony to make sure he buried her there too, alongside their little girl. One of these stakes will be for Diane. But it was private, very private.'

I was curious. 'Was there a ceremony? A funeral? Were you present, Joan?'

'There were two funerals, the first for Hope, and then Diane's only a few months later. I was present at both. They took place just before dawn, and Anthony allowed only two other mourners – Joy and me.'

'Joy?'

'Diane's Toosanik servant woman. She'd have been about thirty when Diane died. I don't know what happened to her after that; a few months later, she just disappeared. And round about the same time, Anthony's apprentice ran off as well; such a nice, good-looking boy. I always wondered if there was a connection.'

Diane's Toosanik maidservant. The woman Merry sent halfway across Europe to have his child.

'I know what happened to her,' I said, looking at Peter, but he was bursting to give us his translation of the inscription.

'I think it says, *Here lies Hope, precious daughter of Anthony and Diane Merry. Aged ten. Rest in peace.*'

'Aged ten,' Jonny repeated sadly.

Gael calculated on his fingers. 'That's two years younger than me!'

I smiled at him. 'Yes, Gael. But it happened long before you were born.'

'Oh yes,' Joan agreed, 'more than twenty years ago. I was young then.'

'So, twenty-two, twenty-three years ago, would you say?' asked Jonny. 'How old were Rory and I?'

'Well, if you want to be exact, it was twenty-four years ago this year,' Joan answered, which of course I knew as well, though it was odd Joan remembered it so exactly. 'Rory's father was Lord of Hambrig,' Joan continued, but I interrupted her.

'I was ten that year, the same age as Hope, and Jonny, you'd have been twelve. I was a page in Hicrown so I knew nothing of this.'

I turned to the second stake, and, as expected, the name Diane stood out, and the same three words in Latin marked the end of the inscription. Peter translated this one easily: '*Here lies the Spirit of Endurance, Diane Merry, beloved and devoted wife of Anthony. Died 2nd January AD 1240. Rest in peace.*'

'Why is she the Spirit of Endurance?' asked Gael.

'If you'd known her, Gael, you'd have understood,' Joan told him. 'She was like a rock. Dependable, solid, practical – everything Anthony wasn't. She helped him organise his jewellery shop in the back of their house. She did all the accounts, looked after cleaning, paid the bills, bought and prepared food, clothes, absolutely everything. He often said he couldn't live without her. And she was the *Spirit* of Endurance, because she was not a strong woman, right from the first, but she never let that stop her doing whatever needed doing. She was dying even before Hope became ill. But she hung on for her child, she wouldn't let go. It was only once Hope was gone that Diane's health became worse. After Hope's death, Diane didn't have anything to live for.'

Could anyone be so scrupulously honest?

'Not even her husband?' Gael asked indignantly. 'Didn't he matter anymore?'

'Oh yes, he mattered. And Anthony told me Diane had made a great many arrangements to make sure he was all right after she'd gone. But she wanted to be with her child, and her child was in the ground under the birch tree.'

'I don't think I want *my* wife to be like that,' Gael said, frowning, and we all laughed.

'What's on the third stick?' Jonny asked, and I handed it to Peter.

'This one's in English!' Peter said in surprise, and gave it straight back to me.

'Well then,' I announced, 'this one says, Here lies the Meridian pathway of long life, great fortune and riches beyond your wildest dreams. Anno Domini 1240.' I looked up at them all and repeated, 'Riches beyond your wildest dreams!'

'*The Meridian pathway*,' Joan confirmed. 'That's what the Toosanik believe, you know. Diane believed that something had gone wrong with a meridian in her body, and Anthony asked her to instruct him in the old healing way. It's called *cheegun*. Diane taught him how to do it, though she didn't really want to. It involved breathing techniques, and a certain way he had to move his hands over her body to encourage the energy to flow uninterrupted along the meridians.'

'But it didn't work,' Jonny pointed out.

'I don't know,' Joan said thoughtfully. 'You see, I believe Diane wanted to die. I told you she wanted to be with Hope. Anthony was beside himself, he would have tried anything to save her, but I think she deliberately blocked his efforts. We'll never know, will we.'

'So where are the riches?' Gael asked, clearly bored with

a conversation on long-ago healing practices. 'Do you know where the treasure actually is, lord?'

I nodded. 'I do know. Merry made a clear translation of the original book, *The Meridian*, and then he added some text of his own. He describes exactly where to find his wealth, which is in the form of precious gold, silver, and jewels, collected from around the world, and worth an absolute fortune.'

I saw Gael's eyes gleam. 'Let's go and find it then!' the boy said, springing to his feet. He'd heard enough talk about dead people.

I considered. I'd hoped to go and see the treasure by myself. I had not intended to take a whole party of folk along. But perhaps it would be better like this. There would be witnesses to the uncovering of the booty; Peter could count the gold in front of everyone, and maybe Patrick should be there too, since he's responsible for the estate funds. Gael was hopping and skipping excitably, so I sent him hotfoot for Patrick.

Carefully, I replaced the lovingly created little markers back in their holes under the birch tree.

'Should we say a blessing?' Jonny asked tentatively.

'No harm in it.' I looked at Joan. After all, she had been closest to this tragic little family. We all bowed our heads.

'Lord Jesus Christ,' Joan began, and she took my hand. 'We ask your blessing on Diane, Hope and Anthony. We ask that their souls may rest in peace with you, and that they may find everlasting life with all the saints in heaven. Amen.'

We echoed the 'Amen', and then began the long trek back to Baudry Hill. I could see Joan and Peter each had something to say. I looked first at Joan.

'It's just a thought,' she said tentatively. 'Could we move

Could anyone be so scrupulously honest?

Anthony's body to the birch tree? Can we lay him near his family?'

'He doesn't deserve any consideration whatsoever,' I said tersely. 'And I'm surprised you think he does, Joan. He tried to seduce your friend, even while he was with you. And then he poisoned her! And suicide is a mortal sin, remember.'

'I know,' she said quietly. 'He was a complex man. I think he slept with Joy too, and possibly others. He couldn't take rejection, not from anyone. But he loved Diane and he loved Hope, he really did. After they died he was just a shell of a man. You know how everyone laughed at him for the outdated clothes he wore? Everything was at least twenty years out of date. Well, do you know *why* he wore those clothes?'

I shook my head. Jonny and Peter, walking side by side, were listening in. None of us had any idea why Merry had made such a laughing stock of himself.

'Well, don't you see?' cried Joan, looking round at us all. 'I told you Diane saw to all his clothes, that she managed everything for him. After she died, he couldn't bear to change anything. He wanted to wear the same clothes she'd made or bought for him. He would not buy new ones. Every time he put on a jerkin she'd made or a hat she'd picked out for him he was keeping her memory alive. And he didn't care if people laughed. It was nothing to do with them.'

'Hmm. I'll think about the re-interment,' I said.

I was also thinking that neither Anthony nor Diane had confided in Joan when it came to the New Beginning. Joan did not know about Joy's pregnancy or her departure for Europe under my father's protection.

It was Peter's turn to speak. 'I've been wondering, lord. How *did* t' Box of Death get from its burial site under t' tree to t' Kyown-Kinnie across t' river? Tha knows t' Kyown-

Kinnie asked that question yesterday? Master Merry buried it here in the hope someone would solve his *People's Puzzle,* find t' Box o' Death, then read *The Meridian* and get t' treasure as their reward. But why did he want someone to do that? Why did he create the puzzle-box-reward trail? Surely the whole point was to get t' Toosanik back here. The reward was the incentive to read t' *Puzzle.* And then, once tha've read t' *Puzzle,* tha feels sorry for t' Toosanik. Master Merry must have been hoping that t' person who solved t' puzzle would have intelligence an' courage enough to make a proper search for t' treaty and then reinstate t' Toosanik into their rightful lands on this side of the Hurogol. *That's* why he di'n't write t' *Puzzle* in plain English; he knew no one would read that. His aim were to create a mystery, to excite people, to make them want to have a go. That's why it's all so convoluted. So who spoilt it? Who dug up t' Box o' Death and then gave it to t' Toosanik, with t' *Meridian* still inside t' secret compartment?'

We all stopped walking and turned to look at him. Peter turned a deep shade of pink, but stood his ground.

'That really *is* a puzzle,' Jonny agreed. 'What do you think, Rory?'

'I just don't know,' I said. 'What about Sammy?'

'What about Sammy?' asked Joan at once.

'Could he have found it and taken it with him across the river? He could have done that, I think. He could have given it to the Kyown-Kinnie to present to Prince Barney.'

'He *could* have, but why?' asked Jonny. 'He had no reason to do that, and he wouldn't have known anything about the Box, or where to find it. No, I don't think Sammy is the answer.'

I heard Joan sigh with relief.

Could anyone be so scrupulously honest?

'Let's leave that for now,' I suggested. 'Instead, we will go and find out how rich we all are!'

Peter already knew the treasure's hiding place, so I took him by the arm and walked him a little way ahead of Joan and Jonny.

'You know where we're going?' I asked in an undertone.

'Aye, I read t' parchment, just as tha told me to.'

It sounded like he was trying to justify reading it. 'Have you been to look yet?' I had to know. My heart had started beating fast and, without meaning to, I'd also quickened my pace.

'Nay, lord, of course not. It's for thee to look.'

But he'd read the manuscript yesterday. He'd had the information before I had it, and he'd had a whole twenty-four hours to find the gold for himself. I gave him a searching look.

He shook his head vigorously. 'I haven't looked for t' treasure, lord, I swear it!'

But could anyone be so scrupulously honest?

37

THE PUNISHMENT SEEMS ENTIRELY FITTING

We marched on in silence.

Patrick joined us in the bailey, and we turned right and headed down the grassy slope, then on towards the stream. We'd missed dinner by several hours. No one mentioned it.

Joan realised where we were going. She gave a little cry. 'No, oh no! You can't believe it's in the *Egg!* It was bad enough to find the treaty had been in my samovar all this time, but not all Anthony's gold and jewels as well! They *can't* be there.'

Her weight dragged on my arm, and for a moment I thought she had fainted. But I pulled her up.

'Joan,' I said brusquely, 'we are going to the *Egg*. Merry is quite clear in his instructions. It remains to be seen whether you also were part of his plan.'

As we neared the little cabin where Joan works, eats and sleeps, I quickened my pace. I flung open the door of the *Egg* and heard it crash back on its hinges. My eyes couldn't see much; the workshop is always dark inside until candles and woodfire are alight. I felt my way to the table, caught hold of

Joan's tinder box and soon had a spark from the firesteel. I blew on the tinder, caught the flame in a splint and lit a candle, my hand shaking. The candle threw strange shadows on the walls of the hut. I was alone. Noises outside the door told me the others had arrived, but hadn't entered.

'It all starts here,' I muttered, turning round and round. 'Sammy grew up here. Sammy *named* this place. Joan was his teacher, his mentor. Then what? Sammy goes to the Nahvitch and becomes their king. Why? Because, unbeknown to me, *the lord of this castle*, the boy's an enemy. He is the son of a Nahvitch chieftain and a Nahvitch princess, so off he goes to make war on us!'

In my confusion and sudden rage I reverted to the old term for the Toosanik, and all the time in the back of my mind were the same old questions, the ones I will never be rid of. *What would my father have done? How would he have dealt with this?*

I pushed the questions away, hating them, for now I had some light and I could see what I was doing. I lit three more candles and placed them around the workshop. The crazy shadows disappeared, and I calmed down a little. I went to the very back of the workshop. Here was the handloom, the spindles and the piles of fabrics in their startlingly vivid colours. Here Sammy used to sleep, curled up on a bundle of woolly fleeces. But there were too many bolts of cloth, too much piled up, and it was impossible to tell what was hidden underneath them all.

Why does Joan have to pile them so damned high?

I began flinging them frantically away: the rugs, the skins, the fleeces, the bolts and bales of stuff and more stuff, and then suddenly Jonny was beside me, and my heart lightened, for it was like the old days, just the two of us against the Mamluks; the two of us, solid, inseparable, looking out for each other no matter what the odds.

'Peter's with Joan outside the hut,' Jonny gasped, grabbing a pile of coarse tweedy stuff and throwing it back behind him. 'I've told them to wait. Is the fucking treasure under all this, then?'

I nodded, barely able to speak. My back was aching from reaching up or bending down to get hold of the heavy blankets and throw them all bodily behind me, and all the fluff had got into my nose and ears and eyes and down my throat, making me feel sick. We kept going, somehow, though it took an age. Eventually, we did it. The floor was clear. Behind us was a mess; utter chaos. Where Joan had had colours carefully separated, her fabrics piled neatly according to colour, type or usage, there was now just a horrible confusion of textiles on the rush floor and across the table. Many of the fabrics were spoilt, having been dragged across dirt on the floor, or they'd got ripped when we grabbed for them.

Bent double, I panted for breath, my hands on my knees, while Jonny knelt on the floor, retching. After a few moments though, we were able to see what we'd uncovered. In front of us were the dusty wooden planks of the workshop floor. Nothing else. Jonny looked at me, waiting for a cue. I rubbed my hand over my face. I didn't know what I'd expected to see – a box, perhaps? Or a chest, encrusted with jewels? Or *something*. But there was nothing here, absolutely nothing.

'You're sure it said it was here?' Jonny asked reasonably. 'This is where he meant?'

'Of course I'm bloody sure,' I snapped back. 'I read it. The back of Joan's workshop, under all the pelts and rugs.

The punishment seems entirely fitting

That's what he said. Oh my God. Perhaps it's all just a joke, Jonny.'

I sank down onto a mess of red-dyed material. 'Perhaps there never was any treasure and it's just a wild goose chase. I bet he's laughing at us right now, if he can see us.' And I gave a short, barking laugh myself.

'He's not looking down on us from heaven, that's for sure.' Jonny wiped his face and sat next to me. 'He never made it to heaven, that man.'

'Well. Let's go and face the music. We'd better tell Peter and Joan there's nothing to be found after all. I won't be building my watermill.'

'Your what?'

'Just a dream I had, Jonny. I wanted to build a watermill on the banks of the Eray. Right here, in fact. When I read about Merry's treasure, I thought – well, it's of no importance now.'

I got up and was brushing my hose down from all the ghastly lint and fluff that had stuck to them, when Jonny suddenly froze. His hand shot out and grasped my arm, pulling me back down again.

'Rory!' he whispered. 'Look!'

I followed his pointing finger, but couldn't see what he meant at first. And then I saw it. A small ivory box. I'd been looking for something big, something that would contain a 'treasure'; after all, hadn't Merry promised *a great reward*, and *riches beyond your wildest dreams?*

But my mouth went dry and my heart started hammering again. Suddenly unable to stand, I crawled forward on my hands and knees, then stretched out to grasp the little box. I sat back on my heels. I looked at my fingers, wrapped around the small container. They were like claws, white-knuckled and shaking.

THE BOX OF DEATH

'I'll get the others,' Jonny said.

By the time everyone had crowded in at the back of the hut, I'd managed to stand up and regain some self-control. Peter's eyes were huge as he looked at the little ivory box. Now that I was holding it, I could see it was very pretty, inlaid with some sort of mother-of-pearl, and glowing in the candlelight.

'What's inside?' breathed Joan. She'd said nothing about the appalling state of her workshop, though she looked completely bewildered. Jonny had fetched a folding stool for her, and she sat in the middle of our little group.

'I have not opened it,' I told them all. 'But it has to be something very small and extremely precious inside, I think you will all agree.'

No one spoke.

I examined the little box to find the way into it. I saw that the lid had a sort of lip, and all I had to do was push on it and wiggle the lid up and down at each side, until eventually I levered it right off. I handed the lid to Jonny and looked into the box. I think I was expecting some rare jewel to be in there, cushioned on velvet, worth a king's ransom. Instead, I pulled out a hen's egg and a small, folded note. I held the hen's egg up so everyone could see it. Jonny swore violently. Peter gasped and reached out to hold on to Joan's chair. Joan's mouth fell open.

'And now the note,' I rasped, replacing the egg in the box and unfolding the scrap of parchment. *'Got Egg Need Teacher? Ha ha! I'll be your teacher now! Follow me to learn something new. From Kit, Duke of Casuel in Smander.'*

For a moment there was total silence. Then Jonny hurled the ivory lid down on the floor.

'This is intolerable!' he spluttered. 'That bloody troubadour, spy, whatever he is! He's found the treasure and

The punishment seems entirely fitting

left this, this fucking stupid joke in its place, that's what he's done!' He stormed out of the cabin. I had seldom seen Jonny look so angry. But he was undoubtedly right: Master Kit had been here before us.

'Do you know anything about this?' I asked Joan.

'No, nothing.' She stared at me in shock. 'I don't understand. When was Kit here? How could he have been here without me noticing?'

It seemed impossible. And then, suddenly, it didn't. 'Where were you during the battle, Joan?' I asked abruptly.

'Oh! On the ramparts, watching. Although most of the time the archers kept pushing me down so I couldn't see much. Why?'

'Because now I know what Kit did. And when and why he came here.'

Joan and Peter looked thoroughly puzzled, but I was remembering Kit two days ago, before he left the castle, telling me about his escape from the dungeon. He looked in the Box of Death, he said, and then he came here. Kit came straight to the *Egg* and found the treasure, which could only mean he'd read *The Meridian*. He left his little riddle-me-ree for us to find. What he'd done with the gold, I had no idea, since he then went back to Arkyn in his dungeon cell. Kit assured me that he stole nothing, but clearly *that* was a lie. Whatever fortune had been in the *Egg* was now gone.

I explained all this to Joan and Peter, and they were aghast. Joan wasn't at the Victory Banquet, so she didn't hear Arkyn in his bid for *Ragnarök*, his description of Kit's escape from the dungeon in the midst of all the fighting. I hadn't believed it was possible to escape; seemingly, it was.

'We must find Master Kit,' Joan cried. 'We must find out where he's put it all. It isn't his! It's Anthony's!'

'Anthony doesn't need it now,' I reminded her. 'And, with

or without the treasure, Kit has gone. I've sent him abroad to make some enquiries. On my behalf.'

'Is this about Kathryn? Oh, Rory!'

'Well, we can do nothing about it until he gets back, and I've given him a month, Joan, so we'd best forget about it for now. One thing we can be sure of: if Kit has hidden it and doesn't want it found, then no amount of looking is going to turn it up. He's much too clever for that.'

Joan nodded, but her mind was not on what I'd just said. She'd hoped I wouldn't try to find Kathryn; I could see that. I didn't know why, and I didn't want to ask her.

Peter was deep in thought. As always, he was far less concerned with acquiring riches than with figuring out how things had happened.

'I think I can see it now, Lord Rory,' he said, wiping his face with one of Joan's colourful cloths. 'Aye, it all makes sense. It must have been Master Kit who dug up t' Box of Death. Tha remembers, we were wonderin' about that? Master Kit dug it up, probably some time ago, perhaps long before he came to t' castle with his troubadour friends. He solved t' *Puzzle* – nay, wait! He di'n't *need* to solve t' *Puzzle!* If he dug up t' Box, an' then he found a way into t' secret part, he'd have t' *Meridian* and t' directions to t' treasure. Then, after he came to t' castle, he took t' treasure for himself. That's it!'

'Yes,' I agreed. 'I think you're right, Peter. Although I don't think he found the secret compartment until he was looking in the Box while the rest of us were fighting for our lives. If he'd found *The Meridian* when he first dug it up, he'd have taken it out then. I think he only discovered it recently. And anyway, it doesn't explain everything, does it. How did Kit know about the Box of Death in the first place? And how did he know it was under the birch tree? How the blazes could he have known about that from bloody Spain? And how did the Box get across the river so that the Kyown-Kinnie could give it to Barney?'

Peter bit his lip. 'I d'n't know, lord. I can't answer any of those questions. There must be *some* explanation though.'

When we were back in the bailey, I found Jonny and asked after Sergeant Alex. He told me Alex was making a slow recovery in regard to his broken bones and bruising. But he had no movement or feeling in his lower body, for I'd damaged his back too severely. He will be paralysed from the waist down for the rest of his life. Jonny gave me the facts in a voice devoid of emotion, which meant he felt very deeply for the young man whose life and career I have ruined. But it is no more than Alex did to mine, and I feel no remorse. In fact, the punishment seems entirely fitting.

38

I WISH HE'D SAID SO IN THE FIRST PLACE

It took just over three weeks, well within the month I'd allowed. On Thursday 14th June, mid-afternoon, a horn sounded from the ramparts. Riders had been sighted from the north.

And so the troubadours returned to Castle Rory. I watched them sweep through the archway, across the bailey and into the castle courtyard as if they owned it. Patrick came to tell me they'd arrived.

'Yes, yes, I know they're here, I watched them come through the gate like the three bloody wise men,' I said fractiously. 'What have they brought? Gold, frankincense and myrrh? If so, I know where the *gold* came from, at least.' The rancour sounded through my voice, and Patrick stepped back in alarm. We've told nobody of the debacle in the *Egg*.

'No, lord, they have not brought you any gifts, I regret to say.' He frowned, as though he might be blamed for this lack of propriety.

'Don't be ridiculous,' I snapped. 'Find out where they went, and send Master Kit to me immediately.'

I wish he'd said so in the first place

'Yes, lord, of course. They did not say much, but they have been to the palace. That is all I know.'

'To the palace?'

'The royal family are in residence, and I daresay they welcomed some entertainment.'

'Damn their entertainment.'

It was supposed to be the position of power. I sat in my carved chair in my library and Kit stood in front of me. He didn't look much like a duke, I decided. With his curly black hair falling over his forehead, and his deep, dark eyes and tanned complexion, he looked more like a gypsy. And his arrogance was as evident as ever, in his impudent stance and challenging gaze.

'I sent you on a mission, Master Kit.'

'You did.' He has never once called me 'lord' except in amused sarcasm.

'Well?'

'May I sit down?'

I remembered having this conversation before. Kit is not prepared to talk except as an equal. He had news I craved, craved beyond living. To know what happened to Kathryn and her baby has been in my mind ever since Joan told me the full story. And somewhere in the back of my mind was the question I didn't want to ask. Had Kathryn loved Alex? Loved him more than she loved me? My need to know was like my need for air to breathe or water to drink. I hoiked over a stool with my foot, and Kit sat down. I knew he would see the hunger in my eyes.

'I do have news,' he began, but then his face became serious. 'She's alive. She's living in a convent in York. I rode to York, leaving the other two at the palace in Hicrown. I didn't tell them where I was going, so they know nothing of this. I spoke with the nuns, and was eventually allowed to see your lady.'

I waited. I could not speak.

'She doesn't want to see you. She was – upset – when I spoke of you. She lives a simple life in the convent, with no possessions of her own, and she's not allowed to see anyone unchaperoned. Another sister was in the room the whole time I was with Kathryn. Her name isn't Kathryn now, by the way. She goes by Sister Clementine, and she barely recognised her old name when I used it.'

'You are *sure* this is Kathryn? My Kathryn?' My voice was a thin, hoarse croak.

'I have proof for you.' He felt in his tunic and took out a ring. He showed it to me, and I gave an involuntary cry of pain. For it was the very ring I had given to Kathryn the day before her uncle came. The last time I ever saw her.

'I said she has no possessions,' Kit went on. 'But she was allowed to keep this ring, though the Mother Superior had it put away in a drawer. Kathryn wants you to have it back.'

The ring had been my mother's; silver, with two fine intertwined bands, doubling around each other in a never-ending circle. After my mother died, my father gave the ring to me. 'For your lady,' he said gruffly. 'If there's any lady in the land will have you.'

I had treasured the ring, and I gave it to Kathryn as a pledge that one day we would be wed. It lay now, in the palm of my hand, a symbol of my complete and utter failure. Before I could stop it, a great sob burst from my throat.

'Is there more?' I looked up at Kit, clenching my hand around the ring.

'Yes, there's more. There was a child. You know about

I wish he'd said so in the first place

that already. It's why you sent me to find the woman you loved.'

'What happened?' I whispered.

'He died. You had a son, but he only lived a few days. That is what Sister Clementine told me.'

'A son?'

'Yes.'

'And – did she say he was *my* son? Or Alex's? Did you ask her, Kit?'

'I asked her. I asked her many things, but we talked in an undertone. She did not want the other sister to hear, and that was quite easy because the other sister sat in a corner of the room, sewing a tapestry and humming to herself. The other sister was a good woman, Rory.'

I wasn't interested in the other sister. I implored Kit to tell me everything he knew.

'Sister Clementine – Kathryn – did not love Alex, she only ever loved you. She could not believe you thought she had betrayed you. When she found she was pregnant, she knew she could not hide it.'

'But how did she know it was mine?' I wanted to scream this question; it was the only thing that mattered, somehow. For God's sake, how could I ever know the truth?

But Kit was speaking again, cutting across the screaming in my head. 'She knows whose baby it was. She was adamant, Rory. It was your baby. When she found she was pregnant, she told her parents Alex was the father. She was protecting you. She didn't want you to get into trouble.'

'Oh, God.'

'What you did to Alex,' Kit said, and then paused. 'What you did to Alex was unforgivable. Wicked and despicable. You listened to Joan and you believed her story. You could have spoken with Alex and heard *his* story. *You should have listened to Alex.*'

Kit got up. He didn't look at me, but walked out of the door. I'd thought I was interviewing him, but it had been the other way around. And I had not even mentioned the treasure or the Box of Death.

For hours I sat in my library, while the sky grew dark outside. The fire burnt out, the candles failed, and the room became cold as a tomb. My limbs turned to ice and my whole body froze, remaining in one position, hour after hour, unable to bend or straighten any joint. I was turned to stone.

I woke naked in my own bed, not knowing how I got there. Someone must have moved me from my library to my chamber; someone undressed me; someone laid me in my bed and covered me with warm blankets. I lay, wide awake, listening to birdsong and the sounds of the castle stirring into action for a new day. Patrick entered my chamber.

'Good morning, lord! All is well!' he said cheerfully. On top of the chest, he put a ewer of fresh water and some clean linen undergarments. He pulled back the bed hangings and bowed to me.

'Did you bring me here?' I asked him.

'I? No, lord.' He looked puzzled, and I did not pursue it. I got up and let him drape a long undershirt over me. After

I wish he'd said so in the first place

that, I dismissed him. I dressed in my hunting gear, dark, practical colours, strong, robust materials, but I finished with my best surcoat, a sign of my rank and nobility.

Still wondering who put me to bed last night, for surely he must have *carried* me there – quite a journey from my library high up in the tower, down the spiral steps, across the dark courtyard, up more steps into the keep and along the passage to my chamber – I descended to the great hall. It was thronged with my household, all of whom stopped what they were doing when they saw me, to bow or curtsy and wish me a good morning. I scanned the hall, as I always do, on the lookout for anything amiss. Although it was another warm day, the great fireplace was crackling and sparking with a fire that had clearly been alight for a few hours. The flames leapt high up the chimney, and gave a glow to the eastern side of the hall. Slightly in the shadows of that glow, stood the three troubadours, together with Amie and Gael. Their songs had power and influence, and they'd caused trouble. I beckoned the cook over to me.

'What are the minstrels planning, Rachel?'

'They are going to perform later today, lord. I believe your steward knows.'

And so he should.

I skirted around the edge of the hall, where Rachel's women were making sure everyone had enough bread and ale. It was, in fact, a typical breakfast at Castle Rory, an informal meal with people coming and going as they pleased, or at least as their work dictated.

Not everyone comes in for breakfast. The Lady Joan, for example, prefers to brew her *Karavanserai* tea in her samovar, and breakfast by herself in the *Egg*. I grimaced as I remembered the mess we'd left there. She'd have had to work for hours to sort all the fleeces and fabrics out and create her ordered piles again. Well, she'd had plenty of time to do it.

Once, I'd suspected Joan of taking the treasure from under our noses. I'd suspected Peter of the same thing. And even now I allowed my stupid suspicions and assumptions to ramble through my mind as I wandered around my great hall, doing my duty as lord of the castle, and resolutely not, *absolutely not*, thinking about my dead son and the woman who had borne him.

Eventually, the company dispersed, still chewing, or brushing crumbs from their clothing and taking a last swig of ale from their goblets. There's no formal end to breakfast, as there is no official beginning; it just runs its course, and everyone knows they should be busy at their work before the sunshine spills into the courtyard.

Patrick and I spent some time in my library going over business accounts and reckoning up taxes, rents due, and other household matters. We have a good system, and with Patrick's flair for organisation and excellent record-keeping, it was done in a couple of hours, underlined with a conclusive 'All is well,' from Patrick.

I asked him then if he'd spoken with the minstrels, and an odd expression came over his face. Grimly, I waited to hear the worst. I would put a stop to all festivities if necessary, I told myself.

'They are hoping to give us some entertainment at dinner, lord. Apparently, it has been specially devised and rehearsed.'

'I'll bet it has.'

At dinnertime, the household entered in dribs and drabs, found seats, talking and stretching after working in the fields or in our barns and workshops. The Lady Joan, to my surprise, was here already, and talking with Sir Jonny at

I wish he'd said so in the first place

the high table. I looked over at the troubadours, standing with Gael and Amie by the hearth. Kit gave me a wink. Bloody cheek.

'What are you giving us today?' I asked him directly, as I approached the group.

'Ah, 'twill be a surprise, a "merry" surprise,' he said with a chuckle. I caught the pun, and it confirmed my fears. This was going to be some sort of satire on the events of the last few weeks, and a warning was needed.

'Your merry surprise had better not be *too* "merry",' I cautioned. 'The castle dungeons are empty at the moment. You five would fill 'em up nicely.'

Gael looked horrified, and Amie bit her lip and cast her eyes down, but the other three just grinned. I nodded to Gael and moved off to take my place in the middle of the high table. Someone sounded a horn, and the food was brought out on great platters.

Some soup was served to us, and we had bread to eat with it. There was venison too, and then fruit and a compote of berries, and while we ate the troubadours got ready for their performance. Patrick looked from them to me, as if weighing up the odds of us all surviving the experience. Again, I considered pulling the whole show, telling the musicians to be on their way and dispatching Amie and Gael to other duties. For some reason, I didn't.

Amie had her harp, of course, but I saw no instruments in Kit's hands this time. Gael had a small drum, and I guessed Kit had lent it to him. As for the other two, they sat to one side, and seemed to be taking no part in the performance.

Kit stepped forward, held up his hand, and the hall fell silent. I think we were all expecting tricks and conjuring, magical wonders and incredible acrobatics. We got none of them. Instead, in response to a simple introductory arpeggio from Amie, Kit began to sing. His lovely voice drifted through the hall, reaching every corner of it. The melody was simple, and Amie played a soft, harmonious accompaniment, so that the words dominated. The company listened, enthralled, to a story no one could have imagined.

> *Now all you good people who dwell here,*
> *Please give us poor minstrels applause!*
> *It's good of you all to welcome us in,*
> *And open your very fine doors.*
>
> *You know that we've come from a distance,*
> *From lands that are far, far away.*
> *And I am quite sure that all of you think,*
> *We're going to return there some day.*
>
> *It's time that you knew more about me,*
> *For I am the Duke of Casuel!*
> *But I was conceived not too far from here,*
> *I started in Hambrig as well.*
>
> *My father was Anthony Merry,*
> *The subject of taunting and jeers.*
> *My mother was just a Toosanik girl,*
> *Who served Mistress Merry for years.*
>
> *My mother was sent on a journey,*
> *For 'Merry' had little of 'Joy',*
> *To Smander she came, the north-west of Spain,*
> *And there she gave birth to her boy.*

I wish he'd said so in the first place

I grew up with royal princesses,
The king told me he had a plan:
He'd give me Casuel, a dukedom no less,
If I were an honourable man.

But honour comes in different guises,
And I have a debt to repay.
The lord of this place gave me a fine start,
So I am his bondman today.

And so, do you see how it plays now?
I'm Hambrigger, Toosanik, both!
I'll serve till my death, for you gave me life,
Lord Rory, I give you my oath.

As he sang the final verse, Kit danced forward to the high table, his arms spread wide. He waited for me to stand and walk round to the front of the dais, and then, suddenly sombre, he knelt and, placing his clasped hands in mine, uttered the time-honoured oath of fealty.

To say I was dumbfounded is an understatement. I heard Jonny behind me muttering something, and then the company broke into spontaneous applause, clapping, stamping and cheering. I raised Kit to his feet and held up my hand to hush the crowd.

'Kit, Duke of Casuel,' I declaimed. 'I thank you for your loyalty. The debt you owe is not to me, but to my late father, who gave your mother Joy an escort out of Mallrovia, through the wild country of Westador and the southern English pastures into France and Spain. I accept your oath, but I release you now from your bond. Only a freeman can be a lord's vassal, and you are a freeman. Return to your fellow troubadours and give us songs and dancing!'

It was the cue they wanted. Kit leapt down and capered back to the hearth, amid more cheering, clapping, stamping and general acclaim. The rest of the afternoon passed in an orgy of music, magic and – what was it? – ah, yes. Mayhem! But on the high table no one paid any attention to the jesters and musicians.

'Kit's the New Beginning?' Jonny asked incredulously. '*He's* the son of Anthony Merry and Diane's Toosanik maid?'

'It seems so,' Patrick responded sourly. 'But I wish he'd said so in the first place.'

39

WE ARE GOING TO YORK, YOU AND I

It seems to me that several more pieces have fallen into place. Kit is Anthony Merry's son. No wonder he speaks in riddles and has no trouble solving puzzles. It all makes sense now.

I thought back to Peter's deductions the day we found Kit's ivory box in the *Egg*. I needed to confirm that what I was thinking was true, so I caught Kit's eye and motioned him to come over. We cleared a place for him to sit with us.

'Kit, you removed the Box of Death from its hiding place under the birch tree, didn't you?'

He nodded. 'My mother knew all about the Box of Death. She told me about my father, and about my sister, Hope. I knew Hope had died in childhood. I knew her mother was dead too. Joy told me about the pact Anthony and Diane made before she died. He was to have an heir. She didn't know about William though. My father already had an heir.'

'Not really,' I said. 'He couldn't acknowledge William as his son.'

'He couldn't acknowledge me either,' Kit said sadly. 'He

never knew me. And I grew up hundreds of miles away. At least William grew up here, in the castle.'

'That he did not,' I said. I myself had known nothing about William until recently.

Joan filled us in. 'William was raised elsewhere. He had foster parents all through his childhood. I visited him every year though; he knew I was his mother. But for a long time he didn't know who his father was.' Joan smiled, but not with her eyes. 'Master Kit, we are not responsible for the circumstances of our conception or our birth, and certainly not for the actions of our parents. Your father must have wanted you to have the best start in life if he sent your mother to Smander when she was pregnant with you.'

'Yes,' Kit agreed. 'My mother had an armed escort, provided by the garrison of this castle. They saw her safely to Santiago das Cunchas, and made sure she would be all right. Rory's father wrote a letter of introduction, giving my mother an excellent reference. He, personally, vouched for her. He gave his officer instructions to deliver my mother straight to the palace. The queen read the letter of introduction, took my mother in and gave her employment.'

'Well, the king and queen of Smander must have taken a liking to you,' Joan said to Kit. 'They gave you everything you needed – even, when you grew to manhood, a large and prosperous dukedom. So *why* did you leave all that and come to Hambrig?'

'I came to Hambrig, lady, to find my father and to repay my mother's debt. I was charged with the task of reinstating my mother's people in the land that is their birthright. When I got here, I found that the lord I owed the debt to was dead, and my father a laughing stock and a murderer. But my mother is a good woman, lady. She told me the truth, or all the truth she knew. She said my father had hidden his treasure, and it was for me that he hid it. I was to dig up the Box of Death from under the birch tree on the Great Plain in Hambrig. Then I was to follow the instructions in an ancient book of her people's history, *The Meridian*. That would lead me to my father's treasure.'

'And you found it?' Jonny had leant forward eagerly, and the question he asked was on everyone's lips.

'Oh, I found it,' Kit said easily. 'Yes, I found Anthony Merry's treasure inside the Box of Death. Obviously, I removed it.'

'Well?' I asked, after an edgy pause.

'It's – well, perhaps I'd better just show it to you. You'll have to come with me.' He looked round at us, as if daring us to follow him.

'I shall go,' Joan said at once. 'I trust you, Master Kit.'

He gave her a friendly grin.

'Then I must also go,' I said, for one of my jobs is to protect the Lady Joan, and indeed everyone in my household. In the end, of course, we all stood up. The merriment in the great hall would continue for hours yet, for the entire company was being well entertained by the troubadours.

Gael has suddenly shot up, and his voice has started to break, so he will no longer sing, but he can turn pretty somersaults and has somehow learnt to juggle. He even brought out his recorder and shyly played a tune, for which he was cheered and delightedly whistled at, which made the boy turn crimson with pride. Acrobatics, magic tricks, music and song, one thing followed another, and I could see that no more work would be done today. No matter. If we were about to get our hands on Merry's treasure at last, I decided my household could damn well have a holiday.

So we followed Master Kit out of the great hall, and I

beckoned to Peter to join us as we passed his table. He's been involved with everything, and it seemed only right he should see the *great reward* now that it was finally going to be revealed.

As we followed Kit across the courtyard, into the bailey and out towards the eastern curtain wall, I realised where we were going. Rachel had housed the minstrels in a disused cow byre. It's only disused in the summertime; the cattle will be overwintered there. But for now, part of the herd was out on the slopes of Baudry Hill, and others beyond that, on the rich grasslands of the Mallrovian Downs. The byre was empty, and Rachel had sensibly told the minstrels they could use it as their own.

Kit took us inside. There was a smell I didn't like, and a rat darted out of the dirty straw.

'You've been sleeping here?' Joan said, startled at the poor state of the place. 'But it's terrible!'

I was shocked too. I hadn't realised how bad this place was.

Kit smiled. 'I've known worse.'

He clambered over some bales of straw and I saw that in a corner of the building was a rickety ladder, some of whose rungs were missing completely. It led to a ramshackle hayloft, and Kit shinned up it. The rest of us stood in the doorway, unwilling to venture into the noxious interior. Joan was quite distressed, and I put my arm around her.

'If Merry's wealth is truly here,' I whispered to her, 'I'll be able to afford repairs to all the castle buildings, as well as build my watemill!'

'You and your old watermill!' Joan said.

Kit scrabbled about in the hayloft for a few moments only, and he soon jumped back down again. We all peered into the darkness of the byre hoping to see the gleam of gold in his hands. I could just make out that he held a small box, identical to the little ivory one we'd found in the *Egg*.

Kit held it out to me, and I took it. I looked round at Peter, Jonny and Joan. We four had come a long way for this, and Joan was the connection between all of us. She'd been Merry's lover, and Princess Eefa's friend. She'd known Joy, the Toosanik servant girl who was Kit's mother, and she'd known Diane, the only woman Merry had truly loved, his Spirit of Endurance.

We stepped outside into the fading light, and the others made a rough circle around me. With a fast-beating heart, I opened the little ivory box. Inside it was a small, many-folded piece of parchment. *Déja vu!* I looked up, scowling at Kit.

'Is this another joke?' I asked angrily. At least there was no egg this time.

He shook his head. 'Read it.'

I took out the parchment and unfolded it. There was a great deal of tiny script, and I began to read it slowly out loud.

Whoever finds this letter has solved a series of puzzles and has shown courage, determination and skill. It is my hope that my son is now reading this, for I buried the Box of Death especially for him. But if through some chance it is someone else reading it, you are to be congratulated, whoever you are, for you have beaten the son of Anthony Merry, and you are a worthy winner. I put my trust in you to find my son and share this letter with him, but you also can gain from the thoughts I have set out here.

For now, I shall assume that my son, who has grown up in the country of Smander, is the first to come upon the Box of Death and its contents, and the first to read this letter.

THE BOX OF DEATH

Welcome! I do not know your name, and perhaps by the time you read this I shall be dead, and we shall never meet in person. That is no matter. You are a Toosanik and a Hambrigger, and that is why you are important. There is a treaty, the Hurogol Treaty, which has been lost. You must direct your efforts to finding this treaty and reinstating the Toosanik people onto their rightful land. That is the mission I now entrust to you. The Toosanik are a proud and ancient people, and they are your people. Your mother is a Toosanik woman, your father is a Hambrig man. You bestride the two worlds, and you must always, always acknowledge both.

But you did not come all this way for a lecture on culture. No, you followed the clues and solved the puzzles because you were promised riches beyond your wildest dreams. And you shall have them. Here, then, is my counsel, and I hereby commend to you my humble works, 'The Book of Truth' and 'The Book of Wisdom'. Both are the products of my life and my experience, and both will show you a treasure many only dream of. You should read them, my son, and then perhaps we will discuss them together. But for now, here is a taste of what is to come.

We will start with the Lady Joan. Joan is my lover, but more than that, she is my friend. She has a son, and he is also my son. His name is William. Find him, he is your brother. This, then, is your treasure. There is nothing more valuable, more worth having, than your family. The Lady Joan is a wonderful woman. Treasure her and honour her, as I do. Hambrig Town, where we live, is in the demesne of Lord Rory. You will find his stronghold at the top of Baudry Hill, south of Hambrig Town. Lord Rory is a brave man. Make him your friend.

My son, I sent you far from home before you were even born. That was to protect you. I hope beyond all Hope, that you have grown up strong and healthy and that you will make this dream a reality. Find the Hurogol Treaty. Look after the Toosanik. Look after those you love. Marry a good woman and have children of your own. I had a daughter once. Her name is Hope. Hope is what I wish for you and for all the displaced Toosanik people, the Hope of a return to their homeland, the Hope of salvation. Carry Hope with you – there is no greater treasure in the whole world.

From your loving father, Anthony Merry

Total silence. Then an exclamation from Jonny, springing forward to catch the Lady Joan who had fainted. Peter was dabbing at his eyes. Kit stood very still, watching me.

'I will put Joan to bed,' said Jonny, and he strode off towards the *Egg* with Joan in his arms.

'I should get back to t' hall,' Peter mumbled. He was quite emotional, and could barely see as he stumbled away. I felt numb. Was that really it? *That* was the treasure? A dream, a hope, and a lesson in family values?

Kit and I were left outside the cow byre. I was still holding the parchment. I re-rolled it, and handed it to Kit.

'You expected gold, emeralds and rubies, didn't you,' I said.

'Didn't you?'

'Yes. Are you angry? You feel cheated?'

'No, I am not in need of gold. But you – you wanted it badly.'

It's true. I wanted it. I'd seen my watermill taking shape, my stables full of beautiful thoroughbreds, my castle walls fortified and strengthened, and all without the King's help. Well. It will have to be Lillian's dowry after all.

'What are you going to do now, Kit?' I asked him.

'Now? I'm going to find somewhere else to sleep. Now

that everyone knows who I am, I should like to become part of your household, and not a visiting troubadour, unworthy of a decent place to lay his head!'

I smiled. 'You shall have a bedchamber in the keep. And I will have a warming pan put in the bed, and a goose-feather quilt laid upon it. You will have luxury as befits a noble Duke of Smander!'

'That is the irony, though,' Kit said seriously, as we began to walk back to the hall. 'I may be a duke, but I am *not* of noble birth. I'm a bastard, whose father was a merchant and whose mother, a servant. I am of mixed race, and my only skills are those of a lowly minstrel. What do you make of that, Rory?'

'I'd say you've shown more than a few skills,' I replied promptly. 'And in any case, there's nothing lowly about being a minstrel. You've been tasked with finding the Hurogol Treaty. Are you aware it's been found already?'

'I've seen it. After our last talk, when I told you about Sister Clementine's baby, I left you alone in your library. Many hours later I returned, and you were still there, but unconscious. You were cold as ice, and I took the lanyard with your keys from around your neck. I found the Box of Death, the gecko and the treaty. I read it. I know exactly what I have to do. After that, I fetched Christopher and Annis, and together we carried you to your chamber, undressed you and got you into bed.'

'What did you do with the Box of Death?'

'I left it in your library, together with all the documents. I read them, that is all.'

I reflected that it was the second time he'd taken my keys without my permission. To be honest, I was past caring. The treasure had, once again, evaporated into thin air. There was a strange, ethereal feel to this whole quest, as when you

We are going to York, you and I

wake from a vivid dream, only to find you cannot remember it, as it shreds itself into gossamer and floats away on the breeze.

'What about Annis and Christopher?' Kit asked me when we'd arrived at the hall. 'Are they to return to the cowshed?'

'No, of course not,' I said at once. 'They must also have a room in the keep. Do they sleep in one bed, those two?'

He chuckled. 'Oh yes. Most definitely.'

During supper a messenger arrived from Hicrown. King Philip has had his secretary prepare a proclamation. It will be sent around the whole country to be read aloud in every marketplace, every town square and in every alehouse.

From his Majesty King Philip of Mallrovia: Be it known that on Sunday the 23rd September in the Year of our Lord 1263 the wedding will take place between our daughter, Lady Lillian, and Lord Rory of Hambrig in Hicrown Abbey.

In the accompanying letter, his Majesty assures me there will be feasting and jousting, archery and tournaments, displays of falconry and a great hunt in the royal forest, while several troupes of minstrels have been hired for the event, which will last two weeks. He also tells me that he will have a special chamber made ready. There will be a great bed, curtained with the finest brocades, and with silk sheets upon it. The detail of this makes clear that by the time the festivities are over, and we pass through the gates of the palace on our way home, he expects the princess to be pregnant with an heir to the lordship of Hambrig.

23rd September? That gives me three months. Three months to achieve the impossible. After supper I made my preparations, and the night passed in a blur of dreaming, waking and nervously pacing around my bedchamber. Just after sunrise I roused Master Kit.

'Come on,' I urged, as he gazed foggily at me from his feather bed. 'Get yourself up and ready. We are going to York, you and I.'

40

IT WAS NO LONGER THERE

Down at the *Egg* I said goodbye to Joan. I didn't have to tell her where I was going, I could see in her eyes that she knew.

She reached up and kissed me. 'If you find her, forgive her, Rory. It was all a very long time ago. Can I ask one other thing? Don't talk about Alex.'

I was silent. I hadn't thought about that – whether and what I'd tell Kathryn about Alex and his punishment. Finally, and truthfully, I said, 'I don't know what I'm going to say yet, Joan. My wish is only to get her back here, and then marry her and look after her for the rest of my life. Kit said she didn't want to see me. But I know she will. Once I'm there, it will be all right. It has to be.'

By the time we were ready to leave, breakfast was being eaten in the great hall. Rachel handed me a cloth bag. 'Rolls, cheese, sausage and bottles of ale and mead. You've a long journey ahead of you.'

I took the bag gladly, but wondered how she knew of the long journey.

She saw my look. 'You are off to York, are you not, lord? Take good care of yourself.' She went back to her kitchen.

Kit was amused. 'Hmm. She's no fool, that cook of yours.'

'She served my father before me,' I said shortly. 'She was here when Kathryn's uncle came to speak with my father.'

Kit gave me a curious look. 'Her uncle? Kathryn didn't say anything about an uncle.'

I was silent for several moments, checking the palfrey's girths and doing other unnecessary things, for of course Eliza had already seen to everything. I'd dismissed Eliza though, so Kit and I stood on our own in the courtyard, the minstrel leaning against the buttery wall, munching an apple. He suddenly pushed himself away from the wall and mounted the steps to the great hall. I waited impatiently, but it wasn't long before he returned and began to unhitch his horse.

'Your cook knows a great deal more than she lets on.' He mounted and turned the palfrey's head towards the gatehouse. 'As I said. She's no fool.'

We set a sensible pace, trotting at first, slowing to a walk on difficult ground, cantering gently over flat plains and rolling downland.

'So, my cook,' I said, for I did not intend to leave Kit's last remark hanging. 'What did she tell you?'

'It's always people like cooks, gardeners or nightwatchmen who know the most about what's actually going on,' Kit said, and I knew this to be true. 'You already told me Rachel was here in your father's time. You said she'd seen Kathryn's uncle come to the castle.'

'What of it?'

'It wasn't Kathryn's uncle, that's what. It was Alex's father. Rachel recognised him. Alex's father begged your

It was no longer there

father to take Alex into the garrison and train him as a soldier. Remember, Kathryn told her own father she was expecting Alex's baby, though I think it was Joan who approached him first, at Kathryn's request. It was all a big cover-up. Then you were packed off to the Holy Land in the hope you'd forget all about her.'

All a big cover-up. A white-hot anger consumed me. What had made them think they had the *right* to deceive me? Joan had reminded me that it was all in the past. But it felt like yesterday as I relived the sadness and the helplessness. Kit kept silent, letting me experience the pain on my own. For that, I was grateful to him.

———◆———

We aimed to cover thirty miles a day. The first two nights, we slept on the ground, rolled in our cloaks, but the weather was kind and there are plenty of watering places, so neither we nor the horses suffered. In fact, it was an enjoyable week's travelling. I got to know Kit rather well, and he would no doubt say the same of me, although we spent many hours riding in silence, as there's no need for constant chatter when you are at ease with someone. And, however improbably, that is exactly what I found – I was at ease with Kit.

He told me more about his childhood in Smander. Growing up in the royal palace was a life of luxury. He expressed again his simple gratitude to my father for making this possible. Without the armed escort, his mother, Joy, several months pregnant, would never have made it to Smander. Without my father's letter of introduction, vouching for her as an honest, capable woman, she would not have found work at all, far less a life in the employ of the royal family. And it was because the Smanderish king and queen were impressed with Joy, and took a liking to her son, that they took him into their own nursery and gave him the same education and advantages that were bestowed on their own children.

'It's like Moses,' I exclaimed.

Kit smiled. 'It is a bit.'

We pressed on, further and further north every day. Kit's talents were extremely useful, and by the third day on the road we found we could earn ourselves a bed for the night and enough food and drink too. Kit's singing opened many doors to us, and we were seen as travelling minstrels. I did not contribute much to this, although I found I could make a reasonable tune on Kit's gittern after some intensive instruction from him. In fact, by the end of the journey, we had an act together, in which I played a tune he'd taught me, and he sang a different but pleasing countermelody. We were applauded, and it was strange to be honoured for what I did rather than who I was. North of Mallrovia, nobody knew me.

As we neared the city of York Kit began to sing a song I'd not heard before. It had a catchy tune, but it was the lyrics I loved. He'd surely composed the song especially for me, I thought.

Gaily the troubadour touched his guitar,
As he was hastening home from the war.
Singing from Palestine, hither I come;
Lady love, lady love, welcome me home.

There were other verses too, mentioning battlements,

It was no longer there

and a weeping, lovelorn maiden. The whole song filled me with delight. Kit promised to teach me to play it one day.

We entered the city through Micklegate Bar just before noon, and walked our horses down Micklegate, the main street. I hadn't been to York before, and found it a similar size to Hicrown, but more crowded. Noisier and smellier too. I followed Kit over the Ouse Bridge, and onward to the city centre. We turned right towards the River Foss, and finally, passing through Stonebow, a narrow passageway, we arrived at a church, where we stopped just outside the precinct.

'Wait here,' Kit said, preparing to dismount.

'Why York?' I asked, urgently. 'Why is she here, in York? You never told me that.'

Standing in the stirrups, he turned his dark gaze on me. 'York? Well. There's a Carmelite monastery here.'

'There's a Carmelite monastery in Mallrovia. What's the real reason?'

He shrugged, and swung his leg over the saddle. 'Just wait, all right? I won't be long.'

I swallowed my irritation, held the reins for Kit, and did as he said. He disappeared into the friary. I looked around. I could see a few friars in the distance, their distinctive brown and white stripes making them easy to spot as they moved from one building to another. There were no nuns, but, as everyone knows, the Carmelite sisters are cloistered.

At first I'd been surprised Kit had been granted permission to see and talk with Kathryn at all, given that cloistered orders are seldom allowed any contact with the outside world. But perhaps nothing should surprise me about that man. I could only hope he would work his magic again.

Nothing happened for quite a while. I was restless and

anxious, but Kit suddenly emerged and walked calmly over to me. I slid down from my palfrey and faced him.

'Keep out of sight,' he said urgently.

I took no notice of this. 'Have you seen her? How is she?'

'Not yet. I hope you heard me, Rory. You mustn't be seen. I'll tie my horse to the fence here, but you must move, immediately.'

We led my horse into Stonebow, where the walls are high and the whole area shadowed.

I confronted Kit. 'Now. Tell me what's happening.'

'I haven't yet been given permission to speak with her. It isn't easy. She's cloistered, which means she's not allowed to speak with anyone or see anyone from outside the order. Last time, I bribed the bishop, but he's away today. So I've been talking with one of the friars – he's a brother in the order, you understand. And he's not so open to making a bit on the side, that's the problem.'

'So what now? If you can't bribe him, what are we going to do?'

'I'm going to lie to him. I'm going to tell him some story about there being bad news in Sister Clementine's family, and throw myself on his mercy. Remember, only Christ and the brothers and sisters are her family in this place. But I thought I saw a glint of humanity in his face when I spoke with him just now, and I'm going to play to that. Thing is, when I do get to see Sister Clementine, we are going to need to act fast.'

'You'll tell her I'm here?'

'No. She doesn't want to see you, she's content here. She won't want to leave. I'll find a way, but you need to be ready.'

'Ready for what?'

'Bloody hell, I don't know yet!'

Kit disappeared again. The narrow passage where I

waited was dank and dirty. There was a filthy channel running down the middle of it, and God knows what was floating down it to the Foss. I'm used to bad stenches and disgusting sights, but usually you pass them by. Here, I was forced to stand and wait in the malodorous passageway, not knowing for how long, trying to keep from freezing.

At some point in that interminable afternoon I decided the only fair thing to do was to walk my horse up Stonebow to the other end, where he could drink from a trough and make himself more comfortable. I tethered him to a post by the trough and ran lightly back down the passage, finishing up crouched low in the entrance, thankful my clothes were dun-coloured. And there I waited.

Night fell in Stonebow before it was dark anywhere else. I heard some noises, and pressed myself flat against the wall. People were talking, men's voices. Brothers perhaps, friars from the order. The voices faded, and again it was silent. I crept out of my hiding place and, bending double, made my way cautiously towards the friary. I heard Kit's horse whickering from the fence to the side, and decided the man must have gained entry, at least. I felt my way to the building itself, and then, hand over hand on the stonework, crept round, keeping in the shadows, pressing myself to the wall.

Eventually, around the back of the building, I found what I was looking for. The shutters on one window had been thrown back, and it was an easy matter for me to climb through the opening. I found myself in a flagged passage, lit by torches in sconces, at the end of which was a closed oak door. Behind the door a voice murmured. Silently, I moved down the passage and then inched the door open. In the room, similarly torch-lit, were several men wearing the brown striped mantle of the Carmelite brothers. They stood as if frozen, their mouths hanging open, and one was cringing back in fear. Out of the corners of their eyes they must have seen me come in, but their gaze was riveted on my minstrel.

On the other side of the room, Kit stood in a theatrical pose, one arm around a nun's waist, pinning her to him, the other hand flung high above his head.

'And now,' he said in his stage magician's voice, 'you will see that I am indeed a messenger from Hell!'

There was a collective gasp of horror from the brothers. The nun he held couldn't move, but she started to scream. Kit clamped his hand over her mouth and whispered something in her ear. At that she looked terrified, but stopped screaming. He was able to remove his hand and wave elaborately at me.

'My assistant, Lucifer!'

The brothers crossed themselves. One of the friars made to move towards Kit, but Kit stopped him.

'No nearer,' he ordered. 'My aura can touch you from here. I will draw a line, beyond which no one may venture, except, of course, my assistant.'

And from his free hand he dropped some small objects. They banged loudly as they hit the floor, and sparks showered the room. *Firecrackers*, I learned later.

Kit's firecrackers popped and danced across the floor. He gave a wicked laugh, and told the brothers that the evil spirits of which he had charge would be contained within the fire. I watched in horrified admiration as the brothers cowered, terrified, in a corner of the room, while Kit began to make his way to the door, dropping more firecrackers as he walked. One friar, more courageous than the rest, moved to block the door before Kit reached it.

It was no longer there

'You may not leave,' the friar said bravely. 'And you will not have our sister.'

'I advise you to move,' Kit said, 'or you will be consumed by my evil spirits. For we are taking this woman, whether you like it or not.'

Kit was now only a few feet from me, and he suddenly hurled the nun away from him. She fell into my arms. 'She's all yours, Lucifer!' he shouted, and then leapt up high and pulled something out of the air. There was a glitter, a flash, a sparkle of movement, and then, to my shocked disbelief, Fiorello appeared, swinging from Kit's hand by his tail.

'Aha!' cried Kit, whirling round to show the gecko to everyone. 'Behold my familiar, *Fiorello!*'

Then Kit spoke softly to the gecko, his voice wheedling, his other hand stroking it lovingly. 'Oh, but he's dangerous! *Soooo* dangerous. If I swing him towards you...' And Kit did just that, swinging Fiorello violently towards first one brother and then another, while I held the nun tightly to me and tried to edge my way to the door.

'If I swing him like *this* and like *this*' – Kit lunged with the gecko as if he held a longsword – 'you will see his murderous eyes fixed on you, and you will know he has marked you for death! Do not let Fiorello look upon you, for if he does, he will *kill* you!'

Somewhere in the friary a bell began to toll. I heard voices and running footsteps. Then a shout went up. The nun and I reached the doorway, but people were fast approaching. Kit was still in the room, executing intricate dance steps, leaping from one side to the other, intoning strange Latin phrases, and finally, heart-stoppingly, throwing the gecko from one hand to the other. These friars truly believed he was the devil, but the alert had been sounded, more brothers were on their way, and we didn't have much time.

At last I was through the door, and no one had stopped me. I heaved the woman over my shoulder, though she bit and scratched in her terror; then I sprinted back down the corridor and climbed out through the window. I raced round the friary, coming eventually to the fence where Kit had tethered his horse. I lifted the nun into the saddle, untied the horse and waited. Kit was only just in time. He exploded out of one of the doors, a pack of brothers in pursuit, the air filled with their shouting.

I threw the reins to Kit, then tore up Stonebow to my palfrey, leaping into his saddle, feet feeling for the stirrups. Kit and I galloped down Micklegate, out through the bar and onto the rolling hills. I was shouting in exultation, and Kit was laughing, great guffaws that split the night sky. We had done it! We had broken Kathryn out of the convent, and we were on our way back to Hambrig. It was a moment of sheer glory.

We galloped for nearly ten miles, until York was far behind us, and it was clear nobody was following. We rode side by side, and the splendour of victory rode with us. Oh, it was wonderful. Kathryn, the only girl I'd ever loved, was coming home. King Philip would not be pleased, but that couldn't be helped, and Lady Lillian would surely not be short of suitors.

In a small thicket of trees we dismounted and, in the moonlight, sorted ourselves out. I lifted Kathryn down from Kit's horse and laid her on the ground. Her habit was torn and she had lost her veil. This was the woman I'd known, the woman I'd loved, but I had not seen her for fifteen years. She'd been a girl then, and I little more than a boy.

'Where's Fiorello?' I turned to Kit suddenly, and was

It was no longer there

disconcerted to see that he'd been watching me looking at the woman on the ground.

'I have him safe. Don't worry.'

'You took him from the Box of Death? The day we talked in my library?'

'Yes.'

'Why?'

'I thought I might need him one day. I was right, wasn't I.'

'That was why you took my keys?'

'That was why I took your keys.'

The day we talked in my library. When I thought Kit had run off with Merry's gold. When I learned that Kathryn was alive, and that I'd briefly had a son. When my feelings had been so unbearable, so painful, that my mind and body had shut down completely.

I bent and loosened Kathryn's shift, trying to make her comfortable. She stirred, and her eyes opened. When she saw me, she started back with a cry of alarm. She didn't recognise me.

'Kathryn,' I said gently, raising her head and helping her to sit up. 'Kathryn, it is Rory. From Hambrig. From the castle.'

'Rory?'

Still no recognition.

Kit held out a flagon of ale. It was a week old and stale now, but we used it to moisten Kathryn's lips, and she swallowed a little.

'We should go,' Kit said. He was right. There would be riders coming after us.

'I'll take Kathryn now.'

Kit helped me get her into my saddle, so I could ride behind her and keep her safe within my arms.

I asked him again where Fiorello was. He indicated his tunic, and I was aghast. 'But you can't have him there!'

He grinned. 'Stop worrying! Fiorello's in a box. The little ivory box, in fact. He can't do me any harm.'

Nothing could do us harm, not now I had Kathryn again.

Of that I was certain.

We needed frequent stops along the way, for Kathryn was unused to riding, and she was recovering from her ordeal. After the third day though, she began to improve, and we found we could go further between breaks. Most nights we spent under the stars again, the three of us. Kathryn and I talked a little, though not as much as you might have expected. So much happens in fifteen years; how can you possibly say everything?

I told her of my Crusade, of coming home to take over the estate, and of some of the changes I'd made to the castle. She told me she'd taken her vows, she was Sister Clementine now, and she had found peace. She spoke in a low, sad voice, and for the first time I wondered if I had done the right thing. Night after night, while the other two slept, I struggled to know if perhaps I should have left this woman to her life of prayer and contemplation. I understood now why she'd been taken to York, nearly two hundred miles from her home. She'd made a new life there. She had a new name, a new family. And the love we'd had for each other? It was no longer there.

41

IT WAS READY

On the fourth day we reached a place called Kirkstead by the River Witham. There's an abbey here, although Kirkstead itself is a very small settlement, and we found lodgings nearby. Kit and I had insisted that Kathryn reverse her robes, so as not to show the distinctive Carmelite striping, and we'd used my undershirt to fashion her a shawl and a new headdress. She had complied with all this in silence. We took lodging in an inn, a room with one small, low, narrow bed. Kit fell asleep in a corner by the door almost immediately, and I sat hugging my knees next to the low bed. Kathryn lay on it, her face turned to the wall. Reaching out, I pulled her shoulder, rolling her over towards me.

'Well?' I said.

'Well what, lord?' she answered dully.

'*Lord?* Don't call me that, Kathryn.'

'What shall I call you then? My abductor? My persecutor?'

'You used to call me by my name.'

'Yes, I used to. You used to love me, we were going to marry. What happened to you?'

I couldn't believe what I was hearing. I put my face close to hers.

'*What happened?* What happened, Kathryn, is that your uncle – no, wait, it wasn't your uncle, it was Alex's father – came to see *my* father. I was not allowed to hear what was said, but afterwards my father told me you were dead. I was sent away to fight the Saracens. I was away five years and barely escaped with my life. When I got home everything had changed. I was Lord of Hambrig, with a million responsibilities, and it was as if you had never been.'

Her eyes filled with tears. 'I didn't know,' she said. 'I didn't know they told you I was dead. I thought they told you I was having a baby, and I waited and waited for you to come and get me. The first year in the convent, I never stopped hoping. I was sure you would ride up on a great warhorse and claim me for your own. But you didn't, and then I gave up hope. Now you've come, but you're fifteen years too late. My baby was born, and lived for two weeks only. After that, I took my vows and gave myself to Christ.'

I was silent. For I *would* have gone to her rescue, if I'd known she was alive. And if I'd known where she was. But there was something else.

'You wanted me to come and get you, even though you'd slept with Alex? Even though I couldn't know whose baby you were having?'

She stared at me. 'You think I slept with someone else? You think I betrayed our love?'

'Alex's father told my father. The Lady Joan told me also.'

Kathryn made a sound somewhere between a laugh and a sob. 'You really believed it then. I would *never* have lain with another man, Rory. Never. I was yours. All I wanted was

It was ready

to be with you, to marry you. I remember Alex, but I never said I'd been with him, I just said a stable boy. I only said it to protect you. I never thought you would believe it!'

'I didn't have the chance to believe or otherwise,' I said angrily, and loudly enough for Kit to stir under his blankets. I lowered my voice. 'I was told you were *dead,* for God's sake! I didn't *know* you were expecting a child. Our child.'

I all but broke down on those words, for I saw now how cruel fate had been. Kathryn had tried to protect me. But my father had also tried to protect me by telling me my girl was dead. And then he'd sent me far away from home. I never questioned the story my father gave me, because he was always honest, he never lied. I put my hands over my face in despair.

I pictured Kathryn thinking I'd been told she'd had an affair with a stable lad. She'd have thought it a good trick, knowing I'd not believe it, certain I'd know it was *our* baby, because we had not been chaste, certain too that I would ride at once to her rescue. And so she waited and waited, never knowing I was in Egypt with Jonny.

Jonny had been my saviour. I had been a mess, but he had been a rock. He told me there were other women; I'd grieve for a while but then I'd recover. And he was so right. It had been exactly like that. What a bloody awful waste.

Long, cool fingers stretched out and wiped the tears from my cheeks. I climbed onto the bed beside Kathryn, and, for old times' sake, I took her in my arms.

Early, before daylight, I crawled out from under the blankets. Kit sat on a pile of rugs on the other side of the room, watching me with his dark, brooding eyes. I crouched down beside him.

'You look like death,' he said.

'I've crippled a man for something he didn't do.'

'He didn't do it? Alex didn't screw Kathryn?'
'No.'
'Did he tell you he was innocent?'
'You know he didn't. I didn't give him the chance.'

I was so wretched I didn't know what to do with myself. After a while, Kit got up and went to wash under the pump in the yard. I closed my eyes, but didn't like the pictures in my head, so I opened them again. All I could see was Alex, lying in the gatehouse arch, his ribs bent and twisted, blood and vomit dribbling from his mouth, his back broken. Paralysed. Crippled. Ruined. And I had exulted.

I awoke to find Kathryn sitting opposite me on the floor, a goblet of small ale beside her and a hunk of black bread in her hand. She offered me the bread.

'You must eat and drink,' she said softly.

I knew at once Kit had told her what I'd done to Alex. An innocent man. I looked away. I could touch no food, but I did drain the goblet. I stood up, aware I was filthy. Outside, I sluiced myself down at the well and then went to see the horses, but Kit had already attended to them. All the time I was thinking furiously, and by the time I'd finished dressing, I'd made up my mind.

I pulled Kathryn towards me and kissed her hard on the lips. I kissed her throat, her shoulders and her breasts. Then I held her at arm's length.

'I'm taking you back to York,' I said. 'Sister Clementine you shall be. You belong there. At least I know now what really happened.'

'You do not want me?'

It was ready

'I want you, Kathryn. I've never stopped wanting you. For fifteen years I believed you dead. I have never married. I wanted only you.'

'So why will you take me back to the convent?'

'I have to. I don't deserve you now, and I have to find a way of making my peace with Alex. I've done a great wrong. I can never put it right, but I must do whatever I can to atone.'

'But you will marry now? You must obey the King, mustn't you?'

'I will marry now,' I agreed. After a pause, I asked, 'Did you give our child a name, Kathryn?'

'I called him Rory, of course. The eldest son of the lord. He never knew his name, he was too little when he died.'

Kit rode on to Hambrig. I made the journey back to York with Kathryn. At the end of Stonebow passage, we dismounted, and I walked my lady to the convent gate. I knelt in the grass and kissed her hand.

'They will take you back?' I asked anxiously. I had not thought of that until now.

'They will,' she assured me.

I watched Kathryn walk through the gate and up the long path to the friary. A door opened, and Sister Clementine went inside.

———◆———

I arrived back at the castle to find that Kit and Patrick had been extremely busy. They'd been consulting the Hurogol Treaty, the map and *The Meridian*, and had decided on the deal to be offered to the Kyown-Kinnie. They were waiting for me to give them permission to proceed. I looked carefully at everything they had done. It was all neatly written up by Patrick, but Kit wanted to explain it in his flamboyant way. I listened to him for half an hour, told him I'd think it over, and then spent a further short time closeted with Patrick, who went through it again with his customary dry precision. Then I sent him away as well, so I could be alone in my library, with Patrick's notes and all the manuscripts on my desk.

Was it watertight? Would it work? Where were the ambiguities? I knew that once the Toosanik established themselves on my land, if there were any loopholes at all they would find them. We had to have everything covered, absolutely *everything*. But my mind would not concentrate. I read the words, but they meant nothing. I read them again, and then again, but it was as if I were reading a different language. Finally, I locked up my library, ran down the stairs, and walked quickly to the gatehouse and the soldiers' quarters above it.

Alex has been moved here, and is recovering slowly. Doctor Bethan tells me she is making him do exercises to strengthen his body, and he is responding well to them. She has found that he does have some sensation; he can feel it when she pricks his left leg with a needle. She can't give him a lot of hope for the future, but it's possible things may improve a little. He's been given a small chamber to himself off the main barracks. I walked in, and found him sitting up in bed just staring at the wall ahead of him. He started when he saw me.

'Alex,' I said, and pulled up a stool so I could sit next to his bed. 'You need something to do.'

'Doctor Bethan visits me, lord. And Captain Kerry is here a lot.'

'Ah yes, Captain Kerry.' Her voice, exclaiming *You have*

It was ready

nearly killed him, lord, haunts me every night. 'No, I mean you need to have something to keep your mind busy. Can you read, Alex?'

'Yes, lord, I can read. Sir Jonny made sure of it when I was promoted archer.'

'Well, you're a sergeant now, so that's even better. I want you to read some documents and tell me what you think.'

He turned a surprised face to me. 'Lord, I don't know nothin' about documents. Maybe you should get a lawyer to look at them. I don't know nothin'. I never went to school.'

'It doesn't matter,' I said roughly, determined my plan would succeed. 'You can read, and you have wit. Put the two together, that's all I want. I will send you the documents and will return tomorrow morning to hear what you think.'

As I left the room, I could feel his eyes staring at my back. Outside the room, I swallowed bile. The man is a wreck, and I have made him one. Even now, I have not apologised. I have offered him work he cannot do, and I've put him in a position where he will fail and feel worse than ever. Crashing down the stairs to the courtyard, I met Captain Kerry on her way up. She stood aside, but I told her to come with me. Out in the courtyard we faced each other.

'How is Alex really?' I asked.

'He is doing well, lord,' she replied, standing to attention.

'Relax, captain. I'm asking you informally, I don't want a medical report. You're his friend. How's he doing, how is he feeling?'

She was silent for a few moments, and I grew impatient. I was determined to do something for this man whose life I had ruined. To make amends. But I didn't know how, and I was frustrated and angry.

Finally, Kerry said, 'Alex has told me he did not go near

your lady. I have talked to him a lot, and he will not budge from his story. I've told him you wouldn't accuse him falsely. You would not have said those things if you didn't know them to be true. Because of that, at first I didn't believe him when he denied everything. But he has never wavered. He says he saw your lady many times in her father's place, which is where he worked as a stable lad, but he's adamant he never touched her.'

She paused. I stayed silent; I could see she had more to say. 'Liars often change their stories, but Alex never has. So, I began to believe him. But if he is telling the truth, then your lady must have lied to you, lord. Alex, Doctor Bethan and I have talked and talked about it. Doctor Bethan thinks Alex might recover quite well in the end, but only if he can make things better in his head. But he can't because he keeps saying he didn't do it, and you think he did, and no one believes him.'

'Thank you, captain,' I said. 'Carry on.'

I watched her run lightly up the gatehouse steps. And then I was violently sick.

Back in my library, I bundled up all the documents and sent Gael off with them to Alex. Gael is delighted I've returned, but Sir Patrick has spoken sourly to me about my page and my bard. Since I've been away, they've been fornicating like rabbits, he said. But the boy is only twelve years old! This is my sticking point. Patrick points out that Gael at twelve is more like I was at sixteen, and it's true he's grown big for his age now.

I was angry with Patrick, although these days I am angry with everyone. Why hasn't Patrick, or Jonny – or Rachel even – put a stop to it? *Fornicating.* What a word to use. Typical of mimsy Patrick, I thought viciously.

'Gael,' I said sternly when the boy returned from

It was ready

delivering the bundle to Alex, 'Gael, you are not to sleep with Amie. You are my page, and you will sleep in my room again now.'

'Yes, lord,' he said dutifully.

But they will find a way of course. I sighed. Why is everything so bloody difficult?

———◆———

I go to Mass in the chapel every morning. Laurence preaches his meaningless sermons, but prayer helps me. I have come to terms with the loss of Kathryn. I know now that I will marry Lady Lillian, and that my heart is free to do so. But I cannot come to terms with the suffering I have caused Sergeant Alex. The day after I sent him the manuscripts I saw tears in his eyes. He told me he'd looked at everything, but there were words he didn't understand, and he has no knowledge of borders, customs, treaties or trade deals. He was a stable hand and then a soldier. That's all he knows. Sadly, I took the documents back, leaving him alone in his room with his black thoughts and his useless body.

Instead, I sat down with Kit and went through everything again. We changed a few things, but finally, stretching and yawning in sheer exhaustion after a whole night of it, we agreed the treaty was the best we could make it. It was ready.

42

THIS IS WHAT HE MEANT

Kit, as the New Beginning, is taking our treaty to the Toosanik. He will have talks with the Kyown-Kinnie. A Spiderboat and its crew have been deployed, my banner at the masthead. Kit is wearing neutral clothes, though the Spiderboat crew are in my colours of red and gold. Recently-promoted Sergeant Sybil and four other soldiers from the garrison are also sailing across to Blurland.

Sir Jonny thought he should go with the treaty, but I want to play down the military presence, and I'm playing down the political presence, too, by not going myself. At first, we called our proposal the Second Hurogol Treaty, but this one was not drawn up on the banks of the river as the first one was, and it is both new and different. It needs a new name. We hope the Kyown-Kinnie will agree to the terms and sign it. A signal has been arranged: Sergeant Sybil has charge of some flares.

These flares! They're new and exciting! They were brought to Mallrovia by merchant ships trading in the Far East of the world. Many wonderful things are imported from Khitai, including silks, precious metals and jewels. The

This is what he meant

people of Khitai make a kind of explosive which we call Black Powder, though William told me that its other name is *fire medicine.* They can put this powder into a pouch and fix it onto an arrow or a lance. At the Battle of Baudry Hill, William's *Senjo* used the Black Powder to launch murderous metal into the Smanderish army.

The flares made their appearance in Mallrovia some years ago, and King Philip has been using them in his Spiderboat fleet ever since. Impressed, I bought a few of my own, though they are formidably expensive. When you light them, they burn with a bright light, but, unlike the Black Powder, they don't explode or cause damage, so they will be useful for signalling from a distance. Sergeant Sybil has her instructions. As soon as the Kyown-Kinnie signs the new agreement, she is to send up a flare.

I saw them off from the landing stage, Kit sitting in the sternsheets, a calfskin bag slung around his shoulders. In the bag was the precious treaty and, of course, the map. My chalk lines have been rubbed off and redrawn more accurately by Joan, using fine Indian ink. The whole drawing now shows every detail, matching up perfectly with our proposal. The Spiderboat shoved off and the crew sculled across to a patch of wind, then hoisted the big lugsail. As the boat heeled over I shaded my eyes to watch them beat across to Blurland, which I could barely see from the landing stage. Jonny, watching from the castle ramparts would have a much better view. I rode back up Baudry Hill and handed my horse over to Eliza. Then I sent for Gael and Amie.

Since getting back from York ten days ago, I've been doing a lot of thinking about Gael. His defence of me that dreadful day in the gatehouse arch still shakes me. It took courage for him to face up to Jonny, to witness my humiliating breakdown and yet still stand by me. I want to reward him for such loyalty, so I've come to a decision, and I want Amie to hear it as well. I will now put away my journal and send for them both.

'Gael, you are twelve years old,' I began, the two of them standing in front of me in the great hall.

'Lord,' he interrupted nervously, 'I am thirteen now. Three weeks ago I had a birthday.'

'Thirteen then. And you are growing tall and strong. Now, I have been thinking a great deal about your future, and I have something very special and exciting to tell you. I am going to advance your training, Gael. You will begin learning to be my squire. We will not wait till you are fourteen, the proper age – we will start now.'

I waited for his delighted reaction, but it never came. Instead, he glanced quickly at Amie, and then licked his lips.

'Lord, you do me a great honour, but...' He stopped.

'What's the matter? I thought you'd be thrilled.'

'Yes, I know. But you see, lord, I don't think I want to be a knight.'

I saw Amie nodding by his side. Obviously, they'd discussed this. But not with me.

I was surprised and disappointed. But I remembered now. Something he'd said in my library a couple of months back. *The Lady Joan told me that one day Amie will be a great bard, even as great as Taliesin of Wales was, and I should be with her as much as possible and learn from her, because I might never be a knight, but one day I might be a musician.*

This is what he meant

'You want to be a musician, then,' I said flatly. It was no life, not compared to being my squire and then being dubbed knight in the King's court. But Gael nodded, his fair curls bouncing all over his head, his hand swinging in Amie's.

'Yes!' he said emphatically. 'It's what I want more than anything. I want to be like Master Kit.'

'Master Kit! He's a *duke,* Gael! He's rich, he has land and property. That's not being a musician. He's just a very clever man who can do anything he wants. Don't be a fool.' I was hurt and upset, but I regretted the words as soon as they were out of my mouth. The boy wasn't a fool, and he wanted to follow his heart. Not very different from Sammy, I thought savagely. What's the matter with the young these days?

'Look.' I took a deep breath. 'Play your music. Learn from Amie, and from Master Kit too. I'll give you a year. You can tell me then if you've changed your mind, and if you have – well, I'll still have you. What do you say to that?'

'Thank you, lord,' Gael answered fervently. 'It is very generous of you.'

Yes, it bloody well was. I could simply have dismissed him from my household and sent him back to his father. If it hadn't been for that day in the gatehouse, that's exactly what I would have done. And it won't be all songs and pretty lays, I thought crossly. I'll find work for him; he'll have to earn his keep. I made this clear, and the two youngsters simply nodded like idiots and looked ridiculously happy. I sniffed and decided I was going soft in my old age. That must be so, for I found myself continuing with the second part of my offer.

'In two years' time, you and Amie may marry.'

Gael looked startled. 'But my father,' he began, his voice

squeaking in alarm, 'my father won't accept Amie as my bride. She is not well born. He won't allow me to marry her!'

'I will speak with your father,' I heard myself say. 'If, in two years' time, you and Amie still wish to marry, I will speak with the baron and he will accept the match. Is that what you both want?'

They nodded again, smiles all over their silly faces. Amie curtsied and Gael made a flamboyant bow à la Kit. I snorted and waved them away.

And realised, alone in the great hall, that I was, indeed, truly alone. No woman, no page, no squire.

But there was still Alex. As the kitchen servants started flooding into the hall to get everything ready for dinner, I made my way slowly to his room and found him playing hazard by himself. I watched for a while from the doorway, before he looked up and saw me there. Immediately, he reddened, and tried to salute. I went in and sat on the bed.

'Sergeant Alex.' I came straight to the point and did what I should have done weeks ago. 'I have done you a great wrong. I gave you no chance to defend yourself and tell me the truth, which is that you did not touch Lady Kathryn. You were a stable lad in her father's household, and she did an unpardonable thing, and used you to cover for me. She should not have done that. The sad thing is that I didn't even know she *had* done it, because I was told a lie. I was told Kathryn was dead. Others did know the story she told about you, but I learnt of it only a few weeks ago. I believed you had slept with her, and in my rage, I attacked you. I gave you no opportunity for self-defence. I am truly sorry, Alex. I know I cannot undo the hurt I have done you, but I will do everything I can to make things come right for you now.'

I locked his gaze in mine the whole time I was speaking. I wanted him to see that I was sincere. But when I finished, Alex looked away, embarrassed. Embarrassed by my apology? Because I was a noble lord and he'd been a stable boy?

I frowned. 'Do you understand, Alex?'

Silence. I tried again. 'Do you have any family?'

'I've a mother still living,' he said dully. 'And a younger brother, but he's not right in the head. He can't do much.'

'Alex, I will provide for your mother and your brother. They can live here, in the castle. They will have everything they need.'

He flared up. 'No! We don't need that. We don't need you to look after us. We've been all right the last fifteen years, haven't we? You didn't care so much about us all that time.'

It was unfair. I care about all my Hambriggers, and I look after them as best I can. My taxes and rents are lower than many other lords charge, which is why there's never any money left over, once all the essential purchases have been made. Once a month I ride round the estate, calling in on as many as I can, offering help where it's needed. And all my vassals know they can come to the castle and talk to me, any time they need to. Alex's family are villeins, they are unfree. I have to find out more about them, where they live and how they fare. Then I will do something for them.

I left Alex to his black mood and his dice game and went to speak again with Captain Kerry. She readily told me everything she knew about Alex's family.

'They live in the town. Alex's mother is very poor. She works for a cobbler, cleaning and fetching and carrying for him, but he doesn't give her much. She has to provide for

Alex's brother, so she never has enough to eat. I know Alex sends all his pay to her, but it's still hard for them.'

'Alex's brother. What's his name?'

'He's called Geoffrey. There's something wrong with him. He's an adult, but he acts like a child. You can't ask him to do anything.'

'You've met him? And the mother too?'

'No, lord, I only know what Alex has told me. But Sir Jonny has visited them, I believe.'

'Thank you, captain. You've been very helpful.'

Jonny confirmed everything Kerry had said. 'Geoffrey's unable to do much, he can't even feed himself properly. Alex's mother works all day for Master Robert, and she worries about what Geoffrey is getting up to while she's away from home. They live in a tumbledown hut, which she can't afford to maintain. I don't know what they'll do now Alex isn't working for you, Rory. He's no longer on the payroll.'

'Then put him back on the bloody payroll,' I growled. 'I want him paid. And I want his mother and this other boy brought here. She will work for us, and the boy will be looked after. Gael can take charge of Geoffrey. That'll keep the young stud busy, won't it!'

Jonny looked up, surprised, but I didn't enlighten him, he can think what he likes. I feel a whole lot better, though; if I personally take charge of and pay for Alex and his family to live under my roof in comfort, I will feel I have done what I can.

This is what he meant

It was three more days before the shout went up on a drizzly, grey afternoon. I hurled myself up to the ramparts and stared over to the Toosanik lands. There it was, a bright, shining light, arcing through the sky. The signal, at last.

'Ah, thank God,' Jonny said beside me. We looked at each other. This could be the start of peace. If the Toosanik settle in Hambrig there will be no more raids, no more fighting, and the River Hurogol will be a safe waterway. It may have taken a hundred years, but perhaps, at last, the war will be over. Not only that, but there will be justice for the Toosanik, and Anthony Merry's long and tortuous campaign will be accomplished, which will please the Lady Joan if nothing else.

From the parapet surrounding one of the gatehouse towers, another flare shot skywards. That was our acknowledgement of the signal, and Kit could now return. And, roughly three hours later, the Watch reported sighting the Spiderboat's lugsail, as, in the gathering dark, the Duke of Casuel returned to the landing stage.

I was there when the boat docked. I grasped Kit by the arm and helped him ashore. He looked exhausted, so perhaps there had been a great deal of talking through the night. Perhaps the Kyown-Kinnie had been a hard man to convince. Back at the castle, I took Kit straight to the great hall. He subsided onto a bench and stretched out his legs.

'It has not been easy,' he said wearily. 'The Kyown-Kinnie wanted changes.'

'What changes?'

'More freedom, more land, less rent to pay you.'

'Hmm. What did you agree to?' But he'd had no authority to agree to any changes.

'I agreed to nothing. The deal stands as we drew it up. We'd not have sent the damned flare up otherwise.'

'But you said he wanted changes! What happened?'

'I persuaded him that his changes were both unnecessary and detrimental to his people's welfare. It just took time, that's all. Time and energy. I find I'm running short of both, these days.'

For God's sake! He's only twenty-two! Still, it must have taken a great deal of ingenuity and clever talking, and exactly *how* Kit had persuaded the Kyown-Kinnie, he wouldn't say. Not with Fiorello, surely. I had a sudden alarming vision of Kit throwing firecrackers around and dangling the gecko in front of the Toosanik chief.

The man read my mind, threw back his head and laughed. 'Oh no! You think I used Fiorello again, don't you. No, Rory, I did not. Fiorello belongs to the Nahvitch, remember? *Fiorello is death to those he looks upon. Except* the Nahvitch! They are immune to his deadly gaze. That's the legend. Remember, I'm half Toosanik, I know how to deal with them.'

Somehow, I had forgotten the gecko belonged to the Toosanik. Kit is always a step ahead of me.

'I have other powers of persuasion,' Kit said cryptically. 'Oh, don't worry,' he snapped impatiently. 'It was very diplomatic and businesslike. We held several long meetings, and there were witnesses and scribes and everything. And the Kyown-Kinnie signed the treaty.'

'When will they be here?'

'Some of them will come very soon, as they want to be settled before the bad weather. Those with building skills will come first. They will start building their huts and their Meeting Place as soon as they can. We'll need to send surveyors to check the boundaries are right. He saw the map. *Very* impressed he was with that. He wants one of his own. They'll be crofting, like they used to, which means small parcels of land, especially if it's good grazing or fertile enough for crops. But that's up to them. They know where they can go; how they divide it between them is their business, not ours.'

'Theirs? Ours? I thought as half Toosanik, half Hambrigger, it would all be "ours" to you, Kit.'

He grimaced. 'I suppose it should be. But I've not lived with the Toosanik. I have lived here for a while now, and I've become...'

'What have you become?'

'Settled, I suppose,' he said, distantly. 'I always thought I'd go back to Casuel. But the one thing I'm *not* is a Smanderino.'

'They gave you a home though,' I reminded him. 'They took your mother in, looked after her, educated you, and then gave you a ruddy dukedom! Perhaps you *should* go back.'

'My mother's in her fifties now. She'll be all right. She has everything she needs. But you're right, the Smanderinos have looked after us and I shouldn't just abandon Casuel. I will go back there. But once I've settled my affairs, and another man has been put in charge of the place, I'll come home to my real people as the New Beginning. This is what my father wanted, Rory. *This* is what he meant.'

43

CROWBARS AND HAMMERS

In the last week the weather has changed. After a glorious summer of bright and breezy sunshine, it has suddenly become wild and cold, which often happens towards the end of August in Hambrig. On the hillside and in the fields, the villagers have been working frantically to get the harvest in – backbreaking work. We'd wheat and rye, barley and oats, to get into the barns for the winter, and the animals have been led to the fields to graze the stubble that's left. Eventually the cattle will be over-wintered in byres, but Mallrovian sheep are hardy creatures, and they will be left out on the hillsides. We started three weeks ago, before the weather turned, and I've been helping all day and every day, as I'm fairly handy with a sickle. Everyone who can be spared has lent a hand. Our soldiers have been in the fields from dawn until dusk, and now, thank the Lord, it is all done, all safely gathered in.

We've had a summer of tremendous activity. After an exodus lasting more than a hundred years, the Toosanik have once more taken over the Great Plain, their rightful home. The building, the fetching and carrying, the general moving and shifting, has been going on for weeks. In my household there are many skilled and experienced craftsmen and women, so I sent them down to the Plain, and their carpentry, their basket-weaving, their log-felling and stone-hewing skills have been put to good use.

We all want to make sure that this Toosanik settlement is no swampland camp, but a permanent and comfortable home. What has pleased me most is the communication that has developed between Toosanik and Hambrigger. The educated Toosanik elders all speak good English, but many clansmen and women only have the Okkam. There is much laughter and confusion as mistakes are made in finding out what people want, but it's always sorted out in the end, and small phrases of Okkam have entered our speech here in the castle. Interestingly, one of these is *Keeshiv*. Whenever I hear this word, it brings poor Davy vividly into my mind.

There was something Sammy said when we rode to meet the Spiderboat.

Well, what was it? What did he say?

He said, you will have a surprise when you see me next. You will all have a great surprise.

Did you ask him what he meant by that? And did he say anything else?

He said one other thing, lord, but I didn't understand it at all. It wasn't in English. It sounded like Keeshiv.

Keeshiv? Are you sure?

Of course, the surprise was Sammy's revelation to us as King of the Nahvitch. Oh, he'd built himself up in his own eyes into a grand and royal personage! Hence the enormous stallion he could barely control, and the beautiful new colour for his coat of arms. And *Keeshiv*? It's Okkam for

'You'll see'. How did Sammy have the Okkam? I still don't know the answer to that. I've asked Joan, of course, and her guess, which is as good as any, is that Eefa spoke some Okkam to James and he picked it up. For the sake of his Toosanik son, he may have used these Okkam phrases with him.

So what with organising and helping with the Toosanik settlement, and then the intense and demanding work of getting all the crops in, at last, on this cold and windy Wednesday at the end of August, I decided I was finally able to relax. And so just before dinner I was sitting in the *Egg*, talking with the Lady Joan. Of course, there was a fire going in the hearth, crackling and sparking; the samovar was steaming happily on the table; and candles threw their suggestive shadows on the flinty walls of the little hut. I wasn't just passing the time of day, though, I had something to discuss.

A messenger from the palace arrived yesterday with a letter from the King. Philip is anxious to let me know that preparations for my wedding are well underway. Various entertainments have been hired, and the Lady Joan will soon be sent for to discuss the princess's wedding outfit. Philip trusts I am making my own preparations for the grand celebrations in three weeks' time.

Well, to a certain extent we *are* ready. There has been a lot of work going on making new outfits for me, Sir Jonny and Sir Patrick. We all have new lined surcoats in my heraldic colours of red and gold. We spent a considerable amount of money in Hambrig Town having these new garments made, with hose to match, and the latest fashion in uncomfortable, pointy shoes. Rachel and Eliza will both be coming to Hicrown, lending their help to the palace staff, so they had to have new gowns, wimples and hats. The Lady Joan was asked to design them, which of course she was happy to do.

But she would *not* have anticipated being asked to make the bridal gown for Lady Lillian, and I felt it was only fair to warn her about that. I brought the King's letter with me, and she read it. I didn't expect panic, and there was none, but Joan did raise her eyebrows and look wryly around the workshop. I guess she doesn't yet have the necessary fancy materials she'll need to make a wedding gown for a princess. But we didn't say much about it; Joan knows I'm not marrying for love. And there were plenty of other things to talk about, one of which has been on my mind for some time. Back in May, the Lady Joan had made a prediction about Gael. *I might never be a knight, but one day I might be a musician.* How had she known?

'Ever since Gael came to the castle,' Joan answered, 'he's wanted to be you. He's seen you striding around the place, he's seen how our people love and respect you. You're strong, you're honest and you're a leader. Gael wanted to be all those things. He's idolised you these last six years. But then he fell in love. No, I don't mean with Amie, although he is undoubtedly besotted with her too. I mean he fell in love with music. Funnily enough, it didn't start with Amie, it started with Master Kit. Kit awakened something in Gael, something that had been lying dormant for years, and suddenly he knew there was only one thing he wanted to do. But he couldn't tell you, and he certainly couldn't tell his father.'

'He told you though?'

'Not in so many words. But he asked me if I thought Amie was a good musician. I told him she's gifted; she could be as great as Taliesin. She puts her whole soul into her music, and she doesn't care if you don't like it. Her music is how she says what she thinks, what she believes. That's what I said to Gael. And he sat here and said he wanted to be as great as Taliesin too. All I did was tell him to follow his heart. If that's what he wants, he should not try to do something different, or pretend to be someone he isn't.'

'Poor Giles,' I said, suddenly seeing how it would be for him. One son dead, the other a musician.

Joan gave me an amused look. 'Being a minstrel is still being *alive*, Rory. Giles won't mind what Gael does, so long as he's happy.'

I disagreed with her, but didn't say so. That might be *Joan's* attitude, but it wouldn't be mine, and it won't be Giles's either. And I've also promised Gael I'll see that his father consents to him marrying Amie in a couple of years' time. Well, that's for the future; anything can happen in two years. I lounged in my chair, stretching my legs towards the fire, luxuriating in its warmth. At least I don't have to worry about Gael's wedding just yet. I've enough to do making ready for my own.

So there we were, Joan and I, looking forward to dinner, relaxing in front of a blazing fire in the *Egg*, and suddenly the door was flung wide, letting in a swirl of leaves and all but extinguishing the candles. Jonny stood bare-headed and breathless in the doorway. He had clearly run all the way down the bailey, for his chest was heaving.

'What the devil?' I jumped up. 'What's happened, man? You look like you've seen a ghost!'

'I just realised!' Jonny panted. '*Oh my God!* We got it all wrong, we were so stupid, so fucking stupid!'

Joan hurriedly cleared some furry stuff from a chair, and I hauled Jonny in from the doorway so we could shut the weather out again. Joan passed him a goblet of something. He downed it in one go and collapsed into the chair.

'*What* did we get wrong?' I demanded. 'What the *blazes* are you talking about?'

'When we looked here for Merry's treasure. You can't have forgotten!' He swept an arm around the *Egg*, and I remembered all too well that frantic hurling around of blankets and materials in our desperate quest to find Merry's hidden riches. All we found was a small box, with Master Kit laughing at us. *Got Egg Need Teacher, follow me*. Load of nonsense.

'Of course I haven't forgotten.'

'Yes, but I've just realised,' Jonny said more calmly; he'd got his breath back by now. 'He didn't mean here. Not *here,* in the *Egg.* Because *it* wasn't here either, not when he wrote his instructions, was it!'

Joan gasped. She'd been holding out her hand for Jonny to give her the empty goblet, but now her hand flew to her mouth. 'That's right! I moved here much later. In '49, I think it was. You were in Jerusalem, Rory.'

It was Egypt, but no matter.

'When did Anthony write *The Meridian,* Jonny?' she went on, turning to him. 'It must have been a good twenty years before, surely?'

He shook his head. 'I don't know. But we know when he buried the Box – Anno Domini 1240. And that's definitely before this cabin was built.'

'It was Rory's father who built my workshop here,' Joan said, thinking aloud. 'It was his idea. Well, actually it was Sir Patrick's, but Lord Rory authorised the building.'

'In that case,' I said in mounting excitement, 'in *that*

case, when Merry wrote that the treasure was buried under the fabrics, he didn't mean here. He meant in your house in the town!'

My stomach had turned over. They were both staring at me: now we knew where it was, what were we going to do about it? I flung the door open and a gust caught it and slammed it back against the wall.

'Come on! Let's go!' I shouted to the wind and the cold grey sky.

We tumbled out of the *Egg*. Lady Joan's skirts blew wildly about her, and I put my arm around her waist to steady her in the gale. We ran up the hill and met Captain Kerry exercising a platoon in the courtyard.

'I want an armed guard, mounted, by the gatehouse in half an hour,' I panted.

'Yes, lord.'

Kerry never wastes your time asking stupid questions.

I sent a lad to let the kitchen know we'd not be wanting dinner. Sir Patrick was informed too, and he would take charge of the castle. Horses were fetched, saddled, bridled and blinkered, and I made the decision that Joan should be mounted behind me on Gael's horse; he was keen to lend her, and keener still to come along himself. I told him no, he was no longer my page, riding by my side. I saw the devastated look on his face; it was a bitter pill, but a necessary one.

With us were Captain Kerry herself and a dozen men-at-arms, armed with lances and spears, and carrying shields. My red and gold banners flew high above us, whipped by the strong winds, the standard bearers hand-picked by Kerry and riding at the head of the column. We were not going to war, but it looked as if we were. Why? Because we hoped to find a fortune, and where there's money, there may be violence.

Joan, when she lived in Hambrig Town, had the house next to Anthony Merry's. And Merry's house was burned. Not burned down, for it's still standing, but it was fired, and there was smoke and water damage to the walls and the floor. With not much space between the two buildings, anything might have happened to Joan's house; in fact, it is no longer Joan's house. It's now occupied by a merchant. Down at the bottom of the hill the wind was less strong, and it was actually possible to speak and be heard without having to shout. I asked Joan if she remembered the merchant's name.

'Possibly it was Master Lewis?' she said vaguely. Her arms were around my waist and I hoped she felt secure, for I'd set a good pace, and the whole column, two abreast, were cantering along behind me. The Toosanik were building their new settlement, and they, along with Hambriggers in the villages of Baudry and Toldesdane, looked up in astonishment as we passed through without a glance. Through Baudry Gate into Hambrig Town, down the main street, past the now defunct courthouse, we trotted into an open square, bordered on two sides by large flint houses, and on the third by the Guildhall. The Merchants' Quarter.

Kerry and her cavalry troop fanned out to face all four sides of the square. They wouldn't miss a thing. Jonny, Joan and I made our way to the house that had been Joan's, and I knocked on the solid beech door. It was opened by a surly old man, unshaven and unkempt in a ragged gown and slippers.

'Wha's goin' on?' he asked bad-temperedly. 'Waddaya want?'

'You fool,' Jonny said, contemptuously. 'Do you not

know your lord? This is Lord Rory. You owe your house and your land to him!'

'Oh. Sorry, lord.' But he didn't sound it. 'D'yer wanna come in? Suff'n wrong?'

I moved him aside and we entered the house. I asked Joan to show us where she and her father had kept the fabrics piled up, and she led the way into the back, behind the hall. The old man, who might or might not have been Master Lewis, followed us, grumbling under his breath. He held an oil lamp, which was useful, as the area at the back was dark and dingy.

'You know, I don't remember it being like this,' Joan said, turning to me. 'This room was always bright with candlelight, and there was a big table just here where Father used to examine the cloth before he bought or sold anything. There was always a fire in the grate, and everything was warm and comfortable. Look at it now!'

I was looking. The room was bare, just a few chests lining the stark walls. The grate was empty and cold, and the only light came from Master Lewis's oil lamp.

'There's nothing here,' Jonny said, his disappointment showing in his voice. 'Nothing! You know what? I'll bet that *fucking* minstrel has been here before us! Kit's taken whatever there was, hasn't he.'

I was about to agree, despondently, when the miserable trader behind us spoke up.

'Noobody bin 'ere, yer graces. Yer ter first ter come. That smook an' fire next door, that pu' everyone off, that do. All my spices smell o' smook. I'm ruined, I am. Ruined!'

I looked at him. 'You're a spice merchant?'

'I *was* a spice merchant, yer honour. But my spices are spiled, and I in't got nuff'n left. I'm ruined, I tell yer.' He subsided onto one of his chests, shaking with misery.

Impulsively, Joan went to comfort him. She wrapped her own brightly coloured shawl around his wasted shoulders and patted him on the arm.

'Well. What now?' asked Jonny.

I had no idea. We'd reached another dead end, it seemed. Could Kit really have been here first and lifted the treasure? But he would surely have at least hinted something about it. He'd shown us Merry's letter, and he seemed to believe that it actually *was* the legacy his father had left him. Joan was talking softly with Master Lewis, asking him if he had any warmer clothes to put on. The weather had got so cold, she said gently. He didn't want to freeze, did he? The man huddled further into her shawl but didn't give an answer.

'Do you have any food?' Joan asked him with concern.

'Lady, there in't nuff'n left,' the old man said tearfully, rocking backwards and forwards on the wooden chest. 'D'n't yer understand? My spices are all spiled an' noobody buy 'em, so what am I s'pposed to do fer food? I in't 'ad nuff'n ter eat fer four days, I in't.'

'What will you do with the spoiled spices?' Jonny asked. 'Are they in these chests?'

'Wha's left of 'em, yes. But the rest I jus' threw down in ter cellar. The rats can 'ave 'em. Spices fer rats! Ha!' He started to laugh, but it turned into sobbing.

But I wasn't listening to him anymore. I was staring at Joan. 'Where's the cellar?' I mouthed. 'You never mentioned a *cellar*.'

Merry had written that his fortune would be found *at the back of Joan's workshop, under all the pelts and rugs*. What if 'under' didn't mean underneath a pile of rugs, but under the floor itself? And I saw Jonny's eyes widen as he also understood, and Joan gasped, and said that yes, there was indeed a cellar, and it was underneath this room and you could get to it by means of a trapdoor which was by the wall just there – in fact, *just there*, hidden by the very boxes on which Master Lewis was sitting, rocking back and forth and crying like a baby.

'Be careful,' Jonny whispered to me. 'If he realises...' Jonny didn't finish. He didn't need to. Here was the destitute spice merchant, literally sitting on a fortune. I bit my lip. We had options here. It wouldn't be hard to force the man to move, to hold him still and then open up the trapdoor. But then he would know more than we wanted him to know.

Jonny went to get Captain Kerry, and Kerry, very formal and professional, told Master Lewis to come outside for questioning. He had no choice but to slide down from his box and shuffle his way out into the square, where he caught his breath at the sight of the magnificent, mounted soldiers, the fiercely waving flags, showing colourfully against the grey, swirling sky, and the whole pageantry of might and power ranged right outside his door. There were other merchants and their families milling around in the square by now as well, and all were anxious to know what was going on. Kerry was spreading some story about, and there was a general air of hubbub and kerfuffle. It would be easy for Kerry to get Master Lewis to join in and be part of the excitement.

In the workshop at the back of Joan's father's old house, though, there was a completely different kind of excitement. The kind of excitement you feel when you have levered up a trapdoor and descended a set of stone steps, clambered over boxes and boxes of ruined condiments, and then – because Jonny thought to do it – frantically shifted a whole teetering pile of musty wallhangings to find the concealed entrance to a narrow passage, where even Joan had to bend low, tallow

Crowbars and hammers

lamps lighting the way, and finally found yourself at the end of the passage, faced with a thick, heavy, locked and very promising-looking door. We had no key.

'What's behind this door?' I asked Joan. 'You've been in here?'

'No,' she answered emphatically. 'I didn't even know it existed! Father used to store bales and bolts of cloth in the main cellar, and I used to fetch them up for him. And then I stored my samples there after he died, but I never knew there was a passageway at the other end. Those tapestries and whatnot must have always been blocking the way in. I'd no idea this place was here!'

I nodded. We only found the passage because we were looking for it, we knew there had to be *something*. It occurred to me that Joan's father might well have known about the passage and this door at the end of it. Perhaps he'd also known Merry's secrets. And then, maybe, he'd deliberately stacked bales of cloth in front of the entrance. Well, both men are dead now.

Jonny broke in on my thoughts. 'So? How are we going to get in?'

'Go and get Captain Kerry. We need crowbars and hammers.'

44

THE ONLY THING TO DO

It took two hours, mostly because the passage was so narrow, small and cramped. None of us could stand upright, and Jonny and I had to bend almost double. Kerry, when she arrived with an enormous crowbar, told us Master Lewis was being held by her troopers; I gather they arrested him on some trumped-up charge. No matter; I'll put it right with him later.

Jonny, Kerry and I took turns with the crowbar, but we couldn't go for long. The lack of space gave the crowbar only a tiny purchase and we were soon slipping and sliding in our own sweat, trying to exert a lever on something that had little hope of moving.

Until Kerry suddenly felt it give.

Joan had long since gone back up the passage. She was sitting in the main cellar, ready to warn us if anyone approached. Jonny was lying exhausted on his back behind me, but when he heard Kerry say it had moved, he jumped up, banging his head hard on the passage roof. We somehow, God knows how, managed to find space on the crowbar for all three of us to hold on.

The only thing to do

'One,' I said, adjusting my grip on the metal bar. 'Two. Three. Heave!'

There was a mighty splintering sound, and we pushed with all our weight, but the passage wall prevented the lever from doing its work, and the door stayed where it was. God, it was frustrating.

'If we cut through the gap,' Kerry began, and I saw at once what she meant. We now had a small gap where the wood had been torn away. It wasn't much, but it might be possible to get a saw into it and then cut down and enlarge the hole.

'Do it,' I said to Jonny behind me, who was the most free to move. I heard him crawling back down the passage, then voices as he explained things to Joan, then silence.

'Can you see anything?' I asked Kerry, though I knew it was a stupid question. The gap was tiny, and if you put your eye up close to it you weren't going to be able to put a lantern there as well.

Jonny returned with a sharp-toothed saw. I didn't ask where all these tools were coming from. It's another thing I'll deal with later. For now, there was a door to open. Only of course, we never did open the door; we sawed away at the small gap and eventually made a hole just large enough to clamber through, and that was all that mattered. One by one, the three of us twisted and struggled and wriggled our bodies into a small stone-walled underground chamber, where we were at last able to stand upright, and Jonny and I held our lanterns high so all could see.

And there it was. The lamplight gleamed on boxes of gold bars, silver bullion, rubies, emeralds and huge sparkling diamonds. There must have been a dozen boxes, all sealed and bound with iron bands, but through the gaps between the wooden laths, precious gems and metals winked and shone. We found we were holding our breath, and for several moments we just stood and stared. It was a hoard, the jewels alone worth many thousands of pounds, and with the ingots of gold and silver added in – an absolute fortune. A treasure indeed.

Kerry commandeered a cart from the wine merchant, and Jonny and I hacked more of the door away to make the hole bigger. Kerry's troopers made a human chain from the strongroom to the cellar, up the steps, through the house and out into the square. It took a long time, but in the end every gold bar, every ingot, nugget, jewel and gem was brought out into the open. The boxes were stacked up neatly in the cart. I saw the soldiers' eyes widen as they handled them, passing them one to another. But these were hand-picked troops, and their behaviour was impeccable.

As twilight deepened over the town, a pair of carthorses was put between the shafts and a large tarpaulin was thrown over the boxes, marlin hitches securing it to the sides of the cart. With the guard mounted and armed in two columns, one on each side of the bullion wagon, we made our careful way back to the castle. Before we left, I authorised the spice merchant's release and gave him half a crown to buy food. He returned to his house still nursing his grievances, but somehow keeping hold of Joan's shawl. She smiled, happy to let him have it. Shawls are ten-a-penny to Joan.

We rumbled into the courtyard long after dark. I sent for Sir Patrick and quickly put him in the picture. I had the pleasure of seeing him, for probably the only time in his life, totally lost for words. Not even an 'All is well!' passed his lips!

The soldiers unloaded the cart, and all the boxes were taken up to my library, where an armed guard now stands sentry. As soon as it grew light again, I dispatched a message

The only thing to do

to the King, requesting that he send a master jeweller to us from Hicrown.

It's 7th September, and Master Bullen arrived this afternoon. He is a dried-up little man, but he knows his stuff. I told him I wanted a valuation on the hoard, and after many hours spent in my library examining each piece carefully through a special lens, he said he was ready. I made him write the sum down.

My heart was hammering, my pulse racing and my mouth was as dry as the dust in Mansurah. My hand shook as I took the parchment the wizened fellow held out to me. While I unrolled it, he polished his magnifying lens and put it away in a small pouch. I had to blink several times as I looked at the number he'd written down, and at first I couldn't believe it.

'Are you sure?'

'Oh yes,' he said, without emotion. 'It's the most valuable collection I have ever seen, Lord Rory. You are a very, *very* rich man.'

And with that, he pocketed his payment, closed up his leather bag, bade me farewell, and stepped unhurriedly down the spiral stairs to the courtyard, where he mounted his small shaggy pony and trotted back to Hicrown. It was as if the valuation were all that mattered; he asked neither where the treasure came from, nor what was to be done with it.

THE BOX OF DEATH

And what *is* to be done with it? That question was on both Jonny's and Patrick's lips all evening, but, to their infinite annoyance, I gave them no answers. Strangely, Joan didn't ask me anything at all, but simply walked back to the *Egg* and made tea.

Four of us found the treasure: Joan, Kerry, Jonny and me. Are we the ones who get the *great reward,* promised in the Fiorello message? My mind goes into a spin as I think of what I can do with a quarter of the wealth calculated and written down by Master Bullen. I see the improvements I'll make to the castle; the repairs and the extra barns we can use; and then – *then* I see my watermill! I will build it by the *Egg,* so the tumbling little River Eray can turn the waterwheel, and Castle Rory will mill its own flour for the first time. The thought is intoxicating.

I let my mind wander to the other three who were with me in Joan's father's cellar. What will Joan do with so much money? How will Jonny spend his? As for Kerry, living on a soldier's pay, this will change her life.

I don't need to re-read the parchment from the Box of Death. I know it by heart now.

> *Fiorello is death to those he looks upon. Only a person of great courage and determination will open the box, but if such a one can be found, a great reward will be his. This message comes from Hope, Endurance and a New Beginning.*

Well, the Box was opened by Barney, Jonny and me. But

The only thing to do

the Kyown-Kinnie had opened it before us, and Master Kit had opened it before that.

So, in my own mind, I know exactly what to do, because it's clear now that Anthony Merry made a complicated trail to his treasure. Solve *The People's Puzzle*, and you will then be able to dig up the Box of Death. Find the secret compartment (but how would you do that, if you didn't even know it was there?), and you will uncover *The Meridian*. Read this manuscript and Merry's additional pages, and you may or may not understand that you have to use it together with *The People's Puzzle* to find a new and deeper code. Break *this* cipher, and you will know that Merry's riches are to be found buried beneath the Lady Joan's bolts of fabric. *Then* have the wit to understand that you need to go back to the house where she used to live and go down into the cellar, where you must deduce that somewhere there is a tiny passage leading to a strongroom which has a locked door to which there is apparently no key.

So who the blazes was meant to do all that? Not your average Hambrigger, that's certain. No. Merry meant this trail to be followed to its end by one person, and one person only, and that was his son, the half-Toosanik, half-Hambrig so-called New Beginning, sent before his birth a thousand miles away to far-off Smander at my father's expense.

The more I think about it, the more I realise the whole thing was *impossible* to follow without some inside information and a particular skillset. You would have to know about the false bottom in the Box of Death; you'd have to be a reasonably competent codebreaker; you would have to know where Joan used to live, and where she kept her supplies. And, most importantly of all, you'd need to have grasped the link between the Hurogol Treaty, *The Meridian* and *The People's Puzzle*.

THE BOX OF DEATH

Only one person could have done it, because his mother would have told him about it. Joy knew about the Box of Death, where it was buried, what it contained and all its secrets. She knew about Joan too. Joy would have told Kit where to go and what to do. Peter was right when he guessed Kit dug up the Box well before Prince Barney, Jonny and I first met him on the Wartsbaye Road, on that long ago day when a rabbit jumped out of the Box and frightened us out of our wits.

I am up in my library of course, my journal open on the desk. I lower myself into my beautiful chair and make myself think it through carefully, the way Peter would: Kit dug up the Box from under the birch tree, and took it to the Toosanik. Why? Because his mother had told him to. She was Toosanik, and she wanted her people to have their history back as well as their land. But how did Kit cross the Hurogol, in two directions, without anyone from the castle noticing? We keep such a good lookout the whole time, one of the Watch would have seen a boat heading to the Nahvitch country, or coming away from it. How could he possibly not have been seen?

Bloody hell! Suddenly I know. I jump up from the chair and, totally forgetting to be Peter, I rummage frantically in the top drawer of the oak chest. It's that damned song! Kit wrote it down for me after we got back to the castle. Four whole months ago that was! I remember throwing it into the drawer thinking it foolish troubadour nonsense. In my head I can see the impudent minstrel again, skipping backwards in front of me, expertly twirling his swagger stick. *You will want to read my song. If not now, then later...*

Finally I find it, rip off the cord that binds it and unroll the parchment. With my heart racing, I read the thing for the first time. And it's neither foolish nor nonsense. It all, quite suddenly, makes perfect sense.

> *Over the mountains and onto the Downs,*
> *Crossing the plains and then passing the towns,*
> *Looking for treetops or under the ground,*
> *Pretty things hide, but they want to be found!*
> *On through the water, but not through the sea,*
> *Splishing and splashing, the travelling's free!*
> *I'm just a minstrel, I'm not some great lord,*
> *Tiptoeing through, that's all I can afford!*
> *Dirty and murky and chiefly I go,*
> *Hither and thither, but you'll never know.*
> *Places and faces and spaces I've seen,*
> *Prancing along like a merry machine.*
> *What a good boy, taking Mother's advice.*
> *You gave me everything, wasn't that nice!*
> *These are my friends who've been waiting for me,*
> *Having a grand time with posh royalty.*
> *So I've returned and I want you to know,*
> *'Mission accomplished' is still 'way to go'.*
> *Dancing or singing or boxing in fun,*
> *Now I've arrived and my journey is done!*

The 'splishing and splashing', the 'tiptoeing through' all point to just one way of crossing the river, and then – 'that's all I can afford' – a pun on the word 'ford', of course. Kit crossed on foot, using the ford in the north of the country. No wonder we'd not known anything about it.

The more I look at the song, the more it appears to tell Kit's Hambrig story. How about 'Dirty and murky and chiefly I go' – a reference to murky Blurland and the clan chief?

'Prancing along like a merry machine' – doing his father's bidding, of course.

'Taking Mother's advice' is obvious, but as to 'You gave me everything', does that refer to his mother, or to my father? Perhaps it's both, for between them they certainly *had* given him everything.

And that word 'boxing' near the end. Of course I thought it meant fighting with fists, but suppose it simply refers to the Box, one of the 'pretty things' that wanted to be found? It now seems like the entire song was one big clue to what Kit has been up to, and it is all getting clearer and clearer. And it has been here, for me to read, all this time. I am mortified. My father would not have made this mistake, he would have read Kit's song months ago.

At least now I know. Kit dug up the box, he crossed the Hurogol by the ford in the north, he delivered the Box to the Kyown-Kinnie, as per his mother's instructions, and then he returned by means of the ford again. He picked up his musical friends from the palace in Hicrown and they all came a-trooping down to Hambrig, leading us to believe they'd only just arrived in the country.

Kit is in Smander now, of course, back with his mother in the royal court, or perhaps in his own territory of Casuel. He told me he would return to us, but I don't really believe that. He knows my draughty old castle and he's seen the relative poverty of Hambrig compared with the land where he grew up.

'Lush', he called it. Well, nobody could ever call Hambrig 'lush'. Cold in the wintertime, buffeted by gales and lashed by rain, while in the summer it's fresh and sun-washed, and sometimes even quite warm, but you'd never call it tropical. I've been across the Med to Cyprus and Egypt – I know the difference. But Kit does not know we have

The only thing to do

found Merry's actual treasure. The 'great reward'. And if he never returns to Mallrovia, what then? Can I justify spending it? Can I justify *not* spending it?

A question pops into my head. What on earth had made Jonny suddenly think Merry's treasure would be in Joan's old house in Hambrig Town?

———◆———

I looked for Jonny at supper, but didn't see him. Afterwards, though, I found him relaxing in the off-watch mess all by himself.

'It was Patrick,' he told me.

'What on earth did Patrick know about it?'

'Oh, he didn't know anything about it. But we were talking about your wedding to Lady Lillian, and Patrick said the Lady Joan might be asked to make the princess a wedding gown, and how good it was that she had her workshop here now, because if it had been in Hambrig Town, as it was many years ago, it wouldn't be so easy for the princess to go for fittings, or some such. I didn't catch everything he was saying; as soon as he mentioned the *Egg* being only built ten or so years ago, it made me think about our frantic search, and then finding Master Kit's stupid joke. And I'm afraid I was very rude, and I didn't stay to listen to the rest of what Patrick was saying, but crashed out of here and ran as fast as I possibly could to tell you. I've apologised to him since, though.'

I subsided into a chair. I'd forgotten all about the wedding. I'm supposed to marry the princess, of course I am. And I even promised Kathryn I would. I ran my hand over my face. The last, *the very last,* thing in the world I want to do is marry that petulant Lillian. And now I don't even need her dowry! As Master Bullen said, I am a very, very rich man. Or Kit is, but he doesn't know it. Perhaps he doesn't need to know it. Jonny was watching me. Somehow, he knew exactly what I was thinking.

'You can't do that, you know,' Jonny said.

'What can't I do?'

'You can't keep it to yourself, Rory. Master Kit has to know.'

'Master Kit! He's a damned duke! He doesn't need gold and silver.'

'It's his though, and you know it.'

It is, and I do.

'All right,' I said, giving in. 'I'll save all the treasure for Kit when he returns, *if* he ever returns. And in three weeks' time I'll marry the princess and have dozens of children. That do?'

Jonny smiled, punched my arm lightly, and we sank a couple of goblets of wine together. Perhaps more than a couple. Sometimes, getting drunk with a very old friend is the only thing to do.

EPILOGUE

I am standing on Baudry Hill, my eyes shaded against the low winter sun, watching two riders gallop over the Mallrovian Downs towards Hambrig. The Downs are a ridge of chalky hills, covered in grass. In the summertime, they look fresh and green, but now they're bare and bleak, the wind gusting and blasting across them. The sun is weak and lacks warmth. Soon it will disappear below the western horizon, for today is the Winter Solstice, the shortest day of the year. Not long until Christmas, I think, as I watch the clouds scudding overhead. The riders are getting closer, and I fancy I can hear the horses' hooves, but I can't really. I know who it must be, although they're still just a blur, and almost seem part of the wind itself, for they are galloping so fast and so effortlessly, the horses appear to be flying.

I have removed my hat and I'm waving it, hopeful they'll see me and know I'm waiting for them. My hair blows wildly in the chill, biting wind, and although I really only have eyes and ears for the horses and their riders, I'm suddenly aware that someone has joined me out on the cold hillside.

'Is it Branca, lord?' Gael asks. 'Branca and Master Kit?' I look down at him, though not so far down these days.

'Yes,' I say. 'Branca and Master Kit are coming home, Gael.'

'Does Master Kit know about the treasure?'

'Not yet. I will tell him about it later.'

'Is it all still there, lord? Or is some of it spent?'

'It's all still there, Gael. It's Master Kit's, isn't it.'

'What do you think he will do with all that money?'

'He'll spend it on the Toosanik,' I say easily. 'They are the reason he's here, Gael. The Toosanik have come home, and so has Kit. He'll spend his fortune on them.'

We stand together, both of us shading our eyes, buffeted by the wind, straining to see the riders and the horses – but mainly the horses. It takes a short while longer, and then here they are, standing before me, steam coming off their flanks, nostrils flaring and ears laid back. Kit is in a sweat too, for he's had to work hard to keep up, but Branca's grinning from ear to ear, and the horse she's riding – that's *my* horse.

It's another mare, a blue roan, though I don't know anything else yet. Branca begins to tell me about her. She was completely wild, and in Smander they call these horses 'mustangs'. Branca chose her for her speed, her strength and her stamina. It took two months for the mustang to begin to trust Branca, and for Branca to be able to approach her. Another couple of months went by while Branca got the horse to understand her and to trust her completely. Finally, Branca decided the mustang was ready, and the two of them set off on the long journey north to Mallrovia.

I am overcome. I have never heard of mustangs before, but she is everything I wanted. I note her short back and her low-set tail, her stumpy ears and her deep girth. She looks strong and intelligent, and I've already seen how fast she is. I cannot *wait* to ride her. Gael is full of questions, but I scarcely hear him. Branca lets him chatter on, and throws him the occasional titbit of an answer, but mostly she is watching me, watching to see how I handle her new creation, for that's what this mustang is. Branca has made this horse, and she has made her with me in mind. She tells me this. She tells me she knows my seat and has observed my style, my cues, my language. She has accustomed the mustang to a life with me. I feel humble as I listen to all this, because there is so much more than Branca is telling me. I can see it in her eyes.

I picture the long, hot days in Spain, horse and rider circling, wary, waiting for a chance. The horse breaking free and thundering off, or throwing Branca to the ground in a terrible temper at having the weight of a person on her back for the first time. Branca, never giving up, knowing this is the right animal for me, knowing she *has* to win. There are weeks and weeks of story in this, but Branca is economical with it, and I hear only a few telling sentences. I am satisfied though. My mustang is strong, fast and disciplined. She is not as beautiful as Guinevere. She is *not* Guinevere and she never will be. She is herself, a gorgeous blue roan, the white flecks shining in her dark coat. I run my hand over the mustang's flank, and Branca tells me the horse will show more white hairs in the summer months, but now it's winter there is less white. I am fascinated.

Branca watches. I mount the mustang and take off into the sunset, the horse rippling beneath me, so much power, so much strength. It feels as if I am riding the wind. Gael is a pale dot on the hillside, Branca another, and I see that Gael has grown as tall as Branca, and will soon be taller still. I wheel round, laughing at the tumultuous clouds, the bleak

Downs, rolling on and on into the land of Westador. It's so tempting to gallop further, but this mare has ridden far today, she deserves a rest. I turn her towards the castle, and we canter sedately back, still laughing, on top of the world.

Below us on the Great Plain, the new Meeting Place is ready. Huts have been built, and the smoke from many cooking fires curls into the air and is shredded by the wind. Everyone has now crossed the Hurogol; there are no more Toosanik in Blurland. The inky lines on the map have come to life, and fences and hedgerows mark one person's croft from another. It still surprises me to hear the Okkam spoken in Hambrig market, and to see Toosanik people coming in and out of buildings in the town. But I like it, and so do my Hambriggers. The Toosanik sell to us and buy from us, and we're talking, learning and adapting.

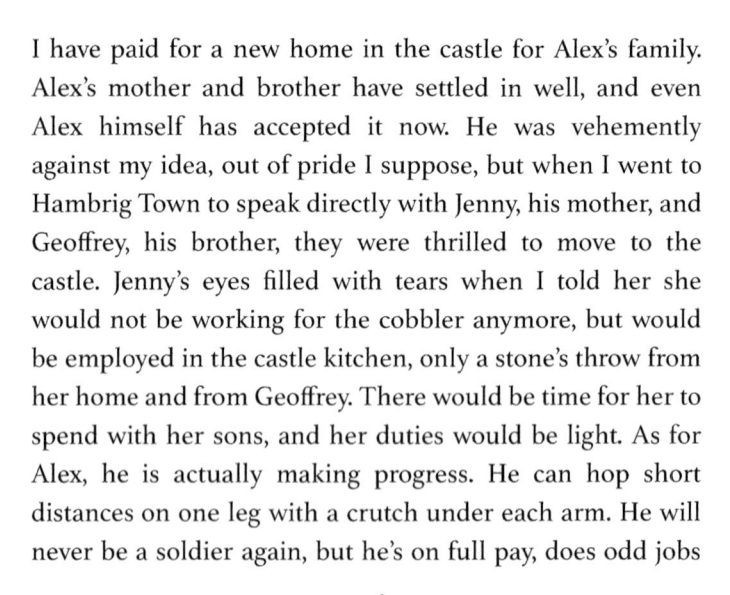

———◆———

I have paid for a new home in the castle for Alex's family. Alex's mother and brother have settled in well, and even Alex himself has accepted it now. He was vehemently against my idea, out of pride I suppose, but when I went to Hambrig Town to speak directly with Jenny, his mother, and Geoffrey, his brother, they were thrilled to move to the castle. Jenny's eyes filled with tears when I told her she would not be working for the cobbler anymore, but would be employed in the castle kitchen, only a stone's throw from her home and from Geoffrey. There would be time for her to spend with her sons, and her duties would be light. As for Alex, he is actually making progress. He can hop short distances on one leg with a crutch under each arm. He will never be a soldier again, but he's on full pay, does odd jobs

Epilogue

here and there, and is regarded by the castle's children as a war hero. Gael takes his duties seriously. He spends a lot of time with Geoffrey, helping him each day, and can even understand his strange way of speaking. In the odd way that boys have, they've become friends.

I give my new warhorse a proud name. I call her 'Blue Wind', because her coat is blue and she rides like the wind, but she will be 'Blue' for short. After taking the mustang to the castle stable, I walk jauntily to the *Egg* to see the Lady Joan. She is making herself a light supper – some bread and cheese, a goblet of mead and a couple of raisin buns. As soon as she sees me, she cuts me some bread and cheese. I'm not hungry, but don't have the heart to say so. I let Joan fuss round me for a bit, and after a while we're both sitting at the table in the firelight.

'Do you miss him?' I ask. 'Sammy, I mean.'

'I know who you mean. Yes, of course I miss him. But he'll be back. And I know now you were right to send him away with William. He knows William's my son, there's a connection. And William knows Sammy is important to me, as his mother once was. I don't miss him as much as I thought I would, because I know it's for the best.'

I am glad of that. I haven't told Joan, but William has instructions to stay away for two years. In two years I hope life at sea in a privateer will turn young Sammy into a man, and into a leader of men. Then I will send him to the Toosanik. The new Kyown-Kinnie will welcome Sammy, and I think there will be another New Beginning. I also intend to dub William knight. Joan will be prouder than

THE BOX OF DEATH

ever to have Sir William for a son, but he has deserved the knighthood ten times over.

———◆———

And now the new year is just one week old, and I am spending a few days on the road, riding north. We go by ourselves, Blue and I, and eventually arrive in York. I speak with the Carmelite friar, who is a reasonable man, and he agrees to my request. I eat supper with the brothers in the refectory, and am given lodging with them overnight. The next day Sister Clementine and I walk slowly, arm in arm, down to the bottom of the sloping friary grounds. Here is the small graveyard, where departed brothers and sisters are buried. We make our careful way between crosses and tombstones, and come to the one we seek. I kneel down on the hard, frosty ground, and Sister Clementine puts her hand on my shoulder. I part the long grass in front of me to find a very small headstone, and I peer at the engraving on it.

In loving memory of Little Rory
Born 25th February AD 1249
Died 13th March AD 1249
I pour out my tears to God

Two weeks and two days. A very short life indeed. I never saw him, never knew him, but he was mine. Kneeling there in the grass, Sister Clementine beside me, I do indeed pour out my tears to God.

Epilogue

I have not married Princess Lillian. Obviously, the King was furious, and I'm told Lillian will never speak to me again, but I can live with that. Something changed inside me after we found Merry's treasure, and I will not marry the princess out of duty, nor because my King wants me to, nor because it will buy me a watermill and the much-needed repairs to my home. I will marry her only if I love her, and I do not love her. And so I remain unmarried.

And what of the Box of Death? All along it has symbolised the resettlement of a displaced people, their return to their homeland and their acceptance here once more. Through the Box of Death we found the Hurogol Treaty, and now we have a new one. It was easy to give it a name: it is, of course, the Treaty of Hope. The Box of Death has been returned to the Toosanik, and its proud *croovbayha* runes have been carved into the lintel of their Meeting Place.

Once, we thought the Box was dangerous. We thought Fiorello was a deadly animal, capable of mass slaughter. We thought the Toosanik were the enemy, the dreaded 'Nahvitch'. We fought for our lives and our land at the Battle of Baudry Hill, and many died that day.

But the Box of Death helped us recover the long-lost treaty, which gave rise to a new and peaceful settlement on the Great Plain of Hambrig. And it brought riches to Master Kit, wealth which will help smooth the integration of the Toosanik even more. Peace has replaced war; diplomacy has replaced fighting. The Box of Death had a personal gift for me too: it brought me knowledge of my Lady Kathryn, and of my baby son.

It's Thursday, 31st January 1264, and in a moment I will put down my pen and close this journal for the last time. It is my destiny to rule here, as my father, my grandfather and my great-grandfather did before me, but my eyes have been opened.

For ten years I allowed things to take their own course here in Hambrig. I tried to act as my father would have wanted, but I was neither challenged nor put to the test until the Box of Death came to the castle. The testing, then, was severe, and I fell short. I did not see what I should have seen. I did not do the things I should have done. The high standards set by my father were not upheld. My complacent attitude was exposed. My self-control was challenged, and it was inadequate. I let my father and my household down.

I now realise that my rule has, all along, been a flawed one, and that conflict cannot always be resolved by the person in charge. I am not the solution to every problem; my power is not absolute. Sometimes, I even make the problem worse.

As the cold and dark of winter descend on Castle Rory, I glance at the indictment I've just written, the ink still wet upon the parchment, and I shiver.

Thank you for reading *The Box of Death*,
Book One in *Tales of Castle Rory*, a saga of Medieval Fantasy Adventures!

Epilogue

Lord Rory's exploits continue in Book Two,
The Soldier of Fortune:

The accusation hangs in the air like a noose: *"Murderer".*

It's 1264, and **framed for the murder** of a girl within his own walls, Lord Rory of Hambrig has no choice but to flee. **On the run** from those who once swore fealty to him, Rory must navigate the fractured kingdom of England, where the **Second Barons' War** pits brother against brother.

Rory's own brother, **Nicholas,** is **caught in the turmoil**, fighting for Simon de Montfort's rebellion in Sussex. But Rory is burdened by the presence of Felix, **a strange adolescent boy** who joins his party and whose unpredictable behaviour causes great unrest. With **danger closing in** from all sides, Rory makes **a desperate bid** to save Nicholas and clear his name.

As dark forces rear their heads, Rory realises that the war outside may pale in comparison to the battles he faces within his own group. The secrets that haunt both his brother and Felix could unravel **everything Rory is fighting for**.

Will Rory's flight from the law lead him to justice – or straight into the jaws of his enemies?

Read *The Soldier of Fortune*, Book Two in *Tales of Castle Rory*.

Did you enjoy *The Box of Death*? Leave a review, and let everybody know!

THE BOX OF DEATH

Want to know what happened to Rory before he became Lord of Hambrig?

Rory and Jonny, barely out of their teens, join King Louis IX of France on Crusade.
This Crusade is a disaster for the Christians, but it forges a tremendous and lasting friendship between Jonny and Rory, who go to war as boys and return as men.
Read about their adventures in Egypt, the women they fell in love with and their miraculous escapes from the Saracens!

This story is told in Mansurah: Jonny's Tale, a free ebook only available to members of **The Household**!

Joining is free and also gives you access to fortnightly newsletters with behind the scenes action, giveaways, fun competitions and much more!

Go to www.talesofcastlerory.co.uk to find out more about **The Household** and get your free copy of *Mansurah: Jonny's Tale*

Go to www.talesofcastlerory.co.uk to find out more about Tales of Castle Rory.

You can also follow me on Facebook.

Epilogue

ACKNOWLEDGMENTS

The inspiration for my writing is, and always will be, my wonderful mum, Joan Marsden. She not only encouraged me to write, but provided the inspiration for me to chronicle these adventures. Without her, Lord Rory's journals would not have come to light, and I would never have been able to publish his *Tales of Castle Rory*. Joan was and is the driving force behind everything I do.

I want to thank Kit Marsden for all his support with technical matters. He is a true friend, as well as being my son.

My daughter, Kerry, has encouraged me, and is a source of inspiration for my work. They have given me many vital insights into feminism, and much of their outlook has informed my vision of Mallrovian society and of the household and garrison at Castle Rory.

Grateful thanks to Peter and Caroline at BespokeAuthor, to Sharon Rutland, my editor and to Rebekah Zink of Rebekah Zink Media. All four did a great job with this book.

Thank you, Arthur Cormack, for introducing me to the wonderful language of Scottish Gaelic, which has featured heavily in this book under the guise of "Okkam". It was your singing which first inspired me to look at the language, and from then on I was hooked!

I'd like to express my gratitude to Debbie Young for her teaching and guidance, and to the team at Jericho Writers for their help.

My thanks also to Bethan and Simon for their invaluable feedback and comments, and to Stephanie for our inspiring discussions and mutual encouragement.

Finally, thank you Patrick – you have been a great friend through good times, bad times and frankly ghastly ones. Your help and support mean the world to me.

AUTHOR'S NOTE

The Box of Death is a Medieval Fantasy Adventure. But how much is Medieval? And how much is Fantasy?

The late thirteenth century comes near the end of the period known as the High Middle Ages, which historians define as lasting, roughly, from AD 1000 to 1300. During this time there was an explosion of the population in Europe, resulting in the building of towns and increased urbanisation of landscapes. In addition, many national identities were established, including the city-states of Italy, the Crusader States in the Levant, and the expansion of the Holy Roman Empire into most of Italy and the vastly enlarged Kingdom of Germany.

In England, feudalism was well established. It had existed during the Anglo-Saxon era (prior to the Norman conquest), but it was the Normans who imprinted their style upon it and made it the rigid structure which was such a feature of English medieval life. It was an immutable hierarchy. Social mobility hardly ever occurred, nor was it encouraged, although slaves could purchase their freedom (manumission) if they were able to raise the funds to do so. But this was rare. Vassals owed allegiance to their lord, and a "commendation ceremony" was conducted, in front of witnesses, to seal this pact. The vassal would then be given land, known as a fief or a fee, in return for his allegiance to the lord, who would call upon him in time of war to take up arms and fight. Villeins were lower in the hierarchy, but they could own land. Slaves, or serfs, had few if any possessions of their own. Above everyone was the king, and even the highest nobles owed allegiance to him, with their own "commendation ceremonies" as binding as anyone else's.

During this period, French became the official language of the country and William the Conqueror, to prove he was now in charge, built a large number of Norman-style castles throughout England. In them, he installed his chosen vassals, lords of vast shires and their citizens. Everyone knew their place, and the castle was the ultimate overlord. These were stone castles, replacing and adding to the previous wooden structures: the motte and bailey forts of the Anglo-Saxons.

Stone castles had a curtain wall – an encircling ring of stone, built high and constructed with a wooden walkway around the top, enabling watchers to see everything from afar. At intervals in the curtain wall, towers were built. They were known as mural towers, and were square in the early days. Later constructions had round towers, which were more resistant to attack. Within the curtain wall, the "castle" was actually a collection of buildings. The main, great, tower was called the *donjon*, a Norman word, naturally, but

Author's Note

in order not to confuse this tower with the "dungeon" which housed prisoners, I've used the word "keep". Inside the keep were bedchambers, and under it was vital storage. Additional buildings included the great hall (where everyone ate, and many slept), the chapel, the kitchen, and numerous outbuildings, workshops and barns. The keep was inside the courtyard, or the "inner ward". Surrounding the courtyard was the bailey, or "outer ward", but there were many variations in this generalised plan.

I have conceived Castle Rory as a typical castle of the time. Its construction began in 1160 and took eight years to complete, which was quite good going for the time. It was built as a matter of necessity, following the Great Flood of 1159, when the people of Hambrig took refuge from the flood waters by climbing Baudry Hill.

And so to geography! Mallrovia is a very small country to the east of England. It is an independent sovereign state, with recognised borders. Its westernmost border, separating it from England, is the River Hurogol, which has its source in the north of England. By the time the Hurogol flows along the Mallrovian boundary it is wide, fast and treacherous. It then plunges through deep ravines and gorges which it has carved out of the rock in Westador, a principality lying to the south of Mallrovia. Westador is not particularly friendly towards Mallrovia, and relations between Prince Elric of Westador and King Philip of Mallrovia are generally frosty, verging on the hostile. This is partly due to Westador being under constant threat of being subsumed by England.

Author's Note

I see Westador as being similar to (although considerably smaller than) Wales. It does not have full independence, although it does have some devolved powers. In this, it's completely different from Mallrovia, which has full sovereignty.

You will see from the map at the front of the book that Mallrovia very much resembles the county of Norfolk (which is where I live!), and Westador is more-or-less equivalent to the county of Suffolk. I have borrowed these two East Anglian counties and created new states from them. This has allowed me to put towns, villages, rivers and forests where I need them, and to create a feudal hierarchy of my own, under the auspices of the volatile King Philip and his family.

In this way, I can integrate the genuinely historical aspects of this period into a fantasy landscape of my own. Or perhaps it is the other way around! This has allowed me to do all manner of things, one of the most important being the elevation of women in what was very much a man's world. There had, of course, been powerful and influential women in England and Europe, women such as Queen Matilda, Eleanor of Aquitaine, Joan of Arc, Hildegard of Bingen and Isabella of France. These women were once-in-a-generation exceptions. I decided to create a society in which women were not only allowed, but encouraged, to pursue careers in traditionally male professions, such as the army, medicine and (in the case of Branca) stewardship of the castle's stables.

Women have always been seen as "healers", which isn't at all the same as "doctors" or "physicians", and there's a popular belief that only men were trained in medicine – in the sense of having undergone formal training at a university. Women, by contrast, would work with herbs and

Author's Note

folklore. This is partly true, but it's also a fact that women *did* train, alongside men, in medical schools, most particularly in the medical school in Salerno, the most prestigious of them all during the High Middle Ages. They trained there and they qualified there.

Doctor Bethan, Castle Rory's resident physician, did not train at the University of Salerno, however. She had a difficult background, and she learnt her craft by studying books, which meant she first had to learn to read. Being a female from a low-born family, she would not have been literate. So first she learnt to read and then she studied the great medical texts of the time. This has given her a somewhat skewed outlook on life, but she is grateful for her position in the castle, where she is well respected.

I have enjoyed putting women into the army in my books. The Castle Rory garrison is small (as they very often were, the castle itself being viewed as the main defensive strategy) and Lord Rory is proud that it contains both male and female warriors. Partly this stems from his admiration for certain individuals within the garrison. To some extent, he is in awe of women generally and female warriors in particular. He grew up in male company, his mother having died while he was young and away from home. But he recognises the value women bring to his household and his garrison.

Rory's greatest friend is Jonny, but Jonny, although commander of the garrison, is lower in status than Rory and this causes a certain amount of tension, given their background. They were friends long ago on Crusade, when

Author's Note

Jonny, as the elder of the two, took a leading role. Rory followed where Jonny led. The reversal of these positions causes Rory no concern whatever, but Jonny's feelings are deep and significant. They are not yet expressed, but they will be.

Finally, a word about the language of Okkam, a corruption of the word Ogham, which was an ancient Celtic language, written by means of runes. I have had a lot of fun with this language, and with inventing the people who speak it.

In 2014 I went on holiday in the Isle of Skye. I found the place captivating, and I fell in love with the language of Scottish Gaelic. I took courses in this language, and made some progress, although I was never as good as I'd have liked to be. When I invented the tribe of Celts who live in Blurland on the other side of the River Hurogol, I decided they would speak Scottish Gaelic. I merged Gaelic with Ogham and created Okkam. Gaelic words have been "transcribed" phonetically to create Okkam words. For example, the clan chief is, in *The Box of Death*, known as the "Kyown-Kinnie". The Scottish Gaelic for a clan chief is "ceann-cinnidh", but if I'd written it like this, would you have known how to pronounce it? Similarly, when Sammy says "keeshiv", which Rory later discovers means "you'll see", he's really saying "chì sibh".

So I want to apologise to all genuine speakers of Scottish Gaelic if I have offended you in any way! My intention was the very opposite: I love your language and I wanted to honour it in my novels. I felt it would be important for people reading them to know how to say the words – not

Author's Note

exactly of course, but as near as I could get. The Nahvitch themselves, who speak Okkam (or who "have the Okkam" as they would term it), describe themselves as the enemy. For years, the people of Hambrig assumed that "Nahvitch" was the name of the tribe. It never was that. The Scottish Gaelic word for "enemy" is "nàmhaid", and the closest I could get to a phonetic spelling of that was "nahvitch"! Later, it becomes clear that the real name for the tribe is the "Toosanik". This came from the Gaelic "tuathanaich". Another example is the Gaelic word "dearc", pronounced "jairthk", which can mean both "lizard" and "berry".

The birch tree is indeed the tree of hope and new beginnings. Scottish Gaelic, like Ogham, originally used trees as letters of the alphabet, and the letter B for Birch tree, was a specific rune, lovingly carved into the lid of the Box of Death.

R. Marsden, September 2024

Printed in Great Britain
by Amazon